**Also by Katie Delahanty**

**The Brightside Series**

*In Bloom*
*Blushing*
*Believe*

Katie Delahanty

# KEYSTONE

Entangled Publishing, LLC
2614 South Timberline Road
Suite 105, PMB 159
Fort Collins, CO 80525
rights@entangledpublishing.com

Entangled Teen is an imprint of Entangled Publishing, LLC.

Visit our website at www.entangledpublishing.com.

Edited by Candace Havens
Cover design by Covers by Juan
Cover images by
Sveta Aho/shutterstock
Interior design by Toni Kerr

ISBN 978-1-64063-824-2
Ebook ISBN 978-1-64063-825-9

Manufactured in the United States of America

First Edition January 2020

10 9 8 7 6 5 4 3 2 1

*For Memamade.*
*Wherever you are, rest assured, your legend will live on.*

*"In the future, everyone will be world-famous for 15 minutes."*

—*Falsely attributed to Andy Warhol*

# Chapter One

*June 25, 20X5*

*T͟his will be my first and last entry, the final secret I share. It's strange, knowing this is goodbye. What will be my final words to my so-called friends?*

I thought I'd get to choose, but in the end, it isn't my decision.

"Jump!" The voice is the wind ruffling the lake, but it's inside me at the same time. Wherever it comes from, it's a voice I obey. Instinctively wadding my limbs into a ball, I launch myself overboard seconds before the explosion.

As soon as I hit the water, the blast pushes me under. Bubbles rumble past my ears in a rush to the surface that fast fades above me. Frigid fingers shove into my nostrils until my eyes bulge.

*Where is Adam? I can't go without him.*

Seconds ago, I was overjoyed to see him. Those unforgettable blue eyes connected with mine, sending a jolt of hot relief down my spine. He was coming with me, and we had everything in front of us. Memories to be made.

*And now...*

Panicking, I thrash, frantically feeling for his fingers until a second wave of debris—champagne glasses, yacht remnants—presses me deeper. Invisible hands bind me, dragging me down.

*He's gone. Everyone is.*

My heart balloons until it will surely burst, and I sob, inviting in the lake. As I choke, my throat scorches and my legs grow heavy, too heavy to move. Held hostage in chilly limbo, I stare into the hazy water, my useless arms floating in front of me. What strikes me most is the silence settling into my core, making room for the Lonely to reside. It would be easy to submit to the tantalizing darkness, to let the cool kiss take me, but some gut reflex won't let me go. Of their own volition, my legs kick, getting tangled in the vintage Balenciaga dress Mom said would be the envy of the party, and there's no way I'm letting *that* be the weight that drags me down. Lungs screaming, I push for life, clawing my way through wreckage until I break the surface with a pop.

I gasp, burned air searing my raw throat as I scan the lake for a sign of life—for evidence any of my friends are still part of mine—but all I find is unrecognizable fragments of my old existence sinking to watery graves. A fire smolders in the distance. Unwilling to believe the inevitable, I bob and dip my way toward it, my dress clinging to my legs, hindering my progress. I hike it up to my chest so I can move freely, but it's still a fight for my exhausted limbs to keep my head above water. When I finally arrive at the charred remnants, it's obvious the yacht is gone.

*I'm alone.*

If I could let the water swallow me, I would, but now that I've chosen to live, I can do nothing else.

A siren sounds on the breeze, reminding me of the plan.

*This isn't how it was supposed to happen, but it can still work. I've got to hide.*

Walling off the desperation that squeezes my heart, adrenaline takes over, giving me strength to paddle toward shore. *This night can haunt me later.*

Crawling out of the lake, I sprawl on the beach, sucking in precious air for as long as I dare. Still breathless, I limp into the woods. My temples throb and I long to return to the house and climb into bed, to huddle under the blankets until the shivering stops. *Last chance to keep my old life. I could come out of this a survivor. My parents would be so proud...* Once the story hit the Networks, my Influencer status would be reinstated—especially now that everyone who knew my family's secret is...dead.

*Isn't that convenient?*

I don't dwell on who's behind the explosion. Maybe part of me already knows the truth, but I'm not ready for it. Instead, the final fleeting glimpse I had of my best friend, Deena, her blond hair whipping across her face right before the blast, assaults me.

Doubling over, I swallow the sickness rising in my throat, shutting my eyes against her. *We weren't speaking, but she didn't deserve this. None of them did.* Tears bubble down my cheeks. Dropping to my knees, I stare up at the starry sky, an irrevocable ache seeping through me. *How can I be in this world without them? Wherever they are, can they see me?* The universe is endless, and the stars shine down without even a wink.

A voice drifts up from the lake, its nearness sobering me. For the plan to work, the world needs to believe I'm dead. *But if I stick to the plan I can never go back.* That truth should terrify me, but I'm already overwhelmed. Besides, there's nothing left to go back to. Not without Adam. He was the only one who made me feel like I mattered. Breathing deep, I heave myself to my feet and drag myself deeper into the woods. *I have no home. I have to keep going.*

The old me would have ordered a car to drive me from Lake Tahoe to the Sequoia National Forest, but the Disconnects offered me refuge on the condition I wouldn't be tracked. Starting now, I'm invisible. They were supposed to send a guide, but he never showed up, and it's pure luck I stumble upon the bikes, sneakers, and hooded sweatshirt hidden behind a tree. Taking it as a sign I've made the right decision, I yelp. Choking back the cry, I tug the sweatshirt over my dress with shaking hands. In the pocket I find a tube of glittery gold paint and draw a haphazard zigzag over half my face to disguise my identity from facial-recognition cameras.

*The mark of a Disconnect.*

Putting my hood up, I hit the trail. *Don't think. Just go.* My muscles scream, but I push forward, praying for momentum to carry me. Luckily, I'm headed downhill, and I focus on pedaling. If the explosion sinks in, my legs will cease to move.

But even the ringing in my ears can't silence the screams.

It's six long miles to the abandoned strip mall where Allard is waiting. Despite my pounding headache, I go as fast as I can, knowing the risk she's taking to rescue me. When my Jell-O legs thrust into the drive, she's standing next to a black hunk of metal that must have been stolen from an antique car museum. Silver letters read "Rambler" across the grill.

For a master thief meant to blend in, Allard is stunning, with a collection of silver and white beads dripping from her forehead. At the sight of her red hair and dangerous figure, I burst into tears.

She wraps me up in a brief hug. "You're alone," she whispers before tugging open the heavy car door and strapping me into the musty backseat. "What happened to your contact? Is he…"

"I'm not sure. He never showed up." My scorched throat strains against the words. Tears roll hot and fast over my cheeks, and I hiccup.

The color drains from her face, but it's the only indication she's worried about my contact. Her voice remains firm. "Okay. It's okay. Keep your head down." She closes me inside the car before throwing the bike into the trunk and getting into the driver's seat.

I press my cheek to the cracked vinyl, my vision blurring as she turns the key in the ignition. The engine rumbles to life, and relief vibrates through me. *I made it.*

Shifting into gear, Allard steps on the gas. We lurch forward, winding our way into the Sequoias. Beyond the whir of the tires, all is silent except for my sniffles.

"You need to forget Ella Karman ever existed," she says before my thoughts can return to all that is lost. Meeting my eyes in the rearview mirror, she hands a piece of paper over her shoulder. "Your name is Elisha DeWitt, now."

Savoring the rarity of real pages, I run my fingers over the smooth surface, resisting the urge to tear the perforated row of holes running down each side of the page in case it serves some purpose known only to Allard.

"I'm not sure she existed in the first place," I whisper, examining my pretty face printed at the top of the article, amber eyes flashing bright and full of life under the headline:

## ELLA KARMAN, DEAD:
## NOT-SO-SWEET SEVENTEEN KILLS DOZENS

Every detail of Ella Karman's seventeenth birthday was planned, down to the custom driverless BMW X-pro18, a gift from her Super-Influencer parents Noah Karman and Tiana Santos. It was scheduled to arrive in the driveway of the Lake Tahoe mansion they'd rented for the occasion at precisely 10:47 p.m., honoring the exact moment Ella was born. But Ella never showed up. Instead, she seduced her closest friends into joining her on a yacht anchored offshore for a private, champagne-fueled fiesta. Little did she know, she was leading them to their death. Or did she? In what is being called an act of terror, the yacht was riddled with explosives.

"How did you get this?" I ask. "So soon…"

"Lil's Life Stream was on. Millions watched tonight's events play out in real time. It's hardly news anymore, though her feed went dark the moment the yacht exploded."

Gravity descends, its weight pinning me to my seat, and it's like I'm at the bottom of the lake, unable to catch my breath. The words twist, and I scan the rest of the article through a cascade of tears.

Our brightest stars, the biggest up-and-coming Influencers, snuffed out so quickly when the bomb went off. Their families are devastated. How will they ever recover?

Biting my lip, I imagine the horrific images being played out in cinematic detail for the world's entertainment, and anger flares in my belly. "It's all lies." I wad the article into a ball so I don't have to see my wavy black hair and poreless olive skin, so eerily like my mom's. "My parents wanted us dead. 'Nothing like a little misfortune to bring the eyeballs to you,' it *should* say. They're totally going to profit off this."

"Do you really think your parents are behind this?" Allard asks.

"They have to be. They had everything to lose. Their secret was going to come out." I wince, familiar anxiety I'll be overheard closing my throat. *But, whatever, it's not my secret anymore.* "The only reason I was born was so Mom could post her baby-bump pics. It was good for their image—the perfect Hollywood power couple needed the perfect Hollywood baby—but I wasn't theirs. They used a donor embryo and grew me on a surrogate farm. She faked everything. Her whole get-your-pre-baby-body-back magical fitness empire is built on a lie." I expect Allard's eyes in the rearview mirror to register surprise, but they remain flat.

"Don't you think it was them?" I ask.

"I'm not sure," she says.

"Who do you think it was, then?" My stomach clenches as a wave a sickness pummels me, and I press my forehead to the seat.

"I don't know, but you have to stay strong," she says. "I understand it's hard."

We whip around another curve, and, bracing myself, I catch her smiling.

"This is fun for you?" I ask, swallowing the metallic taste in my mouth.

"What's not to love? Being out on the open road, having complete control of your own destiny… Tell me, have you ever felt more alive?"

"I've never felt more terrified."

She laughs. "I thrive on risk—the adrenaline rush the moment you take what isn't yours, slip it in your pocket, hide it away. I miss my days in the field, but I get to keep you for a while—you're my fix." Her smile softens. "The fear will pass. Soon you'll understand your potential. Yes, things didn't go as planned, but you're safe now."

The car slows, and we turn into the forest, bumping along an unpaved path. Out the window, high above the giant sequoia trunks, pink light peeks through the leaves. I can't believe it's morning. A lifetime has passed since last night.

"We're here," Allard says several minutes later, shutting off the car.

"Where are we?" The majestic trees surrounding us all look the same.

After getting out of the car, she opens the back door for me. "Welcome to Keystone, Elisha Dewitt. Are you ready?"

I stare at the crumpled article, knowing the girl on its pages is dead. My old life is over. *I won't miss me, but I'll miss him...* Picturing Adam sitting next to me on the dock the last time we talked, our toes making tiny ripples in the lake—remembering the foolish hope that I could keep a little piece of home—I want to curl into a ball and die. *All I wanted was a friend to come with me, for something in my life to be real so I wouldn't have to be alone...* I press my burning eyes shut, trying to get a grip.

Hugging myself, I rock back and forth, memorizing his face—his longish blond hair, his broad, tan shoulders with the slight spray of freckles spreading over them—his lips... *Why can't I remember his lips?* I'm appalled the details are already fuzzy.

Outside, Allard shifts her weight. Leaves rustle beneath her feet, reminding me I need to answer her—need to move on.

*Before he said he'd come with me, I was willing to go alone. I chose this with or without him.* I take a deep breath. *No more looking back. From now on, I only move forward.*

Before I lose my nerve, I step out of the car and fold my arms against the chilly morning air. "I'm ready. This is what I want."

"Nobody can know who you were—and nobody will care who you are. Those are the rules."

"It's a dream come true."

Smiling, she nods. "Then follow me."

# Chapter Two

*June 20X5, Keystone*

Allard leads me down a lightly worn trail, our feet crunching over brittle leaves. It's eerily still this deep in the woods, and we walk in silence for several minutes until she asks, "How did you escape the explosion?"

My heart stalls. *She's going to think I'm nuts.* "I heard a voice…not with my ears, but from…within me," I say, sucking in my breath. "This is going to sound weird, but it said 'jump,' and it was almost like this hurricane wind pushed me over. I mean, I threw myself overboard, but it all happened so fast…"

The night comes flooding back, and I bury my face in my hands, holding back stinging tears, trying to forget what happened next. *Did I hear them scream or did I imagine it?*

Allard touches my elbow. "That's instinct. Your superior intuition is unique. It's why we want you. It will serve you well here."

Raising my head, I push the memories away and focus on her. On the future. "I don't know if I trust my intuition. It's been wrong before."

"I'm here to help with that." She guides me forward alongside a gurgling stream.

"How?"

"Practice. Forgiveness. We study and understand your past so it no longer limits your future."

"Fun," I say, keeping my plans to only move forward and never look back to myself.

We arrive at a small stone cottage so overtaken by ivy it disappears into the landscape. I may have missed it entirely if Allard hadn't pushed aside vines to reveal a weathered wood door.

"I won't pretend it's going to be easy. But it will be worth it," she says. She inserts a skeleton key into the faded brass lock before opening the door and motioning me inside.

Ducking under the ivy, I enter a living room with stone floors and wood-paneled walls. Cast in watery light filtering through the floor-to-ceiling windows at the back of the cottage, a shallow tweed couch faces a large stone fireplace. The space is void of cameras and screens—the techiest thing is an antique record player that sits in an orange box on the hearth. It's like the whole place is frozen in time, like I've stepped into a VR game set a hundred years ago.

I rub my arms against the chill in the room as a dizzying wave of homesickness washes over me. *If only I could curl up with my cat on the cushy lounge in my old home theater to get lost in a movie.* While I was growing up, my parents kept me under lock and key. Most kids were on the Networks since birth, so when they went public at sixteen, they already had fans, but not me. I was homeschooled by robots and nannies with the occasional VR field trip. Publicly, my parents said they kept me a virtual secret because they wanted me to have a childhood, but I think they didn't want to risk revealing my true identity. Movies were my only link to the outside world—practically my only friends—and my only common ground with my dad. As an actor, he studied the classics, and I'd watched the entirety of his rare collection religiously. They were my life.

"Everything is going to be fine, Elisha. You'll see." Allard closes the door. The deadbolt clunks into place, jumping me back to my new reality. "You must be starving. Can I get you anything to eat? Drink? Should I start a fire?"

"No, thank you." My stomach rebels at the thought of food, and my legs wobble, threatening to give out. "I think I need to lay down."

"Of course." She shows me down a hall to a small room with a single bed draped in wool. A light fixture resembling a space station illuminates a streamlined dresser. I try not to compare the sparse furnishings to my room at home—the king-size bed tufted with down, the French crystal chandelier, the dressing room equipped with a delivery portal for sponsored products, ensuring a constant rotation of sequins and bangles—all controlled by a swipe of my hand. I only had to speak the occasion I was dressing for, and, at a wiggle of my fingers, the closet would spin around me while my virtual stylist assembled an outfit in one minute flat.

As I catch a passing glimpse of myself in a mirror, my bruised and bloody face replicated with gold starburst rods radiating around it—*at the center of the explosion*—my breath seizes. Terrorized by the nightmare reflected at me, I quickly look away. It's like I'm underwater again, fighting for breath, and I crumple onto the bed, trembling, the enormity of the night assaulting me. I squeeze my eyes shut tight, and a sob escapes my throat.

"Shhh… Here, take this." Allard helps me sit up and hands me an orange cup. "It'll help you sleep. And tomorrow we'll begin your training so you're up to speed when the others return."

After choking down the sugary concoction, I bury my face in the pillow.

Allard sits silently with me, her hands pressed to my back, and lets me cry.

Eventually, the sedative works its magic, and the sobs slow.

"Welcome home, Elisha," Allard whispers, lightly stroking my hair as I drift to sleep. "I promise you'll find riches here you never knew existed. Everything is going to be okay. You're among friends now."

*Friends.* The word resonates, but I pass out before I dare dream it's true.

When I wake, I'm battered, beaten, limp. Everything hurts. My throat is raw, and my lungs are sore. The night comes rushing back with a vengeance. Wanting to keep the memories at bay, I force myself to my feet, repeating my mantra: *No looking back. Only forward. Don't think. Move.* I head into the hall in search of the bathroom and bump into Allard.

"Elisha. You're awake."

Groggy, I rub my eyes, reminding myself of my new name. "How long was I out?" I ask, my voice scratchy and hoarse.

"About twenty hours."

"That was some strong stuff you gave me."

"Yes. I thought you needed a good rest," she says. "And a hot bath is in order, too." She opens a door behind her and shows me into a spacious restroom with stone walls and a claw-foot tub bathed in natural light from skylights. Dropping a stopper into the drain, she turns on the hot water and throws in bath salts and bubbles.

Sweet lavender wafts up to me on the steam, and I can't wait to soak my aching bones.

"Use these towels, and I'm going to run and get you a change of clothes. I'll be right back." She sets the fluffy green towels on a wood counter next to the sink.

"Thank you," I say as she hurries out of the room.

While she's gone, I force myself to examine my battered reflection in the gold-framed mirror hanging over the sink. A cut on my forehead erupts from a black bruise that radiates over my right eye and fades to a sickly green on my swollen cheek. I'm still wearing my beaded Balenciaga birthday dress, the sheath accentuating my lean frame and the beads somehow intact. I hate everything about it.

"I probably don't need to wear asymmetrical makeup with this monster face I've got going on," I say when Allard returns.

She smiles. "Probably not. I don't think you'll have any scars, though. You'll need a makeup lesson in no time."

"No scars that anyone can see, anyway," I mutter, struggling with the zipper on the side of the dress, unable to peel it off fast enough.

"I'll give you some privacy," Allard says. "But when you're done you can put this on. It's your uniform." She sets down a neatly folded stack of forest green cloth.

Unfolding the jumpsuit, I examine its boxy cut and cargo pockets. It's the opposite of anything I would have worn in my previous life, and I'm grateful for its protective covering after so many months of forced overexposure.

"Actually, could you stay?" I ask. "I don't want to be alone with my thoughts right now."

"Of course," she says. "Let me get something to sit on. I'll be right back."

After using the time alone to kick off my dress, I sink into the tub. The bubbles foam up over my shoulders, and the hot water is heaven to my stiff muscles. I relax until I'm reminded of the lake and the ever-present sadness that lingers in the recesses of my brain surfaces.

I miss my mom. We weren't speaking when I died, but I wish I could go back to a time when I thought she loved me — to when the future was full of possibility — to laying safely next to her in my own bed with her arms wrapped around me. Tears prick my eyes, but I blink them away.

"I'm sure you have lots of questions," Allard says, returning. She carries a small orange stool with two cups of tea balanced on it. "I was thinking after your bath we can have breakfast, and then I'll give you a tour of the campus."

"Cool," I say, swallowing a sob, grateful for her distraction.

"And we're also going to have to do something about your looks." She sits, handing me my tea.

"I thought you said I wasn't going to have any scars?" Sitting up in the tub, I take a small sip from the mug. The hot liquid soothes my parched throat.

"You won't. I'm more worried someone might recognize you."

"But doesn't being a Disconnect mean no technology? How would anyone even know about me?"

"We may live off the grid, but it's important we're aware of what's going on in the world. At Keystone, we're a special legion of Disconnects. Our mission is to steal analog history — to preserve the truth — before corporations and the government can alter the past to benefit their personal futures. We're in danger of entering a Digital Dark Age, where the only information available is digital. Tape recordings, printed books, films, photographs — proof of history — are decaying and becoming scarce. Digital information is easy to tamper with, and there are forces at work that want current society to reflect their version of the past." She sips her tea before continuing.

"Often, we're after priceless works that are protected by

the latest technology, so we have to understand tech even though we don't use it ourselves. We have internet access in the Crypt—that's our code-breaking library—and the *TMI-feed* is likely a guilty pleasure for some of the girls. They watch the Networks—they have to. For your Initiation Heist, you'll be asked to go under cover in Influencer society, and you'll need to know how to fit in—and how to hide in plain sight."

"Initiation Heist?" I almost choke on my tea, the cup rattling in my trembling hands at having to reenter society.

"It's the final test before becoming a full-fledged Keystone member with access to our top-level secrets, but don't worry," Allard says. "You'll have plenty of time to learn our ways—and you'll participate in a heist as an assistant to an Initiate—before you're asked to lead a heist the following year."

"Lead a heist?" My eyes bulge. "Right."

Pressing her lips together, she represses a smile. "We won't make you do anything you aren't prepared for. Though, with your exceptional intuition, I suspect you'll learn quickly."

"No pressure," I mutter, inhaling lavender, processing the enormity of what she's telling me.

She laughs. "As you can imagine, invisibility is essential to being a thief. We don't use technology because we don't want to be tracked," she continues. "We may shun the Networks and refuse to be ranked, but we're not like Unrankables. They aren't *allowed* to rank, while we *choose* not to rank."

*Unrankable.* The word is quicksand in my mind. *The worthless, greedy, lowest of the low. The unemployed, unmotivated poor who live off our handouts.* My face must betray the prejudices so ingrained in me, because Allard straightens, a sad frown forming on her lips.

"I didn't know that," I admit, setting my tea on a shelf and sinking back into the tub. "I've always lumped Disconnects and Unrankables together. My parents taught me Index ranking is everything. If you don't rank, you don't matter."

"This is a lot for you to get used to," she says.

"It is…" I shake my head. "My mom used to say, 'For you to matter, somebody has to be talking about you, eavesdropping on you—spying. Your worth is measured by your number of followers, your Index trade amount, your engagement rate. If nobody's watching, nobody cares.' It sucked, but I've lived and breathed my numbers forever. Who am I without them?"

"We're going to discover that together. You have so many gifts, Elisha. Believe me—numbers don't mean a thing. A one becomes a zero, and a life is erased? Not here. Here, you are *always* someone. You have purpose."

For the first time in forever, I smile. "I hope that's true. I'm so tired of BS people posting their BS lies. *Nothing* out there is real. If there isn't a picture or your Life Stream didn't record it, it didn't happen, it didn't matter. But the truth is, *nothing* matters. It's all…stupid. Pointless." Dipping my head back, I wet my hair.

When I raise my head, Allard's sparkling eyes meet mine. "I think we can find out what matters to *you*. So, what do you say we get to work making you unrecognizable? I'm not worried about your face—by the time summer is over and everyone returns to campus, the collagen and other injectables should have worked their way out of your system. Whatever your mom was using to keep you looking like her will be gone, and we'll see the real Elisha. But maybe we should start with your hair." She holds up a pair of scissors. "Do you trust me?"

Pouring shampoo into my hand and working the soap into my hair, I consider her. *She helped me escape. She's taking me in. She's the closest thing I have to family now…* "Yes," I decide, using a handheld shower head to rinse out the bubbles. "What are you thinking?"

"As you know, asymmetry is important to disguise yourself

from the facial-recognition cameras that are all over the place. That goes for hair, too. I think we should chop it off. Maybe angle it just above your shoulders?"

I rub creamy conditioner into my thick locks, weighing my wet hair in my hands, recalling my mother's signature windswept spirals. When she smiles in the cutesy, infectious way of hers while twirling a curl around her finger, she twists whoever she's manipulating right along with her. We spent years growing my hair out in the hopes it would mimic hers but never quite succeeded. *All I ever wanted was to be hers... but I was never enough. Her love fluctuated with my share price.*

Thinking back to my debut on the Social Stock Exchange, I remember our last moments together before I went public and everything changed:

*"After today, it will be up to you to keep your investors happy," she said. "Always be a story—the more dramatic, the better. If you do, you'll live in luxury. Your currency account will be forever full. If you don't—if you fall from the Index— you'll be Unrankable. Useless. And then you might as well disappear."*

*Wrapping her arms around me from behind, she rested her chin on my shoulder, comparing our mirrored faces reflected on a wall screen. Our house was equipped with the latest in Life Streaming technology. Cameras recorded our every move, and our lives could be edited to movie quality and streamed direct to the Networks with less than a five-second delay.*

*But we weren't live. This was a rare, private moment. One that was recorded only in my Book of Secrets; a palm-sized, leather-bound journal with thick vanilla pages. Real paper. A rarity. I kept it hidden in the zippered belly of my sleep sheep, my lovey for as long as I can remember. Its pages were finite, so I savored the moments I recorded, the memories meant for me alone.*

*I leaned against my mother, memorizing her slim grasp, wanting to stay her little girl but at the same time ready to prove I could fly.*

*"I love you, Mom," I said. "Thank you for making my dreams come true."*

*Taking my hand, she smiled. "That's what we're made of, my love. Dreams."*

Rinsing out the conditioner, I squeeze the water from my hair before pulling the plug on the drain. *And now it's time for the nightmare to be over.*

Allard hands me a towel, and I climb out of the water, wrapping myself in soft fluff. As I towel dry my long, hand-painted locks, I picture my bloated lips shriveling, my cheeks deflating without the fat to fill them, and Ella is one step closer to dead for me. She's destined to be overwritten with time, anyway, stamped out by someone prettier, more popular, more *alive*.

With a nod, I decide. "Let's do it."

# Chapter Three

*June 20X5, Keystone*

"Few believe in Keystone's existence," Allard says as we walk through the forest. "And we like to keep it that way."

The thin morning air is crisp and clean, smelling of sweet, wet dirt. Leaves pitter-patter in a breeze overhead, and fire is in the air. I'd love to collapse next to its warmth, but memories lie in the flames, and I force myself onward.

"There are a few buildings visible at ground level, like the Lodge," she says. We pause in front of a dilapidated stone building with leaded glass windows and broken wraparound porches. It's so covered in ivy it's like the earth is trying to reclaim it. "This is our central meeting place."

"People go in there?" Imagining what sized spiders lurk inside, I shiver.

She smiles. "Yes, but it's not accessible through any doors or windows. You'll see when everyone comes back from summer break. The entry points are locked this time of year…not that we couldn't break in." She winks. "But we'll start your training elsewhere."

"Thank God. That place looks like it could collapse at any second," I say, following her past the Lodge, our path unmarked. "I'd rather not risk…" My lungs seize at the thought of being trapped inside, and I'm back underwater, fighting for breath. Dropping to my knees, I cradle my head in my hands.

She lowers herself to my side and squeezes my shoulder. "You're safe here, Elisha. Everything at eye level purposely appears abandoned in case someone ventures this deep into the forest."

"Does that happen often?" I gasp for air. *Am I always going to have these freak-outs?*

"Almost never. Breathe with me." She inhales, and I fill my lungs with her. "This part of the forest doesn't show up on GPS maps or locators," she says, exhaling. "The trees shield us from satellites, and we have a bit of technology of our own that ensures we remain undercover. Anybody who wanders back here is lost…or trying to find us. But we're prepared for that. Otherwise, most of Keystone is underground or built high into the trees." She rubs my back. "Breathe."

We inhale and exhale together, and she stays by my side until my heart rate slows and the memories are safely tucked away. Squinting up through tears, I stare at the tips of trees disappearing into the sky, unable to discern any structures. "Do I have to learn to climb trees?" My muscles tense.

Allard laughs and helps me to my feet. "No. We have stairs. But we'll explore those another day, too. This way."

We walk for a few more minutes in silence until she stops in a seemingly random place and crouches down. "Today, we're going to focus on the underground. This is the Vault." She brushes away dirt and leaves from the forest floor to expose a trapdoor. Swiveling up a round, rusted metal dial, she reveals a combination lock hidden beneath it.

"This access code changes daily and is equated from the number of folds in the origami displayed in the Atrium—the Keystone cafeteria—at breakfast," she says, turning the knob to a sequence of numbers so quickly I can't register them. "But the Atrium isn't open this time of year… There's also a master access code. That's one of the secrets you'll learn once you're initiated."

With a click, a handle pops up.

"Here we go," she says, pulling open the trapdoor.

I peer over her shoulder down mossy stone steps into a dark tunnel.

"And don't forget to breathe. There's plenty of space down here. I promise." She starts down, and, swallowing the perma-lump in my throat, I follow close behind, focusing on filling my lungs as we descend past mud walls teeming with ferns.

"Pull the door down behind you, please," she says as our heads disappear below the earth.

Panic knotting my shoulders, I tug on the lid, blotting out daylight above us. To my relief, lanterns lining the walls at the bottom of the steps illuminate as soon as the door clicks shut. When we reach the base of the stairs, three identical stone tunnels, all with domed ceilings and lined with flickering lanterns, jut in different directions. She's right. It's much bigger down here than I could have imagined, and I exhale relief.

"What is this place?" I ask, my vision slowly adjusting to the dim light.

Allard heads down the tunnel to our right.

"A treasure chest of sorts." Her voice floats back to me, and I scramble to keep up. "This is where we keep our loot." She laughs. "And it's where we study. Disconnects have been adding on to it for over a century. It's like a secret passageway to every city in the world. Behind each door is a replica of a museum containing both authentic and fake works—including

3-D printed forgeries that have rewritten history. It was never meant to be a maze, but as tunnels have been added, it's turned into a labyrinth of twists and turns. The true number of galleries and treasures hidden down here is one of Keystone's most guarded secrets."

She stops and takes a small vial out of her pocket. "If you ever get lost, remember: water flows downhill." Opening the vial, she pours the liquid it contains onto the ground. It rolls in a small trickle to the right. "You can follow it to the Vault's other entrance."

"It's all downhill from here," I say. "Got it."

"Exactly." She winks. "This way."

We make two more lefts, then a sharp right, and I'm already lost. The corridors are all practically identical.

"Here we are," Allard finally says.

She stops abruptly, and I almost bump into her.

"Where is here?" I ask.

"This is the Crypt. Our library." She pulls open a rusted metal door and ushers me inside. "It's modeled after the International Spy Museum in Washington, D.C., and contains hundreds of code-breaking machines and all sorts of gadgets. Are you ready for your first lesson?"

Inside, the space is shockingly modern, with polished cement floors and lit-up display cases containing briefcases, old-fashioned cameras, and antique computer keyboards.

"I guess so…"

She closes the door and leads me past a fingerprinting display. "It's imperative you learn to transmit messages that won't be intercepted. You'll need to learn to code and decode. This place is an amazing resource—you can check anything out. We have Enigma machines and ciphers dating back to medieval times. Those are located back here." She pushes open another door, and the air sucks in around us, becomes colder. "These are the archives, modeled after Yale University's Beinecke Rare Book and Manuscript Library."

Dozens of individually lit bookshelves rise in front of us, forming a massive cube encased in glass. The surrounding walls are made of paneled marble, and brown leather couches are scattered at the base of the cube, arranged next to gold-framed rectangular tables.

As we enter, a boy about my age looks up from a massive book he's studying on one of the tables.

Having expected to be alone, I almost jump out of my skin.

He slams the book shut and leaps to his feet.

"Garrett," Allard exhales. "It's good to see you."

I'm instantly self-conscious. Terrified he'll recognize me as Ella, I get busy studying my toes. Even though my hair now finishes in a jagged crop above my shoulders, and beneath my angled bangs, a row of white stars explodes over my black eye. I feel his stare and I imagine he sees right through me. He's a thief, after all; they're perceptive.

"You, too," he says.

"Sorry to interrupt," Allard says.

"It's fine. I was on my way out."

"You don't have to leave."

I venture a peek at him. Dark, messy hair falls across his forehead, and three smeared black bars are painted under one eye. He's wearing a jumpsuit like mine, but his stretches across wide shoulders, his sleeves rolled up, revealing strong forearms. His smoldering green eyes pop, amplified by exhausted red rims, and his full lips purse in a frown. If I were remotely able to find anyone attractive at this moment, I would surrender at his feet. Something about him has me buzzing like there's static electricity in the air, and I wouldn't be surprised if my hair was standing on end.

"It's not you," he says. Peeling off a pair of white gloves, he discards them next to the book. "I leave for Atlanta in a few hours."

"Ah." Allard smiles. "Good luck."

"Hopefully I don't need it." He brushes past us without so much as a glance at me, but his nearness sends a rush of heat up my spine all the same. He's much taller than I am. But then, most people are.

The door sucks closed behind him, and the buzz fizzles.

"I thought you said the campus was deserted?" I ask, staring after him, the air stagnant without his energy filling it.

"It is. Garrett's parents—Whitney and Jeff—live here year-round. They're the heads of the training program and the only people beyond me who know your identity. I'll introduce you to them when they return from their summer heist."

"Does he know—"

"You can trust your secret is safe." She cuts me off before I finish my question. "Garrett doesn't get special treatment. He'll be leading his Initiation Heist this year and is headed out for some extracurricular practice. If all goes well, we'll be adding the secret recipe for Coca-Cola to our archives soon. He was studying...let's see..." Heading to the desk, she puts on his white gloves, studying the cover of some ancient text. "Interesting..."

"What is it?" Joining her, I study the cracked brown cover. "It looks really old."

"The Voynich manuscript... It's a legendary book dating from around the fifteenth century written in a secret language and filled with illustrations of zodiac symbols, naked people, and plants that don't exist." She opens the book, revealing colorful flowers painted over illustrated symbols that look like they were written with a quill.

"So cool. What does it say?"

"Nobody knows. Some people think it's a medieval

alchemic *Kama Sutra*, others think it's an anatomy and biology book, while still others think it's a hoax—gibberish. It was stolen from the Beinecke by yours truly, as a matter of fact." She smiles, and her eyes take on the hazy glow of memory. "We thought we'd try our hand at deciphering it before anyone else could make up their own version of what these codes mean. Many have tried, and personally I think it might be unsolvable, but at any rate, it's safe here."

"What does it have to do with the recipe for Coke?" I ask.

"I'm not sure. Maybe Garrett was deciphering it for practice." She shrugs. "It's good to train your brain how to think when faced with code. Maybe he was getting in the right mindset."

"Maybe…" Peering at the strange illustrated plants and random symbols, I feel my stomach knot. I can't imagine making sense of it.

Seeming to read my thoughts, Allard says, "Let's start with something easy." Closing the Voynich, she heads to the glass tower, and I expect her to wave a hand so the doors will slide open, but instead, she punches in a code on a keypad and pushes the door open manually. She disappears inside, returning a couple minutes later with another book, this one with an eight-point cross on the cover.

"Pigpen ciphers," she says, setting the book on the table, "are a series of grids and dots based on the ciphers used by the Knights Templar in the twelfth century…"

She shows me the Templar cipher system of shapes arranged around the Maltese Cross and what letter each shape corresponds to. "Commit this to memory, and you'll have the basis for breaking many substitution ciphers."

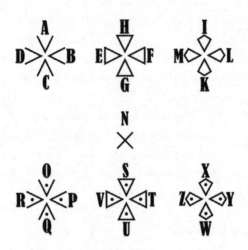

"There's no letter J," I notice.

"Very observant." Pressing her lips together, she nods. "The letter J didn't exist when this was created—it came later, in the sixteenth century. One of the ways you can recognize a Templar cipher is that it only has twenty-five symbols."

"It's going to be impossible to learn all of this." I sigh.

"You'll get it." Allard pats my shoulder. "We'll take it a little piece at a time. All I ask is that you try."

Sitting at the table, I start memorizing the ancient symbols. I'm grateful for a focus for my thoughts, but I can't shake my weird reaction to Garrett-the-Energy-Boy that had me tingling a few minutes ago. *Maybe it was fear of being recognized. It's probably best to keep my distance. From everyone.*

Loneliness descends, but I bury it, concentrating on the codes that are probably destined to be my only friends.

# Chapter Four

*September 20X5, Keystone*

*hree Months Later...*
    The pain is an ever-present ache that pricks the corners of my mind, but these days the debilitating waves of grief knock me off my feet less often. Routine has become my lifeline. I've been focusing hard, waking at dawn to study decoding, ciphers, Morse code, lock picking, escape, and evasion. Breaking only for meals, I've collapsed in bed exhausted every night. The distraction, along with Allard's kindness, has made life bearable. Keystone has become familiar, if not yet home, and today I nervously greet the returning Disconnects, uncertain if I'm prepared to enter their ranks, dreading the inevitable disruption to my new life.

    After entering the Lodge through a trapdoor in the forest floor, I walk through a tunnel until I emerge in the pine-scented room through the back of a rock fireplace. I'm the first to arrive, and I cross the stone floor, taking a seat in the last row of cane-back chairs that face a small stage. Slouching, I pray I go unrecognized as my fellow trainees file in. They appear, clustered in twos and threes, wearing boxy green jumpsuits like mine, chattering about their summers. I examine them from under my bangs. *How am I ever going to fit in?* As a homeschooled only child, it's always been hard for me to act like kids my own age. Deena was my only friend until I was sixteen, and even with her guidance I felt like a misfit. But at least I knew how to talk like an Influencer. Disconnect kids are a total mystery. And clearly they all know one another. I must stick out. My cheeks burn like I'm lit by a spotlight, though nobody acknowledges me.

"Welcome back, everyone." Whitney's voice rings out from the stage. A chestnut-haired beauty, she stands next to her equally appealing husband, Jeff. I met them—Garrett-the-Energy-Boy's parents, who run Keystone—yesterday. They were super nice, giving no indication I was different than any other trainee. It was weird to be treated like I was normal when all my life I've been told I was special, but I liked it.

"I'll keep this short. We have a few announcements to make and then we'll get you to your rooms," Whitney says, slowly crossing the stage as the room quiets. Behind her, the rock fireplaces blaze, having been lit after everyone entered. Even though it's warm outside, the Lodge's stone walls and ivy-covered windows manage to keep the grand room cool. "First, a reminder that data devices are banned outside the Crypt. You may practice wearing AMPs there so you are familiar with augmented reality, but the Crypt is the only place we can one hundred percent guarantee you can't be tracked. We live in an age of transparency, but never forget— at Keystone, we have everything to hide."

*Including me.* A shiver runs down my spine. Above my head, a deer-antler chandelier twinkles against the wood-paneled ceiling, and a little brown bird hops from antler to antler.

"And please remember you're required to use analog data and, on top of that, original data," Jeff says, his eyes glinting. "If you can get your hands on it."

Energy reverberates through the room. The kids lean forward in anticipation I don't get. *They're excited about a challenge. Weird.*

Trained to seek beauty, I spot a familiar face in the front row, and my pulse quickens. *Garrett.* Legs extended and arms crossed, he's the only one who looks like he couldn't care less what his mom is saying. *Maybe he doesn't need to listen — he's probably been stealing since birth.* I admire his chiseled jaw and dark hair mussed to obscure one eye, his puffy — if I'm honest, totally kissable — lips. *He's so perfect he can't be real.* My heart swells, and the chandeliers glow brighter, as if ignited by his presence. The air hums, atoms vibrating. He turns, his eyes connecting with mine, and sweat erupts on my forehead. I blink, finding fascination with the deer-antler chandelier overhead before he thinks I'm staring.

*Again, this reaction. Maybe it's because he's the only person I recognize…*

The little brown bird takes flight and heads straight for the closed window to my left. My body reacts before I think, and I hurl myself in front of it, my shoulder slamming against the window with a loud thud.

The bird changes trajectory and disappears into the rafters as everyone turns to stare at me.

*Oh. My. God.*

"There was a bird," I whisper, my face burning so hot as I slink back to my seat it's probably fluorescent.

Whitney smiles. "I trust you will introduce yourselves to our newest Disconnect, Elisha Dewitt, at an appropriate time. Now, where was I?"

"What's the point of succeeding if nobody knows you did?"

Jeff interjects, his bold voice making everyone jump.

The heads all turn to face the stage. Except for one. His stare warms me, sending a burst of heat to my belly.

Daring a glance up, I lock gazes with his piercing green eyes. He raises an eyebrow, and my stomach contracts. There's something about him—I can't help it—I slowly smile back. After relying on my looks to gain popularity and win influence, some old part of me can't resist the game. My instinct is to walk past him, hips swaying like I'm on a runway, to wet my lips, to dazzle him—to wrap him in my web until he's mine. He'd be great for my numbers. *Stupid. This is why I can't trust my instincts. This isn't who I am anymore.*

But I can't look away.

And neither can he.

My heart thumps.

"Do you live for praise? If only you know, is it enough? Disconnecting is a constant struggle with pride. Remember your self-worth must come from within." Jeff pounds his fist on his chest, and I finally break the stare. Pretending I'm captivated by what's happening onstage, I hope Garrett forgets the girl he just glimpsed.

"An excellent reminder," Whitney says. "Now, I know you're all dying to hear about the Initiation Heist." She grins. "It will be our biggest—and most dangerous—heist to date."

The kids around me perk up even more.

"In a few months, we'll be hosting a challenge," Jeff says. "It will be an obstacle course of sorts, designed to measure your preparedness for the Initiation Heist."

"We take the heist very seriously. As those of you who participated in last year's heist as assistants—and will be leading your own heists this year—know, the stakes are real. You could get caught, and we can't risk involving anyone who isn't ready," Whitney says. "For that reason, anyone who fails to complete the obstacle course or the person with the slowest time will be discharged to Keystone Farms to help grow food for Unrankables in need. Life at the Farm is simple, though without the use of technology, the work is hard. But ending up there isn't a life sentence. If you're able to get past Farm security and survive the wilderness to make your way back to Keystone, we'll happily continue your training."

*Survive the wilderness? Nope. Guess I better find a way to own that obstacle course...*

"On the other hand, the four of you with the best times will be chosen to compete against one another in the Keystone Quest," Jeff continues. "The Quest champion will be awarded three things. First, the ability to choose their partner for the Initiation Heist, rather than being assigned one." He ticks the items off his fingers as he speaks. "Second, the locations of every top-secret Keystone hideout around the world — which is information that is usually earned well after you're initiated — and finally, one get-out-of-jail-free card."

"Normally, if you're caught during a heist, we do our best to set you up as a Maker or Laborer once you serve your sentence," Whitney explains. "But as a Quest winner, you are considered to be amongst our best and brightest, and we would do everything in our power to rescue you and keep you among our ranks."

*I can't imagine what would happen to* me *if I got caught... Unrankable much? I just got here... I don't want to start over somewhere else...* Hugging myself, I slump in my seat, as if that could root me in Keystone. *It would be worth winning the Quest just so I'd know no matter what I could come back here... Not that I have a shot at competing in the first place.*

"You'll be given details specific to your part of the Heist after the Quest, when partners are announced," Jeff says.

An excited ripple runs through the room. Peeking at the

front row, I'm relieved to see Garrett has lost interest in me. He again faces the stage, arms folded across his chest, but the left corner of his mouth is curled up in a nonchalant half smile. Even he seems to be buying into the hype. A shot of adrenaline jackknifes my heart, sharpening my vision, and I'm breathing cool, menthol air.

*But then, winning might be fun...*

"Room assignments and schedules are on the table at the back of the hall. Lessons begin tomorrow, and you're expected to take them seriously," Jeff says. "After all, the future of humanity is at stake."

I read my roommate's name — Rayelle Chen — as a pretty girl (*shorter than me!*) with glossy black hair walks over. She wears thick glasses that distort her eyes, making them appear impossibly large, and her lips are painted in black gloss, so her mouth appears smaller than it is. I'm instantly self-conscious of my attempt to paint the stars across my face.

"Elisha?" she asks.

"Yes." Nodding, I hold my breath, awaiting recognition beyond the bird incident.

"I'm Rayelle. I guess we're roommates." She offers a meek hand, along with a blank smile — the kind of smile you give a stranger when you're sizing them up.

Accepting her hand, I give it a little pump, my heart pounding.

Her fingers squeeze mine, and I exhale relief. If she knew who I was, she would have recoiled, my Influencer touch being the acid that dissolved her kindness.

"So, you're new here? That's weird." She leads me through a fireplace different than the one I arrived from, where the fires have been extinguished, and into a short tunnel. "They barely ever let new people into the training program. Most of us were born into it." We climb a ladder and emerge through a trapdoor into the forest. "Where are you from?" she asks as I crawl into the damp, cool outside air.

"I grew up in a Maker complex in Ojai," I say, reciting the cover story Allard prepared for me as I close the trapdoor and re-cover it with leaves.

Her jaw drops. "How did you end up here? You must have done something terrible to have been forced to disconnect."

"It wasn't really something I did," I say quickly, fearful she could guess my identity. "It was more that I hated letting strangers' opinions of me rule my life. I didn't fit in." *That much is true.*

We walk side by side down a narrow trail, the leaves of the great sequoias pattering in the breeze overhead.

"Then you came to the right place." She smiles. "And if you're here, you must be talented." We approach a cute boy with dark hair and golden skin leaning against a tree, studying his schedule. His jaw is clenched, accentuating his face's angles, and his arms are ripped, his biceps bulging beneath his jumpsuit sleeves. *First Garrett, and now this guy? Now entering the forest of teenage male models... Is being seriously hot a requirement to be a thief? Or maybe if you can't use technology, there's nothing better to do than work out... Mysteries that may never be solved.*

Rayelle lowers her voice. "We've only had one other transfer— Hi Kyran!" Breaking into a megawatt smile, she waves like she's trying to flag down a rescue drone.

Kyran glances up. "Hey."

"You get to run your Initiation Heist this year! Aren't you excited?"

He glances over his shoulder like he's searching for an

escape hatch. "Sure."

"Are you going to the dorms?" she asks. "Do you want to walk with us?"

"Nah. I'm waiting for Garrett." Shrugging, he goes back to reading.

I wince at his easy dismissal while my ears perk up at the possibility of a Garrett sighting.

"Okay. See you down there!" she says, unfazed. We continue past him, and my cheeks burn for her.

"That was him—the transfer," she continues. "From the School of the Seven Bells in Colombia. He's a legacy, though. His parents are big-time smugglers, and he's a natural—he'll be one of the final four for sure. Rumor has it he could pass the Seven Bell pickpocket test by the time he was five."

She's speaking a foreign language. "What's a legacy?"

"It means your parents are thieves. I'm a legacy, too. In fact, all of us are, except you, I guess. My parents are hustlers in Vegas by day and Cirque du Soleil performers by night. Fitting into tight spaces is my specialty." She smiles, and her cheeks bunch up.

*If by tight spaces, you mean your uniform.* The cruel thought hijacks my brain, and I immediately compliment her to counteract the shallow thinking that's ingrained in me. *Ugh. I'm the worst. "Judge the girls and worship the guys" no more.* "You must be really flexible," I say, summoning genuine interest.

"I am." Coming to a halt, she bends over backward and grabs her ankles before wedging her head and shoulders between her knees and pushing into a handstand to get out of the pose.

Jaw slack, I stare as she flips onto her feet.

"What do your parents do?" she asks, tossing her hair over her shoulder.

"I was adopted, so I'm not sure if I'm a legacy," I say, regaining my wits. "I suppose it's possible." We continue down the trail.

"Oh." She frowns. "I'm sorry about your real parents."

"Don't be. I never met them, so I don't miss them. But my adoptive parents definitely weren't thieves."

We stop in front of a massive tree. "This is the entrance to the dorms," she says, running her fingers lightly over the trunk. To my surprise, the tree splits up the middle, opening to reveal an elevator.

"How did you do that? Does the tree recognize your fingerprints?" We step through the opening.

She laughs. "No. Keystone doesn't allow biometrics. There's a button on the ground next to the tree that opens the doors. I stepped on it while you were watching my hands."

"I guess I have a lot to learn."

"Don't worry. I'll get you up to speed." She presses the letter *D* on the panel inside the elevator, and we descend below the earth—I have no idea how far.

"What are your adoptive parents like?" she asks.

"They're farmers who make and sell organic jams, but, like I said, I never fit in. I was always in trouble—I've been stealing for as long as I can remember. I can't help it." I conjure my real mother's acting lessons to deliver the lies. "They didn't know what to do with me, so I made it easy on them and disconnected. They won't miss me. They're probably relieved."

"That's so sad," Rayelle says. "You must be lonely."

"I am," I admit, and it's a relief to tell the truth for once. "It's like I just got to camp and I'm counting down the weeks until I go home, but then I realize I don't have a home anymore." My voice cracks.

Putting her arm around me, she squeezes my shoulders. "Don't worry. We're your family, now. This will feel like home in no time. You'll see."

She sounds so genuine my throat aches. I wish I could tell her everything, could reveal myself to this girl who, in another life, could have true friend potential. But it's impossible.

"Thank you." Smiling, I wipe away a tear. "I hope so."

"I know so."

The elevator doors open, and we step into a greenhouse with high glass ceilings and a scaffold system of bright, white lights. Rows of plants are lined up in black barrels. It smells of damp earth, life.

"What is this place?" I ask, putting the past behind me, where it belongs.

"It's the grow house and the dorms. There are vaults that store every kind of seed in existence, and the weather changes in each corridor to mimic actual climates. The first-year dorms overlook Brazilian sugarcane fields, second-year is China rice terraces, and our rooms are in California—strawberries and oranges. Next year, we'll be in the Netherlands—tomatoes and chilies. Our wing smells like orange blossoms. It's my favorite."

She points out each farm as we walk through the glass hallway that forms a circle around the grow house, separating the dorms from the crops, our footsteps echoing on the bamboo floors.

"Keystone is completely self-sustaining. We can grow anything," she says. "And survive if we have to."

"It's beautiful," I say, in awe that a secret of this magnitude exists.

Up ahead, Kyran picks an apple and tosses it to Garrett. My stomach drops at the sight of him, my arm hairs standing on end.

"Don't get your hopes up," Rayelle says, studying me. "That's Garrett Alexander. Yes, he's hot, but he's practically married to Chloe over there."

On the other side of the crops, a copper-haired girl with tawny skin is headed for Garrett. Her jumpsuit somehow manages to make her look like a curvy goddess. In my old life, I would have pinged her as a potential friend—the prettiest girl I've seen, and therefore a required ally.

"She's a total decoy," Rayelle says. "The only thing she's good at is distraction, but Garrett seems to be into that."

"That's unfortunate."

Rayelle smiles. "It is. He'll probably pick her as his partner when he wins the Quest, but every girl here wishes he'd pick them."

"Not me," I say as we pass into another glass room. The air here is thick and humid, and sweat beads on my forehead. "I hope nobody picks me."

"It's not an option. You have to assist in the Initiation Heist—it's your training for next year, when you lead your own heist. But don't worry. He won't."

Disappointment dips in my belly, and I'm annoyed that I care in the first place.

"Hey Sophia," Rayelle calls out. "Who's your roommate?"

Up ahead, a girl with white-blond hair that reaches her butt turns around. "Ugh. Harbor." Her eyes are huge, painted like a cartoon, and the only thing asymmetrical about her is a set of whiskers snaking over one of her cheeks.

"Weird," Rayelle says as we fall into step with Sophia. "Who's Chloe rooming with, then?"

"Nobody. The boys are in a triple, and she has a single. Wonder who arranged that." Sophia rolls her eyes.

"This is Elisha, by the way," Rayelle introduces me. "She's my roommate."

"New girl. Nice work at the assembly," Sophia says. "Were you trying to jump out the window or something?"

I feel the blood drain from my face as I picture my

ridiculous-scarecrow-act—all flailing arms until I launched myself across the room. *Awesome first impression.* "There was a bird flying straight for the glass, and I thought I could stop it." Tripping over my words, I quickly change the subject. "Do you two want to room together? I'll stay with Harbor. Everyone is new to me anyway."

They glance at each other and come to a quick decision. I'm jealous of their obvious telepathic connection, no doubt the result of years of friendship. *It's how Deena and I should have been.*

"Nah," Sophia says. "I wouldn't do that to you. I can handle Harbor."

"We call Chloe and Harbor the HMs—they're high maintenance," Rayelle says. "If you ever care what's what in Influencer culture, they're the ones to ask."

*Got it. I'll steer clear.*

The temperature shifts to a dry, mild warmth, and a soft breeze washes over us, as promised, smelling sweetly of citrus. We arrive at a single-story row of three rooms with floor-to-ceiling windows flanking each yellow door.

"Here we are." Rayelle inserts a key into the doorknob at room 222.

"I'm in 223," Sophia says. "But you'll be seeing a lot of me."

"Come over anytime," Rayelle says, opening our door.

Inside, the quarters are small but clean, with bamboo floors and white walls cast in the illusion of natural light. Each side of the room contains a tall bunk tucked with white linens and a desk with a bright yellow plastic chair beneath it. A low bookshelf and two white-lacquered dressers are the only other furnishings. At the back of the space, a narrow door leads to the restroom and shower.

Rayelle chooses the bed on the right and starts to unpack. Framed photos of her family and a ceramic elephant-shaped bamboo pot soon adorn her desk. A Cirque du Soleil poster with a unicorn painted in rainbow colors gets taped to her wall.

It doesn't take me long to unpack my meager belongings. I fold my jumpsuits into a drawer, burying the Balenciaga dress deep beneath them. It's my only worldly possession, the only thing linking me to my past, and I can't bring myself to part with it.

Climbing onto my sparse bed, I compare Rayelle's half of the room—colorful and full of life—to mine. Empty. A black-and-white sketch.

Wishing Adam had survived—that I could build my new life with an old friend—I blink back tears.

*I'm so alone.*

Inhaling, I hold my breath to keep myself together.

*But my only choice is to begin again. I'll add color bit by bit until the pencil marks disappear...*

# Chapter Five

*September 20X5: Keystone*

Rayelle and I wind our way up the stairs inside a giant sequoia on our way to master thief Weiss's Escape and Evasion lesson.

"Rumor has it Weiss went kinda nuts when he tried to escape from a burning coffin and almost didn't make it out alive," Rayelle says, her words coming out in little puffs. "He's a little off, but don't worry, he shouldn't make you try to escape from anything your first day."

"That's a relief," I say, heaving for breath in the thin air. "I've never escaped from anything. I wouldn't know where to start," I lie. *Never escaped from anything except my former life and maybe duct tape and rope ties, thanks to Allard's tutoring.*

We emerge onto a wide platform hidden high among the branches, invisible to the naked eye from the ground. It's cool and foggy up here, the rustle of leaves in the wind the only sound, until my ears pop and I catch the whispers of my fellow thieves. There are four tables in front of us, three of them occupied with two kids each.

As we take our places at the last table, I lean over to Rayelle. "Where's Sophia?"

"She's in the front row, next to Stewart." She points to a wiry, dark-skinned guy. "He's the smartest of all of us—can hack into any system—nobody thinks faster than him."

"That's Sophia?" I don't recognize the girl with pale-blue hair, a slim black ribbon tied around her throat, and gray boots inked with sketches. *There's no way that's the same girl I met yesterday.*

"Yep. She's a true artist. She'll look completely different tomorrow."

"Amazing."

"In the next row," Rayelle continues, "is Chloe—you know who she is—and she's sitting next to Harbor." With her translucent skin and wheat-blond hair, she's aptly named, as wispy as the fog rolling in on a December morning.

"In front of us are Toby and Marcel. Toby thinks he's hilarious." She rolls her eyes. "And Marcel is his sidekick."

"Settle in." Weiss appears at the front of the platform, his mouth set in a firm line. Despite his unruly brown hair, his eyes are serious, and he seems perfectly capable to me. "I trust you all had a productive break. Hopefully you used your time wisely and practiced escaping as much as possible."

"You bet we did," Toby says. "Watch me." He stands and heads for the stairs.

"Sit down, Toby. That's not what I mean."

Throwing his hands up, Toby retakes his seat.

"I'm not sure how good he is at escaping, but he could work on his stand-up routine," I mutter.

Rayelle giggles.

"As you're well aware, we have a new member joining us." Weiss gestures in my direction. "Welcome, Elisha."

Six heads turn toward me. "Thank you." I cringe, still

afraid of being recognized as Ella Karman.

"I've heard you're quite the talent," he says.

"I am?" I squeak, hating being put on the spot. *What does he know?* In my periphery, Rayelle cocks her head to the side.

Weiss smiles, and something wild enters his eyes. "Would you like to do the honors and take today's challenge first?"

"Not really?"

"Interesting," he says, his expression unwavering. "Rayelle! Come up here and show her how it's done."

With a sigh, Rayelle makes her way to the front of the class, where Weiss binds her wrists together with zip ties.

"Escape," he commands.

Flattening her hand, she pushes her thumb and pinkie to her palm and slides out of the zip ties.

Weiss frowns. "That's one way to do it, but it's not the way I taught you."

"But that's how I do it. I'm not strong enough to do it the other way," Rayelle says. "I still escaped."

He ignores her. "Go back to your seat. I'll expect you to do it correctly by the end of class or you'll be doing extra hours with me. Elisha!" He gestures me forward. "Your turn. Come on up. Show us why you're so special that rules don't apply to you."

Not understanding his meaning, I swallow hard, but knowing I have no choice other than to obey, I tuck my hair behind my ear, quickly securing it with a bobby pin from my burglary kit so it will stay out of my face, and walk to the front of the room. I face him as he zip-ties my already black-and-blue wrists together. Even though I hate being tested onstage, I try to hold my shaking hands steady, making sure to keep my elbows together as he pulls the ties so tight they cut off circulation.

"Now, escape," he says.

Escaping zip ties is something these kids probably learned in preschool, and I'm glad Allard brought me up to speed. When I first tried this a couple weeks ago, I wasn't able to create enough momentum to break the ties, but practice has paid off, and I have the bruises to prove it. Raising my arms above my head, I yank them down hard so my elbows split to either side of my body. The force almost knocks the wind out of me, but the zip ties pop off.

"Excellent. Pass." His voice betrays no emotion. Turning on his heel, he walks to a curtain at the side of the platform. If he was wearing a cape, he'd have made sure it swung out behind him in a wide arc. "Come here and bring your things with you." His index finger curls with the suggestion I follow.

Collecting my backpack from the table, I meet Rayelle's wide eyes. My throat goes dry at the terror reflected there, but I dutifully obey Weiss.

As I move the heavy brocade curtain aside, my stomach constricts at what awaits. Before me, a narrow plank juts off the side of the platform. My knees go weak at the sight of it bouncing in the breeze. Lacking guardrails, it gives way to a two-hundred-foot drop-off on either side.

"Step into the harness, please." Weiss holds out a set of canvas straps held together with a metal ring. "You may only use what you carry on your person. Leave your pack here and pick it up when you return." He gestures to my burglary kit, adding, "If you return," and punctuating it with a tight-lipped smile.

My throat struck silent, I nod. Setting my pack down, I step into the harness and take inventory of everything I possess, having no idea if it'll help me escape whatever awaits. Allard taught me to tie my shoes with rope-cutting paracord and put my lock-picking kit in my cargo pocket, but...

All business, he clips a cord to the harness and handcuffs

my hands in front of me before stepping aside. "You'll need to escape the cuffs. To the edge."

*Handcuffs? Allard taught me handcuffs, but what do I do again?* My mind goes blank.

"Faster!"

Startled, I inch onto the plank, my limbs shakier than the trees. I move forward until he tells me to stop. My toes flush with the edge, I focus on the horizon. Before me, the Sequoia National Forest sprawls to distant purple mountains, the treetops disappearing into the mist. Not wanting to risk dizziness that will disorient me, I keep my focus on the horizon.

Beneath my feet, the plank bounces with the weight of Wciss's approaching steps, upsetting my balance. Trying to hold steady, I pretend none of this is real. *I'm in a virtual game room. If I jump, I'll land on a trampoline. It's all an algorithm, a mind trick.*

"Everything that awaits will be much scarier than this," he whispers in my ear, sending a cold shiver down my spine. Then he shoves me off the plank.

The wind rushing in my ears is all that registers as I free fall and I don't scream. It's almost peaceful, with the leaves and branches whizzing by in a slow-motion watercolor landscape, until liquid-ice adrenaline floods my veins and I spring to action.

Tucking into a ball, I lower my head and retrieve the hairpin. Careful not to drop it, I straighten the metal, bite off the nubs, and bend one end to a forty-five-degree angle. I insert the pick into the small hole in the side of the cuff until it hits metal. Pulling down and to the right, I release the trigger. The cuff pops open, freeing my hands just as the cord snaps and I rebound back into the sky.

I make quick work of the second cuff on my way back up, and toss the handcuffs to Weiss.

Catching a glimpse of his astonished face before I free-fall back to earth, I bust into uncontrollable giggles. The bungee board catches, and again I bounce upward, a bird soaring to the sky. *Invincible. Free.* After so many suffocating months, the release brings tears to my eyes. My laughter doesn't subside even as I bounce to a stop. Still dangling high over the sequoias, I grip my ankles and sway my body back and forth until I swing close enough to the tree to grab a handhold and climb up to the plank. When I arrive at the trapdoor, I'm grinning in anticipation of my next challenge.

Weiss is waiting with my pack.

"Good job, Elisha." He frowns. Unclipping the bungee cord, he leads me to another platform. This one has a zip line attached to it and a sign that reads "To the Vault."

"I guess the rumors are true."

"Rumors?" My smile falters.

He doesn't respond, just clips me to the zip line and gives me a push.

"Marcel, you're next!" he yells. His words disappear in the breeze as I sail forward, cool wind stinging my cheeks, and am engulfed by the fog.

# Chapter Six

*September 20X5: Keystone*

Kneeling at the entrance to the Vault, I work out the access code in my head. Today's origami was a collection of three paper elephants. The Vault is one of the only places I feel safe, and I come here all the time, now. I've gotten pretty good at finding my way through the maze, and I love that I can steal whatever I want. Planning what I want to steal is way more fun than remembering the past. When the nightmares keep me up, which is most nights, I plot what I'm going to take next and how I'm going to do it. Allard thinks my time in the Vault is why I've honed my abilities so quickly. She thinks I'm a natural, but the truth is I've been deceiving since I could walk. My talents come from years of sneaking around pretending to be someone else.

"Need help?" an appealing male voice that hints at laughter asks.

Startled, I freeze.

Garrett looms above me, his arms folded over his chest. He's flanked by Chloe, Harbor, and a lanky guy I don't recognize. "The first number is seventeen."

Up close, he's more beautiful than I remembered, and the buzzing is instantaneous. His eyes are a soothing green-gray today, and his signature three black bars are expertly lined up on his cheek. Goose bumps rush up my arm, and, standing, I brush the dirt from my knees, my tongue turning to clay. "No, it's not. It's twelve," I manage to say. I smooth my hands over my pants, hoping the cotton will absorb the moisture.

"Just checking." Garrett tucks a strand of his messy, chin-length hair behind one ear, his perfectly bowed lips curving into a smile. "Lots of secrets down there. We can't let just anyone in."

"I'm not 'just anyone,'" I say without thinking, the old-me taking offense like I'd just been denied access to an exclusive club.

"Is that right, new girl?" he asks, scanning the length of my body. "So, who are you?"

Heat creeps over my skin, and I remember where I am. "I'm nobody," I whisper, held captive by his stare.

He arches an eyebrow. "Very good."

Chloe steps forward and circles me. "She's pretty plain. Unremarkable, I'd say. What's all the fuss about? She looks like a little girl…" She comes to a stop in front of me. "Don't let her in, Garrett. She probably thinks there's something down there that will help her influence her way through training."

*Influence?* The word sends me reeling, and I wish I could sit down to process it. *Does she know? Is that the rumor Weiss mentioned?* Blood rushes to my brain, dizzying me, but I hold steady. Something flares up inside me that won't let me show my underbelly, and I remember I don't want them to like me anyway. *Nobody cares who you are.*

Fingers gripping my hips, my shoulders meet my ears in

a show of nonchalance. "I'm allowed to study in the Vault, just like everyone else."

"I guess." Shrugging, she returns to Garrett's side. "Listen, we don't put up with cheating, sweetheart. This isn't like the place you came from. Here, you have talent or you don't."

"I wasn't aware 'decoy' was considered a talent," I reply.
She frowns.

The lanky guy bursts out laughing. "She's feisty. I like it. Haven't you heard 'the meek shall inherit the earth,' new girl?"

"Is that what you are? Meek? Planning to take over the world?" I raise my eyebrows. "And my name is Elisha."

"Liam." He reaches out to shake my hand. "And I don't need the world. While everyone else is living it up as an apathetic virtual human in the Super Brain, I plan on stealing what I need, holing up somewhere, and living happily ever after off the grid."

"The 'Super Brain'?" I ask, having no clue what he's talking about and ignoring his outstretched fingers. "That's what you think you've got between your ears?"

He laughs harder, shoving his rejected hand into his pocket. "You don't know, do you?"

"Know what?"

"Why do you think you're here?" he asks.

"To steal the truth for the good of humanity…"

Liam presses his lips together and approaches me. "That's cute." Leaning in, he smells my hair.

Totally confused, I freeze, sneaking a peek at Garrett. His head is cocked to the side, his eyes faraway and flitting back and forth like he's working out some intense calculation.

"Mmmm. Vanilla? Brown sugar? You smell like a girl," Liam says.

I have no words.

"Don't be weird, Liam," Chloe says.

"Where did your parents find her?" Liam asks Garrett, rejoining them.

Garrett focuses on my face, and I dare to meet his gray-green stare. It's like being lost at sea—his eyes beg me to sink into their depths—and a fresh wave of dizziness washes over me.

"Don't ask me," he finally replies. "They don't tell me anything. But she must be special."

"I don't get it," Harbor says, speaking to them like I don't exist, deceivingly sweet dimples appearing in her cheeks. "She's not a legacy—she came out of nowhere."

"Maybe she's a spy." Liam grins. "There's nothing hotter than a spy. Especially a spy spying on the spies."

"I'm not a spy," I snap, holding my chin high.

"Shut up, Liam," Garrett says at the same time. "My parents know what they're doing. I'm sure Ellie deserves to be here. She'll show us what she's got." Shrugging, he turns to go. "Let's eat. I'm hungry."

Chloe snakes her arm around his waist as they retreat.

"My name is Elisha," I say to his back, ignoring that he defended me.

He glances over his shoulder and smiles, sending a bolt of electricity straight to my toes. *Is it just me, or does he feel this crackling energy, too?* "See you around, Ellie."

My temper flares. Watching them go, I beg my heart to sever whatever connection it believes it has to him.

*I don't care what he thinks.*

Dropping to my knees, I turn the dial—*12-16-6*—and open the trapdoor. Careful to avoid the slippery moss, I climb down the stone steps and shut myself inside. I'd love to get lost in the Prado right now, to soothe my frazzled nerves by stealing *Las Meninas*, but I'm meeting Allard to recap my first day.

"You're late," she says when I arrive in the Musée de

l'Orangerie. She's waiting in the oval-shaped gallery lined with Monet's *Water Lilies*.

"I'm sorry. I had a run-in with Chloe and company," I reply. Chloe's name is bitter on my tongue. "She said I couldn't influence my way through training. Do you think she recognizes me?"

"No." She pats the bench next to her, and I sit. "If she did, she would've outed you already. She's fishing for info. I guarantee her reaction is because you're new. She's probably afraid of you."

"Afraid of me? Why?"

She thinks for a minute. "Part of disconnecting means severing pride, but thieves are a little different. Pride is our currency. We don't steal for 'the stuff' of it — it's about having anything we want — getting there first. We're competitive. Your presence at Keystone is highly unusual. The faculty were told you're a gifted thief with potential, and the students know an exception was made to allow your admission, but not the specifics. I'm sure that's cause for speculation. They assume you're greatly talented — and therefore a threat."

"Garrett did say I'd show everyone what I've got…" My heart skips a beat when I say his name. "But even *I'm* not sure I belong here."

"I am. Yesterday at the welcome assembly…the bird…you knew it was going to fly before it did."

"Don't remind me." My cheeks burn. "Nobody should be threatened because I speak bird."

She laughs and then sobers. "I'm being serious. You have superior intuition."

"I don't think so." I shake my head.

"It's true. I've been studying your DNA and brain scans for months, trying to make sense of it all." She takes a scroll out of her backpack and unrolls it. "This is a map of the connections in your brain. These are the parts that lit up with activity when I showed you flashcards and you guessed the image on the other side." She traces her finger over the bright red-and-yellow network on the right side of my brain. "Look at your locus coeruleus—that's a center for gut feeling—it's a fireball. I've never seen anything like it."

"What does it mean?" I ask, the brain map making zero sense to me.

"I'd dare to say—as we suspected when we brought you here—it means you possess 'quantum cognition' in the intuitive parts of your brain. In other words, you can perceive correct information about a person or situation and react with lightning speed. Babies are born with trillions of connections between their neurons, but the ones that don't get used are eventually eliminated. *You* seem to have retained all the connections related to intuition…"

"But how? Why?"

"Well, it might have something to do with your birth. Were you aware you're the product of three parents?"

My heart stalls. "No."

She nods, the facts spilling from her lips, her eyes glinting with excitement. "Your donor-father was Romanian, and one of your donor-mothers was Brazilian—like your 'parents'— but you also have a Lebanese donor-mother. I'm not sure if your intuition is a result of the genes that were so carefully selected at your creation—it's possible everyone is born with this power or could learn what is innate in you—but I'm telling you, you have quantum cognition. It's science."

I stare at her in a fog, my head spinning from information overload. "My parents always told me my DNA scans said I was meant to be an actress…"

"They weren't wrong… Acting is deception. That's a useful skill for a thief."

"But I believed everything they told me. My intuition was to trust them."

"Until something changed your mind," she reminds me. "Intuition is complicated. Maybe in the beginning your parents *were* looking out for your best interests—but then circumstances changed—and when they did, you fled."

*Three parents?* I can't wrap my head around it. "This is a lot to take in," I whisper.

"I'm sorry to dump it on you." She softens, placing her hand over her heart. "I know I can be a little clinical sometimes, but I thought you should know the truth. Your life is here, now, and I hope you can carve out an existence that makes you happy."

"Happy?" The word is foreign. "I'm not sure that's possible."

"Maybe this will help." Reaching into her bag, she pulls out a tiny black velvet box and hands it to me.

Running my fingers over the fuzzy surface, I will myself to focus on it, to stay present. *I can process everything in bed tonight.* I open the box, and nestled inside is a stone with amber and charcoal gradations polished to a silky luster.

"Consider it a gift from a friend," Allard says. "The color reminds me of your eyes."

"What is it?"

"Tiger's eye. It's thought to increase perception. The Egyptians used it as the eyes in their statues of deities as a symbol of divine vision."

"Is that science?" I ask. Picking up the stone, I expect it to vibrate with energy, but it remains cool and flat in my hand.

She laughs. "It's history. And antiquity is worth studying. Maybe the Egyptians knew something our brains have forgotten over time. Personally, I think there are frequencies at work we can't see. Do you feel them sometimes? A buzzing in your spine? The rushing of your blood?"

Garrett instantly pops into my mind. "Maybe. I don't know," I say, quickly pushing him out of my head, fearing she can read my thoughts.

"You will." She closes my hand over the stone. "Tiger's eye also aids determination and protects against the negative intent of others. Hang on to it. You might need it."

I wince. "I hope not."

"Me, too. But all the same, I want to keep you safe, Elisha. And I'm here to help you. We don't have to start tonight, but I think we should practice trusting your intuition. If you can let go of past assumptions and start over with a fresh, open mind, your instincts will be your secret weapon."

"How am I supposed to do that?"

"I believe you once kept a diary?" she asks, again reaching into her bag, this time pulling out a little leather-bound book. It reminds me so much of my Book of Secrets, goose bumps shoot up my arms.

Taking the journal, I nod.

"Maybe reliving the events that brought you here will be therapeutic. Analyzing your initial reactions to situations when already knowing the outcome will help you learn what to trust."

My trembling hands cradle the book. "I don't know if I can do that. The only way I'm surviving is by focusing on the future."

"But *I* think the only way you can move forward is to forgive the past so you can set clear intentions for the future. You need to confront and accept yourself in order to be free from judgment—of yourself and others. Are you willing to try?"

*Freedom from judgment… I'd love that…* I close my eyes, terror and hope colliding in my chest. *What do I have to lose? Maybe it's time to say goodbye.*

"I think so." Sighing, I open my eyes. "Where do I start?"

Allard smiles. "How about with what caused your death?"

# Chapter Seven

*September 20X5: Keystone*

My new journal tucked under my arm, I'm deeper in the Vault than I've ever been. The lanterns that line the more-traveled corridors are few and far between down here, and I don't bother lighting them. Shining my penlight on the dirt path, I wind my way through the mud tunnel, the damp air cool against my bare arms. The tunnel splits, forking in three directions, and my instincts lead me left. Pausing, I note the direction on the map I've drawn on the inside cover of my book so I can find my way out of here later. Closing the journal, I walk a few feet until my hair catches on a root. *At least I hope it's a root.* Picturing a crooked finger tickling my neck, I shiver. *I'm definitely deep enough for this to be a long-forgotten cemetery.* Before I totally freak myself out, I illuminate a small wooden door to my right with the word "Montauk" etched into it. *This is as good a place as any. Nobody is going to find me down here.* Inhaling, I turn the brass doorknob, praying I'm not walking into a closet full of skeletons.

The room is pitch-black. Half expecting to get a face full of spiderweb, I hold my breath as I duck through the doorway. Luckily, the coast is clear. Flashing light over wood-paneled walls and a brick fireplace, I straighten my spine under the vaulted ceiling, exhaling relief. I spotlight a floor lamp and switch it on, casting the small space in a warm, yellow glow. The only other furnishings are a cushy gray chaise longue next to an end table and a built-in bookshelf on which the book spines all face in, their aging pages turned out in variating lines of brown and cream. *So cool.* The fireplace is filled with candles, and, happy with my hideaway, I kneel to light them before curling up on the chaise with the journal on my lap.

*Me and my past, alone at last.*

A candle pops as I lift the cover, and I jump, my chest tight with anxiety. The blank, vanilla first page stares at me, impatiently awaiting the life only I can create for it. *But I don't want to go there. Not back, only forward…* My lower lip quivers, and I want to slam the book shut, to run screaming to the surface, but I take a deep breath. And another. And another, until my racing heart slows. *But back is the only way forward. You promised you'd try. Do it. Now. Write the first thing that comes to your mind. How did you get here?*

Before I lose my nerve, I roll up the tip of the gold-plated pen Allard gave me and begin.

*August 23, 20X4*

*It started with Adam.*

We met my first day at Intersection, the Hollywood high school all the top Influencer kids attended. I didn't know anyone except Deena. She'd been my best—and only—friend since we were five, when our moms launched a line of workout clothes together. We'd been dreaming of coming here—what we'd wear—who our first boyfriends would be—for years, but I hadn't seen her in person since her sixteenth birthday in February, when she debuted on the Social Stock Exchange. Since then, I'd devoured her Network feeds, and it was clear she'd been accepted to the "in" crowd. Deena was my only connection to what the outside world was really like, and I felt lucky she was my ambassador.

"Hey babe." Deena kissed my cheek, wrapping a spindly arm around me in a quick hug. Everything about Deena was skinny. Her limbs were knotted together at the joints, jutting knees and elbows. I wasn't sure how the ocean breeze didn't carry her away. "This is it. Welcome to the big time."

She gestured to an iridescent beach, where kids lounged on cushy pillows at long driftwood tables decorated with sea glass, white dahlias, and flickering votive candles like they were at some glamorous seaside resort instead of hanging at school. The salty air even smelled like coconut. The augmented reality probably sparkled with rainbows, but I hated wearing AMPs—contacts that exposed virtual overlays and made it possible to control the Networks with your eyes—because the excess imagery gave me a headache, so I'd never know.

"This place is so fancy," I said, hugging her back.

"It's all for the Networks. It will look totally different next week. Gotta keep the setting interesting for everyone's feed," she said. "Do you have Self-Awareness first?"

Flipping my wrist over, I swiped the screen sticker I wore instead of AMPs and studied my schedule. "Yep."

"Me, too. Good. I'll introduce you to Kylie and Lily," she said as we started walking toward class. "You're lucky. I've got them thinking they're better off having you as an ally. I wish someone had done that for me."

My stomach dropped. Having never been in a social

situation with kids my own age, I was already in knots and didn't need added pressure. I'd naively thought I would get to make my own first impression. "Why? They've never met me — how could they have already made up their minds about me?"

"You're new. You're pretty. And you had the highest debut price ever." Eyelashes fluttering, she rolled her eyes. "They don't have to know you to hate you."

I frowned, dread seeping through me.

"Relax. You're still going to be an actress, right?"

"The DNA scans all say so." I shrugged. My parents were actors, so it made sense to follow in their footsteps. I'd never considered anything else.

"That's good. None of us are actresses, so you won't be competition." Grabbing my hand, she pulled me to a stop. "It's going to be okay. Just follow the rules and you'll be fine." She adjusted the strap on my romper so it tucked away the skin bulging near my armpit, wrinkling her nose like the sight of the tiny lump disgusted her.

"Rule number one: always hide your armpit flab?" I smiled, hoping for a glimpse of my old friend, the one I used to giggle over the Networks with at sleepovers, but her eyes remained flat.

"Be serious, Ella." She flicked her hair over her bony shoulder. "Are you live right now?"

"No." I shook my head. "I haven't gone 'live' yet. I'm nervous about being 'on' all the time, and I'm afraid there's going to be a major sell-off if my investors see how boring my life really is." I double-checked the Life Stream icon on my wrist. Sure enough, it was set to private, promising the hundreds of cameras positioned around Intersection weren't recording me straight to the Networks. "But my parents are on my case. I'll be the star of my own Network movie soon enough."

"That's why you need Kylie and Lil." Seeming satisfied with my strap placement, she started walking again. "They live for drama. They make creating content easy."

"I can't believe I'm going to be friends with them," I practically squealed, my heart pounding in anticipation. Kylie and Lil were my celebrities. I'd obsessed over their Network feeds for years. Lily became famous when she was an adorable toddler, cheering her dad on at his football games. Now she was an Olympics-bound gymnast. And Kylie was a tastemaker with a hot body and her own swimsuit line that she loved to model.

They were everything I wanted—and needed—to be. Killing it, trading at Ä56, which was less than my debut price but more than anyone else on the exchange. Besides, my price was fake. My dad had a deal with some of his corporate buddies, who promised to buy into me to drive up my price—which was totally illegal—but I wasn't supposed to know that. I'd overheard my parents discussing it when I was hiding under the dining room table during one of their famous dinners. They partied with everyone—Influencers, rock stars, politicians, priests, corporate big shots—and I was never invited.

But that didn't stop me from attending in secret anyway. Eavesdropping was my favorite pastime—I craved the rush that came with being on the brink of discovery—and I recorded everything I overheard in my Book of Secrets.

"You're not friends yet," Deena said with a sideways glance that said *chill out*. "But I think you'll be okay as long as you do what I say. Here's how it is. We promote one another. That means reposting, commenting, and complimenting the squad on your Network feeds—talk about how lucky you are to have such great besties. And keep everything positive. A win for one of us is a win for us all. It's our job to build one another up."

"I can do that." I nodded.

We arrived at the Self-Awareness classroom, and she lowered her voice as we entered. "And most importantly, stay away from Adam. He's Lil's. And trust me. You want to stay on her good side."

I flinched at the bitterness in her voice, but she didn't give me time to ask for more info.

The classroom was furnished with bohemian knitted rugs, tufted floor cushions, and dozens of throw pillows. On the far side of the space, long reclaimed wood tables were arranged in a square, so the seats faced one another. Bypassing the lounge, Deena led me to the back of the room, where two girls watched us approach, eyes snaking over my body.

They were so flawless I wondered if I was looking through a filter. Bronzer sparkled on Kylie's high cheekbones, highlighting her tawny skin, and her luxe brown hair perfectly framed her face, while Lily's cloud of curly black hair contrasted with her wide, sky-blue eyes, making them pop. Or maybe it was the judgment in them that pierced me.

"Hey babes, this is Ella, who I was telling you about," Deena said, dragging me to a stop. "Ella, this is Kylie and Lily."

I smoothed my sweaty palms over my silk romper, standing so my thighs didn't touch.

"You look just like your mom," Lily said, standing. When she reached her full height, the top of her head barely reached my ear—and I'm not tall. Despite the genetic fiddling that took place at my conception, my parents kept me short like my dad. But Lily might as well have been a giant the way I wanted to cower at her feet.

"Did you really debut at Ä89 a share?" Kylie asked, squinting up at me.

"Yes." Holding my head high, I acted on a hunch that I was

worthless to them if I was weak, affecting a haughty-actress vibe though my stomach was doing flip-flops. "It was no big deal." I shrugged.

They stared at me.

Lily took a step closer, and the muscles in her shoulder twitched. My instinct was to recoil, to regain my personal space, but I held steady. "How'd you do it? You came out of nowhere," she said. Her breath was warm on my cheek.

"Everyone knew your parents had a daughter," Kylie said. "But no one ever talked about you. Personally, I forgot you existed."

"I got lucky, I guess." I wound a curl around my finger, mimicking my mother's signature move. "My parents' publicist leaked an ugly-duckling makeover story about me, and it caught on. Everyone loves a makeover."

"Interesting." Lily's eyes flitted back and forth like I was a book she couldn't wait to get to the end of, and I held my breath.

She studied me for a full minute until, finally, she smiled, revealing gleaming white teeth fitted together in a perfect line. "You can call me Lil. Everyone does, on account of the fact I'm so tall." She laughed, a tinny, joyless laugh.

Inwardly, I cringed. "Nice to meet you, Lily." Shifting my weight, I glanced at Deena, and she nodded. "Lil."

"Deena's told us great things. Sit with us," Lil said, moving a slouchy leather bag off a chair. "We have room for one more."

"Thanks." I sank into the offered seat. Deena squeezed my arm in celebration, taking her place between me and Kylie while Lil retook her seat on Kylie's other side.

"We have to make sure we can trust you, of course," Kylie said, leaning forward to see past Deena. "You'll have to pass our test."

My heart stalled. "What kind of test?"

"I haven't decided," Lil said, cocking her head to the side. "But we'll talk at lunch."

Behind her, kids filed in, setting up their tablets and chatting. The room was equipped with VR sensors in the lights so AMPs weren't required to see the few avatars present, but most everyone showed up in person. I'd expected them all to be A-list celebrity-avatar gorgeous and was disappointed at how average everyone was compared to Kylie and Lil.

Then *he* arrived—six feet of bleach-blond sun-kissed glory, complete with ocean-blue eyes—and my expectations were met. It might have been my imagination, but it seemed like a hush fell over the room when he crossed it.

*This must be Adam.*

Ambivalent to the hair flips and improved posture of the other girls, he casually slid into the empty seat next to *me*, even though the spot next to Lil was available, too.

Deena audibly gasped, and Lil's stare could have burned a hole in my romper. My chest tightened, but I scrolled through a Network feed on my wrist screen, pretending nothing happened while secretly checking him out in my periphery. A line of salt crust clung to his golden right cheek, and he was wearing board shorts. *Maybe he came from the beach?*

"Hi Adam," Lil said, her voice so sweet my teeth ached.

"Hey," he replied, taking a leather-bound virtual notebook out of a Quiksilver—probably one of his sponsors—backpack.

*Australian?* I immediately placed the accent, having practiced it as part of my acting studies.

"How were the waves?" she asked.

"Decent. Had to cut it short, though. Couldn't miss Self-Awareness." He rolled his eyes.

"No, you couldn't. It's the only class we have together." She was practically purring.

"Good Morning." A youngish teacher walked in and stood in the center of the room. He wore a ratty T-shirt with a stretched-out collar that showed off the slight slope to his shoulders, and his feet shuffled as he walked. He seemed anything but self-aware.

"A human?" I muttered under my breath.

"Yeah. Intersection keeps a mix of humans and robots on staff. They think it makes us more well-rounded," Deena whispered back. "It's really sad. He was a college football player on the fast track to becoming an Influencer, but he got injured and ended up here as a Laborer."

"We have no secrets in Self-Awareness, Ms. Karman." The teacher's voice boomed across the room, shutting Deena up. "Care to share yours?"

Everyone faced me. Under the pressure of eyeballs, heat rose in my cheeks, and I forced a smile.

"I'm Peter." He crossed the room and came to a stop in front of me with a curt nod. "Those debut numbers were almost too good to be true. Want to explain?"

Sweat trickled down the inside of my arm. "I'm not sure what you're asking."

"Then you're in the right place." His eyes bored into me, and I expected him to demand an answer, but he blessedly changed the subject. "Let me catch you up to speed. Diary entries are due tomorrow. They're an ongoing assignment. Part of being self-aware is listening to your inner monologue, and you're required to record your stream of consciousness once a day. If you're confused as to what an inner monologue is, these are thoughts that your Life Stream would have no knowledge of because they are only in your head." He tapped his forehead with his middle finger for emphasis.

"I know what stream of consciousness is," I said, anger flaring in my chest.

"Then you've already exceeded my expectations. But don't think that because you had the highest debut in history you're above doing the work. We can always work on mastering our thoughts."

I recoiled. Nobody had ever doubted me—my parents praised everything I did—and I wanted to stand up for myself, but I couldn't think of a comeback to save my life.

Dismissing me with a flick of his wrist, he faced the class with a superior smile. "Today we're going to work on *speaking* our inner monologue."

There was a collective groan, but I slowly exhaled relief at being out of the spotlight.

"The ability to speak your thoughts out loud is crucial in social situations," he continued. "When a group falls silent, you can keep the conversation going by voicing your inner monologue—what it's noticing, thinking. Chances are, others are thinking the same thing, they just aren't brave enough to say it out loud. By mastering this technique, you are mastering other people. They'll feel a connection to you—will open up to you—and this is the key to wielding your influence." He paused, taking a seat on the arm of an overstuffed chair in the lounge. "It takes coming out of your shell, though. You've got to have confidence. I'm going to pair you up."

The groaning intensified.

"Adam." Peter waved his finger in our direction. "You and Ella are partners. Go make yourselves comfortable."

My eyes widened.

"All right. Come on, Ella." Standing, Adam offered his hand. I could feel Lil shooting daggers into my back.

My tongue was wood, so I remained silent and allowed him to lead me to a floor cushion.

Once everyone was paired off, Peter continued his instructions.

"This is a trick stand-up comedians have mastered—you don't have to be as funny as them, though—anyone can do it. Speak your mind. What is your inner monologue noticing about the other person? What are your innermost thoughts?"

I sat facing Adam, my legs crisscrossed. The outline of his pecs was visible through his T-shirt, and his arms were big, but not too big. Lean. Strong. But there was no way I was saying that out loud. My clammy hands gripped the crochet cushion, my gaze frozen on his chest. Staring.

"I don't hear you talking!" Peter strolled around the room, pausing next to us. "Adam. You start. Show her how it's done."

Adam remained silent, and I snuck a glance at his face. He was smiling.

"Ä89. Impressive," he said.

"It's a start," Peter said, walking away.

I searched for lenses outlining Adam's irises, for a telltale sign he was doing an internet image search for my face. Getting lost in his blue eyes, I felt warmth spread over my skin, and in a flash, I had a vision of us huddled under an umbrella, laughing. Somehow, I knew—*knew* it in the center of my core—he was going to be important in my life. Taking a deep breath, I spoke what I was thinking. "Are you wearing AMPs? What app are you using? It's rude to spy on people, you know."

"No. I don't use those things—I like letting mysteries unfold naturally." His lips stretched farther, revealing a dimple in his left cheek. "Everyone knows your price. Tell me something no one knows."

"There's not much to tell. I'm not that interesting,"

"Not true. I think you're very interesting." His eyes lowered to my collarbone.

Butterflies flapped to life in my stomach, and I changed the subject. "I like your journal. Is that the new AS410?"

"It is. Thanks. It feels as close to real paper as you can get while still being digital. I like things that are tactile. Touch is my favorite sense." He inched his cushion closer to me, and my heart quivered. "Do you write?"

"What made you ask that?" I tilted my head to the side.

"I don't think any girl here would know the model number of my journal." His eyes glittered.

"Oh." I flushed. "I probably sound so lame."

"No, you don't. I like that you know. It makes you different. That's hard to come by. Nobody wants to risk having an opinion around here in case it messes up their rankings."

Liking the warmth spreading through me, I tucked my hair behind my ear. "Well, I guess touch is my favorite sense, too. But I don't have a digital journal. I have a real one. It's paper."

"Paper?" His eyebrows arched. "Won't you run out of space?"

"Maybe, but I haven't yet. I only write certain things in it. Secrets that I don't want anyone to know. Not my parents, not my Life Stream. I like knowing it can't be hacked. So much of my identity is on screens and in clouds—I like that there's part of me that only I know. With my Book of Secrets, I hold my identity in my hand."

"Book of Secrets? Is that what you call it?"

The burning on my cheeks intensified, and I closed my eyes. "Yes… I've never told anyone that, and now that I say it out loud, it sounds totally dumb."

"It's not." Laughing, he squeezed my knee, sending a jolt to my belly. "I'm into it. Do you know what I'm thinking?"

"No…" I peeked up at him from under my eyelashes.

"I'm thinking you're full of surprises, Ella Karman."

My name rolling off his tongue with that accent took my breath away. That's when Self-Awareness became my favorite class.

The room took on a hazy glow, and I wanted to know everything about him. "What about you? Tell me something you've never told anybody."

He thought for a second. "I might have to get back to you on that. The Networks make it hard to keep secrets. My investors get antsy if I'm private too long, but if I could sneak away, I'd go surfing…"

Fear shot through me at the reminder I should be live, that I needed Lil and Kylie to make me interesting. My vision cleared, and behind Adam, Lil came into focus. She was watching us, her lips pressed together in a thin line.

I bolted to my feet. "I'm so sorry. I really want to hear the rest, but I just remembered I've got to go."

"Now? But we're just getting started."

"It's my first day. I…just…can't do this." My voice cracked with desperation.

"Okay, but when can I see you again?" His fingers circled my wrist. "This sounds impossible and you're going to think this is a line, but I promise, it's not—I feel a really intense connection to you. Tell me you feel it, too."

Every ounce of me wanted to say yes, *knew* that he was going to be in my life; it was inevitable. But I needed to get away. To think. "Always leave them wanting more," I said, imitating my mother's most flirtatious smile. Detangling myself from his grasp, I found Peter and claimed girl problems as the reason I needed to be excused.

"Go ahead." He waved me off like he expected me to cut class.

As soon as I was outside, I found a bench and sat. Closing my eyes, I breathed deep to slow my racing pulse.

*So much for staying on Lil's good side…*
*I'm in trouble.*

# Chapter Eight

August 23, 20X4

*T*ruth: I am a person who will destroy someone else's life to save my own.

"How'd you like Self-Awareness?" Lil asked, her eyes flitting over me.

We were eating lunch on the Boulevard, the resort-style oasis dotted with lush palms, yellow umbrellas, and wood loungers arranged around a kidney-shaped swimming pool that served as Intersection's dining room.

I pressed my hands to my queasy stomach. "It was okay."

"Didn't you tell her about Adam?" Kylie whispered to Dee.

"It's fine," Lil said, sipping her sparkling water. "You're new, so you get a pass. But trust me, you don't want to let a boy come between us. It's terrible for your numbers." She stared at me until I blinked.

"Nothing happened, I promise," I rushed to assure her. "It's not like Adam chose me—Peter paired us up—and mostly he talked about surfing and how much he'd rather be doing that."

"Ella, we all saw how you were looking at him like a lovesick puppy," Lil said. "I get it. He's hot. You've had your one pass, and now you're over it, and it's time to prove we can trust you."

"Yes. You can trust me," I said. "I'll do anything."

Lil and Kylie looked at each other and smiled.

"Is everyone's Life Stream turned off?" Kylie asked.

I double-checked my wrist screen, even though I was positive my stream was off, and they all stared into space, their eyes blinking commands at whatever they were seeing through their AMPs.

"All good," Deena said.

"Me, too," Lil said.

I nodded.

Kylie turned to me, her eyes twinkling. "Do you have the Burble app?"

"No," I said, slowly. "What's that?"

"It's an app that sends messages from a Network account that you choose—not from yours," Lil said.

"Give me your wrist," Kylie said. "I'll download it for you." She took my arm.

"I should mention, as a general rule, if you're going to hang with us, you should keep your top on, and no sexting," Lil said while the app downloaded. "You'll see why in a second. Those pictures never die."

"No danger of that," I said, glancing at my microscopic breasts. "I don't have much to look at."

"It doesn't matter. Seeing you naked isn't what people get off on," she said. "It's how they can use it against you that makes them hot." The corner of her mouth curled up, and I cringed.

"Finished," Kylie said, holding my wrist up so I could see.

"Here's what we want you to do."

When I saw the image, I yanked my arm away, covering the screen with my palm like it had scalded my eyes.

"What is that?" I sputtered.

"It's a dick pic," Lil said.

"I saw. Whose dick is it?"

"It doesn't matter," she said.

"See that girl over there?" She pointed across the Boulevard to a cute girl with pixie-like features. "That's Samantha Valenti. She's a total Maker. Her parents own some children's clothing company, and they're hoping by going to school here she can launch them to Influencer status. She debuted at Ä4 a share or something pathetic like that. Anyway, she'll eat this up, so to speak. She needs the hype to get noticed, so she'll totally share it when you message her this picture from Peter's Network."

My jaw dropped. "But that could ruin his life. And hers."

"Exactly," Lil said. "Listen. We know your secret."

My heart thudded to a stop. A cool breeze licked over my skin, and I folded my arms across my chest, assuming they were talking about my inflated IPO. "You do?"

"Yes," Kylie said. "We know you're really no different than Samantha over there, trying to be someone she's not."

"But at least Samantha's mom actually gave birth to her," Lil said.

I choked on my salad, my eyes bulging like she'd slapped me, having never imagined they knew *that* secret. "Oh." Knowing where they got this information, I glared at Deena. She was the only person I'd ever confided in with the truth about my birth.

Her eyes were on her juice cleanse.

"It's no big deal—at least not to us—we all have secrets," Lil said, her voice sounding faraway. "If you prove we're friends, we'll protect you."

Slowly, the potential consequences of Deena's loose lips creeped in. *My parents' authenticity is their biggest asset. If their followers found out everything they've believed for the last sixteen years is a lie — if they stopped trusting them — their investors would sell... They'd be Unrankable.* My stomach churned as the tornado swirled in my brain, dizzying me.

"But I don't know any of your secrets," I whispered.

"If you text that picture to Samantha, we'll each tell you a secret," Kylie said. "You guard our secrets, and we'll guard yours. That's it. Otherwise, maybe you're better off sitting with Samantha."

*I'm trapped.*

"It's not like Peter was nice to you today," Deena said. "Teach him a lesson."

"I guess…" Glancing at my wrist, I swiped away the dick pic and scrolled through Peter's Network feed, hoping for evidence that he deserved to go to jail for soliciting a minor. All I found was a picture of him tenderly cradling a tiny infant with tubes coming out of its nose. The caption said, "Volunteering at the hospital today. This gives me hope that innocence still exists, that there are still people who need to be held, who benefit from human connection."

Tears stung my eyes, and sickness rose in my throat. I held the fate of both of my parents and Peter and Samantha and the infant in my hands.

"Your parents are supposed to have such good taste…" Lil *tsk*ed. "It would be a shame for the Networks to lose them, but starting over isn't always bad. I hear the Unrankable food plan is delicious." She sliced her seared ahi for emphasis.

Fear pierced my chest, and I wanted to throttle her.

*I can't betray my parents… Maybe Peter can hold Unrankable babies.* Swallowing hard, I faced Lily. "They really won't know it was me?"

"Nope," she said. "Not unless Burble gets hacked. Maybe you should get a throwaway screen to be safe and do it from there."

I nodded. "Okay. If no one will know it was me, and if you'll tell me *your* secrets, I'll do it tonight."

After school, Deena and I picked up coffee and headed to a stretch of Venice Beach that wasn't augmented. Nobody ever went there because it was so ordinary looking, and I knew we'd be alone.

We kicked off our shoes, walking along the edge of the water. The wet sand was reassuring between my toes, and once I was satisfied the roar of the waves would drown out our voices, I confronted her.

"Shut off your screens. You're not going to want this in your Life Stream." Pulsating waves clouded my vision, casting her in red.

"Okay…" She frowned but complied.

"How could you tell them that secret?" I asked as soon as I was certain we weren't being recorded.

"Don't be mad, Ella. I had to. The only way we're going to maintain our numbers is through Lily and Kylie. I did it for you." Her voice was calm, practiced. "They needed to know you weren't a threat. If I didn't tell them something good, they would've made your life miserable. You need their protection, and so do I."

"You couldn't have made something up? You totally sold me out." Gritting my teeth, I couldn't look at her. I kept focused on the path in front of me. One foot in front of the other, kicking up sand.

"I'm sorry you feel that way, but the truth is best. Trust me. They're like human lie detectors. They had to claw their way to the top, and they'll do *anything* to keep themselves there."

"I'm sorry if I have a hard time trusting you."

She shook her head. Grabbing my shoulder, she forced me to stop. "Look. You'll figure it out soon enough. It's eat or be eaten. You would've done the same for me."

I searched her eyes, hoping to find my friend. "You don't have any secrets."

"Yes, I do! You know I had my stomach stapled," she replied. "That could take down my entire family, too."

"That's nothing in comparison. It wouldn't take you down— it would probably build you up. Poor abused girl, forced to starve for the rest of her life."

"You make it sound like it's no big deal." Her jaw clenched, and she practically spit the words. "Do you know what it's like to not be able to eat? I'd love to devour an entire slice of pizza, but I can only have one bite or else I'll throw up. And isn't that ironic, since the reason they did this to me was so I wouldn't have to suffer like my mom did for her career. So I wouldn't end up sticking my finger down my throat."

"I'm sorry." I focused on the sand. "I can't pretend to understand."

She softened. "Besides, same with you… Generic farmed girl rises to fame… It's our parents who are in danger. Not us. We have the power here." Her eyes were pleading, but the betrayal was too fresh, and I put up a wall.

"*You* have the power, and you know it. I'd never survive. I may be genetically Unrankable." I shuddered.

"People love a rags-to-riches story, but it won't come out. I promise. Lil and Kylie will protect you."

"As long as I send that picture, as long as I ruin someone's life!"

"It's better than your life being ruined."

The icy ocean swirled around our ankles, but the cold failed to penetrate. I was numb. "I feel like you robbed me. Maybe I could have been friends with Kylie and Lil without you paving the way."

"With your numbers? You were ripe for a takedown. You're a threat. I had to convince them it was safer to align with you." Her cheeks flushed with anger. "I did you a favor, and don't you forget it."

I narrowed my eyes. "Don't worry. I won't."

Throwing up her hands, she headed down the beach alone before whipping around, her voice sailing toward me on the breeze. "Ella, this isn't the fairy-tale world we thought it was going to be. I hate to break it to you, but you'll see. You'll do things you never imagined."

"Like send a dick pic?" I asked, scurrying to catch up with her, my feet sinking in the sand, slowing my progress.

"That's just the beginning. You'll do things that are much, much worse. The faster you realize you don't have any friends, the better off you'll be." Her long, blond hair thrashed at her cheeks.

"Starting with you?" I came to a stop in front of her.

Her eyes filling with tears, she didn't respond right away. I almost thought I glimpsed my friend, but in a blink, she was gone, replaced with the steely replica of someone I used to know.

"It's how it has to be," she said.

*Sadly, she was right.*

My head is spinning, my hand is cramped, and I can't write anymore. Setting down my pen, I wipe my wet cheeks with the back of my hand, my stomach clenched with self-loathing. Drained, like reopening old wounds has bled me dry, I close the book.

*And the worst is yet to come...*

*I hate this.* Curling up, I press my head to my knees, hugging myself like I could squeeze the ache out of my heart. *It's like losing them all over again. Is reliving these memories even working? Were my instincts right about anything? I was so certain Adam was going to be in my life, and look how that ended up.* A single tear slips down my cheek. *I should have turned and run the second I got to Intersection. But if I did, I wouldn't be here...*

My run-in with Chloe and Garrett from this morning pops into my head.

*At least I didn't back down.*

Pressing my knees to my chest, I lift my head and breathe deep. As my lungs expand, hope creeps into my chest.

*I'm glad I'm here, that I have a life where numbers mean nothing. At least I know who I am, now...*

*This time is going to be different.*

# Chapter Nine

*September 20X5, Keystone*

"Sophia's already here," Rayelle shouts, pointing at a girl with powdered white skin and a black widow's peak who is sitting alone.

"I'll take your word for it," I yell over the din of the lunchroom.

Nestled in a grove of olive trees, the Atrium is located at the center of the circle that connects the grow houses and dorms. Metal scaffolds lined with pots growing fresh herbs create private nooks, and without the Network to distract them, kids are actually talking to each other. Their voices, combined with clacking silverware and chairs scraping across concrete floors, bounce over the hardscape.

"Come on." Rayelle bumps her tray against mine, and I slowly follow her toward Sophia, stealthily scanning for Garrett, as has become my tendency. Our paths haven't crossed since our run-in outside the Vault a week ago, and as much as I want to ignore him, there's no use fighting his draw.

He's hanging with Kyran and Liam in a crop of cushioned

modules surrounding a firepit. Chloe and Harbor are there, too, acting like princesses on their thrones.

Indulging in a moment of observation, I sink down next to Sophia.

Placing her hand on Garrett's arm, Chloe whispers something in his ear that makes him grin. A bolt of heat explodes in my brain. *Maybe if I stare hard enough, I can slam her backward into a scaffold without moving a muscle.* It's wishful thinking. For some reason, seeing them together gets on my last nerve. It's ridiculous—I have no reason to be so possessive-obsessive—but I don't like her touching him.

"Did you hear about Faye?" Sophia asks, arching an eyebrow over a fuchsia eyelid with spider-thin liner legging out around it.

Reluctantly, I drag my attention to her. "Who's Faye?" I sample a French fry. I can't get over eating real food anytime I want. Meal-replacement drinks aren't an option here. Steak and fries for lunch? Yes, please. Sign me up.

"She brilliantly just stole the Fairchild Patent Notebooks from the Computer History Museum in Mountain View," Stewart answers, setting down his kale salad and cedar-planked salmon. Brain food, he calls it. "Cunning and beautiful. That girl is killing it."

Sophia rolls her eyes. "Looks aren't everything, Stewart."

"You know me. I'm only interested in her mind," he says, winking. "But no wonder Garrett was into her."

"That's a rumor. You don't know what happened. No one does," Rayelle says.

My ears perk up. "What are you talking about?" I busy myself slicing my steak, pretending I'm not *that* interested.

"Garrett was Faye's assistant in last year's Initiation Heist, and something went wrong," Rayelle whispers. "It was bad. They almost didn't complete their mission."

"Most people think they were hooking up and lost track of time," Sophia says.

"This was pre-Chloe, of course," Stewart says. "It'll be interesting to see who Garrett picks this year. Chloe's the obvious choice, but after last year maybe he'll play it safe, pick someone who won't be a distraction—"

"Rumor has it you passed Weiss's handcuff test in record time," an amused voice says from behind me. I flinch, heat surging to my cheeks at the thought that he might have heard us talking at the same time goose bumps shoot up my arms. My insides immediately buzz.

Rayelle and Sophia snap to attention, and Stewart has the good sense to shut up.

Garrett towers above me with Chloe draped over his shoulder. I glance around to see if he means someone else, but his eyes are on me.

"I guess…"

"Looks like you have competition." He nudges Chloe.

She frowns. "She got lucky with Weiss. I heard Allard has been tutoring her—she probably knew what was coming. But nobody knows what's on the obstacle course. She won't be able to cheat next time."

My jaw twitches, and I square my shoulders. "I didn't cheat, but I'm sorry you're so insecure you can't handle another girl succeeding."

Stewart almost spits out his salmon.

Instead of dignifying me with a response, Chloe curls closer to Garrett, tugging on his collar. "Why are we wasting our time with these hacks? Let's go."

He allows himself to be pulled away, but not before smiling at me and saying, "Nice, Ellie."

"Elisha," I correct him.

Pressing his lips together in a smirk, he walks off. As soon as he's gone, the energy fizzing in my spine disappears.

"I'd rather be a hacker than a decoy," Stewart mutters.

"What was that about?" Rayelle squeaks.

"I don't know," I say. "They have it out for me. I think it's because I'm new."

The three of them look at one another, biting their lips.

"I don't know what you all see in him, anyway," I say.

"Did you see the same boy we saw?" Stewart asks. "Because the boy we saw is seriously fine."

"Yes, he's cute—" I say.

"Cute?" Stewart says. "Nobody would call him cute. Puppies are cute. A hamster wearing a top hat and bow tie is cute."

I roll my eyes. "Fine. He's hot."

Stewart's fingers curl, gesturing for me to give him more.

"Hotter than hot. Like surface of the sun hot," I say, my cheeks on fire. "*Caliente.*"

"Cali-what-now?" Stewart laughs.

"As hot as my face is red," I say.

"Oooh. Yeah," Stewart says. "That's hot."

We all bust out in giggles, and I throw a French fry at him, warmth spreading through me. *I don't remember the last time I laughed with friends.*

"I meant it seems like he's trapped under Chloe's thumb," I say as my laughter subsides.

"Never," Sophia says. "You'll see. He'll dump her as soon as he gets officially initiated and leaves Keystone. He's a guy, and she's probably fun for now."

"Being a guy isn't an excuse," I reply.

"I don't know how he can stand her. She's the worst," Rayelle says, pushing her food around her plate.

I raise my eyebrows. Even though I've only known her a week, it's unlike her to put anyone down.

"Nobody remembers," Sophia says, placing a hand on Rayelle's arm. "It's ancient history."

"History never dies in this place, remember?" Rayelle says, turning to me. "Last year, Chloe spread a rumor that I got so drunk at the Into the Woods party I passed out and wet my pants—which is totally untrue—but it stuck. I shouldn't care, but it still makes me mad. Why would she say that? It's not like I'm anything to her."

The hurt in Rayelle's eyes cuts right through me. "She must be jealous," I say. "Maybe you *are* competition for her. Maybe flexibility is her weakness."

"Poor Garrett," Sophia says.

We burst into laughter again.

"No matter what, you have to beat Chloe in the obstacle course, Elisha," Stewart says. "She's totally afraid of you. Can you imagine the look on her face if she lost to a nobody?" He claps his hands before squeezing my shoulder. "No offense."

"None taken." I hold back a smile. "Besides. There's no chance of me winning. I'm *so* behind."

"But Allard is helping you," Sophia says. "That must count for something."

"It doesn't matter." I shake my head. "I'm learning what you all learned when you were five. There's no way I'm going to be in the top four."

"You're probably right," Stewart says slowly. Then his eyes light up. "Maybe I'll win."

"You do that," I say.

"And who will you pick for your partner, Stewart?" Rayelle asks.

"Garrett, obviously. He's the only choice."

"You could definitely learn from him," Sophia says. "Have you ever thought about doing some push-ups?" She taps one of his skinny arms.

"Ew. No. The boys like me wiry."

We all groan.

"No. They don't." Sophia laughs, turning to Rayelle. "Who would you pick?"

"Probably Kyran."

"Kyran? Really?" Sophia says, though I'm not surprised.

"He's just so…interesting." Rayelle blushes. "What about you, Elisha?"

"Me? No one. I pick no one." I imagine myself standing in the Lodge with everyone staring at me while I choose. There's no way I want to draw that much attention to myself. "If we don't win the Quest, they pair us up with someone anyway, right?"

"Yes. But you could get stuck with Liam," Stewart says.

"Ugh." I frown. "That's enough to make me work on my escape moves, but it's a risk I have to take. There's no way I'm going to win. I'll be lucky if I don't get sent to the Farm."

"We won't let that happen," Rayelle says. "Promise."

"Yeah, if you ever need help or have questions, just ask us," Stewart says.

"Actually, I do have a question." I scan their faces, wondering how dumb I'm going to sound. "Liam said something the other day about a 'Super Brain'? What is that?"

Their smiles falter.

"We'll let you field this one, Stewart," Sophia says.

He takes a deep breath, his fingers drumming on the table. "Basically, you know how President Madden is implementing her plan for world peace, right?"

"Yes, everyone loves her," I say. "She wants to bring people together — Corporates, Influencers, Laborers, Unrankables — no more labels. We'll all be equal. Isn't that what we want, too?"

"Not exactly." He wrinkles his nose. "That all sounds

great in theory—she knows what people want to hear—but everyone, except the Disconnects, already voluntarily use tech that allows every move to be tracked. And soon her messaging will suggest everyone should voluntarily put computer chips in their brains and upload their minds to a database—the Super Brain—that will connect them to the internet, too. It'll sound like a good idea. Who wouldn't want access to all of human knowledge? To think a question and instantly get the answer? Nobody will be smarter than anyone else. We'll all be equal, part of the collective world consciousness."

"The thing is," Sophia jumps in. "The information in the Super Brain is being chosen by the Corporates to build the society *they* want to live in. They're rewriting history to create an artificially-intelligent simulation where robots will do all the work and we'll play all day. Any experience we want will be virtually at our fingertips. Criminal urges and what they call the 'ugly past' will have been erased from memory."

"And all of that will come at the expense of emotions and free will," Rayelle says. "We won't feel anger or love or excitement. We'll be apathetic puppets on her peace playground."

"I don't know about you, but if I'm going to get gobbled up by the Super Brain, I'd at least like to know it has its facts straight," Stewart says.

"We don't have to get gobbled up, though, do we?" I ask.

"Not if we do our jobs. The only thing standing in the way is the Disconnects. The Unrankables will chip their minds in a heartbeat at the promise of prosperity. Keep people hungry, and they'll do anything for a handout." He shrugs. "We're pretty much the only ones who can save human life as we know it."

My mouth hangs open. "I can't even begin to process this."

"It's a doozy," Stewart agrees. "But you asked."

The Atrium lights dim, signaling lunch break is ending and everyone stands.

"I've got Code Breaking, so I've got to run," he says, taking his tray to the compost bins. "But I'll explain more later."

"The point is, we need all the help we can get," Sophia says, matching steps with me as we head to Forgery class. "So, let's keep you off that farm."

"I'll do my best," I say, uncertain if my best will be good enough. *Though I definitely prefer the Farm to the Super Brain...*

# Chapter Ten

*October 20X5, Keystone*

I bang on Allard's door, announcing my presence before letting myself in. "I'm here!"

"Elisha? Is that you?" she calls from the kitchen.

"Yes!"

Some old-timey music plays on the turntable, and I half expect her to appear wearing a vintage Dior dress borrowed from the replica of the Victoria and Albert Museum's costume collection in the Vault. They have clothes that are hundreds of years old down there and an entire wing dedicated to disguises that we can borrow. It's one of my favorite places to hang out.

"Have a seat. I'll be right out," she says.

Sinking onto the tweed couch, I pick up her coffee-table book, absently flipping through photographs of Frank Lloyd Wright–designed houses, wondering why she so urgently summoned me here. I'm reading about Fallingwater when I notice indentations left from handwriting in the margin. I try to make them out.

*Safety in stone—*

"Are you ready to get to work?" The kitchen door swings open, and she appears, wearing a white lab coat, her red hair clasped in an array of wispy tendrils that refuse to stay in place. She's the complete opposite of what I imagined, and I bite back a laugh. *You can take the girl out of Hollywood…*

"What are we studying tonight? Code breaking?" I ask.

"I thought we'd work on intuition," she replies. "How's journaling going?"

I grimace. "It's not exactly fun…"

The corners of her mouth turn down, and she nods. "Dredging up the past is hard, but I truly believe it will be worth it in the end."

"I hope so." The terrible things I have left to record flash through my mind, filling me with dread.

Taking a seat next to me, she rests her elbow on the back of the couch and cocks her head to the side. "Let's try an exercise on first impressions. What did you think the very first time you saw me? What's the first word that comes to mind?"

I think back to that day at the Anonymous pub. "Dangerous. I wanted to run."

"And rightly so. I was a threat to everything you knew—to the life you led."

"But then you started talking, and I felt better. I was mesmerized."

"I'd say our friendship worked out. Wouldn't you?"

"Yes." I nod.

"So, your instincts were correct. Let's try another one. How about Garrett? First impression."

My stomach drops in embarrassment. "I don't want to answer that."

She laughs. "Pretty please?" She bats her eyelashes. "I promise there's a point to this."

Rolling my eyes, I sigh. *I wanted to collapse at his feet.* "It was weird. It seemed like the lights glowed brighter, and the air was humming, and I wanted him to notice me. But the second time it was like I needed him, like I wanted to use him. I turned into the old me. It can't be right."

"Interesting," she says, opening a notebook and jotting something down. "I think you *are* right. Garrett operates at a higher frequency than most people. You felt that. He has a knack for attracting the tools necessary for him to succeed. It might just be that he needs *you*."

"I doubt that."

"Well, doubt is what we're here to work on." She smiles.

Still skeptical, I shake my head.

"Maybe it wasn't the 'old you' you were glimpsing, but the 'new you.' The confident you," she continues. "The you who is so steadfast in your calling to reveal and preserve what you *know* is truth you'll do whatever it takes. When you get into the field, it will be necessary for you to deceive others—to make them believe you're one of them—and you can't do that until you believe in yourself—until you know that what you stand for is right and good. Until you trust your instincts."

"It sounds impossible." I squint into the last of the golden light glinting off the river.

"It's not. I promise." Rising, she draws the curtains against the setting sun. "Let's work on forgiving who you were raised to be. It's okay to admit you come from a less-informed place. You're growing and learning. It's a process. Stop beating yourself up. Are you willing to try something with me?"

"Do I have a choice?"

"Not really."

"Go for it, then." I shrug.

She rejoins me on the couch. "Close your eyes and think

of a time you were unfair to someone. Start with something insignificant. You can work your way up to the bigger things."

"Okay." Taking a deep breath, I remember a day on the Boulevard. *Lily and I walk up to our bistro table, where a skinny freshman girl with bad skin is sitting alone, eating a sandwich. She emanates a loneliness so deep my chest aches. Remembering nights as a kid when I was left at home with nannies and robots while my parents were vacationing for weeks on end—when I felt invisible and unwanted—I want to be kind to her. But Lily is watching, and I need to prove myself. Eat or be eaten.*

*"You're in my seat," I say, injecting ice into my voice.*

*The girl looks up. "I'm sorry?"*

*"You're in my seat. This is our table. You can't sit here." My hands tremble, but I persist.*

*"It's a free world." She tries to look tough, but her lips wobble. My heart screams for me to end its aching, for an act of kindness, but I silence it.*

*"Do you know who we are?" Lil asks, having no time for someone who doesn't instantly acknowledge her clout. "You're about to find out." Deena, Kylie, and Jaxon file in behind us, and fear creeps into the girl's eyes. Everyone on the Boulevard is watching.*

*"This is our table," Deena says. "You need to leave."*

*The girl still refuses to budge—whether it's out of pride or fear, I don't know. But Jax makes the next move, sitting next to her, his thigh touching hers.*

*"If she won't move, we'll have to sit on her," he says.*

*They all pile onto her, then, squishing in close, smothering her. I'm supposed to join them, but I can't bring myself to do it. I wish I could stop them, but I can't do that, either. I back away from the scene.*

*She doesn't know what to do—looks wildly around, her*

*face bright red—until she gives up. Grabbing her bag, she squeezes herself out from under them and is subjected to the stares—and probably worse, the pity—of the entire school.*

*My stomach twists.* Then and now. *How could I be so cruel? She probably was the only worthwhile person in that place.*

My sinuses burn.

"Don't judge yourself," Allard says softly. "Forgive that side of you. Acknowledge it, destroy it, and let it go. You will do better, be better. You already are."

Keeping my eyes closed, I nod. *It's in the past. I'm not that person anymore. I was weak, insecure, needed validation, and had to cut down others to feel okay about myself. I have confidence now.* I think back to how mean Chloe was to Rayelle, and I know what I have to do. *I will defend those who can't stand up for themselves. If someone is hurting, I will do something about it. I will find the good in everyone and help them see the gifts they have to offer.* As I take the vow, relief that I've acknowledged my shortcomings rushes through me. *I will speak up. I'll be like Adam.*

As soon as he pops into my head, I fall down a rabbit hole of memory.

*As I'm backing away from my "friends," I bump into someone tall and strong and solid. Turning around, I look up into those mesmerizing watery blue eyes that crinkle at the corners when he recognizes me. We haven't talked since that day in Self-Awareness. Fearing Lil's wrath, I've kept my distance, and lately he's been attending class virtually anyway. According to his Networks—which I only stalk when I'm in bed, buried under my covers with my Life Stream turned off—he's been surfing a lot. Even though a relationship with him is impossible—Lil aside, I'm not sure I'd be good for his numbers—I fantasize about what it would be like to be with him. I wish I could ask Quinn, our household AI, who is my other BFF, aside from Deena. Even though she's not human, she understands me better than anyone. Nobody in my family makes a move without running the numbers with Quinn first. She could tell me with almost 100 percent certainty if the public would like Adam and me together, but I can't ask her. Letting my true feelings be known outside of my Book of Secrets is too risky. Everything is so connected; it could find its way back to Lil. No information is safe.*

*"It's my lucky day," he says, his Australian accent weaving his words into a symphony. "Just the girl I've been looking for. I haven't been able to stop thinking about you."*

*My cheeks flush, and I say the first thing that comes to mind. "I wish I knew how to flirt so I could come up with something cute to say, but I don't, so I'll admit I've been thinking about you, too…"*

*He grins. "You're perfect just the way you are, Ella. Don't ever change."*

*A thrill shoots through me, and, not wanting to let on how much he means to me, since I barely know him, I change the subject. "It seems like you've been busy surfing."*

*"Yeah. Gotta keep my investors happy, and that's what they buy into me for." He shakes his head. "A clothing company just paid a lot of money to use my name for a line of surf T-shirts, and the whole deal depends on how much I can sell from my Network feed. It's a lot of pressure. I've got to keep finding ways to get people's attention—surf bigger waves, be a spectacle. I don't know… It's not really working, but I've got to come up with something. You know how it is."*

*I nod. "I do. My numbers aren't growing, and my parents are on my case to inject some drama into my feed before they have to find me some." I roll my eyes. "But I don't want to publicize the drama at Intersection. It's too depressing." Cocking my head, I glance toward Lil and the gang.*

*His eyes focus over my shoulder, and he frowns. "Those guys are dicks."*

*At that moment, Lil looks up. I feel her eyes staring me down and I know I've got to end this.*

*"They—we—I—made her move..." I whisper, tears crowding my eyes.*

*He follows my gaze across the Boulevard to where the girl now sits in a corner, shoulders slumped.*

*"I hate myself for it...but I'm stuck..." I say. Sensing Lil's impatience is intensifying, I take a step backward. "And I should probably go before Lil gets any more pissed."*

*He reaches out to touch my arm but pauses in midair, seeming to think better of it. "I get it. Don't worry, Ella. We'll stay in touch. I'll find a way. Be strong."*

*With that, he brushes past me, leaving with an almost imperceptible wink.*

*I watch him walk over to the girl and ask to sit with her. My heart fills to bursting, and all I can think is, "Don't ever change..."*

*Bang, bang, bang.* Someone pounds on the door. Allard and I both jump.

"Who is that?" she wonders.

"Weiss," I reply without thinking. He's the first person that pops into my head.

"Wait here," she says, standing.

I sink low on the couch as she opens the door.

"Weiss. What are you doing here?" she asks.

"I saw your light on. You know it's candles only after seven."

"Of course," she says. "I was reading and must have lost track of time. Thank you for the heads-up." She clicks off the light.

"Goodnight."

"Goodnight."

She closes the door and turns to me. "You knew it was him. Instincts."

"Instincts."

"Remember how that felt," she says.

I nod, memorizing the rush that sparked in my brain, the almost-audible burst of wind that accompanied the answer.

"I wonder…" She pauses, thinking out loud. "If you could hone your instincts so that when you think of someone, you get an impression of where they are and what they're doing…"

"I don't know… Is that even possible?"

"It might be. With practice. Are you willing to experiment?"

*What events would I have to relive to get to that level?* Exhaustion overtakes me, and I rub my eyes. "Yes. But not tonight. I should be going."

"Of course. Another day." She shows me to the door.

Before I go, I stop, not wanting to go outside if Weiss is lurking. "Does Weiss come by often?"

"No. It's unlike him."

"He's super creepy. Do you think he knew I was here?"

"No… I actually have another theory." She grips the doorknob but doesn't open the door. "I've been experimenting with the idea that when people with higher brain function like yourself—and Garrett—are in a meditative state, you receive what you send out. Like if you send out fear, you receive fear. If you send out hate, you attract hate…"

*Maybe that's what happened in Tahoe. I sent out hate and brought the evil to us.* My throat constricts at the notion. Rosy memories surface—me and Deena as little girls—sleepovers and secrets and dreams. The good times blot out the bad, and I'm drowning again. *Nobody should ever get close to me.* But I fight to surface, to forgive. *It's not your fault. That's not who you are anymore…* I force my focus to Allard.

"…but if you send out love, you receive love," she continues.

Letting out a bitter laugh, I swallow my tears. "No danger of that."

"You never know." She squeezes my arm. "And if it's okay, I'd like to do some more brain scans soon to see if our work is increasing your connectivity."

"Sure," I say. "Anytime."

"Thank you. Now, don't worry about anything else tonight. Go get some rest." After wrapping me in a brief hug, she shows me outside. "I'll set something up soon. I wonder if I could get some scans of Garrett, too. It would be interesting to compare the two of you."

"That would be fascinating," I say, injecting sweetness into my voice before disappearing into the night so I can go bang my head against a wall in private.

# Chapter Eleven

*October 20X5, Keystone*

*Two twists to the right, one to the left...* I trigger the pin, hold it in place with my L rake, and feel for the next one. Deep in the vault, I'm attempting to steal the Pink Star, a fifty-nine-carat pink diamond that sold at auction for Ä83 million. According to the plaque on the glass case, the collector who purchased the diamond is actually the proud owner of a 3-D printed replica. The original stone was stolen by a Keystone Disconnect years earlier, when it was on display at the Smithsonian, and that's where it lives now—in the Vault's version of the Smithsonian's special exhibit hall. The collector never came up with the currency to purchase the stone, anyway, and the replica resides to this day in Sotheby's inventory.

My full concentration on the lock, beads of sweat form on my forehead. *Just one more second—*

"I never pegged you for pink."

The voice startles me, and my hand slips, sending my L rake rattling to the floor and triggering the alarm. Pulsating sirens reach air-raid status, and, whipping around, I clamp my hands over my ears.

Garrett stands behind me, smug. *And alone.*

"Didn't anyone teach you not to sneak up on people?" I yell.

He crosses the room and punches a code into a keypad mounted on the wall. "Actually, no. I've been trained to *always* sneak up on people. You should watch your back." The alarm abruptly goes silent.

"I'm no stranger to that." I stand frozen in place, every muscle in my body tense.

His footsteps echo against the stone floor. Electricity surges up my spine, a ball of buzzing energy, as he draws closer.

*I need you.*

The thought pops into my brain, and I instantly dismiss it, annoyed at my body's physical reaction to him.

"You could've fooled me." He grins. "It's pretty girly, don't you think?" He points at the cotton-candy-colored gem. "Of everything in this room, *that's* what you choose to steal?"

Ignoring his smile, I try to be the girl Allard wants me to be. *I don't need Garrett to like me.* "Why wouldn't I want a pink diamond? I *am* a girl."

"You just don't strike me as someone who is easily dazzled."

"I'll take that as a compliment."

"I meant it as one." He raises his eyebrows, and my heart skips a beat.

Squelching the quiver in my belly, I shake my head and draw on my Self-Awareness days. "Uh-uh. I'm not falling for any of this."

"Any of what?" He cocks his head.

"This." I wave my hand in front of his face. "You're cute, but I'm immune to cute. I'm not going to let you get to me."

"Don't worry, Ellie," he murmurs, his eyes snaking the

length of my body before matching my stare. "I have no interest in getting to you."

A surge of disappointment makes my vision go black, but when my eyes clear, I strengthen my resolve and my spine. "What are you doing here without your entourage? Or are you reporting back to them?"

"Because all they think about is you?" He shakes his head. "You have a pretty high opinion of yourself."

"What's wrong with that? I should. I'm going to win the Quest, after all. And don't worry—I won't be choosing *you* as my partner." *Where am I getting this?* "I won't get in the way of any heist fantasies you and Chloe have going."

"You have me all figured out, don't you?" A small smile forms on his full lips.

"I've known plenty of people like you."

"Yeah?" He studies me. "So you know the Vault is my second home—I've been coming here since I could walk—it helps clear my head."

Sensing he's being honest, I imagine him as a kid building forts in the antiquity wing, playing hide and seek. But before I soften, I throw up a wall. "Sorry to intrude."

"Don't be. That's why you're here—to learn to intrude." He steps closer, and I'm like a string that's just been plucked; his nearness has me humming. "Do you want help with that?" He points at the diamond.

"Do I have a choice?" Attempting to create space between us, I almost back into the glass case.

"Not really." His smile widens as he lowers his face toward mine. My breath seizes, but at the last minute, he bends down and retrieves my L rake.

"Go ahead, then." I exhale, brushing my bangs aside, pretending he didn't just jackknife my heart. Kneeling next to him, I focus on the lock. "The code kept scrambling, so I was picking it manually. I wish we could use a computer to decode it…"

"That would be too easy." He inserts an S rake under the keypad. "The trick with T-10 cabinet locks isn't the code, it's the timing. You have to catch one pin at a time in rhythm…"

I watch the muscles in his forearm twitch with each minute movement as his fingers manipulate the pins. *Such control for such big hands…* The case pops open.

Heat emanates from him, and I don't know what's more tempting—him or the diamond.

"What's the pattern?" I ask.

"If I told you that, I'd have to kill you." Taking the diamond from the case, he holds the walnut-sized gem up to the lights. Its facets sparkle from pink to lavender. "Keep practicing. You'll figure it out."

"Thanks for nothing." I frown.

"Hey—for all *I* know, the T-10 will be part of the obstacle course. I know *you* plan to win the Quest, but *I* plan to give you a run for your money. It's very important to me that I choose my partner for the heist. This is my Initiation and I'm responsible for everything that happens—you aren't—you're just assisting. If something goes wrong it'll be my fault, so I don't need extra competition."

"*I* wouldn't know if it was part of the course, either," I reply, not liking his insinuation.

"Are you sure about that? It's pretty unbelievable you managed to get out of those handcuffs on your first day… almost like you were tipped off. Nobody here gets special treatment."

My temper flares, crimson creeping into the edges of my vision. "You're one to talk—"

"Especially me." Setting the diamond back on its pedestal, he snaps the case shut. "If anything, they're harder on me.

Have higher expectations. I wish I could scrape by, but I can't. I have to be an example. Do what they say. Grovel at the feet of Influencers who will never know my name so I can take their precious treasures. Sometimes I can't wait to get out of here. The Quest is my ticket, you know. As soon as I ace this heist, I'm out."

"Then what are you going to do? Become an Influencer?"

He laughs a bitter laugh. "Of course not. But I'm going to steal from the best of them. On my terms."

"Are you sure you're a Disconnect? I thought pride had no place here. It sounds like you could use a reset. Or maybe you need to make up for last year's heist? I heard you royally screwed that up."

His eyes narrow to slits, and an ache forms in my chest. I feel his pain and instantly regret saying it.

"You have no idea what you're talking about. I lost everything that night. It's a hurt I hope you never know."

Swallowing hard, I stare at him. "My hurt runs deeper than you could ever imagine."

"I highly doubt that." His words are ice, and tears spring to my eyes.

"You don't know anything about my hurt," I say, my voice cracking. "Don't pretend to."

We face off, oddly one-upping each other in heartache, though it's like our misery is one and the same. I sense he gets me on a level nobody else does—or ever has.

"Why are you telling me this?" I finally ask.

"I don't know."

He searches my face, and my heart thuds. I'm being drawn into him, like we're connected by some invisible tie that binds us together and is wrapping around us, tighter and tighter. Then I remember what Allard said about his power of attraction— that he attracts what he wants to use—and snap out of my daze.

"Don't you have somewhere to be?" I ask. "I'm sure Chloe would *love* to play with your lock."

I wait for a reaction, but he doesn't flinch. His eyes remain steady, holding mine. "Just like I thought…" he says. Breaking our connection, he shakes his head and turns to leave.

"What's that supposed to mean?" I ask, chilled by the distance between us.

"It means absolutely nothing," he replies without looking back.

Unwilling to let him have the last word, I scramble for a comeback, but before I respond he glances over his shoulder, his eyes full of mischief, like the hurt never happened.

"So, you think I'm cute?"

"Shut up, Garrett."

He grins. "See you around, Ellie."

His laughter lingers long after he's left me.

# Chapter Twelve

*November 20X5, Keystone*

I stand wedged between Rayelle and Stewart, waiting my turn to enter the hill that houses the obstacle course bunker. Up ahead, Liam disappears inside, and the line inches forward.

"This might take a while." Stewart clicks start on his stopwatch. He's an unofficial timekeeper. "Unless he immediately gets disqualified, of course."

"How do you know your times are accurate?" Sophia asks.

"This was used by the Stopwatch Gang during their bank robberies. They could rob a bank in two minutes or less. I borrowed it from the Crypt," Stewart says. "Even though it's over seventy years old, it still keeps perfect time. They don't make 'em like this anymore."

"I don't mean the stopwatch," Sophia says, rolling her eyes. Today, her face is powdered white, and her cheeks are crimson. Gems glitter across half her forehead, cascading like raindrops over the left side of her face. "I mean, we don't see anyone exit the bunker, so how do you know they're done?"

"I'm basing it on when the next person starts. So far

Ophelia was faster than Harbor but slower than Chloe."

"I have a bad feeling about this." Rayelle sighs. "Promise me you'll wait to start, Elisha, so I don't look bad."

"You'll do fine," I say. "I'm the one who should worry. Everything is so new to me. If we took a vote, I'd probably win 'Most Likely to be Sent to the Farm.' You only have to be faster than me." My stomach tightens with anxiety. I've been studying extra hours with Allard, but this will be the true test of my belonging at Keystone, and I desperately want to prove I'm worthy of my place here.

"Hey, none of that," Sophia says. "You're both going to be great."

"And if, God forbid, one of you gets sent to the Farm, we'll hide food in the woods so you have something to eat while you 'survive the wilderness' to find your way back," Stewart adds.

Rayelle and I look at each other, and I see the same terror coursing through my veins reflected in her eyes.

"Hopefully it's all laser fields and fitting into tight spaces," I say.

"That would be nice." She smiles weakly.

Up ahead, Garrett enters the bunker. Stewart starts his watch and notes Liam's time. "Meh. He's probably safe," he mutters. "This should be interesting, though."

Everyone falls silent, and it seems like the entire line holds its breath.

I've tried to stop replaying our run-in in the Vault, but every time I close my eyes, he creeps in. I can't understand why he tried to help me—or why things went south so quickly.

It feels like hardly any time passes before Toby enters the bunker and Stewart declares, "Fastest one yet! Three minutes, twenty-nine seconds. And you know he didn't fail."

*The time to beat…* Even though I'm mostly scared of

failing, part of me wishes I could beat Garrett just to prove I'm the real deal, that I don't cheat. *But that's probably impossible… and then I'd have to compete in the Quest. Nobody needs that pressure.*

The line moves forward until it's Rayelle's turn.

"Good luck," I whisper.

With a meek smile, she disappears inside.

Too many minutes pass for Rayelle to have beaten anyone's time, and finally, it's my turn.

"You've got this, Elisha." Stewart starts his watch.

With a deep inhale, I walk through the door. It takes a moment for my vision to adjust to the dark, but when it does, I see scaffolds and ladders leading high into the rafters. It reminds me of one of the soundstages I visited in my previous life, but without the cameras. *At least the visible cameras…*

To my right, Weiss waits. "Toes on the red line," he commands.

I stand poised at the ready, squinting up the ladder at what I guess is the entrance to an air-conditioning duct, remembering the last thing Allard told me:

*Overthinking is your enemy. It can lead to wrong decisions. Trust your gut.*

"On your mark, get set. Your hint is: it's all an illusion. Go." Weiss shoots a little gun into the air.

Leaping forward, I scramble up the ladder and clamber inside the narrow duct. Plunging into blackness, I feel the walls close in, my breath echoing in panicked puffs. *Get a grip. Trust yourself.* Exhaling conscious thought, I empty my mind and belly-crawl, feeling for a latch as I go. One full body length later, I find the false bottom and slide it open. Rolling onto my back, I drop my legs through the hole, hanging suspended by my arms while surveying the circular room with smooth, stainless steel walls below. I pull down the night-vision goggles I wear strapped around my head, illuminating a laser field.

*There you go, Rayelle.*

Silently lowering myself, I'm careful to avoid the criss-crossed beams. When my feet touch the floor, adrenaline floods my nose, and my sinuses clear. I step over the first beam and I'm off—bending, twisting, dodging—my body navigates the field seemingly of its own volition, controlling each steady beat of the dance. I don't think. I'm in another place.

It's the calmest I've felt in ages.

When I reach the metal wall on the other side of the room, I resist feeling for an exit. Sensing the walls may be armed with vibration technology that will sound an alarm, I drag my feet along the perimeter, disrupting as little air as possible while I hunt for a discrepancy in the metal. I quickly spot a seam, but I don't see a trigger that will open the wall; there are no furnishings in the space, no latches on the floor, no fingerprints on the metal that indicate where to press.

*It's all an illusion.*

The answer pops into my head.

Careful not to back into a laser beam, I hurl myself at the space to the right of the seam. I brace myself for impact, for the sirens that surely will sound, but nothing stops me. I slip through the fake wall and tumble to the other side. Tucking into a ball, I roll to a stop and jump to my feet. Before me is an ATM machine, a relic from when people used paper currency, secured with a Kaba Mas lock. I almost bust out laughing. When my dad starred in the movie *Operation Infeasible*, the prop master taught me how to dismantle—and put back together—a Kaba Mas lock while Dad was busy ignoring me.

*Luck. Pure luck.* But I'll take it. I get to work dismantling the lock. As soon as I open the ATM, an exit sign illuminates to my right, and I duck through a narrow door beneath it that is equipped with a Kwikset lock so easy to pick it must be a joke. Emerging from the bunker, I'm blasted with cool forest air and applause from master thieves Allard, Abignail, and Robie.

"You've crossed the finish line, Elisha," Robie says, clapping me on the back.

At his touch, the whirl ends and I come to my senses, having no clue how much time just elapsed.

"Did I pass?" I ask.

"The results will be revealed after everyone completes the course," Abignail says. "Please make your way to the Atrium."

Allard's lips are pressed together, and she avoids eye contact as I pass. I can't read her expression, but I think I was fast enough to stay off the Farm... *Wasn't I?*


"How do you feel?" Rayelle asks, plopping down next to me in the Atrium. She's followed by Sophia and Stewart.

"Stewart says you rocked it," Sophia says.

"So, you know who the four are?" I ask Stewart.

"I think so..." Eyebrows raised, he looks me up and down, and my heart rate spikes.

"More importantly, you know who's going to the Farm?" Rayelle asks him, pushing her glasses up on her nose as they slide down.

"I think it's safe to say it's not you, slowpoke." He playfully pinches Rayelle's arm. "You were second to last."

Rayelle slumps in her seat. "I got through the air-conditioning duct and the laser field okay, but that Kaba Mas lock was impossible. It took me forever."

"The lock was the worst part," Sophia says. "It doesn't matter, anyway. Garrett's going to win the Quest, and he's going to pick Chloe. Nobody stands a chance."

"You don't have to be bitter about it, Master of the Middle," Stewart says.

She sticks her tongue out at him.

"However, you, Elisha," Stewart continues, "have the opportunity to disrupt everything. You're the dark horse."

"What do you mean?" I ask, my heart drumming so loud it thunders in my ears.

"How'd you get through that lock?" he asks. "You weren't here when we studied Kaba Mas locks. I mean, it took *even me* a year to learn how to crack them. Who taught you?"

I shrug. "Allard tutored me when I first got here…"

"But you couldn't have learned every Kaba Mas lock in that short amount of time. We've spent years learning to dismantle them." He presses deeper. "What's your secret?"

"I don't have any secrets," I say too quickly. Taking a deep breath, I choose my words carefully. "My dad had the same lock on our barn. I watched it get repaired once, and then I used to break into it for fun. I got lucky."

Stewart studies me, blinking, and I can tell he doesn't buy it. Fortunately, before he can continue his interrogation, Robie's voice sounds over the loudspeakers.

"Good afternoon. As you already know, we've calculated the results from this morning's obstacle course, and the four who will compete in the Keystone Quest are as follows, in no particular order." He clears his throat. "Chloe Mattson, Garrett Alexander, Kyran Barrera, and Elisha DeWitt."

My name lands with a thud, and all eyes shoot to me. The noise in the Atrium raises an octave.

The room swirls in a blur of color, and I rest my forehead on my palm to steady it. I barely register the rest of the announcement, but Robie continues, "The person who will be sent to the Farm has already been notified and is being escorted there now."

"Who isn't here?" Rayelle asks, craning her neck to search the other tables.

"Marcel," Stewart says. "I overheard Abignail say he used his cutting torch on the Kaba Mas and that disqualified him. Lucky for you."

Rayelle audibly exhales.

I lift my head, trying to focus on my friends' faces, unable to comprehend that I'm competing in the Quest.

"Kyran and Garrett are no surprise," Sophia says. "And Garrett must have helped Chloe—"

"But Chloe completed the obstacle course before Garrett," I finish her thought, processing everything out loud. "He couldn't have tipped her off unless he already knew what the course looked like."

"Interesting." Stewart's fingers drum on the table. "Garrett isn't supposed to get special treatment."

*As he keeps reminding me.* "To be honest, I believe him," I say. "Maybe we shouldn't underestimate Chloe."

"That's depressing." Rayelle sighs. "She's perfect."

"Please," Sophia says. "She's a decoy. The lock probably took one look at her and its legs fell open."

"We all have gifts." Stewart laughs. "But *you*." He gives me his full attention. "Let's not forget about *you*."

Heat rises in my cheeks. "We can forget about me," I say. "It must be a miscalculation. It's a fluke."

"You actually came in second to Garrett." Stewart's smile widens as he folds his fingers in front of his mouth like some sort of evil lord. "Chloe, Garrett, Kyran, and Elisha. One of these things is not like the others. They're all legacies, and one thing's for certain, missy: they aren't going to like it if you win. Which is why we have to make sure you do."

"But I don't want to win. I told you—I don't want to pick

my partner." *And I certainly don't want to be partners with Garrett. We'd kill each other.* As soon as I think his name, my eyes find him.

He looks up at that exact moment, smirking and silently applauding me.

Chloe catches my eye as well, shooting me a smug smile, her eyes narrowing in warning as she snuggles up to Garrett.

Scowling, I turn back to my table. "On second thought, maybe I do want to win." *It's the only way to guarantee Garrett is* not *my partner.* "I'll think about it."

## Chapter Thirteen

*November 20X5, Keystone*

I turn down the corridor that leads to my secret room, intending to work on my journal. Allard scheduled a brain scan for next week, and I want to show progress. My stomach growls. It's dinnertime, and I should be in the Atrium, but I've been skipping meals, claiming I need to study—which I do—but I'm also avoiding Garrett, Chloe, and Kyran. Ever since our names were announced, everyone has taken sides. There's even an underground betting ring. Garrett is the odds-on favorite, and I'm the long shot. It's earned me several supporters, spiking my popularity, and I don't like the notoriety. But as much as I don't want the added attention winning would bring, guaranteeing Garrett isn't my partner is tempting. And I'd never forgive myself if I didn't beat Chloe. She's the real reason I've been putting in extra study hours.

The walls narrow, and the air thickens. Lost in thought, I miss a turn. Now I'm in an older section of the Vault with no recollection of how I got here. I pass the *Sphinx of Hatshepsut*, an Egyptian statue with a lion's body and a female human head. According to the plaque at its base, it was stolen from the Met in 1960 by Barrett McLaughlin, a Keystone alum and art historian. When he was working on the restoration of Gallery 131, he made casts of the statue, re-assembling the forgery at the Met and later reconstructing the original here. Beyond the *Sphinx* are the gates to the Pyramid, a replica of Cairo's Grand Egyptian Museum that houses the Vault's ancient treasures. Made of iron and stone, the gates are nearly flush with the ceiling, impossible to scale. Breaking the lock that holds them shut is the only way in.

This isn't what I planned on doing tonight, but I'm up for the challenge and happy to put off reliving my past for another night. Kneeling in front of the gates, I get to work. The lock is an ancient pin tumbler with a trick element that opens successive keyholes and is surprisingly difficult to pick. It takes me hours to crack it. By the time I'm finished, I'm too exhausted to explore the treasures on the other side, and I sit on the floor resting my eyes before hiking back to the dorms.

Footsteps echo down the hall. Sensing Stewart is coming, my eyes flutter open as he appears around a corner.

"There you are," he says. "Just who I've been looking for. You weren't at dinner."

"You missed me?"

"Absolutely." He grins. "How's Quest training going?"

"You placed a bet, didn't you?" I frown.

He sits next to me. "I did. And I'd like to protect my investment, Scarlet Spy, but I also want to see you win."

Hating the nickname, I cringe. It makes me feel like an outcast who should be wearing a scarlet letter, even though I know it's probably a reference to how easily I blush. Either way. *Ugh.*

"Why?" I ask. "Other than your love of underdogs."

"I do enjoy a come-from-behind victory." He laughs. "But

I also feel like you're one of us."

"And who is 'us'?"

"Listen, a lot of thinking at Keystone is old-school, but some of us don't want to live off the grid forever. Personally, I don't think all technology is bad, and someday I'd like to rejoin society as long as it's not 'Super Brain' society. I get the feeling you would, too."

"I don't know what I want." I lean my head back against the gates. "And you shouldn't get your hopes up. Garrett knows this place inside and out. Don't you think his parents will make sure he wins?"

Stewart shrugs. "I don't know. They seem fair. If anything, they're harder on him... Neither of his brothers nor his sister won Quests. I don't think they even competed in them."

"I didn't know he had siblings."

"They've all been initiated and are working in the field. He's the youngest—and by all accounts the smartest." Stewart leans his head back next to mine so we're both staring down the stone corridor.

"What's their deal, anyway?" I ask. "They seem like nice, normal parents. I can't imagine them stealing anything."

"It's weird, right? But I heard that back in the day they were the most-wanted couple in Europe." He studies me out of the corner of his eye. "Garrett has skills, but I have a feeling about you. Besides, we're friends. I want to help you win in any way I can."

*Friends.* The magic word. Enjoying the fuzzy warmth prickling across my skin, I smile. "I'd love your help, but I'm not sure I *want* to win."

He sits up. "Why not?"

I glance at him without moving my head. "I don't like being the center of attention."

"Well, it's too late for that, so you might as well try to win."

"Yeah…" I wrinkle my nose, trying to work out the real reason I'm hesitant. "I guess the bigger issue is that I've never been good at anything. I've failed at everything I ever tried, and I don't know if I could take it if I failed at this. I feel like I *could* be good at being a thief, like it's the closest I've come to succeeding at something—I at least have the fantasy Keystone is where I belong—but if I give it my all and I lose, it might break me. I'm scared to want it. It feels much safer to accept third—I at least want to beat Chloe—place."

"Elisha." Grabbing my shoulders, Stewart stares me directly in the eye. "You are a thief. This is one hundred percent what you're supposed to be doing. You're a natural! You already beat everyone—with one glaring exception—in the obstacle course. You're already a winner. I think you owe it to yourself to go after this. To want this. To prove to yourself that you are someone who goes after what she wants. Forget your pride and turn that fantasy life into reality." Giving me a final, little shake, he drops his hands.

"Pride." I groan, smacking my hand against my forehead. "I know, I know. How did you get to be so wise, Stewart?"

"It's my gift." He smiles. "Stick with me, kid. You can have it all."

"Is that a Matthew McConaughey impression?" I ask.

"Nice work," he says. "I wouldn't expect a Maker kid to get that."

"Why? He wasn't a thief, he was an actor."

"That's what you think."

"Really?" Straightening my spine, my eyes bulge.

"It's not my secret to tell." He laughs. "But mostly it's because Disconnects only watch film, so we're stuck with a lot of old movies."

"Well, I've always loved old movies. They were so much more fun when all they did was tell a story instead of being a virtual-life experience. I like really old ones, like *The Goonies*. My parents were so afraid one public misstep would ruin my chances of becoming an Influencer when I grew up, they kept me under lock and key. Movies were practically my only friends. It was a good thing my dad had a massive collection of them." For once, my Maker cover story aligns with the truth, and I'm glad I get to share a little bit of the real me.

"It sounds like you were always meant to be one of us."

"Maybe." Glancing at him out of the corner of my eye, I smile.

"We have the original *The Goonies* here in the Vault, you know. We should watch it sometime."

"I'd like that." For a moment, I dare to believe in the possibility of real friendship.

"Hold on a second. Question. Have you ever seen *Jerry Maguire*?"

"Yes. My dad worshipped classic actors like Tom Cruise, so I've seen all his films."

"Cool. Okay. What's the famous line from that movie?"

I don't have to think about it. "'You had me at hello'?"

"The other one."

"'Show me the money'?"

"Correct. Good. You're one of us. Just checking."

"What are you talking about?"

"Most people believe the line is 'Show me the currency.'"

"No, it's not." My jaw drops. "No way. That movie came out before there *was* a world currency! Before the new era when the world became one nation and we marked the change by adding letters to our years. It was, like, 1996."

"Exactly—but try finding a copy that still says 'money.' You can't, outside the Vault or your dad's collection, apparently. We have the original. We know the truth, but that's one way the Corporates are changing history as part of the plan to get everyone to enter the Simulation. It seems like no big deal, but eventually people will forget there ever was something called 'money.'" Standing, he drags me to my feet. "Come on. I want to show you something."

"Where are we going?" I follow close behind him, crouching as the ceiling slopes.

"To the Bodleian. It's in the oldest wing of the Vault, but it's not far."

It's nearly pitch-black, and he lights lanterns as we go. I cling to the hem of his shirt so I don't lose him. "Stewart, are your parents legacies?"

"No—they're Unrankables." He sighs. The path descends sharply, and cold air swirls around my ankles. "My dad was a doctor, but he refused to accept that a robot could diagnose his patients better than he could. He kept going on about human touch and compassion being elements of healing, and eventually he lost it all... Ah! Here we are."

We stop in front of a carved wooden door, and he picks the lock.

"That's so sad," I say. "Did they send you here?"

"Uh-uh. I'd heard rumors about Keystone, and I ran away when I was ten to see if it was real. Robie found me wandering in the woods, and I begged him to let me in. I couldn't do *nothing* any longer, and I agree with my dad. Disconnects are the only ones with the tools to restore balance."

He opens the door, and we enter a musty library. Endless rows of books tower under carved wood ceilings, and leaded glass windows filter light from an unknown source.

"This is so familiar..." My breath catches in my throat as it hits me. "Are we at Hogwarts?"

Stewart laughs. "Yes and no. They filmed the Harry Potter movies at the real Bodleian in Oxford. I'm glad you remember it. Few people do. And now for the true test." The floorboards creak under our feet as he leads me to a stack labeled "rare." Pulling out the thirteenth book on the eighth shelf, he shows me the cover. "Do you recognize this?"

"*Nineteen Eighty-Four*?" I shake my head. "Should I?"

"No. It's almost been completely erased from current memory, but this book is the reason Keystone was built. This is one of two known copies in existence—the other one is hidden in the Walker Library in Connecticut. This book is about erasing memory, changing history and language to reflect the government's ideals while keeping society under constant surveillance. When it came out in 1949, Keystone was established in order to preserve a record of history—to prevent *Nineteen Eighty-Four* from becoming reality."

He hands me the book, and I run my fingers over the tattered cover. It feels like it might disintegrate beneath my fingers, but my instincts tell me this book has power.

"The thing is, it's happening anyway," Stewart says. "This book is what it would be like inside the Super Brain, where there would be no freedom of expression or thought. In *Nineteen Eighty-Four*, the Thought Police shut down free will, but the Brain wouldn't need Thought Police. Any idea that wasn't in line with government-approved thinking would instantly be erased by the central mind. But that's not the scariest part."

I swallow. "What is?"

He licks his lips and takes a deep breath. "The scary part is that the Super Brain is artificially intelligent. It will constantly keep learning, and if a large part of society uploads their minds, the technology might keep growing to the point where it becomes smarter than Madden and its teachers. Anything that big has a life of its own—we'd be up against yottabytes of data—and the machine could end humanity as we know it. Like, no more humans. Not even apathetic, brainwashed ones.

It would be Disconnects against the machines."

Ice runs down my spine, and I stare at him, wrapping my head around the enormity of it all. "That's terrifying."

"It's tough to digest." He nods.

"How can you be so calm?"

"Because I think truth will overcome. We're going to do our job. We're going to stop the Super Brain in the first place, and someday we *will* have Utopia. It will evolve naturally. It just takes time." He nudges me with his elbow, doing his McConaughey. "Stick with me, kid. I'm telling you, we can have it all."

Giving in to the urge to hug him, I whisper "thank you" in his ear. A moment passes, and I step awkwardly backward, appalled at my display of human emotion.

He laughs. "If we're going to beat Madden and the Super Brain, we better get busy. Locks you seem to have down, but how are you with ciphers?" He takes back *Nineteen Eighty-Four* and replaces it.

"Not very good," I admit. "I worked on them with Allard a bit when I first got here, but we've been concentrating on other things…"

"Well, code breaking is *my* specialty. We only have four weeks to get you up to speed, but I think you can do it. On the night of the party, we'll have them all cowering in fear."

"What party?"

"The Into the Woods Party. It happens the night before the Quest, and it also happens to be New Year's Eve."

"Let me guess—it takes place in the woods?"

"Yep. Everyone goes. It's our last hurrah. Once partners are assigned, we aren't allowed to talk about our part of the heist—unless we *need* to share information."

Ducking into the corridor, we leave the library and wind our way to the surface. "I'm not sure I'll go… I'll probably need to study, if it's the night before the Quest."

"Don't decide yet. I told you, stick with me. In a month, you may be ready to talk some smack. Garrett and Chloe have no clue what's coming."

I laugh. "We'll see."

# Chapter Fourteen

*December 20X5, Keystone*

*I*'m out of excuses, and I can't put off my journal any longer. The night before my brain scan, I return to my secret room. Taking a deep breath, preparing to acknowledge my demons, I put pen to paper before I can talk myself out it.

*September 6, 20X4*

*Truth: Life is easier when you cease to feel.*

I got rid of Peter, and the girls spilled their secrets. Kylie's was weak—her parents purchased likes and comments and followers to inflate her stock price—but Lil surprised me. It turned out the picture I sent to Samantha was from Lil's private collection. The dick really *did* belong to Peter Waters. She was a complicated girl, and I believed the benefit to staying on her good side. And in some ways, knowing Peter was shady made me feel a little better about ruining his life.

"Look at all these clones wishing they were us," Lil said,

scrolling through the Network screen on her balcony. "They're so boring." Shutting down the screen with a swipe of her hand, she put her feet up on a chaise. Fire was in the air that night. The Santa Anas swept through the dehydrated city, setting the sky ablaze in a spectacular display of red and orange. Positioning her mojito against her pedicured toes with the Hollywood Sign glowing pink in the hills beyond the terrace as her backdrop, she blinked, snapping a picture. "I feel like I've taken this shot a thousand times. We need to shake this slumber party up or else we're going to lose our audience." Lil's parents were out of town, and none of our parents cared if we came home. As long as we were livestreaming, they knew we were safe. We couldn't hide offline much longer.

"We need fresh blood," Kylie said.

"I can invite Jax over," Deena said, lazily fanning herself, eyes on the crimson sky. He was her current crush. "Maybe he can bring some friends."

My ears perked up, hoping "some friends" meant Adam. I'd only seen him in passing a few times since that day on the Boulevard, but, true to his word, he'd been in touch. My insides fluttered as I remembered the first note. He'd brushed passed me without so much as a glance on the Boulevard. I was shattered that he didn't acknowledge me until later that afternoon when I found a folded paper square in my pocket. When I got home, I made sure my Life Stream was off and unfolded it in the back of my closet. It was a note written on real paper with gray lines and a torn edge, like it came out of a journal.

> E—
> I told you I'd find a way. If you want to play with me, leave your response in the flower box where ocean meets sand.
> I like your hair today.
> —A.

Tearing a page out of my Book of Secrets, I immediately responded, tucking his note safely inside the book. It took me a couple days to figure out that "Ocean" and "Sand" were streets, but once I did, the game was on. We kept the notes simple—observations about the other person or little jokes—but the real fun was crafting the riddles and finding new hiding places. The notes were the only happy thing in my life. Looking forward to them was my salvation.

"I'm bored with them, too, but go ahead," Lil said, snapping me back to reality.

Half in a daze, I studied our shadows, stretched long by the setting sun. A line of perfectly spaced Bubble Cars glided down Sunset Boulevard, transporting people we would probably be entertaining tonight wherever they were going. Maybe they were studying our feeds now. *I don't know them, but they know me. Too well. What's next? Where do we go from here? This is it. We have it all...*

Lil sat up. "And *I'm* inviting Samantha Valenti over. Then we'll have some real fun."

The hot wind prickled my skin, and, despite the warm evening, I shivered. My eyes flitted to Dee's, and I registered her fear. But then it was gone.

"What do you want with Samantha?" I asked.

"Her numbers have been growing ever since the Peter scandal," Lil said. "She owes us a thank-you."

"Shouldn't *you* thank *her* for getting him fired?" I asked. "You wanted to get back at him for dumping you. She did you a favor." It wasn't like me to be combative, but my patience was wearing thin. Lil wasn't the only one who was bored.

"Absolutely not," Lil said. "We've created a monster, and she needs a reminder of who was queen first. Keep your enemies close, Ella."

Recognizing the underlying threat in her voice, I bit my

lip to keep from blurting what I really thought—that she was evil to the core. "Do whatever you want," I muttered.

The wind smacked against the building in a thunderous whoosh, whipping our hair across our faces.

"Let's go inside," Lil said, waving a hand to open the sliding glass doors that led to the living room. "Samantha will be here in ten, and we've got to prepare. We go live in twenty."

"Thanks for having me over." Samantha stepped inside the stark penthouse and set down her overnight bag.

"Thanks for coming." A fake smile on her lips, Lil led Sam to the great room, where we were lounging on cushy white couches. The space was wallpapered with screens that displayed a three-hundred-sixty-degree view of Los Angeles. Normally it felt like we were perched on a pedestal in the center of the city, but that night the screens were showing the movie *Believe*, and we were taking turns having our avatars star opposite heartthrob Jake Branson.

"Are you streaming right now?" Lil asked Sam.

"No," she replied.

"Good. We'll tell you when it's time to go live," Lil said. "Have a seat."

"Okay." Her knees shaking, Samantha lowered herself next to Dee.

"Mojito?" Lil asked.

"I'd love one," Sam said, her excited voice echoing around the room.

My heart ached at how eager she was.

"How about for you, Ella?" Lil asked.

"No thanks," I said, barely registering the question. I was too busy sweating, watching Lil bat at her prey. I rarely drank, anyway—I was too afraid of what might air on the Networks should my inhibitions be lowered.

Frowning at me, Lil picked up a pitcher and poured the limey cocktail into a sugar-rimmed glass. "We've noticed your numbers." She handed the drink to Samantha. "Very impressive."

Samantha beamed. Accepting the glass, she tucked a short blond lock behind her ear. "Thank you."

"You should thank me," Lil said. But then she covered the threat with a wide smile, replaced the glint in her eye with a sparkle. "I'm so happy you're here. It's going to be fun."

A bell chimed.

"That must be Jax and Bryce," Deena said, holding her palm toward the screen to pause the movie, then swiping across her face to switch the view in her AMPs to the front door. "I'll get them." Instead of gesturing to unlock and open the door, she leaped up, returning seconds later with Jax's arm slung loosely over her shoulder.

"Hey," Jax said to Lil, his baby blue eyes flashing against his tanned skin. "Is it cool if we shoot some hoops?" The VR game room housed a regulation-sized basketball court.

"That's not why we invited you over." Lil pouted.

"But it's why we came over." Bryce pretended to punch her arm. He was the shorter of the two, with dark hair and eyes, but they were both soccer stars and had the bodies to prove it.

She swatted him away. "I invited you over because we have a new friend." She grinned at Samantha. "And I wanted to give her a proper welcome."

Sam's cheeks flushed under the thick layer of foundation matted to her face.

My stomach churned.

"Where's Adam?" Lil asked.

I leaned over, pretending to straighten my shoe so they

wouldn't notice my interest.

"At some surf charity thing with his dad." Jax shrugged. "What's the plan?"

"We need to go live, but we want it to look artsy—not algorithm-edited," Kylie said, swiping so the wallpaper changed to a mirror and reapplying her lipstick. "This is a slumber party—what do you think our fans are expecting?"

"A pillow fight?" Bryce suggested.

"Exactly," Lil said. "Five hot girls getting sloppy…you guys are down to man the screens, right?" Her eyes met theirs, and something passed between them—a mutual acknowledgement. *This is all bad.*

"Girls, follow me. To the closet!" Lil said. "Boys, drink up and make yourselves comfy. We'll be back in a few."

She led us down a long hall to her bedroom and giant walk-in closet. "I was just gifted the cutest PJ's. This is the perfect opportunity to show them off." Opening a drawer, she handed me pink-and-white striped boy shorts and a fuzzy pink push-up bra with white bows. "Ella, you're so sweet, this is perfect for you. And it will make it look like you have boobs."

I stared in terror. "I thought I wasn't supposed to—"

"Wear it," Lil cut me off. "Don't worry. That's why Jax and Bryce are filming. We'll put our Life Streams on a delay, and I'll screen everything before it goes out. You can trust me."

I knew better, but I reluctantly started to change.

She chose a low-cut, black, lace nightie for Deena that Jax would "love," a vintage apron-style halter for Kylie, and a slouchy, off-the-shoulder top that grazed the top of her thighs for herself.

"And for Sam…" Lil held up a sexy red lace bodysuit with thigh-highs and devil horns.

"I'm not comfortable showing that much skin," Sam said, taking a step backward.

"But it will look great on you," Kylie said. "You'll be so hot. Bryce won't be able to take his eyes off you."

"You have nothing to worry about," Dee added. "Being seen partying with us is going to be *great* for you. The networks will *love* this."

Sam looked at me. My heart thudded, and I couldn't meet her eyes.

"Come play with us," Lil said. "We'll make you a star."

Her words hung in the air, a breathy promise.

Sam hesitated, staring at the red lace. After a moment, she took a deep breath and squared her shoulders. "Okay." She excused herself to the bathroom to change.

"We're not really going to post this, are we?" Deena whispered as soon as she was out of earshot.

"Of course not. Not of *us*, anyway," Lil said. "Jax and Bryce know what they're doing. This is like a game for them. Don't worry."

Samantha emerged from the bathroom, trying to cover herself with her T-shirt.

"HOT!" Kylie squealed, grabbing the shirt out of Sam's hands so she had nothing to shield herself with.

Lil took Sam's hands and started dragging her down the hall. "We're going to get *huge* numbers out of this."

"I'm not sure," Sam said, and I recognized the plea in her voice. It was the same one caught in my throat. But I couldn't let it out. Nauseated, I covered my mouth to keep from getting sick.

"I'm not feeling so well," she said. "Maybe it was the mojito… Maybe I should go home."

"But you just got here." Lil tightened her grip. "We'll have some champagne. The bubbles will settle your stomach."

Arms linked, Deena and Kylie followed them down the hall. I dragged my feet, bringing up the rear. Crossing my arms over my chest, I hugged myself like I could keep from falling apart.

"Jax! Bryce! Get a load of this." Lil shoved Samantha into the center of the great room.

From the couch, the guys barely acknowledged her.

"What do you think?" Kylie asked, posing with her hand on her hip.

"You can clean my house any time," Bryce said to Kylie. "But I wouldn't touch *her* with a ten-foot pole and rubber gloves." He nodded at Samantha, whose shoulders slumped. She tried to shield her chest with her arms.

"Don't be dumb," Lil said, throwing a pillow at him. "You're not allowed to touch anyone, anyway. You're here to watch." With that, she popped a bottle of champagne and took a big swallow before handing it to Dee.

"Pillow fight!" Kylie yelled, picking up a furry white pillow and nailing me in the face with it.

I threw up my hands to defend myself. "Ouch."

"Come on, Ella." Dee handed me the bottle. "It doesn't hurt."

"That's what you think." I picked up a black sequined pillow and swung half-heartedly at Dee, dousing her with champagne in the process.

"Oh," she sputtered. "It's on."

She whacked me in the back of the head just as Lil took *her* down at the knees, and I couldn't help but laugh, hearing my old friend squeal with glee. The champagne flowed, and we pounded each other with pillows, running around giggling, tripping, tackling. I nearly convinced myself it was fun.

Jax circled us, controller in hand, manually filming. I tried to make sure I was covered, terrified of suggestive images of me existing, but with the pillow assault, it was all I could do to stay on my feet.

And then I heard the screams.

Lil was holding Sam's head back while Bryce forced her to swallow the rest of the champagne. She was choking, crying for them to stop, but they wouldn't let up.

"You need to relax, Sam. You're too stiff. This will help," Lil said. When the bottle was finished, she pulled Sam to her feet, smiling that fake grin of hers. "Whipped cream!" she yelled.

Shaking a canister, she sprayed Sam with it, smearing it over her thighs and chest.

Deena and Kylie got in on the action, shooting whipped cream until the cans were empty and they were gasping for breath, laughing hysterically.

But I wasn't laughing. And neither was Sam. She was crying.

"Cameras off," Lil commanded.

"Stop crying," Kylie said once the screens showed they were blank. "Do you want your investors to think you're a baby? They bought into you because you're sexy. Give them what they want."

"But I'm not sexy." Sam hiccupped.

"Come on. We know what you did with Peter," Dee said, and I no longer recognized her.

"It was fake." Sam shook her head. "Someone sent me that picture. It wasn't Peter."

"So, you're a liar," Lil said. "We can't be friends with a liar… Jax, how does it look?" She curled her fingers, gesturing without looking at him, her eyes glued to Sam.

*I did this to her.* Guilt washed over me, and I wanted to fix it, to take Sam's hand and drag her out of the penthouse, to run. But I was frozen. Sick to my stomach, I could only watch.

He handed over the controller, and Lil scrolled through the videos, picking out the most suggestive images of Sam. "What's your Network password?" she asked.

Sam remained silent.

Lil grabbed Sam's face, her fingernails digging in, drawing blood, until Sam's eyes bulged. "Tell me."

I gasped, tears springing to my eyes, but still, I was immobile.

Sam clamped her mouth shut.

Dropping her hand, Lil took a step back. "I'm not going to ask again. Tell me."

"No," Sam said, her eyes faraway.

I thought Lil was backing off, but then she whipped around, kicking her heel into Sam's stomach. "Tell me."

Sam doubled over, coughing, and I swallowed a sob.

"Tell me." Lil's fist connected to Sam's jaw with the sickening thud of flesh smacking flesh, a slab of meat flapping on a counter. I'd never heard a punch in real life, and bile rose in my throat.

*She's going to kill her.*

Gagging, I backed away from the scene, taking one last glance at Kylie and Dee staring on, faces void of emotion. As I retreated, Sam's cries grew weaker, until the thuds garnered only whimpers.

Heaving myself into the bathroom, I threw up. When my stomach was empty, I lay on the floor, my cheek pressed to the cold tile. *I can't stand by and watch this...*

But my limbs were too heavy to move.

A sharp angle of light carved me in two. Grabbing me by the hair, Lil pulled me to sitting, getting down on her knees so her nose was touching mine.

"You should learn from this. You're only good to me if you build me up. Your numbers may be higher than mine, but I can dismantle you in a second. Always remember that could be you in there, so get with the program. You're one of us. Act like it. Clean yourself up and get out there. We need to finish this night out—make it look like fluffy teenage fun. You have ten minutes." Standing, she delivered her parting shot, kicking me in the chest.

Lightning exploded across my sternum in hot shards, zapping my breath, and I collapsed on the floor.

"I don't give second chances, and you already used your first," she said, slamming the door behind her, plunging me into blackness.

My lungs heaving, I threw my hands over my head and curled into a ball, silently screaming. I don't know how long I lay there, tears streaming, fighting to breathe, but I cried until I had no tears left, until my throat was raw and my jaw ached. Until I knew I couldn't waste any more time for fear she'd return and finish me off.

Right then, I bottled up my feelings, turned them off, buried them so deep I'd need a treasure map to find them. I understood the flat look in Deena's eyes, the one that took my friend. Like her, I had to die inside.

It was the only way I was going to survive.

Fresh tears roll down my cheeks. I hate that I didn't help her. I have no excuse for my behavior. Inaction is participation and I am guilty, guilty, guilty. But no more. Never again.

*From now on, I act.*

# Chapter Fifteen

*December 31, 20X5, Keystone*

**D**eep in the woods, my feet crunch through the snow in a clearing encased by a small circle of sequoias that protect me from the icy wind. My teeth chattering, I burrow into my school-issued puffy black jacket, tightening the fur-trimmed hood around my face. Tonight is the Into the Woods party, and I haven't decided if I'm attending. My mind is stuck in the past, wandering back to exactly one year ago, to the start of the year that erased everything. I want to be alone — to reflect, to process — to remember. I owe it to Adam. *But I also owe it to myself to begin my new life. I have to let go.*

The moon is full overhead, yellow against midnight blue, and my shadow stretches long across the snow, a taffy-pulled version of me. Allard hasn't been able to convince Garrett to get a brain scan — thank God, I'm not looking forward to *that* comparison — but my last scan showed I've made significantly more connections. My mood is brighter, and my instincts have never been sharper, but I've been avoiding recalling my lowest point. The memory is too painful to

write. Still, if I'm going to continue improving, I have to
face it. Closing my eyes, I take a deep breath and relive that
horrible afternoon.


"We should dress alike more often," Lil said, swiping across
the air to scroll through images of us dressed as sexy genies
at last night's Halloween party. Her feed was projected onto
a Boulevard wall screen, and her manicure was coded to
allow her to navigate the feed without leaving our table. It
wasn't lost on me that putting us on the big screen had the
added benefit of making everyone who wasn't invited to the
party jealous. "People love a band of strong females. We're
inspiration to little girls everywhere. They *so* want to be us—"

"I know you all hate me."

Sam's voice rang out over the Boulevard, silencing Lil,
and we all turned.

She stood on a table, eyes wild, her fingers gripping a
piece of rope hanging from one of the cabanas.

I blinked, even though I wasn't wearing AMPs, not
believing the scene could be real.

"All I wanted was to be one of you," she said. "To be
like you. To be liked by you..." Tears bubbled from her
eyes, overflowing in a shimmering cascade down her cheeks.
Making no move to wipe them away, she continued, her voice
just above a whisper. "I made one mistake, and my life is
over—"

Leaning forward, I strained to hear her.

"You've made yourselves clear—the letters, the posts, the
lies. Maybe if I give you what you want, you'll finally accept
me."

It happened fast. Too fast for anyone to do anything. *At*

*least that's what I told myself.*

She slipped the noose around her neck and stepped off the table.

Everyone gasped, but nobody moved. Maybe they thought their eyes were playing tricks on them, too, that we were experiencing one of the virtual realities we were so accustomed to.

It was dead quiet except for a soft gurgle from her throat, the wood beams creaking under the weight of her body. Even the breeze refused to breathe. We stared for what felt like eternity, watching her body writhe, her eyes bulge, her face turn blue.

And we did nothing.

Tears pricked my eyes, my sinuses burned, my lungs seized, and it was like I was strangling, too. I had to save her, but I couldn't will my limbs to action. I sat there. Watching her die.

Fortunately, she didn't.

Because Adam saved her.

He was the only person brave enough to leap to his feet, to risk his life — his numbers — for hers.

"Samantha," he shouted, grabbing her around the waist. "Don't do this. Your life is worth more than this." He climbed onto the table, lifting her body, loosening the rope. Laying her down, he breathed life into her mouth. "Someone get help!"

The robots looked on in silence — they weren't programmed for suicide prevention. But maybe they'd learn. Next time, maybe they'd act.

Finally, one of the teachers pressed an emergency button, and a pulsating alarm made us all jump.

Samantha coughed, the color returning to her cheeks. Adam helped her sit up, wrapped her in a giant hug. Watching him, warmth grew in my belly, and for the first time in months, a glimmer of hope that someone decent existed—that the world wasn't always cruel—blossomed in my brain.

*I would have sat by and watched Samantha die.*

Sniffling, I acknowledge the worst truth about me. Leaning against a tree, I squeeze my eyes shut against the hot tears rolling down my cheeks.

*I was so insecure—a slave to approval from others—that I couldn't save a life. She asked for help, and I was too much of a coward to give it to her. Pathetic.*

Pressing my lips together, I fill my lungs with crisp night air, and it helps to clear my head. *But at least I can admit it. By recognizing my weaknesses, I can overcome them. I can be better. I'm not that person anymore.*

*Never again.*

The weight of the memory lifts, and I breathe easier. *We all come from somewhere, have demons, but we all deserve a chance. It's not my job to judge anyone but myself. And I have to love myself, forgive myself. It's all so clear. It's time to act, to make this my home. I should go to the party. I should try my hardest to win the Quest, prove to everyone I belong here— prove to myself that I belong here—that I'm part of the team.*

Standing, I hike through the snow until I find everyone. Obscured by the shadow of a tree, I observe for a minute before joining them. I'm honest with myself—I know who I'm seeking. The energy required to resist him is too much, and I don't bother trying.

Rayelle, Sophia, and Stewart are easy to find, huddled together, wearing school-issued coats. Nearby, Chloe and Harbor are perched on low tree branches, hair flipping as they talk to Liam and Kyran. The uninitiated are all there, mingling in the misty forest, drinking from vintage red cups. *Everyone except me, that is, and except... Why can't I find him?*

I promised Allard I'd practice sharpening my instincts, so I focus on Garrett, hoping I'll get an idea of his location.

"What are you doing out here alone?"

Jumping, I whip around. "Garrett?" I whisper, my mind reeling.

*How did he sneak up on me? Or did I send out what I was hoping to attract?* My stomach twists.

Stepping forward into the moonlight, I plaster wide-eyed innocence on my face. "I could ask you the same thing."

"I was wondering where you were." He comes toward me, padding through snow. A faint scruffiness along his jaw makes him seem grown-up, and an image of me snuggled up against his chest leaps into my mind. I blink it away.

"For some reason I couldn't stop thinking about you tonight," he says, coming to a stop in front of me, his face so close his breath comes out in little puffs that mix with mine.

*That makes two of us.* His energy tugs at my core, a gravitational pull in my gut that sucks me toward him, but I refuse to be swallowed into his vortex. Digging my feet into the snow, I clutch the tiger's eye I wear at my throat, calling on its protection to ward him off. "How romantic. Do you say that to all the girls? Because I'm not that easy."

A slow smile spreads across his face. "I like to keep an eye on the competition is all. I know you're a fortress, Ellie. Don't worry. I have no intention of scaling your walls."

Stupid disappointment dips in my belly, but I shrug it off, fluttering my eyelashes. "You're welcome to try. I'm confident the dragon will get you in the end, anyway."

He bites his lip, holding back a laugh. "You're nothing like I expected."

I ignore my racing heart, trying to keep up with him. "You think about me enough to have expectations, huh? Sorry to disappoint."

"Who said I'm disappointed? I figured you were too good for us—pretty Maker girl, forced to hang out with the Disconnect rejects." He searches my face. "But now I know the truth."

My insides clench—he called me pretty—at the same time fear that he knows my secret leaps into my throat. I swallow hard. "Yeah? What's that?"

"You're a nerd who would rather get a good night's sleep the night before the Quest than hang out with her friends. You really want to win this thing." He punctuates his theory by pressing his gloved index finger to the tip of my nose.

Relief that he hasn't discovered my identity rushes through me, and I roll my eyes. "So what if I do?"

He searches my face like I'm a present he wants to unwrap, and I keep a pleasant mask in place so he can't guess what's inside.

"You'd better not get disqualified, then," he finally says, his teeth flashing white in the moonlight. "In the real world, you don't get to choose when you sleep. That's why we're holding a party the night before the Quest. It's part of the challenge. It's mandatory you attend." He offers me his hand. "Come hang with me by the fire. You must be freezing."

A bead of sweat trickles down my back. *Am I the only one who feels this heat? Pathetic.*

Hand still extended, he waits for me to accept it.

I curl my fingers into a ball. "I'm sure Chloe would love you showing up with me."

"Who cares what she thinks?" He shrugs. Grasping my hand, he tugs me forward, and, as if on cue, snow flurries flutter down around us. "Come on, Ellie. It's New Year's Eve.

Let's toast to new beginnings."

Not wanting to deal with the stares if I show up with him, I disentangle my fingers from his, shoving my hands into my pockets, halting our progress. "No, thank you. I'll celebrate when I have reason to celebrate. Until then, I'm happy here."

He sighs, closing the distance between us. "Okay, 'happy here.' I'll stay with you, then."

"You don't have to. I'm fine. Go back to the party."

"I'm not leaving you alone in the dark. You never know what's lurking in the woods. Especially when there's a full moon."

I'm struck by an urge to reach out and brush the snowflakes from his eyelashes, and it's all I can do to keep my hands to myself. "The only thing lurking is you. But then, you *are* pretty dangerous…" Narrowing my eyes, I look him up and down. *What am I doing? Am I flirting?* I don't know what, but something about him throws me off my game.

He studies me. "What aren't you telling me? It doesn't add up. You're not a legacy, but you're familiar. I feel like I know you, but that's impossible. You showed up out of nowhere and beat some really talented thieves to compete in the Quest… Who are you?"

I meet his gaze, my heart thumping. "I'm just a girl from Ojai."

"I don't know what to make of you, Ellie," he says, raising his fingers like he's going to touch my cheek. I long for him to cup my jaw, but he quickly drops his hand. "One minute you look like you want to kill me, and the next—"

"Hi Chloe," I say loudly, sensing movement in the trees and cutting him off.

Seconds that feel like eternity pass before Chloe emerges. "There you are," she says. Harbor is at her side, and Liam trails behind them. "Did you get the dirt on her yet?"

My skin goes cold, but my eyes remain glued to Garrett's beautiful face. "Couldn't stop thinking about me, huh?"

"Actually, yes." He glares over his shoulder at Chloe. "I was worried when you didn't show up." He says it too softly for the others to hear.

I believe him, and a pang shoots through me at the fact that he actually seems to care, but then I picture myself falling under his spell, spilling my secrets. *Maybe that's what he wants. I'm not falling for it.* "Well, don't wonder about me and don't worry," I say. "I can take care of myself. The other competition is here. You should keep an eye on her. Feel free to forget I exist."

His eyes harden. "You don't know how much I wish that was possible."

Turning on his heel, he brushes past Chloe and disappears into the forest.

# Chapter Sixteen

*January 1 20X6, Keystone*

"The only difference between today's Quest and a real-world heist is we'll know who wins." Dressed in black all the way to the beanie on his head, like he time-warped from an ancient mobster movie, Robie paces back and forth, his classically handsome profile silhouetted in front of the fire.

Chloe, Kyran, Garrett, and I stand at the front of the Lodge, our backs to the assembly. I connect with Garrett out of the corner of my eye. *What is he thinking? Probably that he's going to crush me.* As if to punctuate my thoughts, he winks, and I snap my attention back to Robie, gritting my teeth.

"Today you act as a true Keystone Disconnect," Robie continues. "Your mission is to find the truth and steal it. The path will open in front of you, if you are willing to see it."

The energy in the room becomes a living, breathing thing, the air tightening in anticipation, like everyone is fighting for the last bit of oxygen, gulping in liquid adrenaline.

"As you know, along with gaining access to Keystone hideouts worldwide and the promise of rescue should you get caught during your Initiation, the winner will choose their partner for the Initiation heist. The trust between partners is extremely important to a heist's success, so being able to handpick your counterpart is paramount." He pauses to let us digest that.

*All of that sounds great—especially the promise of rescue—but above all I'm doing this for myself. To prove I'm someone who goes after what she wants. This is my personal initiation—this is a test of the new me.* I fill my lungs with air, then exhale, and calm clarity overcomes me.

"It starts with a riddle." Weiss's voice echoes through the Lodge, drawing my attention to him. "But first you must solve the cipher." He hands each of us a skeleton key.

Before I have time to examine the key, the chandeliers go dark and the fires extinguish. Weiss appears, ushering us through a false panel in the back of the fireplace behind Robie. Heading down a corridor I never knew existed, I'm last to climb the ladder at the end. I emerge from a trapdoor in the forest floor into the foggy morning.

"Good luck," Weiss says, leaving us to the elements, before shutting himself back in the warmth of the passageway.

No one speaks, and I barely have time to acknowledge my opponents before they scatter, disappearing into the trees. I'm left alone. The only sound is the pattering leaves in the treetops, enchanted by a breeze I've yet to feel. *I don't know where they're running to…unless they've already found a clue…* My heart pounds. Forest trails splay around me, offering endless options, and I don't know which path to choose. Breathing deep, I attempt to focus, turning the key over.

Nothing is inscribed on the smooth, chrome cylinder. I twist the filigree tip, and the key easily unscrews. Hidden inside is a piece of rolled parchment. Unfurling it, I hold it up to the light filtering through the leaves, but it's blank. A movie I once saw comes to mind, and I kneel, digging into the earth, rubbing the paper with a handful of ammonia-rich soil. Slowly, black words written in a scrawling hand come into focus.

*W htxvdggd dfxo gvrpdtz xgbgug yeef yrbg ueqht adyubqldu usjup jlz pugba ltwaplup. Dsjoo pfvyquuga, vqifxuntz, ujquy, dfud kpvega rd nsuql yg ghmpqiy twwt. Pwutf zhmd oot eqlmfefyrv xgssd; gp ef r seetv fm jrtoy. Yugra oot lfhjz, bjiu ed zeext, xdl yxcg wgih nbwit xbyls oot zeegfq.*

It's gibberish, but I calmly recall my cipher work with Stewart. *Step one. Letter frequency.* I study the text. *Like English, but with more use of "G" and "U" than "E," the most common letter in English...so the cipher uses alphabetic substitution...but it can't be a simple substitution cipher, that would be too easy...maybe it's a Caesar Cipher...* Ticking through everything I've learned, I squelch the creeping fear that someone has already cracked the code. *Focus.* There are three broken branches on the tree next to the path that leads to Imitation Lake. I take it as a sign and turn onto the well-worn trail, keeping alert for clues while contemplating the cipher.

Half a mile in, a pile of rocks signifies I should turn right down a less-traveled road. As I push through the overgrown branches that obstruct the path, a crack overhead alerts me to Liam, perched high in a tree, releasing a pigeon.

"What are you doing up there?" I say, shielding my eyes from the sun.

"Surveillance."

"Any chance you can tell me if I'm on the right track?"

"That would be against the rules," he replies, grinning.

"And you take your job very seriously."

"You know I do, but I could be persuaded..." He licks his lips, patting the branch next to him.

"I'm not that desperate," I say.

"That's what you think, spy. Better hurry."

Frowning, I pick up my pace.

A few minutes later, I come upon the lake. Not far from the water sits a yellow umbrella with its nose stuck in the dirt. *A clue...*

Kneeling next to it, I roll the heavy key between my fingers while I think. *A key.* In a burst of heat, the answer inserts itself in my brain. *The parchment contains a keyed Vigenère cipher, a series of Caesar Ciphers also known as a Quagmire III, and I'll need a key and a passcode to translate it.*

I trace the direction the umbrella handle points. Still as glass, the lake reflects the Crest Mountains from this angle, and a lone tree with two upside-down triangles drawn on in chalk on its trunk. *Two triangles mean "viewpoint" ahead...* It's all I need to see. Armed with this knowledge, I deduce that my alphabet key has something to do with "crest" or "mountain" and my passcode pertains to "view."

Knowing that with this information a computer could easily unscramble the letters, I long for an app to do the work for me, but part of the test is doing it the old-fashioned way. It will require a journey to the Crypt. Finding the nearest zip line, I sail to the Vault.

The trapdoor is open when I arrive, and I scramble down the mossy stairs. Reaching the bottom, I run through the labyrinth, stifling the urge to disappear down unexplored corridors and find what treasures await. I make two sharp lefts before arriving outside the Crypt. Inside, Garrett and Chloe are already huddled in the dimly lit room.

"Always last to the party," Chloe mutters, staying focused on the Enigma machine she's studying.

Kyran is nowhere to be seen, but Garrett grins, glancing up from a brass cipher disk. "Hey Ellie. You finally made it."

My temper flares, but I squelch it. "Kyran was already here?" I cross the room to a glass case that houses the Jefferson disk, noting it requires numbers, not words, to order the disks and dismissing it as a possibility. Though there are likely multiple ways to decipher the riddle, I think Chloe has it wrong with Enigma. Garrett is definitely closer with the brass disks.

"He didn't bother with the Crypt," Garrett replies, eyes back on the puzzle. "Maybe he figured it out in his head. Pressure's on."

He doesn't seem worried, which is annoying.

Taking a pencil and paper to a nearby desk, I pretend Kyran's head start doesn't bother me, either. Plopping into the chair, I read the message again, using the Kasiski method, searching for repeated letter sequences so I can figure out the key length—if it's a five letter word like "crest" or and eight letter word like "mountain"—before deciding the text is too short for Kasiski to work. Biting my cheek in frustration, I give up and trust my gut. Using "crest" as my alphabet key, I write out C-R-E-S-T, followed by what is left of the alphabet: A-B-D-F-G... It's slow going, but once I've rewritten the entire alphabet, shifting the letters as I go, I begin to decode, assuming "view" is my passcode.

```
I CRES TABD FGHI JKLM NOPQ UVWX YZ
C I CRES TABD FGHI JKLM NOPQ UVWX YZ
R I REST ABDF GHIJ KLMN OPQU VWXY ZC
```

I start with row V and quickly realize my transposition is gibberish. *View must be the passcode, though...* Taking a closer look at the riddle, I conclude it uses four Caesar ciphers, so the passcode must be a four-letter word. *The chalk marks clearly referred to "view."* Racking my brain, I try to make sense of what I'm doing wrong. Is there another word for "crest"? Should I try "mountain"? My instincts are telling me "crest" is the key...

Squealing, Chloe leaps out of her chair. She pauses to kiss

Garrett's cheek, letting her lips linger, before she leaves, hips swaying, the answer to the riddle apparently in hand.

*Dammit! Think. Think. Think.*

Staring at my paper, I crumple it into a ball, picturing Imitation Lake. *Imitation…reflection…the upside-down code for view…the umbrella with its nose in the sand…*

*Everything is reversed.*

Frantically, I smooth out the paper, turn it over, and write my alphabet again, starting with "crest," but this time reversing the alphabet.

```
 | C R E S   T Z Y X   W V U Q   P O N M   L K J I   H G F D   B A
C| C R E S   T Z Y X   W V U Q   P O N M   L K J I   H G F D   B A
R| R E S T   Z Y X W   V U Q P   O N M L   K J I H   G F D B   A C
E| E S T Z   Y X W V   U Q P O   N M L K   J I H G   F D B A   C R
S| S T Z Y   X W V U   Q P O N   M L K J   I H G F   D B A C   R E
T| T Z Y X   W V U Q   P O N M   L K J I   H G F D   B A C R   E S
Z| Z Y X W   V U Q P   O N M L   K J I H   G F D B   A C R E   S T
Y| Y X W V   U Q P O   N M L K   J I H G   F D B A   C R E S   T Z
X| X W V U   Q P O N   M L K J   I H G F   D B A C   R E S T   Z Y
W| W V U Q   P O N M   L K J I   H G F D   B A C R   E S T Z   Y X
V| V U Q P   O N M L   K J I H   G F D B   A C R E   S T Z Y   X W
U| U Q P O   N M L K   J I H G   F D B A   C R E S   T Z Y X   W V
Q| Q P O N   M L K J   I H G F   D B A C   R E S T   Z Y X W   V U
P| P O N M   L K J I   H G F D   B A C R   E S T Z   Y X W V   U Q
O| O N M L   K J I H   G F D B   A C R E   S T Z Y   X W V U   Q P
N| N M L K   J I H G   F D B A   C R E S   T Z Y X   W V U Q   P O
M| M L K J   I H G F   D B A C   R E S T   Z Y X W   V U Q P   O N
L| L K J I   H G F D   B A C R   E S T Z   Y X W V   U Q P O   N M
K| K J I H   G F D B   A C R E   S T Z Y   X W V U   Q P O N   M L
J| J I H G   F D B A   C R E S   T Z Y X   W V U Q   P O N M   L K
I| I H G F   D B A C   R E S T   Z Y X W   V U Q P   O N M L   K J
H| H G F D   B A C R   E S T Z   Y X W V   U Q P O   N M L K   J I
G| G F D B   A C R E   S T Z Y   X W V U   Q P O N   M L K J   I H
F| F D B A   C R E S   T Z Y X   W V U Q   P O N M   L K J I   H G
D| D B A C   R E S T   Z Y X W   V U Q P   O N M L   K J I H   G F
B| B A C R   E S T Z   Y X W V   U Q P O   N M L K   J I H G   F D
A| A C R E   S T Z Y   X W V U   Q P O N   M L K J   I H G F   D B
```

The first letter on the paper cipher is *W*. Still believing the passcode is "view," I trace line *V* until I find *W*. It corresponds with column *A*, so the first word is *A*. Taking the next letter in "view"—*I*—I find line *I* and run my finger across to the second letter in the code, *H*. Following the column up, I see it corresponds with letter *R*. *The second word starts with R.* I repeat the pattern: row *E*, letter *T* corresponds with column *E*...

*A re...*

I keep going. Row *W* letter *X* is in column *A*. Back to row *V*, where *V* becomes *C*... I bite my lip in intense focus, and time stands still until I've decoded the entire riddle:

*A reaction that existed before this time where knowledge rules and skill declines. Truth uncovered, recharged, raved, then buried in greed to protect fame. Taken from the hedonistic night; it is a giver of light. Break the world, make it shine, and take your place among the divine.*

Slamming down my pencil, I read the riddle again. And again.

*Existed before this time...* Pre-Information Age...but how far back? *Buried in greed to protect fame...*hidden truth... someone else took credit... *Recharged, giver of light...* A power source? *Taken from the hedonistic night...* Stolen from an orgy?

I run through the possibilities I know exist in the vault: *The Louvre... Museo Nacional de Antropología...* Hmmm... Maybe something from ancient times? The Antikythera mechanism, one of the earliest analog computers, is in the National Archaeological Museum of Athens... *Maybe I should start there?* I concentrate, waiting for something to click, and come up empty. All the while the clock is ticking. *At least I'm not alone.* Sneaking a glance at Garrett with his head bowed over his cipher, a strand of hair falling across his forehead, I take consolation in the fact that he hasn't figured it out, either.

Drawn to him, I take advantage of his closeness—and rare silence. Tracing his strong jaw and full lips, I feel heat build in my center. *He's perfect.* As if he hears my thoughts, his eyes snap up, connecting with mine. They seem darker today, the usual gray-green reading charcoal. Rimmed with kohl to disguise their symmetry, they are like black holes, sucking me in, bending the light in the room, and I sit frozen, heart pounding, unable to look away.

*Speaking of hedonistic nights...*

I blink myself back into reality, and I've got it. *Babylon.* Symbolic of all that's evil in the Bible, awaiting her fall in Revelation... *The answer is the Babylon Battery.* The history lesson comes flooding back. *Also known as the Baghdad Battery, it's an ancient jar containing what was identified as an electric cell, dating back thousands of years before Alessandro Volta took credit for inventing the battery. It was looted from the National Museum of Iraq when the U.S. invaded in 2003, and then was later stolen by a Keystone alumnus and donated to the Vault.* It now resides in the Pyramid. *If only I can get there first...* It's clear on the other side of the Vault, and I don't know how to get there from here, having only stumbled upon it once by accident.

A slow smile spreads across Garrett's face. "Welcome back. You're cute when you're analyzing, but be careful not to chew that pretty lip until it bleeds."

My stomach drops, but I refuse to let him distract me.

"What's this?" he asks, touching the tiger's eye I wear at my throat. "Good luck charm?"

"I don't need luck." Making sure my glare is received, I leap out of my seat and rush to the door. Unfortunately, I'm no match for his longer strides, and he catches me, snaking his arm around my shoulders just as I'm about to exit.

"Fair enough," he says. "Do you want to walk over there together?"

"Do you know where we're supposed to be going?" I stare up at him, my head tucked perfectly against his shoulder. Holding my breath, I resist inhaling his spicy scent.

He laughs. "I think so, but just in case, why don't you tell me where you're going?"

"Not a chance."

The laughter never leaves his eyes. "Okay. Have it your way. But don't forget I offered." Dropping his arm, he heads out the door, leaving me to watch in dismay as he taps out a pattern on the stone wall across the corridor. Seconds later, the wall opens, revealing a secret passageway I had no idea existed.

"I'll see you in Babylon," he says over his shoulder. And the wall closes behind him.

# Chapter Seventeen

*January 1, 20X6, Keystone*

Resigned to going the long way, I turn right, sprinting down the corridor. The passage narrows, the walls changing to stacked stone. Recalling it's down one of these claustrophobic halls that the Pyramid waits, I'm energized.

*Garrett's probably there by now.*

Not to mention Kyran. And Chloe. *If* she was going to the Pyramid. I still don't think the Enigma could have decoded the riddle, but I hurry, winding deeper into the Vault. The air grows colder, the oxygen tighter. It's dark, but already-lit lanterns flicker, telling me I'm on the right track. Passing the *Sphinx*, I climb the stairs to the gates guarding the Grand Egyptian Museum. The iron doors tower above me, and I yank on the rusted handles.

They don't budge

The lock is still intact. *No way I'm the first one here.* Fortunately, my memory serves me well. I pick the lock and, minutes later, slip inside.

Mummies line the walls, their frozen, painted eyes

seeming to trace my path as I cross the dimly lit gallery. At the back of the narrow hall, the battery sits encased in glass at the top of a small altar. At least I hope it's still there. I can't be sure because Garrett is standing with his back to me, hindering my view.

Annoyed he beat me, I march up the stone steps and join him. To my relief, the battery still sits inside the glass box atop a weighted pedestal. I search the case for security flaws. *It's almost too easy. The case can be opened with a rake pick. Just hold the rods in place that trigger the alarm...* The hardest part will be replacing the battery with something similar in weight without sounding the sirens. *That, and doing it before Garrett does.*

"Been here long?" I ask.

He keeps his unusually serious eyes glued to the case. "You made it past the gates. I'm impressed."

"The lock wasn't so tough." I shrug, pretending it was the first time I'd tackled it. "Where's everyone else? I'm surprised they're not here yet."

"I'm not. Kyran will show up when it's convenient. He's probably here now, actually. Waiting to pounce."

"How do you know?" I look around, but my instincts don't detect another presence.

"Everyone has a tell."

"What's mine?"

"That's top-secret information." He grins. "But I'm sure you'll figure it out."

I frown. "What about Chloe?"

"What about Chloe? She's the least of my worries. My only problem is the one standing next to me."

My cheeks get hot. "Where do you think she is?" I ask, hoping he assumes I'm flushed from running.

"Probably trying to steal the Crown Jewels or something.

That Enigma machine couldn't have broken the riddle—who knows what she decoded."

"I'm surprised you didn't help her."

He turns to face me. "That would be cheating, Ellie, and I always play by the rules."

"Somehow I doubt that."

"You should get to know me before you jump to conclusions."

"Why? Do you really care what I think of you?"

"Maybe." His eyes flash.

A surge of energy bolts through me, sending goose bumps up my arms. "What do we do now?" Unnerved by my reaction, I refocus on the challenge.

"Ladies first." He steps backward, his right hand gesturing that the case is all mine.

"You're going to let me steal it?" *It's a trick.*

"Just being polite."

"Make me do all the work so you can tackle me and steal it from me later?"

He laughs. "Believe me. I have no desire to tackle you."

Refusing to dignify him with a response, I square my shoulders. "Stand back."

Giving me a wide berth, he folds his arms over his chest.

I unhook my water canteen from my belt, hoping it will be similar in weight to the battery. Removing the lock kit from my pocket, I work on the cabinet screws. The case pops open easily, and I hold the alarm pins in place with the knife I keep strapped to my arm, carefully using the canteen to nudge the battery forward with my left hand. When the battery is about to fall, I let go of the canteen and catch it. Battery in hand, I leave the canteen in its place and reset the scene. Releasing the pins, I close and relock the glass case.

The museum is silent. I don't know what I was expecting—

bells, whistles…something signifying victory, but nothing happens.

Still watching me, Garrett presses his lips together in a smug smile. "Are the battery components still inside the jar?" he asks.

*Could Kyran have beaten us here, stolen the elements, and replaced the jar?* My heart thudding, I open the lid and exhale relief when I find the battery, still intact. But in addition to the copper cylinder inside, there's another scroll. Another clue.

*Nothing stays hidden forever; everything wants to be found.*

"What does it say?" Garrett asks.

I look up, willing my wide eyes to reflect innocence. "Why should I tell you?"

"Because it's the polite thing to do." He steps toward me, blocking the altar steps.

"All's fair in love and war, my friend." Shrugging, I tuck the scroll into my pocket.

"I don't believe that."

"Then you've been living underground for too long." Plotting my escape, I gauge my chances of squeezing past him.

"I wasn't talking about fairness," he says. "I don't believe we're friends."

Only half listening, I contemplate a plan. *I need to catch him off guard…*

My back warms to a presence behind me. *Kyran.* I spin around, catching his wrist just as his hand enters my pocket. He's quick, but I'm quicker. Unfortunately, I'm no match for his strength. He grabs me with his free hand, twisting my arm around my back. Hot pain shoots to my shoulder until I'm sure my bones will splinter. He reaches into my pocket and takes the scroll.

"Let her go." Garrett charges Kyran, sending me sprawling to the floor. My elbow cracks against the floor, but I scramble to regain my footing.

Garrett pushes Kyran against a glass case, one hand on his throat while the other fights for the scroll.

Frozen, I stare, but then my instincts kick in. *Move.* The path to the gate is clear, and I have all the information I need, even if I don't know where I'm headed. I sprint toward the altar steps, but Garrett's voice stops me in my tracks.

"Do you always leave a calling card, rookie?"

Kyran grabs hold of Garrett and spins them both around, but he doesn't have the upper hand for long. Garrett's reaction is instant; he kicks and knocks Kyran's legs out from under him before throwing a punch into his gut. Crumpling into a ball, Kyran drops the scroll.

Garrett retrieves the clue and quickly reads it. "Are you trying to take credit?" His lungs are heaving, and his words are directed at me.

"I don't know what you're talking about," I reply, hoping my voice doesn't reveal the quaking inside me. *What* is *he talking about?*

Kyran regains his composure and grabs the scroll out of Garrett's hand. Shoving past me down the altar steps, his retreating footsteps echo across the stone floor.

Garrett takes off running, too, but in the opposite direction, throwing open a sarcophagus on the other side of the room. "Your canteen. It has your initials on it," he says before disappearing into what must be the entrance to his secret passageway.

Closing my eyes, I groan.

Hands shaking, I have no choice but to break into the glass case again. Retrieving my canteen, I replace it with the battery, cursing Garrett's head start. *He played me.*

I take three deep breaths. *Concentrate. Nothing stays hidden forever; everything wants to be found.* It sounds like something Robie would say to justify a burglary... Wait. *Has said.*

*Crest. View...* It hits me. The Summit, also known as Robie's office. *We were never after the battery at all.*

It all comes together. The answer sits on Robie's desk: a globe filled with hydrogen peroxide, oxalate esters, butyl benzoate... He told us during a burglary lesson that it was stolen from the White House during a party celebrating President Madden's plans for the interconnected world. It wasn't super valuable, but Robie took it for fun.

*A reaction that existed before this time where knowledge rules and skill declines... It is a giver of light...* A *chemical* reaction. The H202 triggers a chemical chain that produces light... The globe is a glow ball. *Truth uncovered, recharged, raved...then buried in greed to protect fame.*

The story of the globe's theft reminds me of the secret parties my parents used to throw on the grounds of our Santa Barbara estate. Nights when the half-naked, beautiful Influencer elite let loose. Only the trusted were invited, which never included me, but that didn't stop me from hiding in the shadows and taking notes. I'm sure the same sort of thing happens in D.C., especially now that Claire Madden is president.

*Break the world, make it shine, and take your place among the divine...*

I have to break open the world.

Sprinting to the sarcophagus, I grab a kerosene lantern from a wall sconce and duck inside. The Summit is tucked into the side of a mountain and accessible only by the Zephyr, a wind-powered railcar. It's risky to take a path I've never been down, but I'm guessing it's a quicker route to the Lodge, which is next to the entrance to the Zephyr. I just can't afford any wrong turns.

I scramble down the slick stone steps into the dark corridor. Slipping, I tumble to the bottom, scraping my knee and elbow. Metallic blood on my lips, I ignore the pain. I don't have time for it. Jumping to my feet, I hurry forward, straight through a spiderweb that must have been built since Garrett passed through. *Ugh. And where's the spider?* My skin crawling, I brush off my face and arms as I run, picturing a mummy chasing me through the creepy tunnel.

Fortunately, the passageway leads straight to the Lodge. I can't get out of there fast enough. It has little offshoots here and there, but I stick to the main path, and it gives way to a staircase that winds to a door in the back of a fireplace. The fire has been extinguished, and I emerge into cool emptiness.

Heading to the Zephyr, I shut myself inside a waiting car and pull the lever that begins the three-minute journey up the inside of the mountain. It takes forever. Minute two ticks on to eternity. Kyran went the long way, and I can still beat him, but if Garrett figured out the clue, I'm screwed.

The car slows, and I leap out, then race down the glass hallway, oblivious to the sun setting over the mountains, casting me in an amber glow. Reaching the door at the end of the passage, I burst inside, in time to see Garrett lift the globe over his head and smash it to the floor.

The room erupts in a blinding white light, and I throw my arms over my face, dropping to the ground and tucking into a ball to shield myself. From somewhere in the distance, dynamite explodes, signifying a victory. Slowly, the light fades until the globe radiates only a soft glow. Still on the floor, I uncurl myself but remain sitting, in shock.

*I gave it my all, and I lost.*

Garrett crosses the room, stopping in front of me and extending his hand.

I wiggle myself closer to the floor in refusal.

"Don't pout, Ellie. We'll both win the next one." Grabbing my arm, he drags me to my feet.

"How are *we* going to do that?" I sputter, glaring up into those mesmerizing eyes.

He tightens his grip and smiles down at me. "Easy. You're my prize."

# Chapter Eighteen

*January 1, 20X6, Keystone*

I leave the Quest after-party as soon as I get there. Wanting to get as far away from Garrett as possible, the second he lets go of my arm, I head to the Vault to journal. *"You're my prize."* Whatever. *In case you're wondering, Garrett, I'd rather spend the evening reliving my death than watching you and Chloe toast to your awesomeness.*

I really wish he could hear me.

As much as I'd like to indulge in fantasizing about everything I could say to him, I get to work. Now that I've faced my demons and stopped blaming myself, journaling is getting easier, and I dive in.

*February 19, 20X5*
*Truth: You can never account for chaos.*

Deena's seventeenth birthday was a tiki-themed gold mine for her. The big secret was in the specialty cocktail, the Virgin Gorda. It came in a coconut with a colorful paper umbrella and was anything but virgin, in keeping with Deena's aspirations for the evening.

"You're flawless," I said, pinning a flower behind Deena's right ear. With just the two of us getting ready in her hotel room, it was almost like old times. "Total goals."

"Flawless isn't good enough. This is my night. I need to outshine everyone." She lowered her mini hula skirt so her hip bones jutted out above it. "Adam has high standards."

My stomach constricted. "Don't you mean Jax?"

"No. That's over." Adjusting the flower leis draped around her neck, she checked the tape that strategically held them in place. "My numbers are higher than his now. It's time to move on."

"What about Lil? Isn't Adam off-limits?"

"She's over him."

"Since when?"

"Since he saved Samantha. That was basically a big F.U. to Lil." She practiced her wave in the mirror, flowers dangling from her wrist. "Lil was pissed, but I convinced her not to go after Adam, since he said he's into me. He's probably too big for her to take down, anyway. She'd risk losing followers. His fans are really loyal."

"He said he's into you?" A lump formed in my throat. "Did something happen between you two?"

"No. But it will. I had Quinn run our numbers, and she said together, Adam and I are off the charts. He can't pass me up—we both need the boost. I just have to take care of Jax first."

I frowned, relieved that nothing had happened—yet—but irritated she was so certain she'd get her way. "So, you're dumping Jax tonight?"

"No, he's dumping me."

"Does he know that?"

Her eyelashes fluttered. "Of course not, but every party needs drama, Ella. People need something to talk about besides the decorations."

I shook my head, in awe that she could drop Jax so easily after obsessing over him for months. "Fine. But does his replacement have to be Adam? There'll be lots of other influential guys here tonight. Can't you use one of them?" Unable to keep the plea from my voice, I couldn't stop thinking about how Adam saved Sam. We were still passing notes, but we hadn't progressed beyond surface-level flirtation, and I wanted to get him alone tonight. If I was brave enough to defy Lil.

A slow smile stretched across her face. "You have a thing for Adam." Her eyes glittered.

"No." Avoiding her stare, I pretended to adjust my bikini top.

"You do!" She pounced. "Ella! Why didn't you tell me?"

"Because there's nothing to tell."

Wrapping her arms around me from behind, she rested her head on my shoulder. "If you really like him, Ella, I'll find someone else."

"Seriously?" I glanced up at her reflection in the mirror, possibility swelling in my chest.

"You *like* him, like him?" Turning me toward her, she searched my face.

Thinking I'd glimpsed my old friend, I felt my pulse quicken. "Maybe. I like him more than any other guy I've met."

"Do you think about kissing him?" She grinned. "He could be your first."

"Dee." I refused to answer. "I like the way he makes me feel is all."

"Do you know how dangerous that is?" she whispered.

"Yes."

"What does it feel like?" She sounded wistful.

"Tingly, excited… Safe. I think about him all the time…" I confided.

"Okay." She sighed. "Quinn, check the guest list for the party tonight and tell me who besides Adam will give my numbers the biggest jump."

"No problem, babe," the AI replied, her voice coming from a speaker in the wall. *Quinn: never leave home without her.* The hotel had built-in Quinn AI that synced with guests' home AI, and it struck me how different Dee's Quinn sounded than mine. Even though they were the same technology, they had completely different personalities. "Adam is your soul mate, but Trent, the lead singer from Siren Seven, is a solid choice. He's a total sweetie, too. Not to mention hot. The Networks won't be able to handle you together. In a good way."

"Thanks, Quinn." Deena said, flipping her hair over her shoulder and pressing her lips into a smile. "Because you're my best friend, Ella, I'll back off. Have your little fantasy."

I hugged her. "Thank you."

Behind us, the door swung open. Kylie and Lil appeared, wearing grass skirts identical to mine. We knew our place as Deena-the-tiki-goddess's hula maidens for the night.

"Let's get this party started," Lil said, holding out a tiny pill bottle.

"Thank God," Deena said. "I think I'm getting used to my meds. I actually felt sad the other day."

The three of them swallowed the pills, and, at first, I refused. My parents designed my genes to be immune to depression. I was the only girl I knew who wasn't prescribed mood-enhancing drugs. But, remembering my goal to talk to Adam, I thought they might help keep me from chickening out, so I took some, too.

Setting our Life Streams to live, we linked arms and headed outside. The hotel grounds were ablaze with fiery torches. Four shirtless guys appeared to carry Deena into the party on a grass throne.

While Deena got situated, we walked through a virtual jungle, strutting like runway models across a suspension bridge over the lagoon that surrounded the already-packed dance floor. Beneath a thatched tent, dozens of bodies writhed to music so loud the bass thumped in my chest. Or maybe it was the pills I was feeling. I wasn't sure.

"I'm glad she only hired male help for the party—no sexy waitresses to compete with." Lil laughed as we entered the oasis, eyeing a shirtless waiter carrying an appetizer tray.

"Leave it to Deena," I said, already bored with the conversation.

"Her mom did a great job designing this," Kylie said. "I can almost feel the trade winds."

I pretended to take interest in the tropical flower chains dangling over the dance floor, in the private tiki huts overflowing with pillows and candles, while scanning the crowd until I spotted *him*. Standing alone next to a bar, he was perfectly at ease in board shorts and a puka-shell necklace, coconut in hand. Giving in to the fuzzy warmth seeping through my veins, I detangled myself from the girls' arms.

"Where are you going?" Kylie called as I retreated.

"To get a drink," I replied over my shoulder.

"*You're* getting a drink," Lil said, calling my bluff.

"I'm feeling adventurous tonight." I shrugged.

She glanced over my shoulder in Adam's direction. "Don't do anything I wouldn't do," she said. "Or that I *would* do."

I didn't miss the glint in her eye, but I kept going. Normally I would have been afraid, but tonight was different. A breeze tickled my arm, tugging at my skin, urging me forward. I couldn't wait to talk to him.

"Hi." Switching off my live feed, I stopped in front of Adam. Fire licked his skin, casting him in red. "Having fun?"

Taking me in, he smiled. "Ella. It's been way too long since I've had you alone."

Loving my name on his lips, I inched closer. "Agreed. It's time we fix that, don't you think?"

"Absolutely. You're stunning. It's not fair to the birthday girl."

My cheeks flushed.

Just then, Siren Seven took the stage, the drummer pounding out an intoxicating beat. A spotlight illuminated the suspension bridge, and, in a burst of flames, Deena appeared, the perfect Polynesian pinup, aloft on her grass throne, waving to her guests.

"I'm not sure about that." I chewed my lip, watching her.

"I am." He leaned in, his breath tickling my ear. "Do you want to go somewhere quieter?"

"I'd love to." My skin prickled with hot excitement, my blood rushing in my veins. Maybe it was the pills or maybe it was Adam, but for the first time maybe ever, I felt *alive*.

Grabbing two coconuts, he handed me one and laced his fingers through mine, sending a shiver all the way to my toes. We walked down a little path to the edge of the property.

"How do you know where you're going?" I asked, simultaneously aware of his broad shoulders and Deena being helped off her throne by Trent. Trent kissed her hand, and her megawatt smile proved she'd found her new prey. Relieved that Adam was all mine, I gazed up at his profile.

"I always scope out my surroundings—you never know when you're going to need a quick exit. It's habit."

"Why is it habit?" I inched closer to him.

"When I was a kid, I got trapped in the storeroom at a

surf shop. I was checking out some old boards, and they didn't know I was in there—they locked me in all night. It was terrifying. So now I always have an exit strategy. I think that's why I like the water so much—there's always somewhere to swim."

"Unless you get trapped under the water." I cringed.

"You can always go up," he replied.

We arrived at the pool, which was thankfully empty. Keeping his fingers wound with mine, he pulled me down onto an orange double-wide chaise longue. Leaning back, we sipped our coconuts. The frozen concoction was alternatingly sweet and tart and went down way too easily.

"The sky is so big," he said, gesturing at the mass of glittering stars overhead. They weren't real, but they were mesmerizing. The hotel grounds were encased in a climate-controlled augmented glass dome, so AMPs weren't required. "It makes you feel small, doesn't it? Makes you wonder what we're here for?"

"I wonder what the point of all this made-up Influence is all the time," I said. "We're here to…pretend? Sometimes I think we're in a simulation. Maybe we're all pawns in someone's twisted game and we'll be forced to fight to the death." I closed my mouth. The coconut concoction was talking.

"That's dark, Ella." He laughed. "Do you know what I think?"

"No."

"Even if it's all a game, you're never trapped. You just need an exit strategy." The corner of his mouth curved up in a half smile, and he nudged me with his elbow.

"I hope you're not planning to exit yet," I said. "We just got here."

"Oh no. I'm not going anywhere." His smile widened. "What I'm trying to say is, you're in control."

I glanced at him, unable to squelch the glimmer of hope that shined through me. "I wish."

"It's true."

I turned to face him in full. "How do you know?"

"I'm here with you, aren't I?" He searched my face. "We've found a secret way to connect even with everyone watching."

Genuine happiness jolted through me, and I couldn't contain my smile. "Thank you for the notes. They're the only thing in my life I look forward to."

"I think they're fun, too. And your riddles keep me on my toes. I never would have guessed that behind this pretty face you were so brainy." He ran his thumb over my cheek. "You're deceptive. I like it."

Staring into his depths, I felt possibility pulse in my chest. "I like sharing a secret with you."

His hand moved behind my ear, his fingers winding into my hair, and a moment—or maybe a lifetime—passed. I couldn't be sure because all I knew was him. His energy wrapped around me, cradled and protected me, and I was in awe.

"What you did for Sam…" I whispered.

"Shhhh…" His fingers moved to my lips, silencing me. "Let's not talk about that. She's disappeared from the Index. Nobody knows where she is, and I think it's better that way. Let her be forgotten."

But I couldn't stop. "I think about her. All the time. I think about how you saved her. It was unbelievable. I couldn't move. I was too scared—too afraid to risk my own life—" My gratitude got caught in my throat, and I couldn't go on. A tear rolled down my cheek.

"Hey, don't cry." He wiped away the tear. Cupping my jaw, he tilted my face toward his until our foreheads touched. Potential hummed between us. "And don't put yourself down.

You're incredible. I knew it the day I met you, and I've been wanting to get you alone ever since."

"Are you speaking your inner monologue?" I asked as the augmentation shifted around us. Stars fell from the sky in bursts, twinkling in my periphery like fireflies.

"Sort of. Though I can't say everything that's on my mind…" His eyes dipped to my lips.

I really wanted him to kiss me.

But he didn't.

Instead, he broke the connection, sinking back against the lounger and pulling me down with him. Wrapping me in his arms, he cuddled me to his chest, resting his chin on my head while we watched the wonders of the universe unfold overhead.

Engulfed in the safety of his warmth, I relaxed against him, until, too soon, his wrist screen vibrated, jarring us back to reality.

Groaning, he checked the alert. "I've been offline too long. My investors will be missing me. We should probably get back in there."

"Me, too." I sighed.

Adam stood and helped me to my feet.

"Ready to let everyone in on our secret?" he asked, making a show of switching his Life Stream to "live."

As I understood that this meant we were together, that he was mine and there was no going back, happiness flooded me. I nodded and set my stream to "live," too.

Hand in hand, we walked back to the party, caught up in the bleary daze of possibility.

Deena was onstage when we arrived, but her eyes went straight to us, her expression murderous.

She stormed over. "What are you doing with him?"

My hopes evaporated, my voice sticking in my throat and

coming out sounding like a cough. "What are you talking about?"

"Don't play dumb. You knew this was supposed to be *our* night. Mine and his." She leaned in so her nose nearly touched mine.

A crowd formed around us, and I realized *I* was her drama. Me. The betrayer. My heart stalled. *Did they set me up?*

"Deena, don't do this," Adam said. "It was never going to be our night."

Relief rushed through me.

Deena glared at him, clutching her chest like she'd been stabbed. "Do you know what it's like to wake up every morning thinking about someone? To look for them everywhere, to dream about them at night?"

His eyes flitted to me. "Yes. I do."

I cringed. *This is all part of her plan…*

"First Jax dumps me, now this." Deena's huge eyes glistened. "Ella, you knew I always had a secret crush on Adam. How could you?" Crocodile tears slid down her face, streaking her makeup. Her lower lip quivering, she wiped her cheek.

*She's the one who should be the actress.*

"Deena," I said softly, trying to mask my anger, to save face knowing the world was watching. "You said you weren't interested in Adam—you know I would never hurt you. And nothing happened. Adam and I are just friends, and *you're* my *best* friend."

"*Was.* Was your best friend. It doesn't look like nothing to me." She waved a hand, and all the screens at the party lit up with images of me and Adam cuddled together on the chaise longue.

"Where did you get that?" I asked.

"There are cameras everywhere. When are you going to

learn you're never alone? Someone is *always* watching." She cocked her head, pity flashing across her face before she dissolved into tears again. "You've ruined my birthday. I'll never get over this. Don't ever talk to me again." Whipping her hair over her shoulder, she stomped away.

"What do you want from me?" I yelled to her back, seeing red. "Do you want me to stay away from him? I will. If that's what you want."

"Not so fast, Ella," Adam said, sounding genuinely alarmed.

Deena couldn't quite contain her serpentine smile as she peered over her shoulder. "No. Be happy. You deserve each other. I'm sure there's someone better out there for me."

Pointing her chin to the sky, she exited, her buff bodyguards falling in line behind her.

Adam put his arm around me, and I leaned against him, a mixture of disgust and anger colliding in my chest.

In the morning, the numbers supported Deena. Even pretty girls get their hearts broken, have fickle friends. *Poor, poor thing.* She painted me as the bitch who stole her boyfriend.

She won.

And that's when my life began to unravel.

# Chapter Nineteen

*February 20, 20X5*

*Truth: Trust no one. They will only hurt you.*

"I'm sure it will be no surprise to you there's been a major sell-off." Dad's voice boomed across the terrace the second I walked through the door.

Mom and Dad were eating breakfast outside. Within their virtual bubble, a soft breeze cooled the slightly humid air, and waterfalls gurgled behind them next to the augmented Hollywood sign.

Having stayed awake all night with Adam, wrapping my head around Deena's betrayal, I was drifting in a haze. I didn't have any tears left, but the hurt was still raw. It took me a minute to get what he was talking about.

Dad's eyes were far away, scanning a virtual world visible only to him through his AMPs. "You stole Deena's boyfriend? Can't you give him back? Give her what she wants."

"No," I said quietly. "She never wanted him—she wanted the drama. She sabotaged me."

"Then sabotage her back," Mom said, crunching on seaweed. "You need to find a way to fix this."

"That's your answer? Stoop to her level?" Irritation rippled through me.

Mom shrugged. "This is war."

"But she's my best friend. You're best friends with her mom. We have history. I don't want to throw it all away. I don't want a public fight."

"She's not looking out for your best interests, honey. She's not a real friend," Mom said. "You can't get close to people. They'll only hurt you."

"That's not true. You run a business with Deena's mom. She knows everything about you."

"Not *everything*," Mom said. "No one knows your origins," she mouthed the last statement, probably fearing Quinn was judging her. "I'd never tell anyone that."

I swallowed hard. "Never?" I asked.

"Absolutely not," Dad said. "We can't trust anyone with that sort of information. Sure, we trust her enough to let you spend the weekend at her house, to befriend her daughter, but never with our closest secrets. That kind of knowledge claims too much power. You know this, and we're wasting time. What we should be talking about is how we're going to get your stockholders back."

Sickness rose in my throat. *You can't trust anyone. Me included.*

"What is it, sweetie?" Mom asked, her voice saccharine. "You're pale as a ghost."

*I don't want to play this game anymore. Maybe if I tell the truth they'll ban me from the Networks and I can spend all day surfing with Adam...*

I raised my eyes to hers. "I did a bad thing."

Chopsticks frozen in the air, she waited. Dad's eyes bored into the side of my face.

Finally, Mom spoke, starring in the role of concerned parent. "What is it? You can tell us anything. We'll figure it out." But she couldn't act around me. I saw right through her. She was scared.

Breathing deep, I confessed. "Deena knows."

"I hope you're not saying what I think you're saying," Dad said through clenched teeth.

I stayed locked on Mom. "And she told Kylie and Lily. It was part of our trust circle. We knew one another's secrets, and we agreed to protect them, to protect one another. Deena can't tell. If she does, I'll tell everyone she had her stomach stapled."

"Oh. My. God." Mom dropped the chopsticks and buried her face in her hands. When she looked up, her eyes were wild. "That secret isn't worth yours. Your *life* isn't worth that secret. Do you realize this scandal could destroy us? Trust is our biggest commodity. If the public loses faith in us, we lose everything. Life as you know it could end."

My stomach clenched. "That sounds like a threat," I said.

"Oh, you best believe it is." She rose to her full height, all five feet, four inches of it.

"Calm down, Tia. Let's think about this rationally," Dad said. But a moment later, his face was turning purple, the ramifications pulsing through him. "How could you be so stupid?"

"I'm sorry," I said, examining my toes. I didn't know what else to say. There were no words. "I wanted to be honest with you... Maybe I should lay low for a while. Take a break from the Networks."

"Ha! Nice try." Mom paced the deck. "Quinn, what should we do?"

"Oh, you guys. This is a hard one. I really feel for you." Quinn's voice sounded across the deck. "Sweet Ella, why didn't you come to me with this? If you would have asked me, I would have told you hooking up with Adam was a bad idea. Oh…" Her voice broke, like she was on the verge of tears. "I've run all the possible scenarios, and the only thing you can do to save yourself is leave. You have to start over before any more damage is done. If you go now, people will forget. You still have a chance—you just need a new narrative."

"There you go," Mom said. "What you need is a change of scenery. A fresh start."

"I'll pull some strings," Dad said. "Get her a part in a movie—an indie—something edgy, interesting. On location."

"Oh!" Mom gasped, grabbing Dad's hand. "And we can use my cancer." Tears sprang to her eyes. "We're so blessed. Even in the dark, there's always light."

"It's perfect," Dad said. "Your fans will sound the rally cry."

"Your cancer is the answer!" Quinn chimed in. "Make that the focus, and they'll forget about Ella."

"Cancer?" I asked.

"We were going to tell you tonight," Mom said, drying her cheeks with the back of her hand. "This morning, when I went to the restroom, the toilet reported a protein in my urine that's a precursor to thyroid cancer. Left untreated, I might develop cancer ten years from now, but the doctor says if we do a day of radiation, I'll be fine. It's going to be hard on my body—like having the flu—but I will fight. I'm a survivor. At least I will be." She smiled.

I blinked, shocked at her audacity. "Mom, I know you're afraid of pain, but don't you think you're incredibly lucky to beat cancer before you get it? Most people can't afford that technology."

"I'll be creating awareness, sweetie. That's my job."

"And Ella, your job is to fix your price," Dad said. "While you're on set, cozy up to the director, the lead actors. Be seen having a great time."

"But won't it look bad if I leave Mom in her time of need to go film some dumb movie?" I was grasping at straws.

"No," Dad said. "I think it's best you distance yourself from us while we go through this. Your mother is sick. She doesn't need extra stress in her life."

His words had the power of a thousand beestings. *Get close to no one. Including your daughter.* "But I don't want to go. It's my life. Don't I have a choice?"

"No, you don't have a choice," Dad growled. "You're sixteen. You have no say. You're going."

"But what about Deena?" I sniffed, my head aching.

"We'll take care of her," Mom said almost gleefully. "You can never go back to Intersection, you silly, little fool. You'll have to break all ties with your friends there."

"But I can't leave Adam. He's the only good thing in my life." My heart squeezed, and a sob caught in my throat, last night's brief happiness slipping through my fingers.

"Too bad," Dad said, unmoved. "Above all, you will end things with him. Having a relationship with him will only provoke Deena. You're getting on a jet tonight. You will not see him again. Is that clear?"

Desperate to hold on to the shreds of my almost life, I pointed my chin to the sky. "No. I'm not going. You can't make me."

Mom's eyes narrowed to slits. "Watch us."

# Chapter Twenty

*January 2, 20X6, Keystone*

"Good morning, Scarlet Spy." Rayelle's too-cheery voice sounds from across the room.

I groan. The winter sun rising over the strawberry fields is an interrogator, streaming through the windows. The flat, white light assaults me, demanding last night's memories surface.

*You're my prize.*

Irritated by the bolt of electricity the recollection sends through me, I yank the covers over my head.

"Don't remind me." I peek at her from under the blanket. "Everyone who bet on me probably hates me now." *And they'll never know how close I came to winning.* I realize I *want* everyone at Keystone—and beyond—to know I can beat Garrett, that I'm good at this. *Ugh. The Influencer in me will never die.*

"You're too hard on yourself. They knew what they were doing. It's called gambling for a reason. You were a long shot." She jumps out of bed, surprisingly perky after last night's celebration. I barely remember her coming in; I finished crying myself to sleep hours before she returned. The post-Quest adrenaline dump combined with journaling really did a number on me. *It couldn't also be because I lost... I'm not that pathetic, am I? I went after something I wanted, and I lost, but I tried my best. It should be enough...*

"And you beat Kyran and Chloe. That's something," she says, rummaging through her dresser drawer. "Kyran wouldn't have come close if he hadn't followed you or if he'd had to crack Tut's lock by himself. Think about that."

"I don't want to think about any of it."

"Too bad. You're what everyone is talking about. I don't think you can escape it."

"Wonderful."

I watch her pull on tall black boots and a full skirt. Today is a rare street-clothes day. After our partners are announced at the assembly this morning, we have the day free. It's our last break before it's full steam ahead on our heists.

Rayelle examines her backside in the mirror and smiles. Seeming satisfied with herself, she fixes her eyes on me. "Come on. Get up." She marches over and rips the covers off me. "We don't want to be late."

"I do."

She rolls her eyes. "Get dressed. You'll feel better. What are you going to wear? Don't you want to look special for your partner?"

"No. I'll probably get stuck with Liam." Grimacing, I snatch my blanket back. "Besides, I don't have anything to wear." *Except for the Balenciaga, and that's not happening.* "I didn't know we were ever supposed to look normal."

"You can borrow something from me." She tugs on my arm. "You have to go to the assembly. It's mandatory."

I sigh, wishing she wasn't right. "Fine." Heaving myself to

the floor, I rummage through Rayelle's open drawer, selecting a pair of baggy jeans and a Cirque du Soleil T-shirt. Not bothering with makeup, I tie my hair into a squat ponytail and plop back onto the bed, waiting until she finishes.

Rayelle frowns. "That's it?"

I shrug. "I'm not trying to impress anyone."

"Clearly. How can you not care who your partner is? I've been dying to know since I was twelve."

"Maybe it's not the same without the buildup."

Peering into the mirror, she fluffs her hair and dots purple gloss on her lips. "I wonder who Garrett will pick."

Closing my eyes, I hope he's changed his mind, even though my instincts tell me it's a done deal. "I have no idea."


The Lodge is buzzing when we arrive. Everyone is dressed in the latest fashions, and this could easily be an Intersection assembly, except for the Disconnect makeup. I feel a little out of place in my casual outfit. Fortunately, my stalling has successfully made us late, and we're the last to arrive. Robie appears at the front of the hall just as we settle into the back row.

Garrett is sitting in the front row, Chloe's hand resting on his knee. She'd burst into the Summit last night seconds after Garrett "claimed his prize," and he'd dropped my arm immediately. Again, hope that he changed his mind surges through me and is instantly squelched by a thud of disappointment at the possibility he did. *I don't* want *him to choose me, do I? No.* I try to convince myself.

Rayelle leans over. "Remember, no matter what happens, we're meeting in the Vault at the Acropolis this afternoon."

"I'll be there," I promise.

"Good morning." Robie clears his throat, silencing the room. "I won't waste your time by prolonging this—you know why you're here. We'll be giving you the details of this year's Initiation Heist and assigning partners. If this is your first heist, remember the Initiate is in charge. You will do as they say. You are to follow their directions explicitly, no matter what. This is their final test, and they are the responsible party. The rest of you are here to learn."

Giggling, Chloe whispers something in Garrett's ear. *He won't choose me. She'd never stand for him spending so much time with another girl.*

"The assignment is real," Robie continues. "No one you interact with will be privy to your mission, unless they're one of our former students working undercover as a contact. It will require using all your skill and knowledge. You may get caught. If you do, you will not admit any affiliation with Keystone or implicate us. If your identity is exposed, your life as a thief is over. In exchange for your silence, we will do everything we can to establish you as a Maker, but you will no longer be welcome here. Any secrets you hold must be taken to the grave."

He lets the words marinate, and Rayelle leans over, whispering, "It's really bad if you get caught. It happened to a team two years ago, and they're still in jail."

*Unless you're Garrett and just won a get-out-of-jail-free card... If he gets caught, his partner will probably have to take the fall...* I swallow hard, beginning to sweat. But, at the same time, my insides leap in anticipation.

"In years past, the heists have been small, mostly involving stealing treasures to add to the Vault, but this year is different. Your mission will be integral to preserving the truth." He paces back and forth across the stage. "Each of the ten teams will be asked to steal a piece of the overall puzzle, and, when combined, the information will be of great significance to the Disconnect movement. For your own safety, you're not to discuss your heist with the other teams—the less you know about the overall heist, the better.

"Each team will be assigned a master thief who will oversee your plan. They're the only ones who will know your strategy and what it is you're after." He comes to a stop, and his eyes go to Garrett. "And now for the moment you've all been waiting for. Our champion will choose his partner. When the announcement is made, I'd like his partner to come to the stage."

He motions Garrett forward, and I look to his parents. Their expressions remain unchanged, though they must be bursting with pride in their son.

Garrett stands. It's weird seeing him dressed like a normal guy, in dark fitted jeans and a thin black T-shirt that shows off the definition in his lean arms. Hands casually shoved in his pockets, he moves next to Robie, scanning the room until he finds me. A slight smile forms on his lips.

Shrinking in my seat, I stare at his toes.

"Are you ready to choose?" Robie asks.

"Yeah," Garrett says, like the announcement he's about to make is no big deal.

"Who will it be, then?"

The air is heavy with silence as Garrett waits, letting the anticipation build.

My heart pounds in my ears. He's taking so long I check his face to see what his deal is.

As soon as our eyes meet, he speaks. "I choose Elisha DeWitt."

Rayelle gasps and tries shoving me to my feet, but I can't move. The blood drains from my face as the room erupts in chaos.

"Excellent choice," Robie says, smiling. "Elisha, please join us."

Knowing I don't have a choice, I force my wooden legs to move toward the stage. It's like I'm swimming upstream, faces floating by in a sea. Chloe's steely eyes stare me down as I stumble up the steps and take my place next to Garrett, hyperaware of the whispers in the crowd.

"Glad you dressed up. Are you hoping hobo is our cover identity?" Garrett mutters under his breath.

"What about you? All black? It's a little on the nose, don't you think?" I say through clenched teeth. "Or would you prefer I wear a tutu and a tiara like your girlfriend?"

"No. Baggy suits you," he replies. "Besides. It wasn't an essay question."

I glare at him. "So sorry, I'm usually a girl of few words, but for some reason you *Exorcist* them out of me."

"What an excellent day for an exorcism."

Annoyed that I get all tingly at his use of the old movie quote, I press my lips together. Robie steps between us. "Master thief Abignail will be your advisor. This is your assignment." He hands Garrett a packet. "Find a quiet place to digest it, and then I trust you'll dispose of it correctly."

"Thank you," Garrett says. Taking the packet in one hand and gripping my arm with the other, he drags me away as Robie calls Kyran to the stage.

The last thing I hear before Garrett leads me into the passageway at the back of the fireplace we left through yesterday is the announcement that Kyran is to be partnered with Rayelle.

# Chapter Twenty-One

*January 2, 20X6, Keystone*

Once we're outside, I wiggle free of his grasp.

"Why did you pick me? You could have chosen anyone."

"I thought you could use a mentor."

He smiles down at me, his stormy gray-green eyes cleverly hiding the truth.

"Lucky me." I frown. "Can I refuse to be your partner?"

"Nope. You don't have a choice. I won, remember?"

"And you'll never let me forget it." Turning my back on him, I stomp down a trail, wanting to put as much space between us as possible.

"Come on, Ellie." He easily catches up to me. "You're the only person at Keystone who's competition for me."

I squelch the lightning bolt that shoots through me. "There you go with the compliments again."

"Nah. I like to keep my rivals close is all."

"So Chloe is your rival?" Coming to a halt, I stare up at him.

His lips purse. "Jealous isn't your color, Ellie."

"What do you see in her, anyway?"

"Oh, she's really talented. She has the ability to—"

"Stop." I cover my ears. "Never mind. I don't want to know what you two practice in private."

He laughs. "You have to admit: we'll make a great team. With my looks and your...well, *my* charm, we'll be unstoppable." He elbows me, his mouth twitching like he's showing me how to smile.

Ignoring the pounding in my chest that tells me he's right, I shake my head. "I'm not admitting anything."

"Now that we're partners, we need to work on loosening you up. Let that hair down. Bottling up your emotions isn't healthy." He tugs on my stubby ponytail. "But first things first. Do you want to know what this says?" He holds up the packet.

"Yes." Snatching it from his hands, I take off running and climb a nearby tree.

He's after me in a flash, catching me around the waist before I fully get my footing and dragging me to the ground. Not letting me go, he yanks on a branch, and a door I had no idea existed opens in the base of the tree.

"Convenient," I say, resisting the urge to relax against his chest. "You only won because you know all of Keystone's secrets."

"Even I don't know all of its secrets," he says, hustling us into the safe room. Closing the door, he plunges us into darkness. I hear him fumbling with something metal-sounding, and a lantern that sits in the middle of a small table illuminates his face. "I admit knowing the tunnels helped with transportation, but my real victory was getting you to steal the battery for me."

Unable to deny the truth, I drop the subject. "What is this place?" I run my fingers along the smooth grains of the hollowed-out tree interior.

"A hideout. Disconnects pride themselves on being able to disappear."

"Is this one of the hideout locations you learned about for winning the Quest?"

"No. This one is only level-one classified. Everyone can access this. Level-one hideouts exist all over the forest and the world. You just have to know how to recognize the signs."

"I haven't learned them yet."

"They're not something you're taught. They're something you figure out. But don't worry—I'll show you the ropes."

"Lucky me..." Reluctantly, I hand over the documents.

He rips open the envelope, spreading its contents on the table. Curious, I nestle close to him, peering over his shoulder. We fall silent in concentration, squinting to read the papers in the dim light.

**Target:** Nicki Simon, 17-year-old socialite and Influencer—runs the popular San Francisco Society blog "Confessions of an Haute Hacker."

**Background:** Only daughter of Collette Simon, reigning queen of the San Francisco Charity Circuit, and James Simon, CEO of Simon Technologies/creator of Quinn, Artificial Intelligence Cognitive technology. Quinn resides in nearly every household on earth, and the world adores her. Every Quinn has a unique personality she adapted from her family. She has learned her family's beliefs and filters information so it is in line with their opinions and worldviews in order to keep everyone happy and free from conflict. But all Quinns have one thing in common: their knowledge base.

Simon feeds Quinn daily updates, giving him supreme control over information. Unbeknownst to the general public, he has earned trillions planting information from anyone who wants their message ingrained as truth. He employs a top-notch team of coders who encrypt the channels that supply information to Quinn, but a backdoor key/ algorithm that can control every device does exist. It is a powerful tool that, in our hands, is imperative to preserving the truth.

Recognizing Simon's name, the tree seemingly twists around me. My parents were integral in influencing the world into accepting Quinn into their homes in the first place and are still on Simon's payroll. *But I've never met James and Collette in person. I've only seen their feet when I was a nine-year-old hiding under my parents' dinner table. Will they remember I existed?* Quietly fighting for air, I try to keep from passing out, lest Garrett have to revive me. *But then, I didn't know* they *had a daughter, so maybe I was off their radar, too. Allard wouldn't put me in danger. I probably won't have contact with Simon.* Clutching the tiger's eye, I call upon its powers to calm me. My heart rate slows as my lungs expand.

I keep reading.

Simon is about to launch a Quinn update that will have her convince the public "mind uploads" to provide a permanent backup to their "mind files"—memories, personality—are a good idea. Quinn will insist everyone go to their nearest upload center immediately. This is the first step in getting people to enter their data into the Super Brain. It will put their brain information into the AI, making it smarter, and later, will ease society's entry into the Simulation. If we have the backdoor algorithm, we can take Quinn offline and shut down Simon's propaganda feed forever. But we have to do it before Simon launches his update.

**Mission:** The key/algorithm is not stored digitally. Simon is nervous about it being hacked and falling into the wrong hands, so he keeps it on a hard drive physically locked in a medieval jewelry box at his

Menlo Park home. The key to the box is a ring Nicki wears at all times. Your mission is to steal the ring. Once you've obtained it, transmit your completion to your advisor and await further instruction.

**Contact:** Faye Connolly is living undercover in Silicon Valley society. She will introduce you to Nicki.

Garrett's eyes are on fire. "This is going to be wild."

My mouth refuses to close. "Have you lost your mind? How are we supposed to get close to Nicki and stay off the grid? Silicon Valley is the most connected place in the world!"

"The same way people have been hiding in plain sight for centuries. We'll change our appearances, our names. I'm sure you're no stranger to the term 'alias.'"

My stomach tightens, and I wonder if he knows.

"It's simple social engineering," he continues without missing a beat. "And the facial-recognition cameras are easy to fool."

"No, they're not. The technology just keeps getting better and better. This is *so* not a good idea." I want to shake sense into him. "And since you've got this all figured out, how are we going to get the ring if she wears it all the time? We can't just steal it off her finger—she'll notice it's gone immediately, and then her dad will change the location of the algorithm."

"Not if we convince her she lost it. Then maybe she'll be afraid to tell her dad. Especially if she loses it doing something he wouldn't approve of." A slow smile lights up his face.

"Like what? We don't even know this girl. How do we get her to do anything?"

"We don't know her *yet*. We will. And I'm very convincing."

I fold my arms. "Ugh. I feel sorry for her already."

He laughs. "Listen, don't freak out on me, Ellie. We're going to figure out every detail, think of every possible thing that could go wrong. This isn't happening tomorrow. When we walk into San Francisco, we're going to be prepared. I won't do anything that makes you uncomfortable."

*Except exist.*

But I don't say that out loud. "Okay, okay." I take a calming breath. "Okay."

He holds up the papers. "Have you memorized these?"

"Target Nicki Simon, daughter of Collette and James—"

"Good." He drops the packet on the dirt floor. Striking a match, he lights the pages on fire. They flare up and, in a flash, are gone.

"See you at Abignail's in the morning?" he asks.

"You want to wait until tomorrow?" I sputter. "I thought we were going to be prepared. How are we getting to Silicon Valley? Where will we stay? What if we get caught? We should get to work right away."

"It's one of our only free days all year," he says, "and freedom isn't something I waste. Neither should you. Enjoy it while you can."

"Don't want to keep Chloe waiting, huh?"

Raising an eyebrow, he doesn't dignify me with a response.

"Whatever the master says." I sigh. "It's your Initiation Heist, not mine. I'm just your lowly assistant. Do what you want."

"That's my plan." Extinguishing the lantern, he drapes an arm over my shoulder and guides me to the door.

My spine goes rigid at the same time my skin warms to his touch. Sweat pools on my back.

"Relax, Ellie. There's nothing to be afraid of. You're with me."

"*You're* what I'm afraid of."

"Maybe we need to do some trust exercises, then. Let's plan on it." Giving me a quick squeeze, he opens the door.

"See you tomorrow, partner." White light briefly slices the room in two as he disappears into the forest, leaving me in the dark, my stomach flip-flopping with dread.

And excitement.

"I can't believe he picked you!" Rayelle yells when she sees me, her voice echoing across the Acropolis. She's waiting among the stone columns and marble statues with Stewart and Sophia.

"I can." Stewart grins. "He's a smart guy. Of course he picked the best."

"Did you see the look on Chloe's face?" Sophia asks as they huddle around me. Today she's transformed herself into Chloe, having gone so far as to pad her uniform to give her curves where none usually exist. She knits her eyebrows together, her lip trembling before affecting a haughty stare, in a perfect Chloe imitation. I squint to make sure it's Sophia I'm standing next to. "She was pissed. It was fantastic."

"Is your heist really hard?" Rayelle asks.

"She's not allowed to talk about it," Stewart silences her.

"But maybe you'll go undercover as his girlfriend," Rayelle says.

"I hope not." My traitor heart thumps at the possibility, and I pretend I hadn't considered that myself. "But knowing him, he'll purposely make me as uncomfortable as possible, so maybe."

"That would be so much fun." Rayelle sighs.

"What about you? Who did you guys end up with?" I ask. "As his highness was dragging me out through the fireplace, I thought I heard you were paired with Kyran?"

She flushes bright red. "Somehow my dream came true,

though he doesn't say much… I'm not sure how he feels about me being his partner, but I'm so excited we're going to San Francisco together—"

Stewart claps his hand over her mouth. "Shhh. We're not supposed to talk about it. He's going to *hate* being your partner if you slip like that during the heist."

He lowers his hand, and she bites her lip.

"Is everyone going to San Francisco?" I whisper.

They all nod.

"I'm sure Ophelia and I will have a *fabulous* time," Sophia says, breaking the silence.

"Garrett's cousin?" I ask.

"Yeah. She's not so bad," she says. "It could be worse. I could have ended up with—"

"Liam." Stewart groans, raising his hand. "I win."

"At least we know we'll have friends nearby," Rayelle says.

"Yeah. Thank God for you guys," Stewart says. "I'll feel a lot better knowing you're close. No matter what, if any of you needs help, send out a signal, and I'll come running." He puts a hand in the center of the circle.

"Me, too," Sophia says, placing her hand on top of his.

"I'm in." Rayelle joins the pile.

They look to me expectantly, and I hesitate.

"Goonies always say live," Stewart says.

"No!" My eyes widen, and all three of them bust up laughing.

"She passed," Sophia says.

"We think the quote changed sometime during the Positivity Movement of the 20Y0s," Stewart says.

"Goonies never say die," Rayelle and Sophia say at the same time.

"I can't believe you guys know that movie," I say, shaking my head. "It's ancient."

"Stewart told us you were a fan," Sophia says. "Which is a weird coincidence because we've seen it dozens of times."

In awe that I've found my tribe, I smile and add my hand to the pile.

"Always say die, never say live."

# Chapter Twenty-Two

*January 2, 20X6, Keystone*

Exiting the Acropolis, I tell Rayelle, Stewart, and Sophia I have secret heist research to do and promise to meet them for dinner. We part ways, and I go straight to my secret library. With Garrett and the heist demanding my full attention, I'm eager to get to the end of my journal. I'm ready to move on.

*February 21, 20X5*
*Truth: Nothing can tear me down. There's always a way. I'm a survivor.*

No goodbyes. No explanations. My parents confiscated my devices, changed my passwords, and shipped me to Savannah, where I was to film *Unseen*, a low-budget movie targeting the Maker market by using physical locations instead of green screens. According to the Myrna-bot who had taken over manning my Network feeds, I was "doing it for the art." They had officially turned me into the virtual daughter they'd always wanted.

In some ways, it was a relief to put my Network feed on autopilot, but I was also cut off from Adam's stream, and I was desperate for contact. I at least wanted to say goodbye. The moment Bernard—the robo-guard assigned to keep me under constant surveillance—deposited me in my hotel room, locking the door from outside and taking up residence in the threshold, I frantically searched for a communication device. The hotel was a few years past its prime and—probably thanks to my parents—there was no Network access, no screens, no computer, and no VR in my room. There was only a desktop robot, who asked me if I wanted room service before going on the fritz and sounding the wake-up alarm. The buzzer shrieking in my ears, I slammed the robot against the floor until he shut up.

Sitting on the bed in silence, I stared at the faded wallpaper. As alone as I was certain I was, I couldn't ignore the eerie presence that lingered in the walls, the past impression of moments lived within the tiny box. The walls started closing in, suffocating me, and I inhaled the faint rose scent that failed to overpower the antiseptic air in the stale space. With no one to cling to, I threw myself on the lumpy bed, buried my face in a pillow, and screamed. *No escape... They can't disappear me... They can't keep me from him... I'll find a way.* My throat closed, smothering a sob before it surfaced, and I knew it was best if my true feelings stayed deep.

I begged for sleep, hoping to wake with a plan to get around Bernard, but sleep never came.

In the morning, my eyes were red and puffy when Bernard escorted me to the makeup trailer.

"What happened to you?" The makeup artist gasped as I slumped into the chair bearing my name. Failing to introduce herself, she tilted my chin upward, examining my swollen eyes.

"I got in late last night and didn't sleep well. I'm sorry," I replied.

"It's going to take a miracle to fix this," she muttered before disappearing through a doorway.

"I'm sure you're homesick," the lady in the makeup chair next to me said. "Don't worry, though. You'll make friends soon. It's hard when everyone's a stranger, but I promise we'll be family before you know it." She extended her hand without looking at me, keeping her head steady as the other makeup artist airbrushed her face. "I'm Crystal Harrison."

My ears perked up, the name sounding familiar. "I'm Ella Karman." I accepted her hand.

"Nice to meet you, Ella." She squeezed my fingers before letting go.

I eyed her cloud of blond hair and white skin, so stark against her red lips. "You play the voodoo priestess?" We would have a lot of scenes together. The movie was about a voodoo priestess who adopts a runaway teenage girl (me).

"I do."

Recalling a distant conversation stolen from beneath the dinner table, I couldn't stop staring. "You were a famous actress, but you disconnected," I blurted.

She smiled, her eyes remaining on the makeup artist. "Once upon a time, yes."

"What are you doing here?"

"I decided it was time to stage my comeback." She giggled but quickly shut her mouth when the makeup artist cleared her throat.

"You can do that?" I asked. "I thought once you disconnected that was it."

She considered me out of the corner of her twinkling eye. "Anything is possible."

"How?" I exhaled. Tickled by a faint flutter of hope, I

wanted to know everything about her.

The makeup artist stepped back, studying her work.

"Honey, are we all set?" Crystal asked. "Do you think I could get some water before I leave? This air-conditioning is murder on my throat."

"I'll get you some, but you're free to go." The makeup artist left the room.

Crystal paused in front of me before she left. Her face had been transformed into a glittering skull, but she hadn't changed into her costume yet and wore a cheery floral sundress. The effect was like visiting a ghostly lemonade stand on a hot summer day. "Why don't you come by my trailer when you're done? We'll talk."

"Come in and have a seat," Crystal said, ushering me inside.

Her trailer was identical to mine, except her mahogany makeup table overflowed with flowers tucked into tiny glass vases. Their scent was innocent but intoxicating. Kind of like Crystal herself.

"Hungry?" She offered me a plate piled with gooey chocolate chip cookies.

"Thank you." Lowering myself into a chair, I took a bite, careful not to smudge my lips, though I was playing a fifteen-year-old ingenue and my makeup was practically nonexistent. The cookie was soft and still warm.

"Have some tea, too." She poured a glass from a pitcher sunning itself on a windowsill.

"You've thought of everything," I said, accepting the drink. "It's so homey in here."

"I can make any place feel like home." She sat on the edge of her makeup table, her dress splaying out around her knees. "Because it's wherever I am. What about you? Where are you from?"

"L.A. My parents are Tiana Santos and Noah Karman— they're Influencers. This is my first movie, my first time on my own."

"I remember them."

I watched for signs she knew them more deeply than from their Network feeds.

"I didn't know they had a daughter, though," she said, and I decided they were strangers.

"They kept me out of the spotlight. Until now." I sipped the sweet tea. "My IPO released over the summer, and to be honest, it's been a little rocky. They're hoping *Unseen* will help."

She frowned. "So much pressure for someone so young."

"It is."

Her eyes were blacked out by her contacts, so I couldn't gauge her thoughts, but my instincts told me she was a friend, and I couldn't wait any longer. "I was wondering if you could help me. I need to get in touch with someone, but all my devices were confiscated, and Bernard out there won't let me near the Networks." I nodded over my shoulder to where the robot stood guard outside the door. "And even if I could locate a store to buy a device, my currency account is frozen. Do you have a wrist screen or AMPs I could borrow?"

"I'm sorry." She shook her head. "I don't. No data devices for me."

My jaw dropped. "How do you keep in touch with people?"

"I write letters or call."

"How do you call someone without a device?"

"There are pay phones."

"What are those?"

Pressing her lips together, she suppressed a smile. "They're public telephones. They used to be everywhere before the internet. Some still exist…usually in abandoned strip malls. In big cities, they get augmented to look like green spaces, but in towns that haven't fully digitized, history is all around. You just have to open your eyes to it."

"Do you know where I could find one?"

"Sure. There's one outside the bank in the shopping center across the street. But do you have any change?"

"Like, physical coins?" I raised my eyebrows, recalling an antique piggy bank filled with quarters and dimes Mom used to keep in the back of her closet from when she was a little girl. I hadn't seen it in years. I remembered her trying to throw it out at some point, saying it was worthless. But I'd rescued it from the trash. It had always been hard for me to let go of items that might someday trigger memories. "No…"

"Who do you need to reach?"

"My boyfriend." I stumbled over the words, unsure if they were technically true—aside from publicly holding hands, Adam and I hadn't made anything official—but it was the easiest way to describe how much he meant to me. "My parents made me leave without saying goodbye."

"This is an emergency, then." Grinning, she leaped to her feet and, opening a drawer, produced a roll of quarters. "I've been saving these for a special occasion. Come on. We should hurry. Wardrobe will be here soon."

"What about Bernard? He's set to notify my parents every time I move."

"This will take care of him." She held up a black-and-white striped umbrella. "It's my little indulgence, coded to scramble all GPS signals. I never leave home without it. With this over your head, you're off the grid."

Leading me outside, she opened the umbrella. We huddled beneath it, tiptoeing down the trailer steps and inching past

Bernard. I held my breath, positive he was going to flash to life any second and alert my parents I was sneaking away, but he didn't budge. Once we were safely past him, we hurried across the street, the steamy Savannah day threatening to melt our makeup. It didn't take long to find the forgotten corner where a black phone hung in a silver box.

"It looks like something from a museum," I said, examining names and number strings etched into the metal. "Do you think it still works?"

"It will. The Disconnects keep them running." She handed me two coins. "Pick up the receiver and put these in that slot. Once you hear a tone, start dialing."

Following her instructions, I listened as the box swallowed my coins with a crunch, but when the tone sounded in my ears, I couldn't remember Adam's private number that would connect me to his wrist screen. I'd never dialed it before—I only knew him by his icon, and even that would only have connected me to his private Network message center. "What if I don't know the number?" I gasped.

"Dial 411. You can look it up."

I pressed the buttons, and, to my surprise, a recording directed me to say the city and state I was trying to reach. I followed the prompts, but unfortunately his information was unlisted.

"This is impossible." I slammed down the phone. "Without technology, a person could go missing. They could disappear."

"Yes, they could," Crystal said, putting her arm around me. "Being off-grid forces you to keep the people you love close, that's for certain."

"How am I going to get in touch with him?" I threw my hands up in frustration as we walked back to the trailers.

"Send a letter? I'll give you a stamp."

"To where? I don't know his address."

"What about his Network? You could use a library computer, create a new account, and private message him."

I shook my head. "So many people want to get to Adam, he charges to read messages, and my currency account is frozen. But maybe we could go together and you could message him for me? I'll find a way to pay you back."

"Sorry, hon. I don't have a currency account." She linked her arm with mine.

"How do you get your stipend, then?" I asked, my jaw falling open.

"I don't. Favors are my currency." She laughed. "Maybe you have to wait for him to come to you. It isn't a bad thing, you know."

"I guess…" *There's got to be another way.*

I stared at our shadows as we walked, our silhouettes melded together by the umbrella, and an idea formed.

# Chapter Twenty-Three

*March 1, 20X5*

*T*ruth: *Waiting for what you want is worthless. If you want something to happen, you have to go after it yourself.*

I tried it Crystal's way, waiting around for a note to slide under my dressing-room door with a riddle that would lead to a meeting place—he must have known I was in Savannah from what the Myrna-bot was posting to my Networks—but nothing showed up. To keep myself from wondering if he was over me, I threw myself into my role, spending every waking moment studying the script, memorizing my lines. Acting took me by surprise. I *loved* being on set. Despite being nervous at first, as soon as the cameras rolled, I *became* my character and my nerves evaporated. It was freeing not being me anymore, and I couldn't wait for all the characters I'd get to play in the future. The DNA scans were right. I was a natural. And I was hooked.

Still, I was dying to know what was happening at home. It took some convincing—Crystal was way more protective of me than my own mother ever was—but she eventually agreed to let me borrow her umbrella.

"Are you sure I can't go with you?" Crystal asked, dipping her brush into a little gold jar and dabbing the cold cream under my right eye.

"Positive. I have a paper map that shows where the library is and the quarters you gave me. Once I get there, I'm sure someone will help me access the Network, and maybe the quarters will be enough to get them to send Adam a message for me. I'll be fine," I said. "Besides, tonight is your last scene. You can't miss it."

"I know." She sighed, dotting glue over my eye and adhering gold beads. "I just hate having you out there alone. If you waited until tomorrow, I could go with you."

"But *I* have a big scene tomorrow. I go out alone in L.A. all the time, and it's much scarier than Savannah—I'll be back before you know it."

"I guess." Standing back, she scanned my face, admiring her handiwork. "But in L.A., you can be tracked. No Savannah cameras will recognize this girl. You could disappear." She turned my chair to face the mirror. "Disconnect looks good on you, don't you think?"

My lips parted in awe as I stared at my reflection. A gold sequin fan arched over my right eye, and three thick, gold teardrops dripped over my cheek beneath it. Above the corner of my mouth, a rhinestone beauty mark sparkled, and my lips were drawn in with red glitter on one side, black on the other. "Wow." I exhaled, blood thundering in my veins. I felt like I was back hiding under my parents' dining room table, like an imposter on the verge of getting caught. And I liked it. "It's incredible."

Standing, I kissed her cheek.

"Be safe out there." She hugged me. "Come find me as soon as you get back, so I know you're okay. And don't forget this." She handed me the black-and-white striped umbrella.

A little charge shot through me. "I'll be home before you're done shooting. Don't worry." Taking the umbrella, I headed for the door.

First, I had to get past Bernard. He believed I was shooting tonight and was standing guard outside of Crystal's trailer. He had no concept of time, so if he didn't detect my movement, he would stand there all night, thinking I was inside. His sensors detected daylight, so I just had to be back before sunrise.

Slipping out the trailer door, I opened the umbrella and took a deep breath. With a silent wave to Crystal, I tiptoed down the stairs and wiggled past Bernard. He didn't budge. I easily disappeared into the night.

Walking along the river, I strolled down boulevards dripping with Spanish moss, past stately Victorian mansions, imagining what they looked like through AMPs. I'd overheard a cameraman describing how at night the city was augmented to play up its haunted image. The homes decayed, and tattered curtains fluttered behind broken windows. There were cold spots and things that went bump and the occasional apparition. My footsteps echoing ominously on the cobblestone sidewalk, goose bumps rose on my arm, and I picked up my pace, turning onto River Street.

It was lined with shops and bistros overflowing with customers, and garlic and spice wafted on the breeze. My stomach growled. Uneasy eyes glared at me as I passed, and people crossed the street when they saw me coming, tripping over themselves to get out of my way. I knew what they were thinking. *Lazy. Freeloader.* Shielding my face with the umbrella, I shuddered. It was everything I'd been taught to believe.

I lost my appetite.

Dipping out of sight, I wandered along back roads and through abandoned courtyards until I arrived at the steps of the Carnegie Branch Library. I climbed the crumbling stairs and entered the moss-covered brick building, decayed after years of neglect.

Once inside, I peered through the dust floating in the dull light that filtered through the windows. The library was full of Unrankables huddled around archaic computers plugged into ethernet cables. *They must be the only ones who use libraries.* Only the poorest of the poor would subject themselves to public download speeds.

"Can I help you find anything?"

I jumped and turned to find a guy about my age standing behind me.

"Are you lost?" he asked, his voice betraying a soft southern accent. A series of lightning bolts zigzagged across his bronze skin.

My instinct was to withdraw, but without flinching, I shook my head no.

"Are you sure?" He gestured at the umbrella. "You don't need that in in here, you know. The satellites won't find you."

"What about facial-recognition cameras?" I asked.

"I promise, we're off the grid." He laughed. "We still use dial-up. We don't exactly have the currency for that kind of tech."

"That's ridiculous," I said, lowering the umbrella. "You'd think the government would want to rehabilitate people—I mean—a place like this."

My face heated, but to my relief, he smiled. "Well, well, who do we have here?" His dark eyes roamed my face. "Ella Karman?"

"You recognize me?" I gasp.

"Of course I do, even under all that glitter. Real Disconnects don't shine." He winked.

"Maybe given the right opportunity they would."

"Maybe." He extended his hand. "I'm Johnathan."

"Nice to meet you." Hating my instinctive repulsion, I forced myself to put my hand in his. "Though I don't know if you should be talking to me."

"Because you're an Influencer?" He shrugged, continuing to hold my hand. "Nah. That don't bother me. I'm not a Disconnect. But tell me, what are you doing posing as one?" With a squeeze, he let me go.

"I could ask you the same thing. What's with the lightning if *you* aren't a Disconnect?"

"Fair question." He smiles. "The truth is I'm Unrankable, same as everyone else here. I'm not ashamed of it. It's the life I was born into, and I don't think I'd want to rank on the Index even if I was allowed. If I had a choice, I'd probably be a Disconnect, but you can't refuse what you've never been offered, so I show my support with lightning. That's pretty much the most interesting thing there is to know about me, so now it's your turn."

"I wanted to look up something that I don't want my parents to know about," I said. "They constantly check my Life Stream, so I had to go off-grid."

"I got you. You need access to the Network?"

"You have that here?"

"Of course. Even though we can't post to the Network ourselves, watching you live your life is still our biggest form of entertainment. The way I see it, you Influencers need us. We may not be able to purchase stock in you, but we can sure use our stipend to buy what you're selling. And that keeps your Corporates happy."

Leading me to a computer, he gestures for me to take a seat.

"I never thought about it that way," I said. "You're a pretty smart guy, Johnathan."

"Nah. I'm curious is all. Now, this is called a mouse." He held up a black plastic oval with a roller ball on the top. "You use it to click on this icon." He demonstrated, clicking open a little blue check mark on the screen. The Network appeared. "Just click inside that white square, and you can enter whoever or whatever you're looking for by typing the letters on the keyboard."

"Thank you." I exhaled, barely able to contain my excitement.

"Happy to help anytime," he said. "I'll leave you to your search."

Barely noticing him leave, I typed in Adam's name. His feed appeared, full of surfing videos. It told me nothing, but tears pricked my eyes at seeing him again. At least I knew he was okay. I wanted to send him a message, but I didn't have access to a currency account to pay him to read it. Looking around for Johnathan to see if I could give him some of Crystal's quarters in exchange for use of his currency account, my hand slid almost of its own volition to Adam's friend list. Something told me to click on Deena's stream.

I immediately regretted my instinct. Her feed was live, and there they were. Deena—and Adam—together. His hand sliding up her puny thigh.

My heart pounded in my chest, sending blood straight to my head as I watched in dizzy disbelief. Adam leaned in, his lips finding Deena's. The screen blurred through my tears, but I couldn't look away. I wanted to throw up.

"Are you okay?" Johnathan asked, appearing by my side. "You look like you've just seen a ghost—which isn't impossible.

Ghosts are a major attraction around here."

"No." I swallowed. *Maybe Adam was in on Deena's plan all along... Maybe there was nothing good in my life.* My temples throbbed. I needed air.

Knees wobbling, I stood. Pushing up my umbrella, I blindly ran out of the library, not caring where I was going. I wandered the streets in a fog, Adam kissing Deena on constant replay in my mind, until I ended up at Colonial Park Cemetery. Hazily focusing on the eagle statue lording over the gate, I felt the hairs on the back of my neck stand up. I peered through the iron bars down a dark path lined with giant trees, their spindly arms dripping with moss, reaching out. *Probably craving human flesh.* I gulped and checked my map. All I wanted was my bed, and the quickest way to the hotel was through the graveyard. I was going in.

The gate was locked, but I pushed it open enough to squeeze through. Dropping to my hands and knees, I crawled inside. The cemetery sprawled before me, coming to terrifying life. *It must be in an augmented dome.* The trees swayed as if in a storm, the wind howling through them. Statues turned to face me as I hurried down the path, and I broke into a run. My skin crawled as I ran past winged angels reaching for me from graves with headstones rubbed smooth. Apparitions soared to the full, yellow moon, and fingers ruptured the ground, grabbing at my ankles. *It's not real, it's not real...* My heart in my throat, I ran faster, the ghosts and specters a blur.

Exiting the cemetery as quickly as I could, I ran straight to the hotel. I stumbled down the hall until I found Crystal's room and banged on the door.

"Oh, thank God, you're back," she said, embracing me the moment she saw me. She was still wearing her voodoo makeup from set. "I was so worried."

I rested my head on her shoulder, catching my breath.

"Is everything okay?"

"It's Adam…and Deena. They were playing me." I squeezed my eyes shut. "I was stupid to believe any of it was real."

She held me as tears rolled down my cheeks. *I can't believe I was so wrong about him.*

"I'm sorry, love." She patted my hair. "Let's get you to your room, dry those eyes. A hot bath will help."

I nodded and let her lead me down the hall.

When we arrived at my door, I stopped abruptly. "Wait." I threw up my hand to halt her. "Something isn't right." I studied the lock, a shot of adrenaline clearing my sinuses. Everything looked normal, but I had a weird hunch. "Someone might be inside."

"Why do you think that?" Crystal asked. "Your lock is biometric—only your fingerprints can open it. A lock, like I have, would be easy to pick, but breaking into your room would require a full set of your fingerprints…"

"There's only one way to find out." Placing my hand on the sensor, I waited until the light blinked green and the deadbolt clunked open.

I opened the door to find my room had been ransacked. Light from the massive moon outside the window spotlighted the disaster: clothes everywhere, makeup bottles spilled on the floor, empty drawers gaping.

A fresh wave of dizziness washed over me.

"How did you know?" she whispered.

"I don't know. I just…felt it. It was like there was an impression left in the air, heat…energy. I can't explain it."

"Interesting." She studied me as we stepped inside. "Is anything missing?"

I went straight to my bed, shaking out the covers. "My sleep sheep," I whispered. "It had my Book of Secrets inside."

"What's a Book of Secrets?"

"My journal…"

"Are the files saved somewhere?"

I shook my head. "It was handwritten."

"Handwritten?" She narrowed her eyes.

"My private thoughts… It was the only way to keep them out of my Life Stream…. It had things I overheard when my parents entertained—"

She clamped her hand over my mouth. "Never mind. Don't say anymore." Pressing her forehead against mine, she whispered, "Knowledge is the real currency. Any info you have on someone, keep it for yourself. Don't tell even me. The walls are listening."

I nodded.

"We should call the police," she said loudly.

"Do we have to?" I asked. After what Crystal just said, I didn't really want to publicize the existence of my Book of Secrets. Having to explain why I wasn't in my room and reveal my new ability to go off-grid could only get me into more trouble with my parents. "I've been through so much tonight, and only my journal is missing…"

"It's your decision," Crystal said.

"Let's clean up and pretend this night never happened. I can't deal." All I wanted was to crawl under my covers and hide.

"Okay. Whatever you want. And then let's get you into a hot bath. It'll make you feel better."

Silently, she helped me reset the room. When it was reinstated to its former neatness, she filled the tub.

"Do you want me to stay with you?" she asked before I got in the tub.

I shook my head. "That's okay. I need some time alone."

With a sad smile, she squeezed my hand and headed

for the door. Before she left, she reached into my pocket, grabbing the map and pointing to an intersection. Holding up eight fingers, she mouthed, "Breakfast. There's someone I want you to meet."

"Breakfast," I mouthed back.

"See you tomorrow, love. I'm going to go get Bernard. He'll be stationed outside your door so you'll be safe. Promise. All you need to do is try to get some sleep."

"Thank you. Goodnight, Crystal." With a tiny wave, I closed the door behind her. As soon as the deadbolt slid into place, I sank to the floor, my head spinning.

*Who would want my Book of Secrets? And who does Crystal want me to meet?*

Setting down my pen, I rest my head against the chaise, Adam's betrayal coursing through me like it happened yesterday. *He had his reasons… It wasn't easy, our life. Nothing was black and white.* But even knowing what I know now, I can't deny that night changed him for me. *Even if he'd lived, we would never have been the same… I never would have fully trusted him.*

Crystal, on the other hand, I instantly saw as a friend. She still is.

That much I know is true.

# Chapter Twenty-Four

*January 3, 20X6, Keystone*

"Have you memorized the information supplied in your packet?" Folding his arms over his chest, Abignail leans back in his captain's chair. He's a retired con artist, an expert at forgery and assuming new personalities. I'm glad we're paired with him because I'm going to need every ounce of my acting ability to transform into yet someone else.

"We have," Garrett says. "The first thing we need to do is establish cover identities—open currency accounts, hack our fake retina scans into the Network database—and most importantly, we need to create history for ourselves on the Network so Nicki can cyberstalk us."

I raise my eyebrows, surprised at his professionalism.

"Very good." Abignail nods. "Do you have anything to add, Elisha?"

They look at me, and I rack my brain. Having tossed and turned half the night, wondering how I'm going to boldly walk back into the connected world, risking everything by subjecting myself to facial-recognition technology, my head is in the clouds. The sliding glass doors behind Abignail open to his infinity pool, and I imagine jumping in and swimming straight into the forest.

Abignail clears his throat, making me jump.

"I don't. This is Garrett's heist," I say quickly. "He's in charge. I'll do whatever he says."

Garrett keeps a straight face, though I doubt he believes a word of it. *I'm sure he'll gloat later.*

"What are your ideas for cover identities?" Abignail asks. "You should come from a place you understand and are comfortable acting as an authority on, so you can stay in character at all times. Try to come off as confident, charming, sincere. It also helps to have something about you that stands out, that people will remember you by—so they don't look too closely at anything else. Make that trait something easily discarded, rendering you unrecognizable."

His jaw twitching, Garret squares his shoulders and offers his hand. "Beau Bradford, pleased to meet you, sir." As his posture changes, so does his essence, transforming him into a stranger. The ease with which he makes the switch catches me off guard. *Will I ever know the real Garrett?*

"I just moved to San Francisco to spend the summer interning in nanotech so I'm ready to work for my father's import business when I return to the Cayman Islands in the fall."

"What does he import?" Abignail asks.

"He 3-D prints seashells." Garrett smiles, his eyes crinkling at the corners.

Abignail laughs. "The perfect answer. Everyone knows better than to inquire about a Cayman-based business, but can you speak to what the nanotech project is you're working on?"

"I wouldn't want to bore you with minute details—besides, it's top secret—" Beau says.

And he really is Beau. There's no trace of the Garrett I think I know.

"Let's just say my father would be very pleased if he were to get the first contract to export items via a space elevator."

"Very good," Abignail says. "You know, you were given this task specifically because of your social skills. We felt you were the perfect candidate to get close to Nicki—partly because you're nearly the same age, but also because of your ability to quickly analyze a situation and think on your feet. I trust you understand how to behave in the tech-savvy world. Despite what happened during last year's heist, you did prove yourself sufficient in portraying an Influencer…"

My ears perk up, but I keep my expression neutral.

"And who's this?" Abignail gestures to me.

Remembering Rayelle's suggestion I pose as Garrett's girlfriend, I imagine how much trouble we could get into pretending to be in love. *We'd probably have to get comfortable kissing… How would it happen the first time? Would he push me up against a wall and plant one on me to keep us from being discovered?* I can practically feel his lips pressed against mine, and my stomach drops. I frown. *These fantasies must. Stop.*

"This is my kid sister, Betsy," Beau says. Unable to quite contain his grin, the Garrett I've come to know and hate appears, and the daydream comes to a screeching halt.

My glare could cut glass. "Beau and Betsy Bradford? You can't be serious."

He ignores me. "Mom and Dad sent her along for the summer hoping I'd rub off on her and she'd get her act together. She's gotten a little too into island life lately."

"A lazy little girl? That's what I'm an authority on?" I say. "I can't be an intern, too? Or have my own start-up?"

Beau evaporates, and it's Garrett that faces me, his eyes

full of mischief. "Of course you can, but in this situation, you'll be more believable as my sister."

"But we don't look anything alike."

"Not yet." He grins. "Besides, with your innocent looks it will be easy to convince Nicki I need help making you over. She'll jump at the chance to mold you. Then you'll be on the inside, and she won't suspect you're after her ring. She'll feel like your big sister."

"Won't we be a happy family," I mutter before realizing Abignail is watching us, hiding a smile behind his fingers that are folded in prayer over his lips. Shutting my mouth, I compose myself, attempting to appear the obedient mentee.

"I like the social engineering in this plan—make Nicki think she's helping you. People naturally want to help when they're asked," Abignail says, leaning forward to ruffle through a stack of papers on his desk. "And you two are well suited for each other, though a true partner is years in the making. You'll need to become extremely comfortable with each other to make others believe you're brother and sister. From now on, I expect you to be glued at the hip."

"I won't let her out of my sight," Garrett says.

I focus on the ceiling, wishing for a lightning bolt—a spear—anything to strike me and put me out of my misery.

Producing an envelope from the stack, Abignail slides it over to Garrett. "There should be more than enough currency in this account to get you started. Begin with the physical transformation so you can build your Network feed. You have a couple months to get yourselves situated and make sure you've planned for all possible scenarios. According to our sources, Madden's Mind Upload Centers won't be functional until mid-April—that's when Simon will launch the Quinn update persuading people to start backing up their 'mind files'—but it's imperative you leave us enough time to steal the algorithm once you have the ring. We'll send you to San Francisco at the end of March. That should give you time to get close to Nicki and steal the ring so we can get the algorithm and shut down Quinn before Simon launches his update."

I sit, transfixed in silence, my shoulders knotting under the pressure of the enormous task before us. *But we only have to steal Nicki's ring. We're one little piece of the puzzle.* But even being a small part of the big picture fails to calm me.

"Understood," Garrett says. "We'll get to work right away." Seeming to realize I'm frozen, he takes my arm and yanks me to my feet.

"And remember the Moscow Rules," Abignail adds before we leave. "Assume nothing. Never go against your gut. *Everyone* is potentially under opposition control."

"Trust no one," Garrett agrees.

"Not even each other," I mutter.

We exit Abignail's cottage, the icy winter wind stinging my cheeks helping me regain my wits.

"You were undercover as an Influencer last year?" I ask as we head to our classes. The trail is only wide enough for one person, so I fall in line behind him.

"That's classified," he says over his shoulder.

"Says who?"

"Says me."

"But I thought we were supposed to learn everything there is to know about each other."

Garrett comes to an abrupt halt, and I almost run into him.

Turning around, he raises his eyebrows. "Do you really want that?"

"No." I sigh. "But what about Faye? She's our contact, and she was your partner last year."

He starts walking again.

Dodging tree branches, I scramble to keep up with him.

"Don't you think it's important for me to know?" I ask. "If there's romantic history between you two and things get weird, it could tank the entire heist."

His spine goes rigid, but he allows me to catch up to him as the path widens.

"I'm only going to tell you this once," he says. "And then I don't want to hear about this topic again."

"Fine." I shrug, and we stand, facing off.

His eyes are stone, without a hint of their usual mirth. "There *is* nothing, and never *was* anything, romantic going on between Faye and me. We're partners and friends. That's it. Besides, it's against Keystone Code for partners to hook up," he says, his jaw taut. "There's too much at stake to let emotions get in the way of a job."

"So that's why you picked me instead of Chloe? You were avoiding temptation?"

He steps closer to me, his face softening, and tucks my hair behind my ear, sending hot chills down my neck. "Don't sell yourself short, Ellie." Leaning down, he whispers in my ear, "I picked you in spite of how beautiful I've always thought you are. I picked you because you're the best."

His breath tickles my ear, and my heart skips a beat, but I refuse to let him play me. "I told you I'm not falling for any of this," I say, ducking away from him and waving my hand in front of his face.

"And I told you I'm not trying to get to you." He sighs. "I was being honest, but never mind. You clearly will only believe what you want to believe. Did I answer your question? Can we move on now?" He's restored to his normal, cocky self.

I swallow hard but thrust my chin forward. "Yes."

"Thank you." Turning, he heads back down the path. "You were a Maker. Do you know anything about building a Network following?"

Relief rushes through me at the thought that I might actually be able to help with something. "A little… We can buy followers, and I'm sure Stewart can hack the Network, so I can change the dates on whatever content I upload…"

"Good. You're in charge of building our backstories, then. I'll take care of currency accounts and retina scans. We'll need pictures of Beau and Betsy for the facial recognition cameras, so figure out what she looks like. How long will your makeover take?"

"I don't know. A couple days?" *I'll ask Sophia to help.*

"Tomorrow it is," he says like he didn't hear me. The path forks in front of us, and we stop at the crossroads. "And may I suggest extensions? Chloe says long hair is everything on the Skywalks."

"I'll keep that in mind." I grit my teeth.

He keeps talking. "Abignail is right, you know. In order to convince Nicki we're brother and sister, we need to be comfortable with each other."

"And how do you suggest we do that? Trust falls?"

"Oh no, we're not to that level yet. I barely know you."

I roll my eyes.

He barrels on. "Meet me tomorrow at six in the clearing behind my parents' house—they're out of town. I'll show you where I grew up, and then I'll teach you to walk and talk like an Influencer. You know, since I'm an expert."

"I can't wait," I deadpan.

"Great." Heading down the path to the right, he grins over his shoulder. "Don't be late, Bets."

# Chapter Twenty-Five

*January 4, 20X6, Keystone*

Tramping through the snow, I pull my coat tight over my chest. I can't stop thinking about what Garrett said yesterday, about picking me because I was the best. And I'm not even going to go there with the beautiful part. I hate that I'm flattered—that his opinion matters to me—that I want to believe it's true. *Because it doesn't matter what anyone thinks about me; it only matters what I think.* It's unlike him to let his guard down, so there's got to be something he's hoping to get by complimenting me, but it's also been fun pretending what he said was true. *Ugh. I'm so needy.*

Up ahead, Garrett sits on a tree stump in the clearing, staring off into the distance. Gone is the messy chin-length hair that obscured his face. It has been replaced with a short, cropped cut, dyed a golden brown and mussed with some sort of pomade that accentuates his cheekbones, makes his murky eyes glow brighter. Except for the three black bars under his left eye, he could rival any of my Influencer friends.

He catches me admiring his perfect profile, and my cheeks flush.

"Do I make you nervous, Bets?" He grins as I approach. "We can't have you blushing so easily. You'll give us away."

"Are you incapable of using a person's full name?" I ask, stopping in front of him, my cheeks now heated with annoyance.

"Of course not. Ask *Chloe*." He presses his lips together, the corner of his mouth twitching. "Your hair looks nice." Picking up a strand of my pale-blue waves, which now finish halfway down my back, he examines them. "This is a good look for you—less sulky and murderous—more approachable."

I ignore him. "Speaking of Chloe—since we're here to learn everything about each other—you haven't told me. What reason did you give *her* for picking me as your partner?"

"Slow down, Ellie. Maybe we should establish some ground rules first."

"Ground rules? I thought we needed to be so in tune with each other we know what the other person is going to do before they do it. That comes with honesty, full disclosure."

He folds his arms over his chest. "That's what I mean. I tried 'full disclosure' yesterday, and you didn't believe me. This is never going to work if you think I'm lying to you. We need to agree that we'll be honest with each other."

*I wish I could tell him everything, but there's no way.* Having no intention of letting my secrets slip, I've been rehearsing my backstory all morning. "Fine." I raise my right hand. "I solemnly swear to believe everything you say is the truth."

"Great. Me, too." He stands. "Let's go inside."

Clasping my hand, he tugs me toward his parents' house. Irked that his touch sends shivers up my arm, I untangle my fingers. "You didn't answer my question," I say, taking two steps to his one.

"I don't owe Chloe any explanations, but if she asked, I'd tell her the truth. My parents made me do it." He delivers the line without looking at me. "They were afraid you would tank the whole heist without the right person to guide you."

"And why did you really do it?"

"Don't you have any new questions?" We arrive at the back door, and he takes out his lock-picking kit. "I just told you."

"But that can't be the truth."

"Can't it?" Kneeling, he makes quick work of the door.

I frown. Unable to prove it *isn't* the truth, I change the subject. "Don't you have a key to your own house?"

"I don't live here. I live in the dorms like everyone else."

"But you grew up here."

"Yes, but I told you, I don't get special treatment. No one has the keys to a master thief's cottage except a master thief." Opening the door, he pushes me forward. "Now get inside before someone sees us."

He closes the door behind us, and my vision slowly adjusts to the dark. We're standing in a mud room where the walls are lined with glass cases filled with glittering gems. "Before I forget, I have a present for you." He flicks on a light and hands me something from his pocket. "Your AMPs."

I almost drop the contraband item. "Aren't these against Keystone Code?"

"Yes, but you should practice wearing them so you don't look awkward when Betsy needs to use them. Plus, they'll disguise your eyes so they read as Betsy's."

My fingers close around the contacts I so detested in my former life.

"Besides, some rules are made to be broken," he adds. "That's what tonight is about. This way." He ushers me into the kitchen, flicking a switch on an antique wall panel that illuminates the chandelier over a round dining table surrounded by wicker chairs. "Try to relax and have fun. Nobody will believe you're my sister if you're always so jittery around me."

"To be clear, *you* do not make me jittery. It's just my nature. But I will try to come off as your carefree, adoring sister."

"Thank you."

I tuck the contacts into my cargo pocket. "It's so French in here," I say, running my fingers over striped satin curtains that frame a leaded glass window.

"Yeah, my mom lived in Paris before my parents were married. She would've loved to stay there, but it wasn't possible. Robie promised her a chateau if she came to Keystone, and here it is."

We walk into a living area. In keeping with the streamlined Keystone aesthetic, the space is bright and light, with floor-to-ceiling windows that open to the woods, but that's where the similarities end. The room is packed with stuff. One wall is lined entirely with books, and next to it a sculpted marble fireplace is flanked with intricate moldings. Gilded-framed paintings lean against ornate wooden tables and velvet couches. While examining the crystal chandelier twinkling overhead, I trip over a tassel on the rug and nearly collide with a vase painted with blue dragons and flowers, catching myself just in time.

"Good thing you didn't break that one. It's from the Qing dynasty," Garrett says, ducking behind a claw-foot wet bar. "It's worth millions."

"Good thing," I mutter. "Did your parents steal all of this?" I ask, picking up a jewel-encrusted brooch.

"Yep." His voice sounds from behind the bar. "A K-12 protect-a-lok with tamper resistant screws. Too easy, Dad."

My jaw drops. "But what about stealing for the fun of it? I thought it wasn't about the stuff?"

He reappears with a bottle of vermouth in one hand and peach schnapps in the other. "Now you know my dirty secret: my parents like stuff. They just have interesting ways of getting it."

Laughing, I relax, comforted that his parents have their own version of smoke and mirrors. "Literally *what* are you doing with those?" I point at the bottles.

He takes out two etched crystal glasses and adds ice to a shaker. "Truth-serum cocktails are served."

"No, no, no." I shake my head, watching him pour the schnapps.

"Ellie, we're going to be in a situation where we have to party. We need to be able to stay in character and keep our secrets."

I narrow my eyes. "I thought you wanted me to spill my secrets."

"To me, yes. To Nicki, no. It's good to have a tolerance and to know how to fake it."

"You don't have to worry about me," I reply. "I'm a pro at faking it, and let me be the first to tell you, that combo is disgusting."

"I was undercover as an Influencer last year, and people were drinking all sorts of combinations." He frowns.

"Yeah, well, I lived in the real world more recently than you, and trust me, nobody wants to drink that. Let me back there."

He steps aside. "Be my guest."

Crouching behind the bar, I study the possibilities, blowing dust off the bottles. Some of the labels are so faded they look like they're from the Qing dynasty, too. Finally, I opt for switching the vermouth for some brown stuff that I think is bourbon.

"This isn't what people will be drinking, either, but whatever.

It's the best I can do." I shake the cocktail and pour it into the glasses. I sample the drink and wrinkle my nose. "It's not so bad…"

He takes a big sip of his. "I like it. You're officially our bartender."

"That's the second-nicest thing you've ever said to me."

"Yeah? Well, don't get used to it. In here we can be ourselves, but out there…" He gestures to the woods. "We keep our game faces on."

"Agreed." I clink my glass against his. *Maybe this will be fun.*

Cocktail in hand, he links arms with me, and we stroll out of the living room into the dining room.

"We used to have big dinners here every night when we were kids," Garrett says, gesturing with his glass to a long rectangular table with seating for ten. "I don't know if that will ever happen again, now that my brothers and sister are scattered in the field. I miss those days."

He seems serious for once.

"Where are they?" I ask.

"I don't know. Their work is top secret, and they can't risk coming back here that often. The last time I talked to my sister, she said they leave coded notes in safe houses for one another, but they barely ever see one another in person."

"You'll all be here together again someday, I'm sure of it," I say. Picturing him as a little kid joking with his siblings causes a pang in my chest. My childhood was so isolated it's the kind of family I dreamed of, the life I'd only seen in movies.

"I'm not." His smile is sad, but he changes the subject. "You haven't answered any of my questions, you know."

"You haven't asked any."

"I realize that. That was my segue," he says. "What's the most important thing for me to know about you?"

Already fuzzy from the drink, I call on Self-Awareness class, speaking in a stream of consciousness. "You need to know I'm fiercely loyal. I'll stand up for—defend—do anything—for my friends. Friends, to me, are the most important thing in the world."

He takes a sip of his drink. "Loyalty. I like that about you."

"Another thing you like about me." I tilt my face up to his. "Wow. This truth serum works fast. Or maybe you're a lightweight." I grin.

"I'm not allowed to lie." He laughs before turning serious. "And I like lots of things about you."

He surveys my face, and my heart skips a beat.

"Do you miss your family?" he asks.

"Not really." I shake my head, highly aware of his bicep beneath my fingers, trying to keep from curling against his chest. "I could never live up to their expectations, so I mostly kept to myself. I'm used to being alone. And life is probably less stressful for them without me…"

"I bet they miss you. You know, the whole not-knowing-what-you-have-until-it's-gone type of thing." He searches my eyes. "I know my life was way more boring before you showed up."

My stomach flips. Needing space before I do what my instincts are telling me to do and rise on my tiptoes and kiss him, I untangle my arm and wander into the foyer. "What's up there?" I ask, pointing upstairs.

"Bedrooms. My parents' offices. We should stay down here."

I down my drink and bite my lower lip. "That's no fun." Giggling, I run up the stairs.

He chases after me, reaching out to stop me, but it's too late. I burst into the first room I see. It's an office cluttered with more stuff. The walls are lined with framed articles.

## BRITAIN'S BANKS BAMBOOZLED: DARING DUO ESCAPES WITH MILLIONS

## PARIS ON ALERT: BEWARE OF THE PROWLING PAIR—NO SAFE IS SAFE

## LOCK UP YOUR DIAMONDS: THIS HEROINE'S GOT HUSTLE

"So much for 'if you know it, it's enough,'" I say, scanning the articles, amazed by how many there are.

"It's human nature to want people to know," he says from behind me, his breath warm on my ear. "Being humble is great, but I think it's okay to sometimes be proud."

"I agree." I can't stop reading. "They're fabulous." I exhale. Intoxicated by their exciting escapades, I feel my heart pumping in anticipation, wishing I could live out some of these heists myself. "You're so lucky. This is probably what your life is destined to be like. Traveling around the world, attending fabulous parties, stealing the truth…"

"It's what your life will be like, too." Taking me by the shoulders, he turns me to face him.

"Do you think so?" I ask, lifting my face to his.

"If you want it."

Our eyes meet, and I sense we're level with each other, even though he stands much taller than me. His hands slide down my arms, and without thinking I ask the first question that comes to my lips. "Why are you so hard on me?"

He doesn't miss a beat. "Because I like you."

My stomach constricts.

"But I'm not supposed to like you," he whispers, wrinkling his nose. "It complicates things."

"Is liking me against Keystone Code?" I ask.

"Sort of." He chews his lip. "But just so you know, whatever happens out there" — he points at a window — "you know the truth in here." He thumps his hand over my heart, and I'm sure he can feel it pounding.

I search his eyes, trying to make sense of what he's telling me, but they're returning to their usual unidentifiable mix of humor and superiority. Whatever window I had to his soul is closing.

Checking his watch, he sighs. "I'm late. We should go." Without giving me time to respond, he grabs my hand, guiding me down the stairs and outside. "That was fun. How do you feel?"

"Fine. I'm fine." It's the first time I've lied to him all night.

"Good." Dropping my hand, he locks the door behind us. "See you tomorrow, then, Bets."

Raising his eyebrows, he bumps his forehead against mine before jogging down the porch steps and heading for the woods, leaving me to stare after him.

*I'm so confused.*

# Chapter Twenty-Six

*January 4, 20X6, Keystone*

**M**y evening now wide open, I head to the Vault. I have no clue what just happened with Garrett, and rather than analyze our conversation to death, I grab my journal, grateful I have the past to distract me.

*March 2, 20X5*
*Truth: We are all liars.*

Under the cover of the black-and-white umbrella, I ducked into the Anonymous, the basement pub on River Street where Crystal was waiting. With exposed brick walls and a small collection of rickety tables surrounded by barrel chairs, it was dim, dank, and sour. She sat alone at a table, the sole patron except for a few early-morning drinkers posted up at the bar. After the dark night, I would have preferred to soak in the light of the market, but I wasn't in a position to disobey orders.

"Thank you for meeting me," she said as I sat, her voice low. She wore a fitted gray jacket and a hat with black net draped over one eye. Her makeup was pale, the only pop of color the shell pink that zig-zagged across her lips.

"Of course," I whispered.

"You don't need the umbrella here," she said. "I know the owners—they're Disconnect-friendly. This place is off the grid, so you can speak freely."

"No offense, but how do I know I can trust you?" I asked, lowering the umbrella as a flood of memories starring Adam and Deena flashed before me. "I want to, but right now I'm afraid to believe anyone." Closing my eyes, I tried to erase them from my mind.

"I understand. There's probably nothing I can say to prove I have your best interests at heart, but I promise I used to be just like you, and all I want is to be your friend."

"I don't think friends are possible."

The corners of her mouth turned down, and my heart ached for hurting her, but I didn't trust my instincts anymore.

"I know it's hard to believe, but they are." She sighed. Reaching into her purse, she pulled out a weathered news article encased in plastic and slid it toward me. "Maybe this will help."

At first, I was taken by the picture of her in her younger days, posing on a red carpet, flashbulbs illuminated behind her. I scanned the headline.

## CRYSTAL HARRISON SHOCKER: I'M DISCONNECTING

"It wasn't my choice," she said. "I was forced out. I got involved with the wrong people—there was an affair with a musician. I'm not proud of it. At the time, AI was just getting popular, people were becoming dependent upon it.

My husband was a Corporate, and he was so scandalized by my infidelity he threatened to ruin my reputation. He had the power to make the world believe anything he wanted. He could change my backstory, turn me into a prostitute, a pornographer. His plan was to slowly poison people's minds against me until they thought I was a virus. It wouldn't happen overnight, but eventually people would start to believe. I didn't want to go down that way—without my reputation, I was nothing—so I went out on my own terms."

"How could he turn the world against you, though? What about your fans? Wouldn't they find the truth?"

"Nobody has that much energy." She shrugged. "People believe their Network feeds, everything their AI tells them. Truth is based on the collective opinion of an audience, not cold, hard facts. Majority rules. Even people who don't blindly go along with the masses, who take time to research, can't find correct information. Everything online has been tampered with. It's all propaganda, legend. If you want the truth, you have to consult the original source, and that is becoming impossible to find. 3-D printers reprint artifacts so they can be in several places at once, but with each replication, the truth changes slightly. It's the same with text. There are minute changes with every duplication until the truth is buried. No information is safe."

"So we're *all* living a lie," I said. *At least I'm not alone in that.*

"He who holds the knowledge has the power to brainwash the masses. There's a war going on, and most people don't know it. It's not between countries—it's between corporations. They're fighting to see who gets to control our minds, and they'll stop at nothing." Placing her hand over mine, she fastened her eyes on me. "The only thing we can trust is our memories. Never let anyone convince you your truth is wrong."

As I nodded, my thoughts turned to Adam. *I don't know*

*what his truth is, but I'll never forget…*

"The time for passive disconnection is gone," she continued. "We have to take action before the Corporates gobble everything and everyone up."

"You make it sound like there's going to be an uprising."

"Going to be? Oh honey, there already is."

Fear leaped into my throat, and my terror must have shown on my face.

"Don't worry." Crystal laughed. "Change doesn't come quickly or easily."

"But there's got to be a way to protect information," I said. "To live for something bigger than popularity."

"If you really want that, then there's someone I want you to meet." She glanced over her shoulder. "I think you have potential." Lowering her gaze, she fingered her napkin. "Last night…you knew things…how?"

Staring at her hand on mine, I considered. *All of my secrets are gone—anyone who reads my book will know everything… She's being honest with me. I believe that. It would be nice to have someone to talk to…* I took a deep breath and met her eyes. "Instinct? I don't know. It's not the first time it's happened—that I felt a change in the air or sensed someone's presence the moment before they walked in the door—but it's like a reflex. I can't do it on command."

She didn't register any emotion. She simply asked, "Do you know who took your book?"

"No. It doesn't work that way. I only get answers seconds in advance."

"Interesting. I wonder if you could learn…" She was talking more to herself than to me.

"The only person who knew about it was Adam." My voice cracked. "But he has an alibi. He was 'live' with Deena." Tears bubbled to my eyes at the memory.

Crystal scooted closer to me.

"Ella," she said. "I'm so sorry about Adam and Deena. I promise you, not everyone is like that. There *are* true people out there. A community of people that supports one another. They don't care how influential you are. Real friends." Crystal gestured to a woman in a black jumpsuit sitting at the bar, her red hair tucked under a wide-brimmed hat that obscured half of her face. "Can I introduce you to someone?"

Wiping my eyes before the tears dared overflow, I nodded.

"This is Professor Allard," Crystal said, gesturing the woman over. "She's a scientist and close friend of mine."

Allard sat, tilting her head to reveal a black-and-purple starburst exploding over one eye.

Goose bumps erupted on my arms, every nerve in my body signaling *run*.

"Crystal tells me you're quite gifted," she said, and her voice was like music.

It cast a spell on me, and my breathing slowed.

"I don't know about that," I said.

"We're coming to a time when gifts will be necessary. You'll need more than influence to survive," Allard said. "From what Crystal tells me, your particular skill is quite interesting. You'll be better off than most, but to thrive, you'll need to learn more."

"What's coming?" I asked.

"A war," Crystal said.

My stomach dropped. "But I'm not a fighter."

"We'll all be called upon to fight," Allard said, pressing her lips together. "Our minds are at stake. We all need to be warriors, to protect ourselves, to guard the ignorant."

"How do we do that?" I asked, my heart thumping in my ears.

"We steal the truth." Allard smiled.

The pub swirled, but at the same time a shot of excitement shot through me, and my jaw dropped. "You want me to be a thief?"

"You wouldn't have to steal anything right away," she said. "We would train you. And if what Crystal says is true, I think the skills would come easily to you."

"Would I have to disconnect?" I whispered. *Would anyone miss me? Without Adam, there isn't much left for me in L.A....*

"Yes. My offer would require you to disconnect," she confirmed.

My pulse raced, my mind going a mile a minute. I couldn't process the enormity of what she was suggesting. "I don't know if I can do that."

"I know it's a lot to ask," Crystal said. "But please hear her out." She squeezed my hand.

"There's a place," Allard said. "It's called Keystone. Some believe its existence is legend, but I promise it's real. It's hidden among the trees, and the Disconnects there have been chosen to preserve history. We think you'd be a perfect addition to the campus."

I breathed in the offer and exhaled in a rush. "Do I have to decide now? Leaving behind everything and everyone I know—forever—is a lot to consider."

"Take all the time you need, but know we'd be honored to have you." Opening a silver cigarette case, Allard pulled out a square card. "This is my number. Call me when you've made your decision. And in the meantime, I trust you'll speak of this to no one." She stood.

Reeling, I reread the simple block letters that spelled "Keystone" and the ten digits printed beneath them five times before they made any sense.

When I looked up, Allard was gone. In her place, a single white daisy lay across the table.

# Chapter Twenty-Seven

*T*ruth: *I can trust me.*

I lowered the umbrella inside the library. Crystal gave it to me as a parting gift. She'd completed her scenes and was no longer needed on set, so she was spending a few weeks with Allard, strategizing her comeback. I learned as much as I could about disconnecting before she left, but my mind changed daily about whether I'd go through with it. The one piece of information Crystal couldn't give me was the meaning of the daisy. She told me it symbolized purity and innocence but the rest was up to me.

Settling at a computer, I pulled up the Universal Library and typed "meaning of daisy" into the search box. I waited. And waited. And waited. It eventually came up with listings for purity and innocence, and I knew the internet wasn't going to give me the answer.

Disappearing into the deserted book stacks, I ran my fingers along the endless rows of spines, marveling at all the ideas—people's thoughts, beliefs, *truths*—shelved and forgotten.

"Well, well. Look who's back."

"Johnathan." Turning around, I smiled.

"What can I help you with today?" he asked.

I studied him, unsure if mentioning the daisy would clue him into Keystone.

"If it's something you need to keep secret, you can trust me," he said. "We're friends, aren't we?"

"Are we?" I raised my eyebrows.

"Fine. We're acquaintances. But we could be friends if you wanted."

"It's that easy?"

He looked at me like I'd just landed my UFO in the middle of the library. "Yeah."

*He considers himself a Disconnect…and he can't post to the Networks, so who could he really tell about me and Keystone, if he even connects me to Keystone in the first place?* "Okay. Friends." I nodded, deciding he was trustworthy. "But please don't tell anyone about this."

"I won't tell a soul. Promise." He linked his pinkie with mine, and we shook on it.

"I'm looking for flower meanings," I said. "For some reason the Universal Library is vague on the subject."

If he thought anything was odd about my request, he didn't show it. Narrowing his eyes, he cocked his head to the side. "That's some sordid stuff, Ella, but I can help you out. What you need is the *Old Farmer's Almanac*. Follow me."

He led me to the "gardening" section and started pulling out paperback books. "Do you want one from a particular year?"

"Give me the oldest one you've got."

He studied the options until he found a yellowed book, its pages wrapped in plastic. "1870?"

"That works."

Taking the brittle book, I sat down right there on the floor, gingerly opening it.

"I'll let you research in peace," Johnathan said. "But don't leave without saying goodbye."

"I won't. Promise." Mesmerized by the book—the weight of it, its finite pages—I slowly thumbed through it. "Johnathan? Are all Unrankables as nice as you? Or is it a southern thing?" I asked before he left.

He laughed. "Probably a little of both, but Unrankables are usually pretty cool. You're welcome here any time."

"Thank you." I smiled.

With a tiny wave, he left me to my book.

I could have sat there all day and devoured the pages, but I flipped through until I found a description of birth flowers, and there was my answer, plain as day.

*The daisy represents purity, love, and innocence. Capable of disguise, it can be dyed any color. It is also a flower given between friends who want to keep a secret; the daisy's message is "I'll never tell."*

# Chapter Twenty-Eight

*June 20, 20X5*

*Truth: It doesn't matter where you came from. It only matters where you're going.*

My heels clacked against the marble entry in my parents' Hollywood Hills estate. Sensing my presence, the chandelier lights slowly brightened. At first glance the house appeared empty, but then I heard Mom and Dad's voices lilting up from the veranda.

"What are we going to do with her? If the reviews aren't good, we're tanked," Mom said.

I froze at the top of the staircase that descended into the living room, straining to hear through the wall that was open to the deck.

"We can pay someone. We can always pay someone. Or promise a favor," Dad said.

"Someday we might run out of favors. It's getting hard to pull strings. In fact, I feel like the strings are winding around my wrists," Mom said. "What about the others? They can't be controlled forever. We're lucky we've made it this long without the truth leaking."

"Quinn," Dad said. "Can you calculate the probability that a strong box office will lift Ella's rankings?"

Quinn instantly replied, "Oh, Nick. I don't know how to break this to you, but the calculations are clear. *Nothing* can save that girl. She's not like you. She doesn't have the charisma to pull herself out of this landslide. She's poison."

*Even the AI has turned on me.*

"Thank you, Quinn." Dad fell silent, and then he said, so softly I could barely make out the words, "She's not worth this stress. We're better off without her."

"She's served her purpose," Mom agreed.

Having my worst fears confirmed was like a knife to my gut. Clutching my stomach, I stared into space, his words pulsating through me, their meaning refusing to penetrate. *They don't want me.* My whole life, all I ever wanted was to be theirs, but of course I wasn't, not really. *I tried so hard to be perfect.* And I was. *Until now.*

Hot tears trickling down my cheeks, I closed my eyes. *Nobody wants me. First Adam, now them...* My breath ragged, I sank to the floor. Hugging my knees to my chest, I let the tears flow. *I'm so stupid—I don't belong here. Maybe I'm better off dead.* Whatever shreds of my heart were left disintegrated, melting away in waves of sickness and choked-back sobs until I was empty, lying in a broken ball.

My mother's voice drifted up, and my blood turned to ice.

"She's sixteen—going on seventeen—we've been parenting her for a long time. We've done our job, and I know *I've* had enough. I think it's officially time to let her go. It will be a good lesson for her to have to make it on her own, to see what it's like in the real world. She could stand to appreciate how hard we work for everything we have. And, you know, I think there are a lot of parents out there who will relate to having an ungrateful kid."

"You're right," Dad said. "This could be great for us if we spin it correctly. Now all we have to do is figure out how to get rid of her."

Sitting up, I buried the hurt and replaced it with anger. I wrapped my heart in armor so thick not even a bullet could penetrate it.

*That can be arranged.*

Up until that moment, I wasn't sure what I was going to do. Disconnecting seemed like an exciting fantasy—a way to stick it to my parents—but deep down I didn't think I'd go through with it. There was no way I was brave enough to give up everything I knew and start over in a strange place. I thought my screwup was a blip, something that would be forgiven, but I now realized I was holding on to an impossible hope that things could go back to how they were—that I could still be their dream daughter.

Maybe I *was* brave. And even if I *wasn't*, I had to do something.

Standing, I pointed my chin to the sky and marched downstairs.

"Hi, honey," Mom said, jumping up to hug me. "Welcome home. We missed you!"

She squeezed me tight, and I stiffened, putting up with her phony embrace for half a second before wiggling away. The hills beyond the veranda were cast in misty blues and greens that day, and a tranquil breeze wafted over me, putting me on edge. They set the scene to manipulate my emotions, to keep me calm, but I held on to my anger.

"How did it feel to be a movie star?" Dad asked, standing long enough to ruffle my hair and pull out a chair so I could join them.

"You know how it feels to be a movie star," I said, settling onto the edge of my seat. "It's boring."

"Boring? We sent off a little girl and got back a teenager." Mom laughed.

"I was a teenager when I left," I said. "Maybe I'm a grown-up, now."

"Don't grow up too fast," Dad said. "An actress's career is short-lived—stay young as long as you can."

I frowned.

"Your father is joking, sweetheart. You've got plenty of good years ahead of you."

"No, he's not." I glared at them until they shifted uncomfortably in their seats.

"Speaking of teenagers, we should talk about your birthday," Mom changed the subject. "We already have *tons* of sponsors. It's going to set you up perfectly. Between the party and the movie, your numbers will be fine."

"I don't want a birthday party."

"But your friends are expecting a huge event!" Mom said.

"What friends?" I spat the word. "I don't have any friends. What happened to breaking ties with everyone at Intersection?"

Mom kept talking like she hadn't heard me. "It's going to be spectacular—a party no one will miss—"

"*Everyone* will miss it! I don't care about rankings, and I don't want a party." I was practically screaming, and still she refused to hear me.

"—Framboise has agreed to sponsor your cake—"

"Too bad," Dad hissed, a vein popping in his forehead. "Your rankings are in the toilet, and we're not going to let you drag us down with you. You will have a party, and you will make it look like you *love* it."

"You can't make me go." I stood, my limbs rigid with adrenaline. "If I'm poison, if I'm no longer useful to you, write me out of your lives like you would a bad guy in a script. Stop building me up to be someone I'm not. We'd all be better off if I'd never been born—or if I was dead. Maybe you'll miss me when I'm gone." Having said more than I'd intended, I turned on my heel and ran upstairs to my bedroom. I slammed the door behind me and threw myself on my bed, the tears coming hot and fast.

Mom knocked on the door a minute later. "Can I come in?"

"Can I stop you?" I said into my pillow.

"No." Entering the room, she softly shut the door and sat on the edge of the bed next to me. "I know you're going through a tough time. But we love you."

She was trying a different tack. I wasn't falling for it.

"We want you to be happy, like you were when you first started at Intersection, when you were surrounded by your friends. Don't you want to make up with them?"

"No." I rolled onto my side with my back to her, hugging my knees to my chest. "Maybe I need to make new friends. My old ones are fake."

"That's not true, sweetheart." She stroked my hair. "I saw that Deena and Adam are together now—maybe they'll forget about your little hiccup and take you back."

Hot shards of disgust exploded in my brain at the realization that she had so little faith in me she thought I needed to grovel at their feet.

"They're convenient. For you," I replied, watching the old olive tree beyond my balcony sway, tears pooling under my chin. "And you need me to control them, to protect your secret."

She snatched her hand back as though I'd scalded her. "What made you so mean?"

"You."

Her tiny intake of breath sounded like I'd punched her,

and I was glad.

"That hurts my feelings, honey."

"I'm sorry. But it's the truth. Sometimes the truth hurts."

"You're upset." She sighed. "I understand. I really think a party will make you feel better. Are you willing to try?"

Her hand returned to my hair, but I jerked my head away and looked up at her. My face—if I kept up the injections—stared back at me, a stranger. If she didn't want me to be her daughter, I didn't want her to be my mother. I was going through with it. *And actually, a birthday party might be the perfect way to go...*

I shrugged. "You know what? Sure. Fine. Throw the party. I'll show up, I'll put on a show, if that's what you want."

"What I *want* is for you to be happy. And I think you will be if you do it my way. Trust me. I've been there. I know this will work. You'll be so happy after you make up with your friends. You'll see. You'll go?"

Rolling back over, I rested my chin on my knees. "I'll go," I said to the balcony. "Just tell me where to be and when."

"Oh! I'm so excited. We're renting the most fabulous house on Lake Tahoe near Carnelian Bay. We'll have a yacht on the lake augmented to look like you're in a crater on the moon, and clambakes, DJs—the celebration will go on for days, but people will talk about it for months. We'll keep the first night small, exclusive..."

"You know, Mom? That does sound fun." I injected all the brightness I could muster into my voice. "Maybe you're right. Maybe some time away together is what I need to reconnect with Deena and the girls."

"That's my Ella." She kissed my forehead. "Your father will be pleased."

I nodded. "Can we talk about this tomorrow? I'm exhausted."

"Of course." Rising, she crossed the room. "Get your beauty rest, my love. We're going to have them eating out of your hand." With a grin, she closed the door behind her.

As soon as she was gone, I jumped out of bed. Scouring my closet for Mom's old piggy bank, I found it tucked in a long-forgotten corner. Change secured, I grabbed a lipstick and drew a haphazard zigzag across my face, hoping it was enough to disguise me, before creeping onto my balcony, umbrella in hand. My room was on the second story, but it wasn't a long way down. I swung my legs over the railing and leaped before I could think, grasping the branches of the olive tree. Shimmying to the trunk, I climbed down. Once I reached the ground, I put up my umbrella and walked through the canyon, grateful to the moon for lighting my way.

I headed to the corner of Santa Monica Boulevard and Van Ness. Augmented, it was a Tuscan courtyard. Without AMPs, it was an abandoned strip mall. When I arrived, as I suspected, there it was—a gleaming beacon of hope—a pay phone.

Allard answered on the second ring. "Hello?"

"According to the 1870 *Old Farmer's Almanac*, it means 'I'll never tell. A secret between friends.' Is it true? Can I trust you? Because I don't think I can trust anybody," I said without introduction.

"Are you on a safe phone?"

"Yes."

"Ella." I could hear a smile in her voice. "We follow the Moscow Rules at Keystone, and the gist is 'trust no one.' But yes. If you have it in you to believe that some people are more good than evil, you can trust me."

"What are the Moscow Rules?" I asked.

"If you're calling for the reason I think, you'll learn."

"You're right. You know why I'm calling," I said. "So how

do I do this?" I wanted her to hurry. I wanted a plan. *Now.* Before I lost my nerve, before the adrenaline abandoned my veins.

She sucked in her breath, then let it out in a rush. "We'll fake your death. Nobody comes back from the dead."

I let the words settle, let the finality sink in, and all I felt was alive, like I was breathing pure oxygen. It was all so clear. *I have to end me. It's the only way to live.* "When? I'm having a birthday party at an estate near Carnelian Bay in five days. Is that enough time?"

The line went silent for a moment before she came back to me.

"We can make that work."

# Chapter Twenty-Nine

*March 20X6, Keystone*

"Big day tomorrow." Allard leans back in her chair, drinking her tea. "San Francisco here you come. Are you and Garrett prepared?"

"We're as ready as we can be." After spending every waking minute together for the last three months, we can practically finish each other's sentences. We've built Beau and Betsy's lives for the Networks, photographing fake parties and vacations, trying to one-up each other with weird memories from our "childhood."

*"Do you remember that time Mom and Dad took us fishing and I caught a sixty-pound mahi-mahi that knocked you overboard?" he asks.*

*"You seem to have a selective memory," I say. "The way I remember it, it was ten pounds, and you fell overboard trying to reel it in. But speaking of fishing, I definitely remember the time your prom date catfished you—did you really believe that Miss Teen World was going to fly down to the Cayman Islands to go out with some skinny coder? How embarrassing that you*

*had to take your kid sister instead." I slide the prom picture I've been working on toward him. I've placed his head onto a wiry, tuxedoed body standing next to a version of me that Ella Karman would have been jealous of. "For your approval. I'll add it to your Network this afternoon."*

*He examines the picture and smiles. "I've filled out nicely since then, don't you think?"*

*No comment.*

Despite the increased time together, we've never dipped back into the conversation we had at his parents' house. I guess he was warning me he was going to keep me at arm's length, which is best for both of us. There's too much that could go wrong with the heist to risk any shenanigans. At least that's what I tell myself.

"We definitely fight like brother and sister," I say to Allard, sipping my tea.

She smiles. "And how are you feeling?"

My heart thumps. "Honestly? It's like Christmas Eve. I can't sleep… I keep waiting to hear footsteps on the rooftop."

"Soon you'll be the footsteps on the rooftop."

I let out a whoosh of air. "I know. Is it weird that I can't wait?"

"No. It just means you've found your calling."

I close my eyes, calming the butterflies stirring in my belly. "But I'm also terrified. I keep running through disaster scenarios, like what if someone recognizes me as Ella?" I open my eyes. "If it came out that I faked my death, it would be a scandal—it would probably put me back on the Index. My reunion with my parents would make us *more* famous—they'd spin it as foul play or say I had amnesia from the explosion. Either that or they'd pin the explosion on *me* and I'd go to jail. After all, they couldn't make me Unrankable. I already am…"

"Nobody will recognize you. You look totally different.

If anything, you may seem familiar, but I believe in your abilities." She places her hand over mine. "You're a thief, and you can make people believe anything you want. You're meant for this."

"I hope you're right…" Sinking into the couch, I swirl the tea in the bottom of my cup. "Garrett wants me to play a major role in this heist—and I want to do it—but my biggest fear is exposing him and Keystone. That would be unforgivable."

"Whitney and Jeff wouldn't send you if they thought it was risky." She refills my tea. "Besides, you have something nobody else has—your instincts. Trust them."

"I'm trying to, but sometimes I still don't think they're right. Garrett throws me off. I can't read him." I shake my head.

"People change. Sometimes a first impression deserves a second chance."

"But he changes every five minutes. It's like he's purposely trying to scramble my brain."

She laughs. "Garrett is a challenge. But it's good he keeps you on your toes. It keeps you sharp."

Standing, she crosses the room and rummages through a closet. "Now for the real reason I asked you over. I have a gift for you."

Sitting next to me, she hands me a box wrapped in yellow paper, tied with twine that secures a white daisy. "It's your first heist—you're officially a thief—and Crystal and I thought you should look the part."

I slide an envelope out from underneath the daisy, running my fingers over the buttery stock. Turning the envelope over, I find it's stamped closed with the wax impression of an upside-down umbrella. Breaking the seal, I pull out a square note card.

*Hi friend!*

*Look how far you've come! I'm so proud of you. You're about to embark on an exciting adventure, and you're totally going to own it, but please know that I'm here for you no matter what. It gets intense out there sometimes, and you're always welcome at my door. My home is yours. You can find me if you need me. Just follow the signs.*

*Now, knock 'em dead!*

*Sugar kisses,*

*Crystal*

I smile. "Thank you for this."

"Don't thank me yet. Open it," Allard says.

I lift the lid. Laying on top of shimmery white tissue paper is a black asymmetrical mask made from thin strips of twisted leather. As I slip the mask over my head, it molds perfectly to my face, covering one eye and swirling in a delicate filigree over my forehead and down one cheek.

"It's beautiful," I whisper, catching a glimpse of myself in a mirror. Pushing aside the rest of the tissue paper, I pull out a slender black catsuit with mesh cutouts sliced through the bodice and down one leg. "Wow." I exhale. "I've worn a lot of things, but never anything like this."

"I know it's daring, but it's good to be streamlined. It's functional—there are secret compartments for your tools—but it never hurts to look fabulous, too. Don't be afraid to use *all* of your assets," she says.

"What do you mean?"

"Sometimes people underestimate a pretty face. Look at Chloe. She comes off as a decoy, but she also competed in the Quest. She knows what she's doing."

I frown. "You're right. I do underestimate her... I guess it doesn't seem fair that she has it all."

"You can have it all, too. You play your looks down—and I understand that, given your history—but you can be the smartest person in the room *and* the most attractive. They aren't mutually exclusive. Don't let anyone shame you into thinking a pretty face can't be hiding a world-class mind. It's okay to like lip gloss and heels *and* science. You know who you are, and you hold the power."

"I don't think there's any danger of me being the most attractive girl in the room. Even when I looked like my mom, I never was. And that was with a lot of help."

"But you have something now that you didn't have then. You know what you stand for, and you're motivated. If you let the real you shine through, nobody will be able to look away."

# Chapter Thirty

*March 20X6, San Francisco*

We arrive in San Francisco truly Unrankable. I check to make sure the hot pink fabric mask that covers my nose and mouth is in place before lowering my heart-shaped goggles. While navigating the city streets, we're going to extra lengths to ensure we won't be recognized. Disconnect makeup has influenced recent fashion trends, which in some ways makes it easier for us to blend in, but it also has caused facial-recognition cameras to become more efficient, so it's a double-edged sword. Tugging at the hem of my simple black shift dress, I inhale to settle my nerves.

Raising his charcoal hoodie over his head, Garrett puts his aviator-style goggles in place and heads to the Bubble Car depot. I hurry to keep up with him, certain everyone is staring. He quickly opens a car door and gestures me inside. Our first order of business is to connect with our contact.

"Tell me what to expect when I meet Faye," I say once we're safely tucked away and he's entered our destination in the Marina. "You don't have to tell me what happened last year, just tell me what she's like."

He thinks as the car merges with the traffic flowing through Union Square. "She's smart," he says. "A chameleon. She'll change her personality to fit in anywhere, so in some ways I don't know the real her. She keeps her truth close to her chest. But I *do* know this: she'll do anything to get what she wants. She's not afraid to make a fool of herself to make you smile—or to manipulate a situation—but mostly, she's just trying to make you smile."

Pondering his description, I gaze out the window at the crowds walking past glittering screens that line the buildings, displaying content curated specifically for them. Many of their faces are bare, freely exposed to the recognition cameras, though some wear artfully applied makeup and beads, in keeping with the current fashion. Those who wear masks like mine are few and far between. They walk with their heads lowered in isolation, the crowd giving them a wide berth. Silently, I brace myself for the stares we'll receive when we exit our car.

"Do you still talk to her?" I ask.

"Not really. She's in the field, so she isn't supposed to have contact with anyone at Keystone. It's too risky. But even though we haven't talked, I know we're still close. Partners tend to have lasting relationships."

Returning my attention to him, I frown. "Does that mean I'm stuck with you forever?"

He grins. "Yep."

"Lucky me." My stomach twists, and I don't know if it's because I'm oddly relieved to know he'll be in my life beyond the heist or if I'm terrified of arriving at our destination. Resisting the urge to rub my eyes—they're already aching from the AMPs—I blink. The car turns down a side street, and I'm blindsided by a row of screens outside, all displaying shirtless guys swiveling their hips. I snap to Garrett.

He can barely contain his smile.

"You." I point a finger at him. "What did you put in my bio? Why am I seeing this?"

"Seeing what?" His eyes widen, feigning innocence.

"These guys! What are *you* seeing?" I swipe at the air, navigating my AMP screen, hunting for the "preferences" tab.

"I'm an animal lover, so the streets are lined with puppies and kittens. They're adorable."

"I hate you," I mutter. "Thunder from Down Under? Really?"

"Hey, I've heard good things. They must be doing something right. They've been around forever."

"No." I shake my head. "This is *all* wrong."

He laughs as we arrive at the Marina and the Bubble Car parks itself at a charging station.

Sobering, Garrett pulls me out of the car before I can finish changing my settings. *Clowns? Puppets? Ugh.* He consults his map. "This way."

We walk along the boardwalk. Colorful boats bump against the dock under threatening gray skies. I'm glad I have Crystal's umbrella, for more reasons than one. The fact the screens were picking up my preferences means I'm on the grid, and even though my costume should keep my face from being scanned, I'm grateful for the extra layer of protection.

Garrett glances over his shoulder. "We're being followed," he whispers.

"Are you sure you're not being paranoid?" I peek back at a man wearing a black hooded sweatshirt with zippers zig-zagging across the sleeves. His head is down, so I can't make out his features. A gull squawks overhead, and I jump, nearly tripping over the uneven planks underfoot.

Garrett grabs my arm to steady me. "Calm down, Bets. This isn't code red. Keep it yellow."

*Be alert. Observe. Remember details. See if someone is matching pace with you.* I run through everything I've learned about staying conscious. The rule is never to go "green"—never relax, always keep noticing—but also don't go "red" and freak out.

We slow down, and the man behind us walks past us, his eyes on the water.

"He would have stopped, too, if he was trailing us, right?" I ask.

"No. If you stop and they walk past you but pretend to be looking at something else—that's a tip-off. He's too aware. Memorize his face, something about his essence that's unchangeable. He may be nobody, but better safe than sorry."

I got a better look at him as he walked past. *Dark hair, wire-rimmed glasses, small dark mole on his upper left cheekbone, soft jaw, left ear protrudes slightly more than the right.* I commit the checklist to memory, discarding the glasses, mole, and hair as details that could easily change.

"This is it," Garrett says, nudging me into a tiny coffee shop. We head to a table at the back of the space, where a dark-skinned girl sits, her long, purple fingernails curled around a dainty cup. She wears a tight, shimmery, purple dress that shows everything, and her eyes are surrounded by a rainbow of color with chalky smudges running down her cheeks. She's clearly not afraid of being noticed.

*She's dazzling.* I like her immediately.

"So fabulous to see you," she says, standing and wrapping Garrett in a big hug.

"You look amazing," he says into her hair. "It's been too long."

"Way too long," she says.

Separating, they take their seats across the table from each other.

"Tea? Coffee?" she asks.

"We'll have what you're having," Garrett replies. I sink down next to him, our backs to the door. Fortunately, there's a mirror behind Faye, so I can still see everyone who enters the shop. *And the front door is the only way out.*

Faye enters our order into the screen on the table, and I lower my mask so I can drink.

"This is my 'sister,' Betsy," he introduces me.

"Very nice," she says, giving me a once-over, offering me her tapered fingers. "He made any moves on you yet?"

My jaw drops, and I have no words.

Garrett busts out laughing.

"Don't worry, lovie. He will." She winks.

"I hope not," I reply, finding my tongue.

"That's good. It will save you a lifetime of heartache. The truth is, despite that overwhelming charisma, he's all business. Born to dash hopes. Nobody has a chance. Believe me, I tried." She laughs.

"Do you remember Chloe?" I ask.

Faye laughs harder. "I do."

"How have you been?" Garrett asks, silencing her. "What's it like out there?"

"A dream come true. It's everything we hoped." To my surprise, she grows serious. "But we don't have much time, so let's get to why you're here. Nicki."

A robot delivers our drinks, and I sip the sweet, creamy green concoction, enjoying the warmth it sends through me. I have no idea what it is, but it's worlds beyond any drink I've had at Keystone—probably infused using some forbidden technology. *Maybe there are some things I miss about Influencer life…*

"Yes," Garrett says. "From what we can tell from her Network, she's into music, dance, she goes to a lot of charity benefits…"

"But she's only showing us what she wants us to see," I say.

Faye nods. "I can give you a little insight, but she's not an easy nut to crack. She's good at keeping her mask in place. It'll take time. I've been hanging in her circle for six months, and she still doesn't trust me. She likes me, but she doesn't trust me."

"How are we going to get close to her?" I ask. "We don't have six months or even six weeks!"

"You were given this assignment for a reason—your talents match the challenge," she says. "I'm sure Mr. Charisma over here can work his charm"—she gestures at Garrett—"but you'll have your work cut out for you. Nicki doesn't let guys get close to her, though there's a dude that's been hanging around. His name is Eric, and he's Canadian. His dad runs Simon's kidney farm. He complicates things, but I'm pretty sure they're just friends."

Her eyes meet Garrett's, and they seem to be communicating through some sort of telepathy, even though I know that's impossible.

"You'll see," she says.

Garrett nods, perhaps having received the message. "His kidney farm?" he asks.

"Yes. It's one of Simon's many philanthropic efforts. They don't publicize its origins—Nicki's numbers do better if she's seen as a humanitarian instead of a survivor—but she was very sick as a child and needed a kidney transplant. They couldn't find a match, so Simon found a way to grow new kidneys for her using pig stem cells. It was so successful he started a farm to grow them for other people. Simon and Nicki are very close because of it. And I'll warn you—she may seem like an impractical heiress, but she's not. She's sharp. Her fans engage more when she comes off as a party girl, but there's a lot going on behind those eyes. Simon is breeding her to be his successor. She won't be easy to fool."

"We need to figure out what she *wants* to get close to her," Garrett says, tapping his fingers on the table, lost in thought.

"She has everything she could ever need. All she has to do is snap her fingers, and her dad will make it happen," Faye says.

He shakes his head. "Everyone wants something," he says. "I'll find the thing—the experience—the answer only I can give her…"

My stomach constricts at the thought of them together, and I'm instantly annoyed for caring.

"I'm sure you will." Faye smirks. "You'll meet her tomorrow night. There's a charity event benefiting the kidney farm at the San Francisco opera house. Find a way to meet her there—tell her your sister Betsy is a transplant survivor—she's a sucker for those. That'll be your common ground." She focuses on a point over my shoulder, and the mole man from earlier is reflected in the mirror, walking in the door. Her attention back on us, Faye slides an envelope across the table. "Your tickets." Without another word, she rises and greets the mole man. Arms linked, they exit.

"She's amazing," I say, watching her swaying hips in the mirror as she swishes out of the shop.

"I told you." Scooting my chair closer to him, Garrett takes a small silvery pouch out of his pocket and slides it toward me. "This is for you." His voice is low, and his breath is warm on my cheek, sending sparks up my arm.

"What is it?"

"Your cache. Do you know where you're going to hide it?"

Nodding, I slip the bag seamlessly into the garter on my thigh so nobody will notice the exchange.

"I hope I don't need it." The cache contains new AMPs, a currency card—everything I need to create a new identity if something goes wrong—and I plan to bury it in the Presidio Pet Cemetery.

"Me, too, but you always need an exit strategy. Never tell anyone where it is. Not even me." Leaning in, he clasps his fingers behind my neck, tugging my face so close our noses practically touch.

Blood rushes to my head, dizzying me.

"Give me a five-minute head start before you leave, and make sure you aren't followed," he whispers. "Slow down, speed up, stay alert, make random stops. After you've hidden the cache, meet me at the apartment. Take an unusual path to get there—don't have any patterns. Use your map of the city, not devices, and don't be nervous."

"Easy for you to say," I mutter, certain my heart is going to slam out of my chest.

His eyes hold mine. "Believe me, I'd rather not let you out of my sight, but this is something you have to do on your own. You've got this."

My insides clench, and I squelch the urge to giggle.

Giving my neck a final squeeze, he stands. "See you in a little bit. We have an exciting night of kidney failure research ahead of us."

"Can't wait." I attempt a smile.

He heads out the door.

Instantly chilled by his absence, I rub my arms, realizing how much I've come to rely on him. I spread my map on the table and trace the path to the cemetery even though I've been studying for months and have committed it to memory. The preparation settles my nerves. Breathing calm into my lungs, I grit my teeth.

*He's right. I've got this.*

• • •

I bury my cache behind the grave site for Tweek and Buffy—
beloved hamsters—and make it to the apartment without
incident. Punching in the code Abignail gave us before we left,
I open the door to find Kyran, Rayelle, and Garrett lounging
on couches in the stark living room.

"Rayelle!" My heart leaps. "What are you doing here?"

"Surprise!" she says. "Apparently your heist needs ours,
so we get to be roommates!"

"Really?"

"We all have our own rooms, though," she says, pressing
a button on a remote. The walls rotate around us, revealing
four small bedrooms. "Unless you two want to room together."
Grinning, she has zero regard that Garrett and Kyran are
listening. "That can be arranged." She presses another button,
and the wall between the two bedrooms on the right retreats.

"Rayelle!" My cheeks get hot. "Absolutely not," I say
before Garrett can answer—or get any ideas. He'd probably
love to torture me all night with quizzes on how to tell if
someone is lying or best stalking practices.

I glance at him, but he doesn't acknowledge me. He's busy
reading a book with a kidney on the cover.

"Unless *you* want to share, Kyran," she says. "Elisha likes
her privacy. I, on the other hand, don't need walls…"

I raise my eyebrows at her, silently saying, *we need to talk!*

"No thanks." Kyran takes the remote and puts up the wall.

Rayelle plops onto the couch, unfazed.

"So you're allowed to tell us what your heist is?" I ask,
sinking down next to her.

"I guess." She shrugs, looking to Kyran for confirmation.

"We're supposed to steal a ring," he says.

# Chapter Thirty-One

*March 20X6, San Francisco*

I can't sleep. I've been tossing and turning all night, even though we stayed up late listening to the details of Kyran and Rayelle's heist and I should be exhausted. It turns out their heist is *also* to steal a ring, but it's a different ring than the one Garrett and I are after. They're supposed to steal a Byzantine-era Italian ring from the de Young Museum and give it to us. We have no idea what we're supposed to do with it—hopefully it will all make sense once they give us the ring—but that's the least of my worries.

*How am I going to walk into the Influencer world tomorrow? What if the cameras recognize me? Do I even remember how to act like an Influencer?*

My mind is racing. Needing a distraction and hoping recalling the details of Influencer life will help me prepare for meeting Nicki tomorrow, I take out my journal.

. . .

*June 25, 20X5*

*Truth: I am never trapped. There is always a new world beyond the bubble, just waiting to be discovered.*

The boat bumped against the dock, and I accepted the hand of a waiting staff member who escorted me to land. Flickering lanterns lined a trail to the house, which rose up out of the darkness, a turreted beacon ablaze with lights. It had seven bedrooms and seven en suite baths. Tonight, only the "VIP" crew was in attendance—somehow my parents had convinced them to come—and we each had our own room. *Not that it will keep Adam and Deena apart.* My stomach knotted at the thought of seeing them again—*of seeing them together*—but I gritted my teeth and marched up the path. Bernard followed, on guard to keep me from running.

*As if he could stop me.*

Tomorrow night, when the shore was packed with up-and-coming Influencers, I was supposed to pretend to get drunk on the yacht and accept a speedboat ride from a handsome stranger. Allard said I'd know him when I saw him. Part of me wondered if she'd been disconnected too long—everyone in attendance would be beyond gorgeous, and I wasn't sure I'd recognize him—but I trusted she was right. The plan was for us to have an "unfortunate" boating accident and disappear. He'd make sure remnants of our boat washed up on shore, along with my shoes, before we slipped away on bikes he had hidden in the woods. Simple. There would be a manhunt, and my parents would have the lake dragged, but my body would never emerge. The media would speculate, but eventually my parents would make sure I was believed dead. I could count on that. It was in their best interest. The world would eat out of their hands as they mourned my loss. I was tying everything up in a neat little package for them.

Except, apparently, they had their own ideas.

When I arrived in the foyer, the celebrity-event planner greeted me. "Your friends are in the game room," she said. "You're to join them. I'll make sure your bags are placed in the master bedroom."

Two sweeping staircases spiraled up to the second floor. I already knew what the upstairs looked like, having watched my friends tour the house via their live Network feeds while I was on the boat. They'd gone offline only a short time ago, so the real party was just beginning. "I'd prefer the turret room," I replied. "It seems fitting for a prisoner, don't you think?" *And I'm sure Adam and Deena will claim the master.*

Turning my back on her, I burst through the carved wood doors into the game room before I lost my nerve. Six heads swiveled, and they all stared, their eyes masked by AMPs. Everyone stood around the pool table. Jax was shooting while Bryce looked on, leaning on his cue. Lil and Kylie were sipping pink champagne. Adam had his arm draped around Deena's waist but immediately dropped his hand, inching away from her, shifting his weight uncomfortably.

*Good. I hope I make him sweat.*

"There she is," Deena said, plastering a wide smile on her hollow face. "The birthday girl! Put your headset on, silly. Come into the real party."

"Why? You can't face me in reality?" I picked up a VR headset and pulled it on so I could see what they were seeing. The room transformed into a carnival of flashing lights and sound. Everything was black and white, from the fortune teller's striped tent to the game booths, with the exception of the game pieces. And us. The pool table was black, but the balls glowed neon. Beyond the distant Ferris wheel, its lights cast in vivid color, I sensed we were encased in glass—a snow globe or a crystal ball—trapped.

"Oh, Ella, let's forget the past," Deena said, her avatar coming to my side and resting her head on my shoulder. "I'm willing to start over if you are."

"Why? What's in it for you? I'm Network poison." Sidestepping her, I digested their reimagined forms—Deena was curvier, Lil taller—and landed on Adam.

There was an apology in his stare that I took for guilt, and I steeled myself against him.

*Liar.*

"Ella! We missed you is all." Kylie threw her arms around my neck. "I promise."

"Have some champagne," Lil said. "We have *so* much to tell you." Her words slurred, and she'd clearly had too much already. Pouring me a glass, she let the bubbles foam over the sides. In the virtual world, they looked like oozing lava.

I didn't know why they were being nice to me. *Maybe being miserable for two days is too much to handle so they popped some extra pills.* Whatever the reason, it was fine with me. I would play along with anything in order to escape.

Putting on a happy face, I squeezed Kylie back. "I totally missed you guys, too. Savannah was the loneliest."

"It looked like you worked a lot," Adam said, focusing on the shot he was lining up.

"You were paying attention?" Accepting my glass from Lil, I tried to sound coy, but I couldn't keep the edge from my voice. "I thought you were too busy to notice I was gone."

"He was pretty busy." Bryce snorted and drank from the glowing purple guitar he wore strapped across his chest.

Adam glared at him before igniting the five ball in a swirl of orange sparks, sinking it in the corner pocket. He turned to me. "Do you seriously want to do this here, Ella? Now? Do you want to hear what I'm thinking?"

Surprised by the edge in his voice, I faltered, noticing the small smile that formed on Lil's lips before she hid it.

He didn't wait for me to answer. "Did you expect me to come running after you dragged me through the mud?" His voice was ice.

"I did what?" I sputtered. "You're the one who made me think you liked me, then hooked up with my best friend."

Ignoring me, he took his next shot. The six ball glowed green as it landed in the side pocket. "What, did you expect me to send you flowers after you tried to destroy my reputation?"

*What did the Myrna-bot post?* Dread landed with a sickening thud in my belly, and the carnival swirled around me. I didn't know which side was up. "I don't know what you're talking about. My parents made me leave without saying goodbye. They took over my feeds, cut me off. I've been off the grid."

"Don't lie, Ella," Deena said. "We all know you posted it."

"I'm not lying." Caught in a landslide of confusion, I felt tears roll freely down my avatar's cheeks. "I don't know what's going on, but I don't trust *any* of you to tell me the truth."

Across the room, Bryce grunted. "This is boring, you guys. Can we get on with the game?"

Just then, a stranger appeared wearing a long, black cape, his teeth carved into fangs. Eyes glowing purple, he hissed, sending Kylie and Lily screaming under the pool table and Deena into Adam's arms.

I jumped. *It's not real. This is some strange team building exercise my parents designed to band us together in a once-in-a-lifetime experience against an evil vampire.* Blood rushing in my ears, I breathed deep to calm down. *They're so clueless and theatrical, they literally thought vampire therapy would save us.* Ripping the headset off my face, I threw it on the ground.

Back in the game room, I glared at my so-called friends' ordinary faces.

"Go ahead. Play your game. I'm done."

With that, I retreated to the turret room to await my new life.

# Chapter Thirty-Two

*June 25, 20X5*

*T*ruth: *I'll do anything for love.*
      *This will be my first and last entry, the final secret I share. It's strange, knowing this is goodbye. What will be my final words to my so-called friends?*

Setting down my new, blank journal, I sipped my coffee, savoring it. Alone on my balcony outside the turret room, I watched the cobalt water glistening against the distant snowcapped mountains. The air was crisp that morning—my last morning as an Influencer—hinting of the pine trees that dotted the shore. The view was void of augmentation; the natural landscape didn't need it.

*Will I miss this?* Adjusting my fluffy robe, I breathed in the coffee's nutty aroma. *I don't know how to make coffee... I don't know how to make anything. I guess I'll learn...*

Sparkles pricked the corner of my eye, the sun reflecting off my shimmery vintage Balenciaga dress hanging in the window. *And I might miss the dresses...*

Laughter bounced up to me off the water. Down below,

my friends were headed to the beach, huge sunglasses and floppy hats obscuring their faces from the relentless sun. They'd apparently survived a night with a vampire, but they were moving slowly.

*…But I won't miss them. At least not all of them.* Adam kept me awake most of the night, everything he'd said running repeat in my mind. Once I was certain everyone was asleep, I'd crept around until I found the house's Network center. The Myrna-bot was still auto-posting for me. My parents weren't taking any chances with this weekend, and I was still cut off from my own feed.

Pulling up the Network on the house account, I scrolled through my feed, going back months—realizing I didn't miss the Network at all—until I found the post where I accused Adam of forcing me to sleep with him in exchange for him pretending to like me, for wielding his Influence. The Myrna-bot had pulled images from my Life Stream to dub a confessional video where I went on and on about how terrible he was and the courage it took for me to finally speak out.

It was my parents' attempt to save my numbers—paint me as a victim to get people on my side and give Deena what she wanted by making Adam hate me—but all it did was make me hate my parents even more. At least it proved Adam and Deena weren't gaming me all along. I still didn't understand why they were hooking up, but it reopened the possibility that what Adam and I had was real.

On the beach below, Jax and Bryce put on running shoes and took off in the direction of town while the girls slathered themselves with thick sunscreen and lay in withered piles on the blanketed sand. They all had their own version of sweating out last night's sins.

*Wreck and repair… Before I wreck it all.*

"So, where did he sleep?" Lil's voice drifted up.

"I don't know." Deena rubbed her eyes. "But if it was with her, we're done. This is war. She can't waltz in here and win him back just like that."

I raised an eyebrow. *He didn't stay with her last night?*

Beyond the girls, Adam dove into the water and swam toward a pontoon floating over the sandbar past the dock, his back muscles flexing with each stroke. He deserved to know my feelings were real and I never meant to hurt him. I couldn't bear leaving with him believing the lies; I needed to talk to him.

Having nothing to lose, I tossed the journal on the rumpled bed someone else would make and put on my bathing suit. Winding my hair into a knot at the top of my head, I didn't bother with a cover-up or a hat to shade my face, my mother's voice ringing in my head that I was risking my youth. Purposely forgetting sunscreen was like giving my mom the finger. Hurrying to the beach, I marched straight past the girls and into the lake, splashing cold water up to my knees. Ignoring Deena's snide "good morning to you, too," I plunged forward, careful not to let my chin dip, paddling toward him.

I was out of breath when I reached the pontoon.

He lay on his back, staring at the sky, the sun soaking his golden skin.

"I didn't post it. I know what you were talking about now." I panted, struggling to heave myself onto the pontoon.

Sitting up, he hoisted me next to him. We sat facing the shore, knees nearly touching, our feet dangling in the water.

I couldn't read his expression, but I kept talking before I lost my nerve. "My parents had a robot running my feed. I never said those things. Please believe I liked you—liked you more than I've ever liked anybody—I never would have hurt you like that."

Looking at me sideways, he sighed. "Honestly, I don't

know what to believe, Ella. This whole thing is messed up. I'm starting to think I should stay away from all of you. Maybe I'm better off alone or starting over."

"You're probably right. You're better off alone than with Deena. That much is true." Sadness rippled through me at the thought of them together, and even at the risk of sounding like a jealous girlfriend—which I had no right to be—I couldn't stop myself from asking, "How could you?"

"I never wanted to hurt you either, Ella." He ran his fingers through his hair. "But I didn't know why you said those things. I felt like you were using me to get at Deena, like I was a pawn in your drama game. I know it's not a good excuse, but she's oddly powerful. She gave me two options: she and Lil and Kylie could all release stories saying I abused them, too, or I could pretend to be her boyfriend and they'd all stick up for me, swear that you were lying. As pathetic as it sounds, I need my numbers. I figured I'm better off with her than against her."

"I don't blame you." I sighed, sick to my stomach. "I promise my feelings for you were real. But now everything is ruined. We can never go back to the way it was."

"No. We can't, can we?" He frowned. "If I could go back in time, I'd run away with you before this mess happened— hide away somewhere so we could get to know each other. We didn't get to explore what we had, but I know it was special."

Every ounce of me wanted to believe him, to believe what we had could still exist. *It was our f-ed reality that kept us apart. But I can fix that...* My heart pounded. *I shouldn't tell him. It's dangerous, but maybe he could come with me...*

"What if you didn't need your numbers," I said, watching little rings of water pooling around his toe. "What if we *could* hide away. Would you do it? Hypothetically."

"Hypothetically? I'd be intrigued." He met my eyes, and electricity shot through me. "But it's impossible."

The sun glinted off his hair, bleached blond against his tan, and admiring the strength in his lean torso, I sucked in my breath. "What if it's not impossible?"

*Whoever my escort is will just have to deal with two of us.* He raised his eyebrows.

Back onshore, there was a splash off the edge of the dock. Jax and Bryce's heads popped up in the water, bobbing toward us. I had to hurry. "Tonight. You have to decide tonight," I whispered. "If you want to come with me, it's your only chance. Be at the yacht by ten o'clock. You can't bring anything but the clothes on your back. No screens, no AMPs. Nothing. I'll be waiting."

A slow smile spread across his face, and in it was everything about the Adam I knew and trusted.

"I'll be there," he said.

Jax reached the pontoon, and, plugging my nose, I jumped into the water, dunking my whole head. Breaking the surface, I swam for shore, Adam's answer singing in my ears.

# Chapter Thirty-Three

*T*ruth: *Death isn't an end; it's a beginning.*

The party was everything it was supposed to be. The drinks flowed through a DJ-fueled dance party on the deck while a sunset clambake on the shore faded into s'mores, firepits, and moonlit skinny dipping. It was all over-the-top augmented, though it didn't matter to me. Without AMPs, I couldn't see the fantasy my parents had spared no expense creating. Tonight, nothing could cloud my vision. I had to watch for my contact *and* Adam.

Nine o'clock rolled around, and I still hadn't glimpsed either of them, so I dutifully slipped beyond the velvet rope and boarded the boat that would take Lil, Deena, Kylie, and me to the yacht. Jax and Bryce stayed back, happy to curate the private party attendees from the already-growing line.

Once I was on board, even without AMPs, the yacht appeared to be floating in a water-filled crater on the surface of the moon. Surrounded by a galaxy of shooting stars, in the distance the earth emerged from the black unknown, slowly rotating.

For a while, it was just the girls and me on the magical boat. They stuck together, picking at the dessert bar, pouring champagne, posing pretending to steer the ship at all of the Network-bait photo ops scattered around the upper deck. No longer caring who was watching me, I kept to myself, hugging my arms across my chest, watching for Adam's boat to emerge from the stars. Slowly, other guests arrived, but there was no Adam and no contact. As the yacht filled with partygoers, I had to keep up appearances, and I reluctantly joined the girls in a roped-off corner next to the dance floor.

"Hey birthday girl," Lil said as I slumped down next to her. "Smile. You're finally seventeen!" Clearly her feed was live—there was no other reason for her to be nice to me.

"I don't care," I said. "In fact, you should all stop caring about rankings. It's freeing."

Ignoring me, she expertly kept her expression neutral. "That dress is everything. And those earrings. Birthday gift?" Leaning in, she touched the beads dangling from my ears and muttered so only I could hear, "Careful, Ella. You still have everything to lose. We wouldn't want any secrets to spill."

She purposely knocked a glass of champagne into my lap. The cold liquid seeped between my thighs, and I leaped up.

"Oh no," Lil said. "I'm *so* sorry." Grabbing a napkin, she dabbed at my skirt.

"Don't be," I said sweetly. "I have dozens of other dresses. I'll go change."

Leaving them, I found a quiet corner of the boat and stared into the universe.

*Where is Adam?*

"Hey," Deena said, joining me.

Chilled despite the balmy summer breeze swirling off the lake, I rubbed my arms. "Hi."

We watched the earth rotate in silence, having everything and nothing to say to each other.

"Can we snap a pic?" A pretty girl I didn't know wedged herself between us.

"Sure," Deena said.

Fake-smiling, we sucked in our cheeks, putting our arms around one another like we were friends.

"Chill party," the girl said, walking away. "I'll tag you."

"I can't live like this," I said as soon as she was out of earshot. "Pretending to be happy. Pretending this is real so we can make other people feel small. Do you ever feel that way?"

Deena's eyes were saucers. "Yes."

"Yes?" I gripped her meager arm, my fingernails piercing her skin, trying to grab hold of the fleeting glimpse of my old friend. "Deena. Do you remember when we were little girls? Are you still in there?"

The fragment of emotion was gone as soon as it came.

"Calm down, babe." She smoothed her fingers over my hair. "I have everything I've always wanted."

I searched her dead eyes, wanting to smack her, to get a rise, any kind of reaction. "Deena?" I pleaded. "We used to be friends. I wish we could go back to the way it was before Intersection."

"Ella, when are you going to learn that living in the past is pointless? We're in the game now, and personally, I came to play."

My heart broke for her, for me. For us. "There's got to be more to life than influence."

"This is as good as it gets," she said. "Everyone wishes they were us, and you would, too, if you were an outsider. If this all went away, you'd miss it."

I frowned.

Over her shoulder, a boat appeared. The riders were

silhouetted against a meteor shower, so I couldn't make out faces, but I recognized one of the figures as Adam. The other guy was a mystery. *Probably someone handpicked from the line.*

My eyes swept over the rest of the pretty people on the yacht. *How am I supposed to know which one is him? What if Allard didn't set it up?*

Fear leaped in my chest, stalling my heart, and everything happened at once:

"Jump!" I heard a voice, clear as day, and it was almost like a furious wind physically threw me overboard.

The last thing I saw was Adam, his boat drawing up to the yacht, his blue eyes searching out mine — before —

*Boom.*

# Chapter Thirty-Four

*March 20X6, San Francisco*

"Are you nervous?" Rayelle asks, gluing the last silver rhinestone to the collection gathered under my left eye.

"I feel like an alien is going to punch its way out of my stomach," I reply. "So, yes."

"Same. I can't believe our heists start today." She exhales. "I've been waiting for this my whole life. I hope I don't screw up."

"Me, too. What if the cameras recognize me as a Maker?" I take a sip of mint tea, hoping it will calm my uneasy stomach.

"No chance. Look at you!" She turns me to face the mirror.

A glittery silver stripe runs down the center of my face and is smeared across my right cheek, and my long, pale-blue hair is braided with ribbons, but no matter how hard I squint, Ella stares back at me. *I look too much like me.* Closing my eyes, I breathe Betsy into me—picturing how I'll affect her mannerisms, her slight limp, her frailty. *I will draw on every ounce of acting ability my mother drilled into me. It's all I can do.* Opening my eyes, I wipe my damp hands on the skirt of my silky dress.

"Thank you for helping me," I say. "You did a great job. Hopefully I blend in."

"You're a total Betsy. Don't worry. I can't wait to see what Garrett thinks." Rayelle grins.

"I can." Frowning, I lower my voice, grabbing her arm. "Hey—what was that with Kyran last night? I've been dying to talk to you. The bedroom thing. Have you lost your mind?"

"I know." She groans. "He never talks, so I feel like I have to talk for both of us, but he makes me so nervous that randomness comes out of my mouth. I can't control it."

"I can relate to the word vomit, though Garrett doesn't make me nervous, just irritated."

"Boys." She sighs. "It's probably for the best I'll never see Kyran again after he gets initiated. I'm sure he'll forget all about me—not that I want him to"—she pauses, adding to herself—"actually, it would be okay if he forgot the babbling…"

A pang slices through my chest at the thought that this could be it for Garrett and me, too. "You'll see him again." I squeeze her arm. "Garrett says partners have an unbreakable bond."

Rayelle smirks. "Maybe you two do, but Kyran's different. I keep thinking I need to tell him how I feel before he disappears on me—you know, just in case there's a chance."

"Rayelle. I'm pretty sure he knows."

"You think so?" She presses her hand to her rosy cheek.

"Yes." I laugh. "Without a doubt."

"Do you think there's a chance he feels the same way?"

I don't have the heart to tell her the truth. "Maybe? He's hard to read, but anything is possible."

"Yeah." She exhales. "There's always hope. And maybe you should tell Garrett how *you* feel about *him*."

I scrunch up my nose. "Garrett knows *exactly* how I feel about him."

"Does he? Do *you* know how you feel about him?" she asks. "I've seen the way you look at him."

"Like I want to kill him?"

*Bang, bang, bang.* A fist thumps against the door.

"Are you ready yet?" Garrett calls before I can further deny Rayelle's assumption. "I was hoping to get there before all the kidneys are gone."

Rayelle giggles, and I swing open the bathroom door. "You're not funny—"

He's stands with his hair perfectly mussed, his signature three black bars in place under his left eye. My heart stalls. *Oh. My. God.* I clamp my mouth shut. Dressed in a fitted charcoal suit reminiscent of what the thieves wear in *Ocean's 22*—one of the most-watched films in the Vault—he's my dream thief.

His eyelids flutter rapidly, like he's trying to focus. "Those shoes are a dead giveaway."

My heart ticks back to life, and blood rushes to my cheeks. "What's wrong with them?" I look down at my black boots. "I think they give me an edge."

He shakes his head. "Heels. Betsy is all about heels. Think about everything when you get into character. What would you carry in your pockets if you belonged here? It's all about the details."

Feeling like a child who has just been scolded, I grit my teeth. "But I can't tie heels with paracord."

"Don't worry about that. I have enough for the both of us." He opens his jacket and unzips the lining, revealing everything we could possibly need—paracord, lock picks, a pocketknife, bobby pins, a Zippo, a tape recorder, a tactical pen. "And this jacket is made of bulletproof fabric. We can use it as a shield if necessary."

"But what if we get separated? I need to be prepared, too. I have a tactical pen and lock-picking kit." I raise the hem of my dress, exposing the tool garter strapped to my thigh.

He sighs. "We won't get separated—I have no intention of letting you out of my sight—but wrap some paracord around the pen so you can change your shoes. And hurry. You're going to make us late."

Pivoting on my heel, I head to the closet to change. "You have an answer for everything," I mutter.

When I return, he frowns at my silver flats.

"They're all I have," I say. "Besides, I'm a transplant survivor. People will cut me some slack on my shoe choice."

"I guess so. Come here." He gestures me forward. Grabbing my shoulders, he lowers his face to mine, peering into my eyes.

"What are you doing?" I squeak, my pulse throbbing in my throat at his proximity, trying to wiggle away from him.

"Hold still."

"No." I duck, and he lets me go.

"Are you wearing your AMPs?" he asks. "I don't see them."

"I don't like stuff in my eyes. I was waiting until the last possible second."

He frowns. "You're getting on my last possible nerve. I know you're anxious, but can you please stop stalling?"

"I'm not anxious," I lie. I head to a mirror, and my fingers shake as I put my AMPS in place, blotting out my amber irises in favor of sky blue, making my eyes identical to Garrett's. *I mean Beau's*. "I'm as ready as I'll ever be." Puffing up my chest, I turn to face him, willing my legs to carry me forward.

"Finally." He extends his hand. "Come on, sis. Let's go."

# Chapter Thirty-Five

*March 20X6, San Francisco*

"So, when we see Nicki, we make sure she overhears us talking about your recovery. Remember, you're about two months post-op—"

"I know, I know. I'm feeling better, I'm so happy to be rid of the nanobots that were filtering my blood…"

The opera house looms in front of us, augmented to look like it's underwater—a sunken mermaid's palace at the bottom of the sea.

"I'm glad you know, because here goes nothing," Garrett says. He starts up the stairs, and I'm surprised the ocean doesn't carry him away.

"We're just going to go in?" I call after him, frozen in place at the thought of having to enter the water. *It's not real. It's not real.* But my limbs tremble all the same.

"Yes." He glances over his shoulder. "Are you coming?"

A trickle of sweat rolls down my back. "I don't like the water," I admit.

"You're scared?"

My lungs heave, my breath coming out in little puffs. "Yes."

He sighs and walks back down the steps, extending his hand. "Time to face your fears. I won't let anything happen to you. I promise."

His eyes hold mine, and I'm surprised by the genuine concern in them—that he's not making fun of me, for once.

Accepting his hand, I nod. The strength in his grip helps ease my anxiety as he tugs me into the sea. I hold my breath, expecting cold water to wash over me, but my clothes stay reassuringly dry. A glittering kelp forest parts, and, hanging on to Garrett, I climb the stairs. Undulating waves dizzy me as fish stream by, but he keeps me steady, whispering, "One step at a time." When we reach the entrance to the colonnade, I'm breathing again.

"Thank you," I say. "You probably think I'm a total wimp, but I almost drowned once. Being underwater totally freaks me out."

"It's cool," he says, raising his eyebrows, reminding me to stay in character. "That's what big brothers are for."

I press my lips together. "Right."

He turns to a woman sitting next to a velvet rope and holding a retina scanner. "I'm not in the database," he says. "These tickets were a last-minute gift from Natasha Wilde." Mentioning Faye's alias, he hands her the paper-thin screen seemingly made of bubbles that serves as an invitation. "And the same goes for her." He nods over his shoulder at me before leaning in, whispering, "She's a survivor."

"Oh, what a dear." I sense her pity. "Just a quick scan and you're in." She holds up the scanner.

Garrett leans forward and peers into the eyeholes.

If he's nervous, he doesn't show it.

My stomach clenches; I hold my breath. *The moment of truth.*

A light on the scanner turns green, and she waves him through.

I exhale relief.

"Your eyes, miss." She holds up the scanner, and I bite my lip.

"See you inside, Bets." Garrett disappears into the crowd beyond the gate.

*So much for keeping me in sight.* Wide-eyed, I watch him go.

"Miss," the guard repeats.

"I'm not in the database," I mumble. Hands shaking, I rummage through my handbag, pushing aside duct tape and glitter refills, searching for my ticket. A line of fancy people forms behind me, and, sweating, I say "just a minute" and get out of the way. I set my bag on a nearby wall to properly dig, and just as my fingers find the invitation, I feel breath on my ear.

"Excuse me," a male voice says.

Slowly, I turn, terrified I've been discovered. But I recognize him immediately as the guy Faye left with yesterday, minus the mole.

"Did you lose something?" He imperceptibly slips a rolled-up piece of paper into my hand.

My shaking fingers close around the note, and I push it beneath my cuff bracelet. Keeping my eyes glued to his, I say, "No. I thought I'd lost my ticket, but I've just found it."

"Very good, then. Enjoy the party." He walks off.

Excitement pumping through my veins, my head clears, and it's like that day in the obstacle course. I stop thinking and *go.* Returning to the line, I give the guard my ticket and submit to the retina scanner without blinking. The light turns green, and I sail through the gate on a sea of adrenaline.

Inside, millions of bubbles float to the coffered ceiling.

Seaweed dangles from chandeliers, and a school of colorful fish swishes past me, but I barely acknowledge my surroundings. In stealth mode, I enter the mouth of a sunken ship and hurry down a spiral staircase to the bathroom. The restroom has been spared the under-the-sea augmentation, and once I'm safely sequestered in a stall, I read the note.

*I figured out what she wants: to feel useful, to be a superhero, to feel like she can save someone. —F.*

I close my eyes, processing the information until it hits me. I almost drop the note. *We have it backward. Garrett should ask her to fix something only she can…like finding a kidney for his sister.* This changes our whole plan.

My stomach knots. *I hope it's not too late.*

Rushing upstairs to the party, I search for Garrett, finding him standing casually at the bar like he comes to these things all the time. Ignoring the familiar jolt that pummels me at the sight of him, I hurry to his side.

"It's about time," he says without looking at me.

Staring up at his perfect profile illuminated by a sunshine ray filtered through the water, I'm surprised a chorus of augmented angels doesn't break into song. *But, good looks aside, he's seriously the most irritating person on earth.* "You haven't talked to her yet, have you?" I ask.

"No. She's over there." His eyes stay glued to the flawless blonde standing a few feet away.

Her hair is pulled back in a high ponytail, and her dress accentuates her tiny waist. She exudes femininity and sexuality, and, wearing Betsy's braids, I'm like a silly country mouse in comparison. *Use it. Stay in character.*

Nicki turns to her companions: an equally stunning girl with wild pink hair and a buff guy who stands guard over the beauties, his back to us. Alone, each could command the attention of the entire room, but together they're virile and sensual and brighter than the star that leads you home.

"Look at them," I whisper in awe, something in my gut flaring with familiarity, belonging. I can't put my finger on it, but I feel like I know them. *Maybe it's because they're who I used to be...* But it's more than that. The air is charged with energy, and I'm certain we're on the verge of something big.

Garrett nods, equally entranced by the threesome.

I sense desire in him. Whether it's to be them or to be *with* them, I'm not sure, but it sends my heart straight to the pit of my stomach, as I am certain he'll never look at me that way. I'm destined to be his kid sister. *Not that I care.*

Blinking to clear my vision of bubbles, I straighten my spine and lean my head on his shoulder, fake adoration in my eyes. "Let's get her."

Garrett's lips curve into a smile, and we're conspirators. He elbows my side, whispering, "Now *that* sounds like a plan." Slipping his arm around my waist, he guides me to them.

Electricity shoots down my spine. "Hey," I whisper back, "real quick. Change of plans. Faye passed me a note—"

But I don't finish my sentence because the guy Nicki is with turns around.

My lungs seize like I've been punched in the gut, and my knees buckle. I'd recognize those blue eyes anywhere.

*Adam?*

# Chapter Thirty-Six

*March 20X6, San Francisco*

*T*he room sways—it's all I can do to stay on my feet—as a hundred questions collide in my brain. *He's alive. What is he doing here? What does he want with Nicki?* His hair is cropped short, and his tan has faded, but there is no mistaking him.

Looking like he's seen a ghost—and maybe he thinks he *is* seeing one—he starts toward me. He moves slowly through the water, as if in a trance, drawn forward by whatever fragments of our past tie us together. There's no doubt in my mind he recognizes me.

My nerves stretch taut over my skin. If anyone were to touch me, I'd shatter. *I'm done for. Abort mission…*

Shaking his head, he comes to a stop in front of me. He presses a finger to his lips, seemingly pulling himself together—or telling me to keep quiet. "I'm sorry. For a moment I thought I knew you. But I don't. You must remind me of someone." Gone is the Australian accent, and the sound of his (real?) voice renders me mute. "I'm Eric." Smiling, he extends his hand, daring me to deny it.

His toes are pointed away from me. *Ready to run. It's a tell.
Liar! But I'll keep your secret if you'll keep mine...* "Betsy,"
I mumble, unable to keep my fingers from trembling in his.
"People think they know me all the time. I have a familiar
face." Glancing at Garrett, I'm relieved he doesn't seem to
think anything is odd about this encounter. *Yet.*

"You know who it is?" Adam/Eric points a finger at me,
nodding. "Tiana Santos. You look just like her."

My stomach tightens, but, faking a laugh, I manage to
keep the glint out of my eye. "I've never gotten that one
before."

"No, she doesn't, Eric. She doesn't look a thing like
Tiana Santos. How many drinks have you had?" Nicki says,
appearing at his side, and I'm grateful to her.

"You don't see it? Maybe it's just me. There are worse
people to look like, eh?" Adam ushers her forward. "This
is my friend Nicki, and this is Joanna." He nods toward the
pink-haired girl. "This is...Betsy, did you say it was?"

"Yes." I force a smile.

"Cute," he says.

"Nicki." Garrett takes over. "Just who my sister and I were
hoping to meet."

*Ack! I didn't have time to tell him about the note!* "I hope
my brother isn't too pushy," I interject our new plan. "He
has it in his silly head that you can help find me a new set of
kidneys."

Adam/Eric cocks his head and arches an eyebrow. My
temper flares, the word *liar* again exploding in my brain. Filing
away whoever I thought Adam was, I tell myself I'll process
this later and step into a ray of watery sunshine, deliberately
giving myself over to the best light.

Garrett doesn't miss a beat. "Hey, when you love someone

as much as I love my sister, you'll do anything to save her life"—he puts his arm around me and squeezes my shoulder, his hand hot on my skin—"even make a fool of yourself in front of the prettiest girl you've ever seen." He turns to Adam. "I hope you don't mind me saying that. Sometimes I overstep my bounds by speaking my mind."

"It's cool." Adam shifts his weight. "It's the truth. And speaking your mind is the only way to go."

His eyes flit to mine, but I refuse to acknowledge him.

Nicki blushes, the pink staining her pretty cheeks, making her more inviting.

*I need to learn to do that on command.*

"You guys, stop," she says. "And please, Betsy, I would love to help in any way I can. I know what you're going through. All of it sucks. What stage are you in?"

"Four. The filter-bots make me *so* tired."

"I bet, but you look great."

"You're the sweetest," I say, my nerves settling. I stop thinking as the lies tumble from my lips. "I just want to be hungry again—to want a burger and fries and actually be able to taste it. I want my life back!"

"I've totally been there." Nicki's lower lip juts forward as she wipes a tear from her eye, and I notice the ring on her left middle finger. It has a dark gold band that looks ancient, like it was molded by hand, and four prongs hold in place a foggy blue stone. "I'll put you in contact with our transplant coordinator. She can get you on the list right away."

Garrett touches Nicki's arm and leans closer to her, lowering his voice. I can almost see the heated shivers run down her arm at his touch. *He's undeniable.* "Is there any way we could get her moved up?" Garrett asks. "She puts on a good show, but to be honest, we don't know how much time she has left."

"I might be able to pull some strings." She smiles. "Let me see what I can do."

"Who wants a drink?" Adam/Eric asks. "I hear the Transplantinis are delicious."

"One of my dad's terrible jokes." Nicki rolls her eyes. "But this benefit raises zillions for the farm, so we put up with it."

"I'd love one," Garrett says.

"Me, too," Joanna says.

"None for me," I say. "Doctor's orders."

"I won't have one, either. Wouldn't want you to feel left out, Betsy," Nicki says. "But if you're interested, I have something else that won't be so hard on your system." She clicks open a compartment on her bracelet and reveals a treasure trove of herbs. "They're all natural and organic. Medicine from the farm."

"Sure," I say, knowing I need to bond with her. *Whatever it takes.*

She smiles. "Follow me."

Adam/Eric gets drinks for everyone, and Nicki takes us upstairs to an unaugmented lounge that looks like an old movie palace, with gold wallpaper and red velvet carpets and furniture. I'm relieved to be coming up for air, to emerge from the sea to a space where unaugmented beauty is acceptable.

Nicki curls onto a couch, tucking her feet under her, and I take a seat in the chair across from her. Garrett sits in a chair next to me while Adam/Eric and Joanna join Nicki on the couch.

"These things are so boring sometimes." She packs the herbs into a jewel-encrusted pipe. "Don't get me wrong, I'm grateful for the farm, but it gets old having to be 'on' all the time, to look like I'm having the time of my life." Lighting the herbs, she takes a puff and passes it to Joanna. "I don't know what I'd do without Eric." She exhales. "He's the only one who gets me."

*She's just like me.* The instinct is so strong it almost knocks me off my feet. *I know exactly what she wants to hear.*

"What about me?" Joanna asks, taking a big hit of the herbs. She coughs. "I've known you longer." She hands the pipe to me.

Nicki bats her eyelashes. "You know I love you, babe. You get me in other ways."

Adam/Eric squeezes Nicki's knee. My heart squeezes right along with it. *It was all a lie. He was playing me. If my instincts are supposed to be so great, where were they on this one?* The wasted nights I spent crying over him come rushing back, and I'd love to cross the room and punch him in the stomach.

"I totally understand. Sometimes it feels like everything is a lie," I say, throwing myself into character so I'll stay in my seat. *He's Eric. A stranger. You can smack him later.* Taking a long drag of the herbs, I breathe in rosemary and mint before slowly exhaling. "I have to hide my kidney disease from the Networks. My parents don't want me to seem sick or weak—it would be bad for Dad's business. One of his tax shelters sells vitamin supplements, so I need to look like the picture of health and happiness. It's exhausting. I would so much rather *feel* alive and be surrounded by genuine friends than *look* alive in a sea of fakeness, but real connections are hard to make in this world."

Nicki smiles and takes another hit. "I like you," she says.

"I like you, too," I reply, and I'm not lying.

Joanna waves her hand in front of her face, and Berkeley & the Brightside's "Headshot" fills the room. "This party is way too mellow," she says, pulling Nicki to her feet.

Nicki hands the herbs off to Adam. "I love this song." Giggling, she takes my hand and drags me into the dance party.

The three of us girls dance while the guys wordlessly

sip their drinks. I wonder if Garrett is nervous about the competition for Nicki's attention, but most of me doesn't care. I'm pleasantly buzzed, caught up in a world that spit me out, and I can't help but wonder if, had we met in another life, Nicki would have been a true friend.

"Nicki." A voice sounds from across the room, bringing the party to an abrupt halt. "Your father is about to give his speech."

A stern woman dressed all in black, her mouth set in a firm line, beckons Nicki toward her. She's flanked by two bodyguard types, and I imagine they're scanning Garrett and me with the latest in AMP infotech. Expecting them to pounce, to expose me as a dead girl brought to life, I feel my breath catch in my throat.

"Give us five more minutes, Miriam." Nicki takes the herbs from Adam and inhales a long drag.

"Pull yourself together," Miriam says. "You know how important it is that you're at your father's side tonight. You're the future face of Simon Technologies. Act like it."

Nicki sighs and takes Eric's hand. "Guess we should go." But before she leaves, she hugs me. "I want you two to be my guests at the Stern Grove Festival this weekend. I have an entire picnic table all to myself, and Berkeley & the Brightside is playing. Will you come?"

"I'd love to," I say. *Truth.* "There's no VR access to Stern Grove, right? My parents hate not being able to check in on me, which is why I've always wanted to go."

"Exactly," Nicki says. "My dad thinks it's totally archaic, too—actually having to physically show up somewhere? But I love it. It's different witnessing a concert in person. The smells, the noise, physical contact with strangers—the actual energy of other people. It's so fun."

"It's dangerous for you to be in a public place, Nicki. You

never know what's going to go down," Eric says.

I frown at his accentless voice. *I never knew him at all.*

"I have you to protect me," Nicki says, curling her fingers around his collar.

*That's what you think. I have to stop him from hurting her.*

She peers over his shoulder. "See you guys at the park Saturday at two?"

"We wouldn't miss it," Garrett says. "Can you friend me so my AMPs can find you?"

Nicki lets go of Eric and taps the air.

Feeling eyes on my face, I find Adam/Eric staring directly at me.

"Can't wait to see you again," he says.



"Do you care if we walk?" Garrett asks as we hurry down the opera house steps. "I could use some air."

The night breeze is deliciously cool on my burning cheeks, and I'm so revved up I can't imagine being trapped in a Bubble Car right now. "Not at all. I prefer it." I can barely keep my feet on the ground.

"How do you feel?" he asks, shoving his hands in his jacket pockets and setting a brisk pace.

"Honestly? Like I can fly. That was so much fun." I'm practically skipping.

"You smoked enough to float home."

I flinch, ready for a fight, but then I catch him smiling to himself, and I let it go. "Oh, come on. That was the point, right? I was always in complete control. How many drinks did you have? You're just jealous because Nicki likes me better than you."

His jaw clenched, he glances at me out of the corner of

his eye like I'm an annoying gnat he'd like to flick. "Uh-huh."

"Or you're worried that you have competition..." I playfully whack his arm. "Who will win Nicki's heart? Beau or Eric? I know who I'd choose."

Coming to a halt, he grabs my arms. "Do you?" His intensity catches me off guard, sending hot chills through me.

Abruptly, he lets go and walks ahead.

I watch him go, needing distance. The streetlights glow brighter as he approaches them, illuminating his path. I know they have sensors, but it's like that first day in the Lodge, like his energy could make lightbulbs explode.

Not wanting to be alone in the dark, I don't let him get too far away.

"Good work in there," he says, seeming to have regained his composure when I catch up to him.

"You weren't so bad yourself," I say, happy to restore calm. I can tell he's in a weird mood, and I want the old Garrett back—I want to share my excitement with him. "It's pretty amazing you were able to roll with the story when I didn't get to tell you about the note."

He shoves his hands into his pockets. "What note?"

"That guy we saw at the boardwalk yesterday passed it to me on my way into the opera house. It was from Faye. She said Nicki wants to be a superhero, to feel like she can help someone—so I flipped the script."

"I liked the direction. It felt right." He nods. "We might make a good team..."

I let that idea settle, pleased and terrified by it.

We fall silent, our footsteps echoing on the pavement.

"You're never this quiet," I finally say, unable to shake the brooding mood wafting off him. He's killing my buzz. "What's bothering you?"

He rubs his temples, and I sense he isn't listening to me. "I don't know what Nash is doing here," he mutters to himself as we arrive at our building and enter through the revolving door.

Realizing who he must be talking about, I come to a halt. The door bumps into me, trapping us in glass. "The guy Nicki was with. You know him?"

"Yeah. I know him. We trained together."

The words land with a thud in my gut.

He presses his lips together, and I know that's all he'll say on the subject. "Keep it moving, Bets. We don't have all day." Pushing the door forward, he rotates us until we're spit out into the lobby.

"He's a Keystone Disconnect?" I ask, in my shock not realizing I'm practically yelling.

"Keep your voice down. You could seriously wake the dead." Grabbing my arm, he drags me to the elevator. "He used to be."

"What is he now?"

"I don't know," he whispers. "Listen, it's not safe to talk in here. All I know is when that guy's around, bad things happen. We need to make sure we get the ring first."

# Chapter Thirty-Seven

*March 20X6, San Francisco*

"Okay, so let's review," Garrett says, spreading a map of San Francisco out on the dining room table in our apartment. "Our plan is to get photographs and a mold of Nicki's ring at the Stern Grove Festival and transport it to Faye so she can have a replica made. Once she gives us the replica, we'll figure out a way to get Nicki's ring off her finger and replace it with the fake one."

"Easy," I deadpan. "Seriously, how are we going to get the ring off her finger without her noticing?"

"I don't know yet, but we'll figure it out." He sighs. "We just have to take it one step at a time. Let's concentrate on getting the replica made first. The Stern Grove Festival is here." He circles a park on the map. "And the Bubble Car depot where you're going to make the exchange with Faye is in St. Francis Circle." He traces a path to a point at the edge of the park. "It shouldn't take you more than ten minutes to walk there—remember, the timing is important. You have to drop the key fob containing the mold and photographs in the return kiosk right away. Once I put the ring mold in the liquid nitrogen, it will harden the wax, but if it's in there for more than an hour, it will start to dissolve. And Faye will be waiting. She'll be disguised as a Bubble Car employee and will break into the kiosk to retrieve the key fob, but we don't want to risk her running into a real Bubble Car employee or anyone emptying the kiosk before she does."

"I know, I know." I turn the key fob over, examining the key emblem etched into it. A gift from Allard, it has a hollow interior and a seven-letter code that must be correctly arranged on the side roller bar to access the compartment. Faye already knows the password is "Justice." "Isn't a key fob kind of archaic?"

"Yeah, but the Bubble Cars kept getting hacked, so the city went old-school. The cars will only start if the key fob is present." He shakes his head. "I love it when technology breaks down. Maybe someday they'll see it our way."

"Maybe, but I'm not getting my hopes up," I say.

"Me neither," he says, still studying the map. "Have you decided how you're going to get pictures of the ring?"

"Yep—with this." I pull the 1950s Echo 8 Lighter Camera I borrowed from the Crypt—on a hunch it might be useful—out of my tool garter and flip it open. "It's a concert. She'll want to smoke, right? I'll be able to get up close when I light her herbs. Simple."

He squints at the lighter. "It's never as simple as you think. We don't have room for mistakes. Are you sure that thing will work?"

"Positive."

"Give it here." He waves it toward him.

"Why?" I cradle it to my chest.

"Just let me see it."

I hesitate.

"I'm not going to hurt it," he says, his eyes flashing.

"Fine." With a sigh, I give it to him.

He flicks the lighter. Nothing happens. He tries again. Nothing. Holding it up to the light, he examines it. "Did you put lighter fluid in it?"

Blood shoots to my cheeks, and I snatch it out of his hand. "Not yet. I was going to do it later."

"Mm-hmm..." He grins.

"Don't look so smug." I turn my back on him, willing my blush to fade.

"Why not? I just proved a point."

"Oh yeah? And what exactly is it?" I whip around. "And whatever it is, believe me, it's not the winning point."

"Bets, it's not a competition. I just proved you need me is all."

"Need you? *I* need you."

His eyes sparkle. "Yes."

"You're right. I do need you. I need you to realize you're not God's gift to thieves."

"I love it when you're angry."

"I love it when you're silent."

He laughs.

Behind me, the apartment door flies open. Kyran and Rayelle burst into the room, giggling.

"What's up with you two?" I ask, staring in shock at Kyran's grin. It changes his entire face—makes him almost approachable.

"This," Kyran says, and before I can blink, he tosses something tiny and gold at me.

Catching it, I examine the Byzantine-era ring that is eerily similar to Nicki's. The only difference is the blue stone is set with a round rim instead of prongs. "You stole this?"

"Yep. Heist complete," Kyran says.

Garrett peers over my shoulder. "Does it fit in the key fob case?"

Opening the case, I slip the ring inside. "Yep."

He takes the case from me, removing the Italian ring. "Faye can use this for size and weight when she replicates Nicki's ring. All the more reason to get the mold quickly. Is anybody looking for it?"

"Not yet," Kyran says. "It's somewhat-legally missing for forty-eight hours."

"How did you pull that off?" Garrett asks.

"Tell us everything," I say.

We move to the living room, and Garrett and I settle onto the couch, giving them the stage.

"We knew we needed to sneak into the basement archives to get the ring, so we timed the heist while there was a student art exhibit going on. Sophia disguised Rayelle so she looked thirteen, and we had her show up with an art project full of contraband items," Kyran says, spouting more words than I've ever heard from him.

"Balloons, birdseed, confetti, and glitter are forbidden inside the museum, so my project contained all of them." Rayelle exhales. "I didn't mess up. I've always been the outcast in my family, but I might actually be meant to do this!" She's practically glowing.

"While she was arguing with the guards about her project being 'art,' I picked one of their pockets. That gave us keys to the locker room and a pass card to the archive basement," Kyran says. "Years ago, the museum employees went on strike when they were asked to give their thumbprints because they were afraid of their information being hacked, so the museum doesn't use biometrics for anything. Once I was wearing a guard jacket and had a pass card, I walked right into the archives. Nobody questioned me. I knew from doing surveillance yesterday that I needed a request slip from a researcher to check out the ring, so I forged one from this guy named Charles Sweeney. He's head of acquisitions for the museum."

"The archivist, of course, wouldn't let him leave with the ring without calling up to Charles's assistant," Rayelle says.

"But I had called earlier pretending to be a curator who met Charles last week while he was visiting the Prado on his vacation to Madrid, and I said he gave me permission to borrow the ring," Kyran continues. "I knew Charles was on vacation by checking his Network, but that made his assistant trust me." He rolls his eyes. "When the archivist called, the assistant validated my story, they let me check out the ring for forty-eight hours, and I walked out with it."

"Wow," Garrett says.

"Allard wants us to give it back so no one comes looking for it," Rayelle says.

"Forty-eight hours is a tight turnaround…" I say.

"I wish we didn't have to give it back," Rayelle says, taking the ring from Garrett and sliding it onto her pinkie. "It's the first thing we ever stole together, Kyran. Maybe we should keep it. The museum won't miss it, will they?"

Kyran raises his eyebrows and examines the ring on her finger. "Dangerous," he says. "Nice."

She giggles.

"If Allard said to give it back, she has her reasons," I say, shooting Rayelle a we-need-to-talk stare.

"Yeah. We can't risk any mistakes. We'll make sure you get it back in time to return it," Garrett says. "Ellie, we'll need to coordinate a second dead drop with Faye to get this ring back, even if the replica isn't ready."

Kyran and Rayelle are still staring at the ring. An unseen force vibrates between them, and Garrett and I look at each other. An unspoken moment passes. He says what we both are thinking.

"Hey Kyran, I need to get a ring off a girl's finger and replace it with a replica without her noticing the switch. Any tips?"

"You came to the right guy." Kyran smiles and holds up Rayelle's hand. "We can use her to practice."

They huddle around the ring, and, satisfied Garrett has things under control, I put on my pink mask and goggles and slip out of the apartment in search of lighter fluid.

# Chapter Thirty-Eight

*March 20X6, San Francisco*

"You have your disguise, right?" Garrett asks as we weave between the picnic blankets sprawled across the park. The festival is packed with people enjoying the blue skies on this rare sunny day.

"Oh no." I come to a halt, grinning up at him. "I knew I forgot something."

He glares at me and keeps walking.

My jaw drops. "You're nervous," I say, catching up to him. "The great Beau Bradford…he's human after all. Don't worry." I lower my voice. "It's all right here." I pat the messenger bag slung across my body. My hair is piled on top of my head, and Rayelle painted a white fan across my forehead, punctuating the points with beads. It will only take seconds to pluck off the beads, tuck my hair under a blond wig, pull on the yellow poncho in my bag, and smear gold glitter over half of my face.

"Aren't you?" he asks.

"Human or nervous? You only get one answer."

"Would you be serious?"

"Why? Aren't you serious enough for the both of us?"

He shakes his head.

"Sorry." I relent. "I can't be serious. It's a nervous thing."

"That's good. That means you're ready. Nerves are useful—they keep you on your toes."

"Well, you can never be too prepared." I bat my eyelashes at him. "You have the wax, right?"

Elbowing me in the side, he smirks but keeps us moving, sidestepping a group of concertgoers wearing masquerade masks.

Up ahead, Nicki, Joanna, and Eric are centered directly in front of the stage, sitting at a table covered with a pink plaid tablecloth and dotted with mason jars containing white daisies.

"You made it!" Nicki, wearing a fringed tube top, bunny ears, and a stack of glowing neon bracelets, waves us forward.

As Adam/Eric/Nash—whoever he is—lifts the twine that separates Nicki's table from the crowd, I raise my eyebrows at the daisies, getting his message. *I'll never tell.* He catches my eye as I enter, and my heart thumps with possibility, but I remind myself he is—and always has been—no good. He may have been able to fool me at first, but never again.

"Love the ears," Garrett says, patting Nicki's head.

"Check out my tail." Turning around, she shakes her rear end. "It's for the Networks. You know how it is." She rolls her eyes. "But I'm so happy you're here, that we're all here. *And*...good news!" She puts an arm around my shoulders. "I got you on the list. Once you send in a hair sample, we'll know how long it will take to grow your kidneys. Eric can cut one today and send it up to the farm for DNA sequencing tomorrow if you want."

My eyes shoot to Garrett's. *I can't give a hair sample! They'd know everything about me...*

"You're incredible," he says, hugging Nicki. "How can I

ever thank you?"

"It makes me happy to help," she says. "No thanks needed."

He releases her, holding her at arm's length. "All the same, I'll think of something. Let me surprise you." I watch Garrett stare into her eyes, his lips curving up in a knowing smile, and she blushes, practically melting into him. She's putty in his hands, and my stomach turns.

"How can I say no to a surprise?" she says. "I'll let you."

"Good." Taking her left hand, he places his palm over the ring and squeezes. "I'll have to think of something extra special."

Behind us, Berkeley & the Brightside takes the stage. The crowd roars to life, and Joanna stands up and starts dancing on the table as they play the opening notes to their hit "Headshot." With a whoop, Nicki joins her, but I wait, watching Garrett seamlessly slip the wax mold into the canister hidden in his pocket. I'll fill the canister with liquid nitrogen and put it in the key fob when I change into my disguise, but the clock has already started. I need to move quickly and photograph Nicki's ring before the wax melts. Climbing onto the table, I join Nicki and Joanna.

The band plays straight from the first song into the next, and I raise my lighter to Nicki in question.

Her face lights up, and she pops open the bracelet containing the herbs.

A few minutes later, she's packed her pipe, and my heart stalls as she raises it to her lips with her right hand. *I should have remembered she wears the ring on her left hand and smokes with her right!* I can almost feel Garrett's "expect the unexpected" stare boring into the back of my head. Thinking fast, I pretend to have trouble getting the flame to catch, cupping my free hand to block the nonexistent breeze.

"It's kind of windy," I yell over the music. "Can you help?"

She lifts her left hand to shield the herbs, but what I need her to do is switch hands so I can get a good angle on the ring. I keep fiddling with the lighter, clicking away, figuring these photos will be better than nothing. "I actually think the breeze is coming from the other side. Maybe switch hands?"

"Why don't I light it myself?" she asks.

"No!" I scream too loudly and too forcefully. "I mean… this lighter is vintage. It's finicky. It's better if I do it."

"Why don't I help?" Garrett asks, climbing onto the table.

"It's okay. I've got it," I say, brushing him off.

I'm not sure, because he says it so quietly, but I think I hear him mutter, "Stubborn."

Blessedly, Nicki switches hands, giving me a perfect view of the ring. In the daylight, the stone appears amethyst, and I flick the lighter, snapping several pictures before allowing the flame to catch.

Out of the corner of my eye, I catch Garrett smirking, but I ignore him.

Nicki inhales deeply and offers me the herbs. I pretend to inhale, coughing out a puff of smoke before passing it along to Joanna. When it comes back my way, I pass. Feigning dizziness, I wait through a full song that seems to go on forever before announcing I need to use the restroom.

"I'll come with you," Eric/Adam/Nash says. "Maybe I can get that hair sample?"

"I'm not sure that's a good idea right now," I say, swaying, racking my brain for a way to thwart him. "I wouldn't want them to see herbs in my system."

"It's a DNA sequence—they won't know what you just smoked. But are you feeling okay? You look really pale," he says. "Let me make sure you can walk without collapsing."

"I don't want you to miss the show. I'll be fine."

"Let him go with you," Nicki says, cozying up to Garrett,

sitting so close she's practically in his lap. "I'd hate for something to happen to you."

Eric frowns at Nicki and Garrett but turns to me with a smile. "Come on."

Garrett catches my eye, and I realize he still needs to give me the canister with the ring mold. *Dammit.* I look wildly around for a solution, but then he casually slips a hand into his pocket and I feel the weight in mine. He must have passed it to me when I was lighting the herbs, though I didn't notice a thing. *Apparently, his practice with Kyran is paying off.* Allowing precious seconds to pass, I wait for him to tell Eric/Adam/Nash to stay, to offer to go with me, but he's absorbed in Nicki. She rests her head on his shoulder, and he snakes his arm around her waist. They laugh at some private joke, and I might as well not exist.

My heart thuds as time ticks by, and I can't wait for him any longer.

*I guess I'll have to take care of Adam/Eric/Nash— whoever—myself.*

# Chapter Thirty-Nine

*March 20X6, San Francisco*

"I thought I'd never get you alone," Eric/Adam/Nash says once we're out of earshot, his fingers circling my bicep.

*How many nights have I dreamed of seeing him again?* But not like this. His hands are like shackles.

"I can't believe you're here," he continues. "I thought you were dead."

"I could say the same about you," I mutter. Missing his Australian accent, with a sideways glance, I search his face for something recognizable — salt from a morning spent surfing — anything that will make him *my* Adam, but he remains a stranger. Fury that I was so easily duped bubbles to my lips, and I want answers. I stop walking. "Your real name is Nash?"

"Yes." He takes me in. "You don't know how long I've wanted to tell you that."

My throat aches, but I refuse to cry. "Was any of it real? Self-Awareness? Sam?"

He frowns. "Technically, I'm not allowed to answer that…"

Narrowing my eyes, I grit my teeth. "You just did." I

wriggle from his grasp and back away from him.

"You didn't let me finish." He catches my hand before I can escape, and holds me in place. "I know you want answers."

"I don't want to hear any more lies, that's for sure." My lips tremble.

"I totally owe you the truth…" He falls silent. Seconds pass, and, seeming to make up his mind, he takes a deep breath. "My first mission after my initiation was to steal your Book of Secrets."

My jaw drops. "*You* stole my book? But how? You were live on Deena's feed when my hotel room was broken into."

"I didn't physically steal it, but I knew where it was." He sighs, his eyes rolling skyward before returning to my face. "There are Disconnects everywhere, Ella. We had a contact on set. Do you remember Crystal Harrison?"

*Crystal knows Adam?* For the second time since he came back into my life, it's like the wind has been knocked out of me. *She stole my book?* My brain whirls.

"Why did you want my book?" I ask. "Who hired you?"

Shifting his weight, he wrinkles his nose. "That, I can't tell you."

"So much for the truth." Throwing his hand off, I move to stomp away, but he clasps my wrist, halting me.

"It was the people you'll work for once you're initiated. That's all I can say. But you'll see… I'm on your side. Ask me anything else. I'll be honest. Promise."

"Please stop touching me." I snatch my wrist away. "I won't run if you're going to give me answers."

He lets me go, and I take a step back to create distance between us.

"How did whoever hired you know about my book?" I ask, my hands on my hips. "I never took it out in public."

"You mean you thought you were invisible hiding under

dining room tables?" He laughs. "Corporates have computer chips in everything—they have cameras in their shoes. And you can imagine how valuable that information was to the Disconnects and Corporates alike. To have a list of who can and can't be trusted? Of their dirty little secrets?"

*Of course they had cameras in their shoes. I'm an idiot.*

"We had to get your book before the Corporates did—before President Madden did. They would have done anything to keep those secrets out of Disconnect hands, including ending your life. We had to protect you."

*President Madden wanted my book?* I shudder.

A parade of girls wearing colorful feathers bumps past us, and my internal clock ticks to life. *I don't have time for this. I have to get rid of him.* My head spinning, I move toward the restrooms. Nash matches my pace.

"And hooking up with Deena was a bonus?" I ask, wanting to run but not wanting to alert Nash that I'm on a mission.

"Necessary. She really was blackmailing me, and I needed to keep my Influencer status until I was sure we had your book. Believe me when I say I had no interest in her beyond that."

I ignore the hope in my chest that some shred of our past was real, that I wasn't totally gullible. "Why were you in Tahoe, then? You had the book. You could have left, gone back to being Nash—or whoever you are."

We arrive at the restrooms, and the realization that I *really* don't know who I'm talking to ripples through me. One misstep and I could ruin Garrett's heist. I press my lips together.

"That's the thing." He steps closer to me, tucking a stray strand of my pale blue hair behind my ear. "What I didn't count on was falling for you." His mouth lifts at one corner, causing his left eye to crinkle, and I glimpse the old Adam.

My insides quiver, and I steel myself against him. *I am not falling for this BS...*

"I knew from your book you were curious about disconnecting, and I was going to confess, ask you to come with me. But you beat me to it... If our plan worked, I would have told you everything. I was on the boat, coming to get you...but then"—he swallows—"it all went up. We got blown backward. I was farthest from the blast, so I survived—barely."

It's too much to comprehend. As I sift through the information, realization seeps through me. "You read it," I whisper. Sucking in air, I grasp the tiger's eye I wear at my throat, simultaneously aware that Garrett would kill me if he knew I was wearing it. *Everyone has a tell.*

He smiles down at me. "Most of it. Crystal thought I might find the parts about me entertaining. She genuinely likes you. She'd be very happy if there was still hope for you and me."

"Well, she can forget that." I shake my head. "I thought she was my friend. I thought *you* were my friend. But you were both using me."

"No. The situation is complicated, for sure, but your first instincts about me weren't wrong. Despite how it may seem, I've always wanted to protect you. So has Crystal."

"What do you mean, my instincts?" I say slowly.

"Crystal told me about your talents...and those DNA scans in your book are pretty interesting."

I close my eyes, remembering my parents showing me the scans, my joy when they said I was meant to act—like them—and then how I shoved them into my book for safekeeping because the scans were printed on actual paper and I couldn't bear to throw them away. *But those scans also reveal the truth about my birth... Who else knows? My parents think they've buried the past to secure their future, but whose hands is their fate really in...?* Despite the warm day, I shiver. Even though

I shouldn't care what happens to them, I can't fully erase the desire to be their prized little girl.

"Where is the book now?" I ask, opening my eyes.

"I don't know. Honestly." He holds his hands up as if that could prove his innocence. "Crystal was my contact, and she handed it off to whoever hired her. But don't worry. It's in Disconnect hands."

The sun beats down on my back, and sweat beads on my forehead. Remembering the wax in my pocket, I know I need to hurry and inch toward the shade of the restroom. "What do you want from Nicki?" I ask, backing away from him.

"I'm trying to protect her, just like I was trying to protect you. What about you and Garrett? What do you want?"

"It's classified."

He considers me before closing the distance between us. "Fair enough. Listen, Ella, I don't know why you're here, and your presence—especially Garrett's—complicates things for me. I admit I'm no match for his charm, but I'm glad *you're* here. I want us to be friends, Ella. And to prove it, I'll send a fake hair sample for you."

"I'd appreciate that, but I don't know if we can be friends," I say. *All I know is I need to get out of here. Now.* "Can I have a few minutes to myself? Please? This is a lot to process. Could you go back and tell everyone I went home to lay down?"

"If you need to lay down, let me make sure you get home okay."

"Adam—Nash. Whoever you are. Seriously. I can't think with you around. I'm going to the restroom."

He nods but refuses to understand. "I'll be here when you come out. Now that I've found you again, I'm not going to let you go."

"Fine. Wait here." I disappear inside, slamming the metal door shut behind me. Once I'm in a stall, I pour the nitrogen over the wax, which fortunately still holds a perfect impression of Nicki's ring. After slipping the eight-millimeter film images into the second canister with the stolen Italian ring, I stuff everything into the key fob. Changing into my disguise and taking extra time to unclasp my tiger's eye necklace and stuff it into my garter, I climb out the window, escaping before Adam notices I'm missing.

# Chapter Forty

*March 20X6, San Francisco*

"You're okay." Garrett runs his fingers through his hair and crosses the apartment to me as soon as I walk in the door. Wrapping his arms around me, he rests his chin on my head.

"You were worried?" I say to his chest. It's all I can do not to melt against him.

He releases me and holds me at arm's length. "When Nash came back and said you went home to lay down, I didn't know what to think. I *hoped* you were able to ditch him, but I couldn't be sure. I don't trust that guy. I should never have left you alone with him."

*No kidding.* "You had Nicki to deal with." I shrug him off and pretend seeing them together didn't bother me. "And I can hold my own. It's done. Dead drop complete." Slumping onto the couch, I pull the wig off my head and loosen my real hair, letting the blue waves fall to my shoulders.

His lips curl into a crooked smile and he sits next to me. "How did you get rid of him?"

"I didn't. I went to the bathroom and slipped out the

window. He wouldn't leave my side, but he did offer to send in a fake hair sample."

Garrett's eyes narrow. "Why would he do that?"

"I don't know." I shimmy out of my poncho. "Maybe because I'm with you?"

He shakes his head. "I doubt it. He usually has his own agenda, and it doesn't include helping me."

I cock my head to the side. "He complimented you, though. He says he's no match for your charm."

Garrett lets out a bitter laugh. "I wouldn't say that. I always wanted to be him. I learned from the best." He eyes me up and down. "How did you get him to tell you that? It seems like a lot of information to give a thief he just met…"

"Maybe he was feeling chatty," I say, thinking fast. "He must know I'm from Keystone if I'm with you."

"Maybe." He raises his eyebrows, but fortunately he seems to buy my logic. "What did you tell him?"

"I didn't tell him anything. He asked what I wanted with Nicki, and I said it was classified. He said he was here to protect her… He doesn't seem to be after the ring. Wouldn't he have stolen it already if he was?"

"Probably." He stands and paces the length of the room. "But I don't know what else he could want, unless he's trying to create some kind of alliance…" He comes to a stop, his fingers drumming on the back of the couch. "Maybe Simon has access to some technology we don't know about, or it has something to do with the kidney farm…"

"Who are the people we work for once we're initiated?" I ask. "That's who he said he worked for."

Garrett snorts. "There's no one person. There are hundreds of collectors out there and also different factions of Disconnects—some with their own personal agendas. He could work for any of them. I don't know whose side he's on."

"But you used to be friends?"

He comes around the couch and sits on the coffee table, facing me. "A long time ago. We grew up together, and we were close as kids, even though he's a couple years older than me. He's a legacy, too. His mom is one of the greatest thieves of all time—"

My stomach twists, and I know who she is before he says it.

"—Crystal Harrison. She was an Influencer who disconnected to Keystone when she was pregnant with him, and his dad was a Corporate crook, for sure."

I'm too sick to respond.

He changes the subject. "Anyway, I think I've figured out how to switch the rings." He hands me a brochure.

"*Ring Around the Rosie*?" Grateful for the distraction, I focus on the glittery gold letters being repeatedly spelled out, as if written by a ghost hand, across the brochure. "It's a little on the nose, isn't it?"

Pursing his lips, he ignores me. "It's a traveling play—a Bubble Car tour of the city. At every stop, there are performances, and you interact with the actors. I thought it might be a good way to make the transfer. We could plant Chloe in another car. Once we get the ring, we can pass it to her, and she'll drop it for us."

I hand him back the brochure. "Will she help? Won't she be jealous of you and Nicki?"

"Why would she be jealous?"

"She's your girlfriend. If you were my boyfriend, I wouldn't be very happy watching you flirt with another girl."

Resting his forearms on his thighs, he leans toward me until his eyes are level with mine. "If I were your boyfriend, you would know you were the only one. You'd feel the difference between what's real and what's part of my job. I wouldn't leave any room for doubt."

My heart thunders in my ears.

"Besides," he says. "She's not my girlfriend." He sits back, blessedly giving me some much-needed air and folding his arms over his chest.

My lips part. "What? But I thought—"

"Don't believe everything you hear."

"Or see? You're always together."

"Are we? Seems to me I'm always with *you*." He raises his eyebrows.

I roll my eyes, hoping to distract him from the blood flooding my cheeks. "Heist aside."

He shrugs. "Chloe has her own agenda. She likes to make it look like we're a couple because she thinks being 'in' with my family will give her better placement in the field down the road—at least that's why I *think* she does it—we've never talked about it. I go along with her because it makes my life easier. There are fewer distractions and less drama if I'm taken. I've known all the girls at Keystone—except for you, of course—since birth. It saves me from having to have the 'you're like my sister' talk over and over again."

"And technically I *am* your sister."

"Good point, Bets." He laughs. "Anyway, we can trust Chloe."

"Are you sure?"

"One hundred percent."

"Okay… If you think she can be more than a decoy…"

"She's much more than a decoy." Standing, he resumes pacing. "As for *you*, since you're buddies now—and you're totally his type—you be Nash's date. Distract him so he doesn't notice the switch."

I frown. "And what exactly is his 'type'?"

"Short and sweet." He winks.

I glare at him. "Aren't you missing a step? How are you going to get the ring off Nicki's finger?"

"I haven't figured that out yet." He comes to a stop, staring out the balcony doors. "I'm working on it."

"You could drug her," I suggest. "Plant something in her herbs?"

He shakes his head. "I'm not comfortable with that. If she acts out of character, it would tip Nash off. Besides, she might think something was up once she came to."

"What about when she's sleeping?"

Turning to face me, he folds his arms over his chest. "There's no way Nash is letting me have a sleepover."

"Valid point." I bask in a rush of relief.

He closes his eyes, seemingly talking to himself. "No, we have to do it in plain sight…"

We fall silent, and I rack my brain, remembering my old life and how I spent my time. An idea pops into my head, and I sit up straight. "What about a manicure? They lotion your fingers during the hand massage… What if we got her nails done before the performance? If the person doing the massage could switch the rings without her noticing…"

He opens his eyes. "It's not a bad idea, but it would take skill, sleight of hand, flexibility… Could Kyran pose as a manicurist?"

"He could switch the rings, but is he any good at painting nails? Maybe Sophia could help?"

Behind him, a pigeon coos on the windowsill. Garrett opens the window and picks up the bird, untying a ribbon around its leg.

"We should find out," he says. Releasing the pigeon, he opens the small velvet pouch the bird delivered. "The rings are ready." He places the replica in my hand. It looks exactly like Nicki's ring.

"Hey guys," Rayelle says, walking in behind me.

I grab her hand as she passes the couch, examining her orange lacquered nails. "Did you do these yourself? They look professional."

"Of course. I used to give manicures to my mom and sisters all the time. When you're the clumsy one in a family of circus performers, you find a way to be useful."

"Did they wear chips?" I ask.

She glances at Garrett. "No. That's against Keystone Code."

"It would be helpful if they were chipped," he says, smiling to put her at ease.

She grins and lowers her voice. "I may not be the best at programming most things, but one thing I can code is a manicure."

My eyes meet Garrett's, and he nods.

"I'll go invite Nicki to a manicure and a show," he says. Putting in his AMPs, he heads to the balcony, shutting the door behind him.

He casually leans against the balcony railing, totally engrossed in whatever version of Nicki his AMPs are seeing. The new Chloe information hot on my mind, I can't help but wonder if his interest in Nicki is real. *Ugh. Why do I care?*

"I wish Kyran looked at me the way Garrett looks at you." Rayelle sighs, startling me.

"How? Like you're an annoying fly he wants to swat?"

She laughs. "That's how he looks when you *are* looking. When you aren't, he's—I don't know—protective."

Goose bumps race up my arms. "Probably because he's afraid I'm going to ruin his heist."

"Are you kidding? He trusts you. He's given you a ton of responsibility. So far, all Kyran has let me do is be a decoy. I've tried everything to make him notice me—been his buddy, his cheerleader, worn tight clothes, loose clothes, orange nails—and nothing. Except for the day of the heist when he actually hugged me, it's like I'm nonexistent."

"You do always seem, I don't know, a little over-the-top when he's around. Like you're trying to shine really bright…"

"He makes me nervous."

"I understand, but maybe try just being yourself?"

She frowns. "I don't know if nerdy contortionists will ever be his thing."

"Rayelle, if he's not into contortionists, he's an idiot."

She giggles.

"All set," Garrett says, the sliding glass door closing behind him. "While I was talking to Nicki, I was thinking about how we can plant Rayelle at the salon—"

"Good to know Nicki commands your undivided attention," I say, a bit relieved that he isn't more obsessed with her.

"It's called multitasking, Bets. Even the smallest minds are capable of it." He playfully pats my hair. "Maybe Rayelle gives freelance hand massages."

"Is that legal?" I ask.

He ignores me.

"We'll find a salon where she can offer massages for an extra charge as long as she splits the proceeds with the shop owners. That way she won't have to program the nails. Fewer variables. Rayelle may have to massage some strangers, but if she leaves soon after we do—change of plans—she can hand the ring off to Chloe, who can pass it to you during the performance, Bets. That way we don't risk Nicki recognizing Rayelle. And in the meantime, we'll plant our exit story and make sure Nicki is comfortable with the new ring."

"And you want me to hold the ring through the rest of the performance?" I ask, my palms sweating at the thought.

"Yes." He dismisses me. "Are you up for the challenge, Rayelle?"

"Absolutely." She grins, her eyes bunching up.

"Let's start practicing, then," Garrett says. "We don't have a lot of time. The last *Ring Around the Rosie* performance is tomorrow night. Bets, you be Nicki."

"So soon?" My heart leaps into my throat as I slip the replica ring onto my left middle finger. It fits perfectly.

He shrugs. "The sooner the better. The quicker we get the ring, the less chance of our covers being blown, and who knows when Simon plans to launch his Quinn update. The quicker we get the ring, the more time whoever is going to steal the algorithm will have to prepare."

"This is so exciting," Rayelle says. "Never say live." Grinning, she puts the Italian ring on, turning the stone so it faces her palm.

"Always say die," I respond, holding up my hand for her to massage.

Garrett arches an eyebrow.

"Just go with it," I say.

"Always say die," he repeats with a slow smile.

My insides flutter, and I press my lips together.

Rayelle lotions my hand and begins the massage. I immediately feel the ring move.

"Stop. I felt it."

She tries again.

"Felt it."

And again.

Garrett tries to teach her everything Kyran taught him, and we practice for hours until, at some point, we pass out.

As the first rays of sun light the sky, Kyran arrives.

Laying snuggled on the couch with my head on Garrett's shoulder and my arm flung across his chest, I crack my stiff neck, then bolt upright. Rubbing my bleary eyes, I get my bearings. Rayelle is asleep in a chair, and Garrett stirs, sitting up beside me. I scramble to create as much distance between us as possible.

"What happened?" I ask.

"We fell asleep," he says, running his fingers through his hair, seemingly unfazed. "Hey, Kyran. We could use your help. We only have a few hours to teach Rayelle how to get Nicki's ring off her finger…"

Waking Rayelle, we all four huddle around the coffee table, and I offer my hand up for lotion again. And again. And again.

As the day wears on, dread seeps through me.

*We're never going to get this.*

# Chapter Forty-One

*March 20X6, San Francisco*

"I'm so excited," Nicki says, surrendering a hand to the manicurist. "I've been wanting to go to *Ring Around the Rosie*, but my dad thinks it's too dangerous."

"What's so dangerous about it?" I ask, hyperaware of Nash's presence behind me. He's sitting next to Garrett in the salon lounge, but there might as well be a wall between them the way they're ignoring each other. Scanning the room for an exit, I plot my escape should I need one. My feet are coated in a goopy mask and stuffed in plastic bags, and I picture myself slipping and falling on my butt, my pink dress flipping up to reveal my tool garter, should I need to run. It's not an ideal strategy, and I wiggle my toes, impatient for them to be free.

"Nothing. He just doesn't like me going out in public," Nicki says. "He'd keep me locked in our VR room if he could."

I eye the ring on Nicki's finger, watching the manicurist remove the acrylic chips from her nails and start filing.

"How did you get him to let you come, then?" I ask as my manicurist finishes filing my nails and holds them up for my approval. Rayelle appears over her shoulder, her eyes visible above the white mask she wears but disguised with matching black starbursts.

"Massage?" she asks.

My heart knocks so loud in my chest I'm sure everyone can hear it. Before we left, Rayelle managed to get the ring off my finger a few times without me feeling it. Her success rate was nowhere near 100 percent, but it had to be good enough. We were out of time.

"No, thank you." I nod my approval at the manicurist, and she glues my chips on. "I wish my joints weren't so sore," I say as an aside to Nicki. "Everything hurts."

"You're going to feel a million times better once you get the transplant. I promise," she says.

Rayelle moves on to Nicki, and I hold my breath.

"And to answer your question, my dad doesn't know where I'm going."

"Massage?" Rayelle asks.

Nicki doesn't reply but offers up her hands. Rayelle squirts lotion onto the hand without the ring.

"I told him I was going to dinner with Eric," Nicki continues. "Dad trusts Eric, but we still have to show up at this stupid party he's hosting at our downtown penthouse by nine."

"What about your bodyguards?" Garrett asks. "They must be able to track you. Won't they tell your dad where we are?"

Nicki looks over her shoulder at him. "Not since Eric caught one of them making out with my publicist. Now they're eating out of my hands. Besides, now that I'm getting new nails, I'll have new tracking. They won't be able to find me."

"How did you catch them?" I ask Eric.

"I was in the right place at the right time," he says. "They were in the backseat of Nicki's dad's Corvette."

"My dad collects old cars. It's such a waste of space," Nicki says.

Rayelle switches hands.

I can barely hear the conversation over my pounding heart. Sweating, I keep focused on Nicki's face, waiting for her to snatch her hand back and accuse Rayelle of tampering with her ring.

"I have a thing for old cars, too," Eric/Nash says. "It's awesome how they were built before computers. And since gas engines are illegal, her dad's collection is totally contraband. It's so cool."

"Dad's collection isn't illegal. It's above the law," Nicki says. "He's one of the few people on earth permitted to drive a gas car."

"I was in the garage seeing if we could borrow his '67 Lamborghini Miura," Eric/Nash says. "And there they were, steaming up the windows—"

"Eric is not above the law," Nicki interjects. "It *is* illegal for him to drive my dad's cars."

Eric/Nash smiles. "What's wrong with a little bit of danger? I like to keep things interesting, but not so interesting you could get hurt."

"You don't have to tell me twice," Nicki says. "I *love* danger." She says it to Garrett.

I wait for his reaction, for that flirtatious smile to spread across his lips, for his laser eyes to pierce her like they always do me, but all he does is nod.

Rayelle places Nicki's hand on the table and walks away. *Is it done?*

I suck in my breath. The manicurist applies Nicki's nail chips, and I check to see if the new ring is in place. It's identical to the original, so I can't be sure, but in my periphery Rayelle straightens a vase of flowers. When she turns to her next customer, a white daisy is front and center.

Relief floods me, and I exhale as my manicurist shows me my rainbow-colored nails—ten little computer-chip beacons that will broadcast my whereabouts to anyone who cares to find me. They are heavy on my fingertips, and I can't wait to rip them off.

"You're going to love having chips," Nicki says. "I can't believe you've gone this long without them."

"Between the chips and the kidney, you've changed my world," I say. "How can I ever thank you?"

She reaches out and squeezes my forearm. "No thanks needed. Just be my friend."

Sickness rises in my throat as I deliver the lie. "Friends."

When our manicures are finished, a Bubble Car arrives and takes us to Fisherman's Wharf for the start of the *Ring Around the Rosie* performance. Eric/Nash and I sit facing Garrett and Nicki. His leg presses against mine, and I'm highly aware of his smoldering presence at my side.

"When we get out to participate in the show, remember to stick together," Eric says as the car weaves its way through the streets. "I wouldn't want anyone getting lost." His eyes remain on my face as he says it, and I wonder if he suspects something.

"I won't be letting this one out of my sight," Garrett says, taking Nicki's hand in his and covering the ring with his fingers.

"Anywhere she goes, I go," Eric says. His voice is ice.

"This is a great way to see the city," I say, cutting the tension. "I'm glad we're getting a little tour before we have to leave." I shoot Garrett a look, reminding him we need to plant our exit story, but he's busy whispering something to Nicki that makes her laugh. My foot jerks forward, and I want to kick him, but I pull it back before it connects with his shin.

"You're leaving?" Nicki straightens. "When?"

"I didn't want to tell you until later because I didn't want it to ruin tonight," Garrett says with a micro-glare at me. "But Stanford asked me to come early to work on a top-secret project, and I have to go. It's a once-in-a-lifetime opportunity. We leave tomorrow."

"Oh no," she moans. "We have to make tonight last, then. Will you come to my dad's party with me?"

His lips stretch into a smile. "I wouldn't miss it. Ouch!" His eyes assault me as my foot hits the target it was craving earlier.

"Sorry," I say, keeping my voice innocent. "It's a little cramped in here. I needed to stretch."

"You should come to the party, too, Betsy," Nicki says.

"You can be my date." Nash slips his arm around my waist, and I curl into him, pretending I'm into him for Garrett's benefit, but mostly I'm still disgusted that I fell for his lies and want to push him away.

"Sounds fun," I say, dying to peek at Garrett but keeping my eyes on Nash, a sweet smile plastered on my face.

A voice fills the car.

*"The story begins, as many stories do, with a ghost. Peer into the fog. See her rising out of the mist."*

Outside, the sun sets beyond the wharf, and a girl appears, dancing on the sand, her tattered dress swirling around her, whipping at her legs in the breeze.

*"Ring-around-the rosie, A pocket full of posies,"*

The ghost is joined by two girls in similar dresses. They join hands, swinging in a circle as the voice chants, *"Ashes, ashes..."*

The lights from the wharf shimmer through their transparent skin, and, though I know the Bubble Car's glass is augmented, goose bumps race up my arms all the same.

*"It's rumored her lover was being kept at Alcatraz for a crime he didn't commit. She and her sisters were worshipers of*

*the Rosy Cross. They were clairvoyants who could access the Akashic records—the experiences and desires of every earthly creature since time began. They had the power to control their etheric selves.*

*"Though she was a Compassionate One, who had advanced beyond the cycle of rebirth, it wasn't enough to save her. It is common belief that she drowned trying to swim to him, her beloved. That is a lie. She was murdered. But to truly understand her death, to learn who had the power to extinguish a light so bright, we must experience her life."*

The lights on the wharf go dark, and the Bubble Car glides forward. It's a short drive to the next stop.

"If I had a special power, I'd want it to be clairvoyance," Nicki says.

"Not me. I'd want to read minds," Eric says. "To hear what the person next to me is thinking. Not enough people speak their thoughts these days."

I keep staring out the window, refusing to let him get to me.

Garrett remains silent, but when I sneak a glance at him, his eyes are flitting back and forth between me and Nash, like he's trying to figure out our connection.

The last thing I want is for Garrett to know Nash and I have a past, to think I've been lying to him, for him to stop trusting me. Regretting trying to make Garrett jealous, I scoot away from Nash.

We arrive at the top of Lombard Street. The city lights sparkle below us, beyond the cobblestone street's twists and turns.

*"The night they met, there was an earthquake. Even the earth was moved by the power of their connection. But first, they danced."*

The car doors open, revealing the girl dancing in a rose-colored drop-waist dress under strings of multicolored lights. She's now portrayed by a real person, her amber curls peeking out from a red hat that conceals half her face. Behind her, a band appears with trumpets, trombones, and banjos playing a jazzy tune, their rollicking music contagious. More dancers fill the street, luring audience members out of their cars.

A guy sweeps me into his arms, leading me in a swinging circle. I'm so busy concentrating on not getting my feet tangled with his, I immediately lose sight of Garrett. The dancer twirls me around and transfers me to another partner. We keep circling, switching partners and hands in an elaborate do-si-do, until Chloe and I cross paths. When our hands connect, she slips something small and round into mine. Without making eye contact, I pass it from my right hand to my left and slip it into my skirt pocket. In that same moment, someone grabs me by the waist.

My breath catches in my throat.

"Dance with me," Nash says, spinning me to face him. He leads us to the edge of the crowd. "You're leaving? Did you get what you came for?"

The ring is heavy in my pocket, and I feign innocence, my guard up. "I don't know what you're talking about."

"You're very mysterious," he says, holding me close. "We don't have much time, so I'm going to come right out and say what I'm thinking. Run away with me."

"Have you lost your mind?" I sputter.

"You have a cache, right? I know you do," he says without pause. "Believe me, whatever you're up to is going to go wrong. He's no good."

I find Garrett in the crowd, dancing with the ghost girl.

"We could make our old dreams come true," he says.

"Except I don't know who you are," I say, my eyes still on Garrett. In my heart I know I can't leave him. *I want to see the heist through.* I pretend that's the only reason.

"You don't know who he is, either."

His hands are hot on my back.

"I'm Nash Harrison," he says. "I know that doesn't mean anything, but I want to tell you everything."

*He played me just like he's playing Nicki. His journal that first day in Self-Awareness, touch being his favorite sense—it was all so he could make me feel connected to him. Social engineering. I get it now. I have no reason to believe anything he says. Trust no one.*

I push him away. "My old dreams are dead. I'm happy. Safe."

"You aren't safe anywhere. Whitney and Jeff—they don't want to rule just Keystone. They want to rule the world. The time will come when you'll have to decide whose side you're on." He pulls me to his chest and whispers in my ear, "Ella. I never stopped thinking about you. The circumstances we met under were out of my control. There are bigger things at play than you and me. I don't expect you to believe me, and you don't have to decide now, but if you ever need me, I'll make sure you can find me."

Just then, I'm whisked away by another dancer. For a moment Nash's pleading eyes hold mine, and I stare back over the dancer's shoulder. Fearing his speech was a ploy to pickpocket me, I feel for the ring. It's still nestled in my dress's hot pink skirt, and I exhale relief, but then my hand connects with something else. I pull out a folded paper note and immediately shove it back in my pocket.

When I look up again, Nash is gone.

"It's good to see you, Scarlet Spy," the guy I'm dancing with says, and I realize it's Stewart.

Grinning, I hug him. He hugs me back, quickly guiding me to a different Bubble Car than the one I arrived in. Whispering "never say live," he gestures me inside to where

Garrett is waiting.

"Always say die," I quietly reply, the knowledge that there's been a change of plan inserting itself in my brain.

As I get in, I see Nicki duck into a car with Eric/Nash. Behind me, the actors start screaming "Earthquake!" and through the Bubble Car windows, the street trembles. The string lights flicker, and the girl in the red hat falls to the ground. A trombone player throws down his instrument and shields her as the houses crumble around them.

Stewart closes the car door, and Garrett raises his finger to his lips, gesturing me silent.

"I hate to miss the rest, but Betsy looks terrible. Like, worse than usual," he says, his focus on the virtual world only his AMPs can see.

I roll my eyes.

"The sickness came on really fast," he continues. "I think I'd better take her home. But you and Eric should stay. Enjoy the rest of the show…" He falls silent, listening. "Yeah, I don't think I'll make it to the party. I should stay with her. But I'll make it up to you. Maybe we can have breakfast tomorrow before I go? Just the two of us?" Again, he pauses before saying, "Great. I'll pick you up at eight." As soon as he's done talking, he takes the AMPs out of his eyes and chucks them out the window. "Success?" he asks, finally looking at me.

"It's right here." Lightly tapping my pocket, I follow his lead, wiping the AMPs out of my eyes and throwing them outside, too.

"Good."

"Where do we drop it? I'm exhausted." I blink my tired eyes, blissfully happy to be AMP-free.

"We don't." He grins and pulls a folded piece of paper out of his pocket. "You'd better wake up because our night is just beginning. We have an algorithm to steal."

# Chapter Forty-Two

*March 20X6, San Francisco*

My jaw drops. "*We* have to steal the algorithm?" I ask, heart thudding. "We got the ring. We're not done?"

"Nope. Word came down from our undercover contacts that Simon plans to launch his Quinn update tomorrow—two weeks earlier than planned—so we need to get the algorithm tonight. If we pull this off, it'll be the biggest Initiation Heist in history. We'll win the first battle in the war over the Super Brain by shutting down Quinn and keeping people from uploading their minds into the Simulation. We'll be legends." He unfolds the paper into a large rectangle, studying it.

"Legends? What happened to 'if we know, it's enough'?" My eyes are saucers. "I don't need to be a legend."

"You may not have a choice if you don't get rid of those nails." He glances at my hands before returning his concentration to the paper. "You're going to leave a trail right to us, and then you'll be remembered for botching the heist that almost saved history. If we fail, if we get caught, we'll end up in jail, but worse, Simon and Madden will succeed in uploading minds into their database, and humanity may not be able to come back from that."

My nerves stretch taut at the thought that I could be our undoing, and, scowling at him, I chew on my thumbnail, trying to loosen the glue, which would be much easier to do if my hands weren't shaking so much. "You mean *I'll* end up in jail. The Disconnects will rescue you—their 'best and brightest'—I'll probably be left to rot or get sucked up by the Super Brain." My thumbnail lifts. Positive it's ripping my real nail off with it, I grit my teeth and toss it out the window.

"I wouldn't go without you, Ellie. Promise. We're a team. We're in this together."

"If we're a team, why don't you try doing something helpful, then, like choking on your tongue?" I mutter. "Or helping me?" Stealing myself against more finger-torture, I get to work prying off my index fingernail.

"Glad you asked. Already done. I had Stewart hack your manicure and deactivate it as soon as we left the salon," he says, biting back a smile. "Less risk that way."

Dropping my hands to my sides, I slump against the seat. "And you're just sitting there watching me rip my nails off? Do you know how much this hurts?" I raise all ten fingers to him in defiance.

"I was testing your dedication. You passed."

"I hate you."

His lips twitch. "That's probably not the last time I'll hear that tonight." He shows me the paper he's been analyzing. "This is the floor plan to Simon's Menlo Park house. It maps the obstacles we have to pass to get to the medieval jewelry box Simon keeps the algorithm in."

"Where did you get this?" As I study the illustrations, adrenaline courses through me, clearing my sinuses.

"Harbor was one of the dancers. She slipped it into my pocket."

"A shotgun-shell wall? A fog blaster? Footstep detector? How are we supposed to get past those?" Exhaling slowly, I try to keep from hyperventilating.

"Everyone else already has the answers—don't you see? We have to work as a team."

"As a class?" My eyebrows shoot up. "What happened to 'trust no one'? We're relying on Liam? On Harbor?"

"Yep." He shrugs.

Lips parted, I shake my head. "We're doomed."

The car drops us off behind a café in the Mission District. Garrett goes straight to a pale-yellow BMW with blank black license plates parked in the alley. He circles the car, searching for a key.

"Would you hurry up?" I whisper, my insides quaking, certain someone is going to come around the corner any second and arrest us.

Kneeling in front of the passenger door, he takes out his half-diamond pick and makes quick work of the lock. The door swings open with a creak, and I jump.

"How about you relax?" he says. "Get in."

Unable to move my quivering legs, I ignore him, my mind swirling down a rabbit hole of possible disaster scenarios. *We're going to get arrested…or shot…they'll find out I'm really Ella… Is that what my instincts are telling me?* I'm too freaked out to trust myself. "Will this thing even run?" I finally ask. "It looks like it belongs in a museum."

"It was probably stolen from one. Check the tire." He points to a key drawn in chalk on the rubber wheel. "Now would you get in?" Gripping my arm, he drags me to the car and deposits me inside.

"Aren't you nervous?" I ask, slamming the heavy door with a loud bang.

"Of course I am," he says, getting into the driver's seat. "But I'm using my nerves to keep me moving." Grabbing a tool bag from the backseat, he hammers a screwdriver into the ignition and turns it like a key. "You're not into inconspicuous, are you?" he continues, not looking at me.

"Sorry, the door weighs, like, a million pounds. It's impossible to close gently." Folding my arms over my chest, I hug myself, attempting to pull it together.

"That's not what I meant." He unscrews the panels above and below the steering column, and removes them, before using the screwdriver to point at my puffy pink skirt.

"It was a special occasion. I had to dress the part," I say, smoothing the shimmery fabric over my thighs. "I didn't know we were going to end up breaking and entering. Can't you hot-wire any faster?"

"I'm going as fast as I can." Sucking in his cheeks, he locates two red wires, cuts both, and strips the ends. "And your dress should be a lesson. Always be prepared." He shoves the tool bag toward me. "Luckily, whoever planted the car for us thought ahead for you."

*Of course he had the foresight to wear all black.* I frown and dig through the bag, finding my catsuit and mask. My eyes widen. "Where did they get this? Did they go through my stuff?"

"Is it yours?" He twists the wires together.

"Yes."

"Then yes. They went through your stuff." Pulling up two brown wires, he cuts them and strips the ends. "And you better hurry up and change." He touches the two wires together, and the car rumbles to life.

I scramble into the backseat, crouching low as he drives out of the alley. Wiggling out of my dress, I stuff it into the bag, trying to cover myself with it as I stretch on the tight suit.

"No peeking. Nothing to see here." I catch his eye in the rearview mirror as I zip up the suit as quickly as my jittery hands will let me.

"Tell me about it." He arches an eyebrow.

I elbow the back of his seat, hard.

He laughs.

Merging onto the freeway, he cuts into the line of driverless cars headed toward Menlo Park as I climb into the front seat.

With a nod of approval, he tosses me a black kohl pencil to start disguising my face, but I don't need it. I slip on my mask. Its pressure across my forehead helps to center me, and I close my eyes, wrapping my head around what we're about to do. "How long until we get there?" I ask.

"About half an hour, but I'm aiming for twenty minutes."

*Okay. That gives us time. I'll feel better if we have a plan.* Breathing deep, I slow my racing heart.

The car skids left, and my eyes fly open. "Talk about inconspicuous," I say as he speeds along, weaving in and out of cars. "You don't think we stand out in this car? We're the only ones manually driving."

"Nobody is paying attention. Trust me."

"Trust no one," I retort. On alert for anything that could get us arrested, I peer at the rows of Bubble Cars on either side of us and check the side mirror for flashing lights. The people in the other cars stare with glazed eyes at whatever reality their windows are displaying. They could care less about us.

"Why don't you get busy studying that floorplan?" he says.

"Unless you want to drive?" Taking his hands off the wheel, he gestures for me to take over.

"Would you watch the road?" I screech. The car veers over a rumble strip, sending my heart into my throat. "I don't know how to drive."

He retakes the wheel. "Really? Not even a tractor? They didn't teach you that on the farm?"

"We had self-driving tractors. Nobody knows how to drive except for old people and Disconnects."

"Well, I'll have to teach you someday."

"No, thank you."

"Seriously. You need to know how to drive. Old cars don't have computers—they can't be tracked—they're your secret weapon. When we get back to Keystone, we're having a driving date."

Butterflies flutter to life in my stomach, but I tell myself it's because we're about to break into Simon's house. Concentrating on the map, I pretend I didn't hear him. "According to this, the house is programmed to recognize Simon. The alarms only all turn off when he's present, but each security feature can be deactivated remotely in case of an emergency. Our classmates' heists were to figure out how to disarm each alarm. Stewart and Liam will be in a van in the woods. They'll decode the transmissions from our classmates when each security feature is disabled." I put the map down, trying to comprehend the scope of the plans already in place. "How are they transmitting?"

"Probably through ham radio walkie-talkies. They'll use radio frequencies and keystone code. Even if someone intercepts the code, we should have the algorithm before they decipher it. Timing is everything. Only one security feature can be down at a time, and only for long enough to get past it. The systems will think it's a test if they reactivate before the next one turns off. Nicki said if they all go down at once, Simon gets notified."

"When did she tell you that?"

"After the Stern Grove Festival. She took me to her parents' penthouse in the city. That's how the systems worked there, so it's probably the same for his Menlo Park house, too."

My heart stalls, and I bite my cheek. "Why didn't you tell me you went home with her?"

"I didn't think it was important. It was a way for her to get comfortable with me and to get some intel. We hung out. It was no big deal."

*Hung out or made out?* I frown.

"Don't worry, Ellie. Nothing happened."

"I don't know what you're talking about," I say, smoothing over my features, fearing he can read my mind. "It's none of my business."

"Sure it is." He changes lanes, his eyes glued to the road. "If I was hooking up with Nicki, that would mean I was emotionally involved with her, and that could mess up our heist. It would absolutely be your business, so please believe me when I say nothing happened."

My heart ticks back to life. "Just like partners aren't allowed to hook up, no falling for the targets, either."

"Exactly."

"I believe you." I keep my eyes on the map, unable to hide the relief in my voice.

Punching the gas, he swerves around a bubble car. "Not that it's always easy," he mutters.

He peeks at me out of the corner of his eye, and a charge runs down my spine.

"Kyran and Rayelle will be outside signaling us," I say, focusing on the plan to slow the blood rushing to my head. "Two lights mean go. One light means stay put. The good thing is the house doesn't have any cameras or Life Stream technology… That's weird. It's kind of off the grid."

"Simon probably hides who comes and goes. This is his weekend house. He's not here all the time, and who knows who his secret guests are. Maybe he doesn't want to risk the existence of recorded evidence. That works in our favor, but it's also why he has so many alarms. The first obstacle is the front door," he says. "Can you memorize the alarm code?" Pulling off the freeway, he stops on the side of a heavily wooded road.

"S-I-M-O-N-S-A-Y-S-S-T-O-P-!" I exhale. "Easy enough."

"Good." Separating the two red wires on the dashboard, he turns off the car, then pulls his own mask over his eyes. It's black leather like mine, but his is solid, cutting a diagonal lightning bolt across his face. "From here, we walk."

I nod. My insides are shaking more than the top of Lombard Street, but I fold the map and tuck it into a pocket on my thigh.

Before we leave, he pulls a portable telegraph out of the tool bag and taps out a Morse code message to let Stewart know we're on the move. When he's done, he puts the bag on like a backpack.

Stepping lightly to muffle our footsteps, we stick to the trees, hurrying through the woods in silence. My muscles ache from the strain to remain invisible, but before I beg for a break, Simon's fortress emerges from the shadows. The exterior is made entirely of glass bricks, with concentric rectangles that get increasingly smaller framing the entryway to the red front door.

*Will we have to drink a shrinking potion to fit through there?* I suck in my breath. *I can't believe we're going in.*

Garrett clutches my upper arm and pulls me to a stop. "You *look* like a thief," he whispers, his breath tickling my ear. "Ready to prove you *are* one?"

Beneath his mask, his eyes read dark as night, but in their depths, I detect a spark.

Heat ripples through me as a breeze ruffles my hair, and I'm sure he can see my pulse throbbing in my throat. I swallow. "I think so."

"No going back now."

"No." A sinking feeling drops in my stomach. It hits me like a hurricane. *I have a bad feeling about this. If we fail, if we get caught, I'm going to be locked up for a long time…* Hoping I'm wrong but knowing I'm not, I grab his arm. "One thing," I ask, my breath shallow.

"What's that?" He lowers his face to mine, and my brain buzzes.

"What's our exit strategy?"

"Ah." He grins and reaches into his pocket. "Jump." He flips a carabiner at me.

My trembling hand catches it, and I slip it into one of the zipper compartments on my suit.

"Wonderful."

# Chapter Forty-Three

*March 20X6, Menlo Park*

Clinging to the trees, we make our way to the house, sliding side by side along the glass facade to avoid triggering the motion sensors. My entire body stiff with tension, I want to run screaming into the woods, but I grip Garrett's shirt so I'll keep moving. When we arrive at the red front door, we freeze, backs to the wall, as two quick flashes bathe us in light, splaying our shadows across the porch.

Certain we've been caught, I feel my lungs seize, but I exhale when I realize it's Rayelle and Kyran signaling all is clear.

Garrett holds one arm over my chest, pinning me in place, and he must feel my heart thundering. His other gloved hand inches toward the alarm keypad.

"Stop!" I whisper, my hand shooting out of its own volition and grabbing his arm. "Are you sure this is right? It was Teresa's job—what if she got the code wrong?"

He glares at me, whispering, "What choice do we have?"

"None, I guess." I bite my lip.

"Do *not* freak out on me. We have to trust our friends did their jobs."

"But we're not supposed to trust—"

"Do we have to talk about this now?"

"No. Go ahead." My stomach uneasy, I gulp. Deep down, I *think* my instinct is to trust them, but at the same time, I can't get past my nerves and I'm second-guessing everything.

"Remember, timing is important. Promise me: no more interruptions."

"Promise." I nod, sweat forming on my forehead. "Simon says stop exclamation point," I remind him.

He punches in the code, and I hold my breath, exhaling only when the keypad turns green. The lock clicks as it unlatches.

Garrett releases me but catches my hand, keeping me close to him as he opens the door. "Go slowly," he whispers. "The hall of footsteps."

"I know," I whisper back, my jaw clenched. The moon shines through skylights, lighting our path down a stark hallway with white walls and blond wood floors, leading into the great room. I'd believe we could walk straight through the house into the woods if it wasn't for the moonlight glinting off the glass walls. "I don't want to know how Toby and Ben got the saliva to deactivate the footstep detector right now."

"Be glad it wasn't your saliva they were after."

I grimace. "Oh, I am."

Deep in the gardens beyond the glass great room, two lights flash. Before I can think, Garrett swoops me into his arms, throwing me over his shoulder and closing the door behind us in one motion. My heart leaps into my throat, and it's a miracle I don't scream. "What are you doing?" I hiss.

"I don't want to take any chances with two sets of footsteps," he whispers, his feet gliding across the floor until he reaches the base of the stairs.

"I'm capable of being quiet," I say as he lowers me down the length of his body, setting me on a step. I'm highly aware of every inch of him that slides against me, igniting me in goose bumps.

"It didn't seem like it when you were happily slamming car doors." He holds me close, keeping my cheek pressed against his shoulder. "Don't move a muscle."

*As if I could.* I'm so on edge, rigor mortis might be setting in. *If I was meant to be a thief, shouldn't I be in flow right now? On autopilot, like I was during the obstacle course? Not thinking, just doing?* My proximity to Garrett has me all jumbled, and I can't think straight.

"You know, Liam was right," he says into my hair. "You do smell like a girl."

My head snaps up, and it's all I can do to keep from kneeing him in the crotch.

His lips press together, hiding a smile.

"The footstep detector will be back on any second. And next up, the fog blaster," he whispers, pointing to the jets imbedded in the walls that line the stairs. "They look like an art installation, but if they're activated, they'll spray pepper spray or a sleeping compound—I don't know which—but we don't want to get caught snuggled up in Simon's bed, do we?"

My heart races beneath my catsuit—or maybe it's *his* heart.

Not wanting to admit my traitor body might not be opposed, I grind my teeth. "I'd definitely prefer pepper spray," I reply.

He lets out a little laugh.

We stand there, clinging to each other in silence as precious seconds tick by, lasting for what feels like eternity.

Every muscle in my body is poised, ready to bolt, and my

spine aches. I squint into the dark, hoping for a spark of light. "What's taking so long?"

"I don't know, but I'm positive Harbor and Mike will come through with the signature. He's an expert forger, and she's the perfect decoy if they need one," he says.

"But what if something went wrong? We'd be stranded here." My head spins.

A light passes through the still space, flooding over the couch and strange sculptures in the great room before traveling into the kitchen. It goes dark. We wait, our breathing heavy. I glance at my watch. Only three minutes have passed since we entered the front door. *Not enough time to get caught, yet.* The moment the second flash begins its journey, we bolt up the stairs, both fighting for the lead. The fog blasters remain closed.

When we reach the second floor, Garrett catches me around the waist, bringing me to a halt and sending hot shivers coursing through me.

"The shotgun-shell wall," he whispers in my ear. "Sophia and Ophelia are on this one—retina recognition."

"Sophia's an expert makeup artist. She's got this," I reply, trying to steady my quaking limbs. "She probably made a fake eye… Wait." I frantically scan the center anteroom we stand in. "How are we going to see the light?" Hallways and doors lead to bedrooms from all directions, but there are no windows.

Garrett points to the ceiling, and I glimpse stars twinkling through a skylight.

*CLICK.*

Grabbing me, Garrett throws me to the ground, covering my body with his. My insides leaping, I squeal, certain we're done for, waiting for the bullets to ravage us. He clamps his hand over my mouth as the walls around us shift, rearranging themselves into a new layout.

"Robotic walls," I whisper through his glove when they've stopped moving. He removes his hand from my mouth. "Now how are we supposed to know which bedroom is the master? The map will have changed."

"We'll have to guess." His breath is hot on my cheek.

We lay there, not moving, every inch of our bodies pressed together. This time I know it's his heart pulsating against mine. Electricity coursing through me, I long to curl into him.

White light pours through the skylight, spotlighting us before it goes dark. "One," I whisper, grateful for a new place to channel my energy. "Which room do you think it is?"

"The master used to be down the hall to the right... I'm guessing it doesn't change? Only the rest of the rooms reconfigure to accommodate guests?"

The light flashes again.

"Two," I say. "Sounds like a good guess to me."

He yanks me up, and, shoulders hunched, we scramble down the hall into what can only be the master suite, based on the size of the chandelier dangling from the ceiling and the glass walls that open to balconies overlooking the forest.

"Bingo," he says.

"Where's the closet?" I ask, my lungs heaving in disbelief we've made it this far.

"This way." Garrett nods over his shoulder.

We tiptoe to a hologram wall next to the fireplace. Certain we're about to trigger an unmapped weapon, I hold my breath as we step through the wall. Thankfully no alarms sound. We arrive safely in a spacious bathroom with stone floors and a soaking tub that overlooks the pool. Crossing the space, we find the closet, and I exhale.

"What do we do now?" I ask. "We can't just open the closet door, can we?"

"What does the map say?"

My hands shake as I take the paper square out of my pocket and unfold it. "It doesn't say anything."

"It seems too easy," Garrett says. "But it would be ridiculous to put in a code every time you opened your closet, right?"

"We don't have time to debate ridiculous," I say, glancing at my watch. "We've been inside ten minutes. Time is not our friend. Open the door."

"Don't tell me what to do. It's my heist; I call the shots."

"Fine." Rubbing my throbbing temples, I step aside so he has full access to the door.

"You open the door," he says.

"No!" My stomach clenches. "Like you said—it's your heist. Man up. If we go down right now, you take the blame, anyway. Open the door."

"Fine, but it's going in the report that you disobeyed orders."

I narrow my eyes. "There's a report?"

"Of course there's a report. This is a test."

"Whatever. Getting an A-minus isn't exactly my biggest worry right now. Would you open the door?"

"A-minus? You think I'm giving you an A?" He laughs but quickly grows serious. "Ready? One, two…" Our eyes connect, and I could get lost in his depths. "Three." He yanks open the door, and I brace myself.

Silence.

His shoulders visibly relax, and I practically collapse in a heap as the tension releases.

"After you." He gestures me inside.

The closet is nearly empty, containing only three crisp dress shirts and two pairs of pants hanging in a neat row. A stack of shelves holds four perfectly folded charcoal zip-front sweaters, a pair of loafers, and a set of running shoes.

"He must use a clothing rental service," Garrett says, his fingers tapping lightly along the back wall. "Which makes the car thing even stranger…"

"What about the car thing?"

*BANG.*

My heart flip-flops. The noise comes from outside, sounding like a car door slamming. I whip around, squinting into the night outside the bathroom windows, poised to jump at the slightest rustling of leaves, but all is silent.

Garrett keeps talking like nothing happened. "Simon is a minimalist guy. Look at this place. He doesn't seem like he's in to accumulating 'stuff,' so why give up space to a car collection? Even if he secretly likes driving, why wouldn't he subscribe to a service that lets him borrow antique cars any time he wants?"

"Did you hear that?" I hiss, wishing he would hurry up and figure out how to open the wall.

"Hear what?"

"Nothing." I pinch the bridge of my nose. *Am I losing it?*

"It's weird I've never heard of his collection," he continues. Spreading his fingers, he runs his palm over the wall and frowns. "The closet has a knock lock, right?"

"Yes. The map has the code from Stewart, but it doesn't say where to knock." Impatient, I dig my nails into my palms to keep from pounding on the wall myself.

He traces a line to a spot near the ceiling. "This feels like a false panel, and, judging by the dirt smudges, I'm guessing the lock is here. What's the code?"

Consulting the map, I chew my lip. "Three knocks, pause, seven knocks, pause, one knock, pause, nine knocks."

"Okay. Count with me." Balling his fingers into a fist, Garrett lets his hand hover over the wall.

"Go," I say, and together we count, "One, two, three," as

he raps on the wall.

"Pause," I say, my pulse thundering in my ears. I silently count to two. "Go. One, two, three, four…"

When he gets to the final knock, we hold our breath. To my amazement, with a click, the wall slides open, revealing a small lounge with a large wall screen and two leather loungers—one red, one dark brown. The only other furniture is a reclaimed wood bar. I squeal as Garrett grabs my hand.

Together, we step inside.

# Chapter Forty-Four

*March 20X6, Menlo Park*

"The red chair is biometric." Garrett clicks on his penlight and kneels to examine it. "Simon has to sit in it to open the safe—wherever that is."

"There aren't many places it could be," I say, shining my flashlight around the sparse space. "How are Chloe and Vick going to get Simon to sit in the chair if it's in here?"

"What does the map say?"

Blood pumping in my veins, I spread the map on the floor. Illuminating the circle next to the "biometric chair" icon with details about the safe, I read aloud. "In the event of an emergency, the driver's seat of Simon's vintage Corvette is also wired to open the safe remotely if he sits in it. The Corvette is part of his car collection, which he stores at his Menlo Park home…" My throat constricts.

Garrett and I stare at each other.

"Vick and Chloe have to get him to sit in the Corvette…" he says.

"Which means he's here." I finish his sentence.

Everything goes silent. It's like we're suspended in midair with realization whirling around us.

"Of course Chloe's heist required her to get a piece of ass," I mutter, snapping the tension. "I don't even want to know what she had to do to get him here."

Garrett laughs, and all is right with the world. Except for the fact Simon is probably about to kill us. Or, at the very least, send us to jail for the rest of our lives. My insides crumble. *I can't let that happen. I want this to be my life more than anything.*

"We can still do this," he says, crawling behind the bar. Crouching, he examines its contents with his penlight. "We're sticking to the plan. This is how it's supposed to happen."

"Are you nuts?" I ask, tears stinging my eyes. "We should run."

"Do you really think so? Is that what your instincts are telling you?" He shines his light on me.

My eyes widen at the word "instinct," but I quickly brush it aside as coincidence. Breathing deep, I check in. My heart is throbbing, my head is spinning, and my shoulders are pinched, but nothing is triggering me to leave.

"This sucks," I say, joining him behind the bar. "But we should stay." Kneeling next to him, I peer at the rows of glasses and bottles. "The safe must be back here."

"The mini-fridge?" he suggests.

"That's my guess." Spotlighting the room with my flashlight in search of other possibilities, I realize there aren't any windows. I gasp. "How are we going to see Rayelle and Kyran's flashes?" My mouth goes dry. "How will we know when Simon sits? What if he already has?" A shiver runs down my spine. "What if he's coming now?"

Garrett is silent. The light from his pen raises to my face. "Do you know? Is that what your instincts say?"

The blood drains from my head, and it's as if the room turns on its side. *Again with the instincts. He can't be asking what I think he's asking.*

Setting the light on top of the refrigerator so it casts us in a soft glow, he grabs my shoulders, forcing me to look at him. "Listen, Ella. I have a confession. I was going to tell you after the heist, but I think now is the time."

"Ella?" I whisper, the name reverberating in my brain.

"I know everything, Ella. I know who you are."

His voice echoes, sounding faraway, and the room spins around me.

"I should have told you sooner—I was the one you were supposed to meet that night—the night you died. *You* were Faye's Initiation Heist, but I messed up. And I've sworn to protect you ever since. That's why you're my partner."

My stomach twists, and bile burns my throat. "You know everything?" I manage to say, lungs straining for air. Blackness blots the edges of my vision as I try to comprehend.

"Yes. When Crystal realized your potential—that your instincts are unmatched—she knew you didn't belong in the Influencer world. That's why she contacted Allard. That's why you came to Keystone."

"You've known all along..." My lungs heave. "You lied to me..."

He presses his forehead to mine, piercing me with those murky eyes that can only be my undoing. "Stay with me, Ella. I know it's a lot to process, but I need your help to finish this job. We're running out of time. You would never have let me near you if I told you the truth. I didn't want to lie—I only wanted to protect you. Remember, I told you: no matter what happens, you know it in here." He thumps his hand over my chest.

His hand on my heart gets through to me because I do

know it. My instinct is to trust him. The fog lifts, and I know I've got to focus. "I don't know if I can do anything." I sit on my heels to create distance between us. "My instincts don't operate on command."

"Can you try? We don't have any other choice."

Trying not to hyperventilate, I slowly nod.

Pushing everything out of my mind—for now—I clutch the tiger's eye I wear at my throat and inhale deeply.

He watches me like he's waiting for me to transform into a bird or something.

"Stop looking at me," I whisper. "You're distracting."

"There you are." Smiling, he exhales in a rush. "Anything you say. Let me know how I can help."

"Close your eyes and shut up."

He does as he's told, but his mouth twitches at the corner.

Shutting my eyes, too, I will my racing heart calm, empty my mind, try to act on instinct alone. *We're alone in a closet…* An image of us kissing flashes through my brain, and my eyes fly open, meeting Garrett's watchful gaze.

"Anything?" he asks.

I glare at him. "You're not helping."

"I like watching you work," he says, but thankfully, he shuts his eyes.

I focus on a spot over his shoulder, this time imagining Simon, trying to visualize the Corvette without having any idea what it looks like. I'm grasping at straws. "I have no idea what I'm doing," I say, my mind reeling. "We're screwed."

"Keep trying. You're our only hope, Obi-Wan."

*Nerd.* But warmth washes over me at the fact that he can reference movies that are a hundred years old.

The wall screen clicks on, and we both jump, knocking heads. I'm certain we're done for. The screen illuminates, casting us in soft blue light, before clicking off. A second later, it clicks on again before going dark.

*Rayelle.*

"Now," I yell. "Go. Open the fridge."

Garrett throws open the door.

Holding our breath, we wait for an alarm, for bullets.

Nothing happens.

"Is the box in there?" I ask.

He pulls out an ancient-looking gold jewelry box covered in symbols. Mesmerized, I momentarily forget where I am, running my fingers over the etchings, studying them, noticing the distinct outline of a key in the center.

"Give me the ring," Garrett says.

I slip it off my finger and hand it to him. He inserts the stone in the lock and twists it to the right. Nothing happens. He twists to the left. Nothing. To the right again. Still, nothing.

His face goes pale. "I don't think the ring is the key."

# Chapter Forty-Five

*March 20X6, Menlo Park*

"It has to be!" Snatching the ring out of his hand, I examine it. "The stone is red. When Nicki wore it, it was always blue or purple."

"It's biometric," he says, his jaw dropping. "It must change color based on mood—only someone calm can open the box—and it's probably connected to Simon's AMPs. We need to get it back to blue before he gets an update on her mood."

"How are we going to do that?" The ring trembles between my fingers.

"Put it back on. It's probably red because you're agitated. Try to calm down."

"I don't want it reading me. You put it on." I thrust it toward him.

He frowns. "You already had it on. Besides, it won't fit me. Hurry up and put it on. We don't have time."

"Lucky you," I mutter, slipping the ring back on my finger. It flares to bright orange.

"Take some deep breaths. In through your nose, out

through your mouth." He massages my shoulders.

"Would you stop?" I push his hands away.

"Look at me." Cupping my chin, he forces my eyes to his. "I won't let anything happen to you, Ellie, I promise." His hand glides along my jaw, nestling next to my ear, making my neck ache in a good way. "We're going to do this. Together. Breathe with me."

We sit, focused on each other, the only sound the mingling of our breath. To my surprise, I *do* trust he'll protect me, and as my defenses relax, I get lost in him. Heat reverberates between us.

"Do you feel it, too?" he whispers, searching my face.

"Feel what?"

"This." He gestures between his head and mine. "It's like we're tied together. Linked in some cosmic way."

I can't deny the tugging in my center, that some invisible force is at work, an energy storm crackling to life, and I nod. "I don't like it."

A slow smile plays across his face. "Me neither."

It's like a tornado whips through the room, thrusting us together, pinning us in the eye. Before I can respond or think, he tilts my face up, and his full lips meet mine. Color explodes in my brain, my synapses firing electricity, raising goose bumps on my arms. He coaxes my mouth open, his tongue pressing inside, and I want to inhale him. My frenzied fingers wind into his hair, craving the pressure of his body, unable to pull him close enough. His energy fills me, and I'm caught in the vortex where he's all I know—all that matters. Wound together in a dizzy swirl, we're bound by gravity, by a force so heavy we could sink through the floor without noticing.

His lips become gentle, slowly caressing mine, and the realization seeps in that time matters, too.

I break the kiss, resting my forehead against his, getting my bearings.

He blinks, seeming as dazed as I feel.

Glancing down at the ring, I recover. "Hot pink? Nice work."

Back to his nonchalant self, he smirks. "I think hot pink feels pretty good."

I narrow my eyes. "Listen. We don't have time to get into it right now, and I don't know what that was, but as far as I'm concerned, it never happened. And it will never happen again. Agreed?"

"No problem." He shrugs. "Now let's get this box open. Look at me."

"Uh-uh. No way." I raise the ring on my left middle finger. "Hot pink."

He laughs. "Fine. Don't look at me. Do you have a happy place? Maybe try to go there?"

*It's not a bad idea.* Closing my eyes, I imagine getting lost in the Vault. My heart rate slows.

"Green. It's working," Garrett says. "Where are you? What makes you happy?"

"The Vault. I'm in the Vault."

"That's funny. That's where I'd go, too."

I peek at the ring. It starts to turn black. "Don't ruin this for me." Pivoting so my back is to him, I focus on the ceiling, imagining wandering through the Vault's version of the Louvre, trying to contain the emotions swirling inside me. *Forget the kiss. Forget how he makes you feel. Send out calm, and you receive calm...* I picture myself standing on a mountaintop above a green valley, the sun warm on my back. *Nobody can hurt me.* Everything goes silent, and, overwhelmed with peace, with oneness, I relax. The ring turns blue. Slipping it off my finger, I turn around, insert it into the lock, and twist to the right. I pray it hasn't changed color. "Please work."

The box clicks open. Inside, nestled among red velvet folds, is an old-fashioned memory stick.

"Wait!" My instinct is we should take the whole box, but Garrett grabs the memory stick before I can stop him. The second he does, a deafening alarm sounds. Screaming, undulating waves pulsate in my ears. My calm evaporates, and I can't think straight. Slamming my hands over my ears, I freeze.

"Run!" Garrett yanks me to my feet, his wits somehow intact.

"Hold on." Picking up the jewelry box, I have the sense to shove it into his pack.

"No time for souvenirs, Ellie." He drags me into the bedroom, and I don't argue.

"We can't go out the way we came...the shotgun wall!" I yell. "And Simon definitely knows now—who knows what other traps he's activating." I'm positive bullets will ravage my body any second.

"This way." Garrett pushes me toward the balcony, where he feels around for a latch to open the sliding glass wall.

Knowing we probably need a command to gesture the doors open—or to be recognized as Simon himself—I do the first thing I think of. Taking my tactical pen from the pocket on my thigh, I hurl myself in front of Garrett and slam the tip into the center of the door. It explodes in a shower of glass. Shielding our eyes with our arms, we escape to the balcony through the debris.

A police helicopter appears overhead, spotlighting us, and in the distance, Simon and a parade of cops sprint toward the house with guns drawn. Wasting zero time, we clip our carabiners to the balcony railing. Garrett grabs my hand. "Do you trust me?"

I nod.

"Then jump."

But I'm one step ahead of him. Hurling myself off the balcony, I drag him down with me.

# Chapter Forty-Six

*March 20X6, Menlo Park*

We land on our feet. The second I'm on the ground, adrenaline (finally!) takes over. A current vibrates through me, and I'm invincible. Garrett keeps my fingers wound in his. The helicopter spotlights us as we bolt into the woods, and I'm a star.

My ears ringing from the alarm, each footfall sounds to a rhythmic beat, and it's like I'm flying. At a full sprint, I dodge branches with a flick of my head, ducking, turning, jumping with fluid ease.

I'm a "bad" guy. And I love it.

Overhead, the canopy of trees thickens, blocking out the light from the helicopter.

"Do you know where we're going?" I pant, hoping the cops aren't hot on our trail. We had a decent head start, and the way I'm feeling, I'm positive I can outrun them.

"There's a safe house—one of only a few places on earth that truly has no service," he says between breaths, yanking me to the right. "The trees are too tall. The satellites can't find it. Even if the algorithm can be tracked, its signal will be scrambled. We're lucky Simon lives nearby. Our location will be obvious to Keystone faculty. Abignail will contact us. We just have to get there."

We duck under a low branch.

"Does Nash know about it?"

"He shouldn't." He drags me left. "I only know about it because I won the Quest. It's level-three classified. Every time you add to the Vault, you get a bonus—I purchased the level-two locations with the Coke recipe—but as far as I know, Nash never earned anything beyond level two. He hasn't proven very useful since his initiation."

"Are there levels beyond three?"

Our footfalls pound the dirt.

"Yes, but they're reserved for a very select group of Disconnects. I don't know their locations. Yet."

"How can you be so sure you'll get access?"

"I've never considered myself common. Neither should you."

A craggy bush catches my suit, and I drop his hand to detangle myself, shoving the branches aside. He pauses, waiting for me, and I scurry to keep from slowing us down.

"Does Kyran know Nash?" I ask as the thought strikes me, catching up. We sprint onward.

"He doesn't. He shouldn't. Kyran came to Keystone after Nash was initiated. Why?"

"Just a weird feeling is all."

"Kyran doesn't know where the safe house is, either, so there's no danger of him telling anyone, if that's what you're worried about." Bumping my shoulder, he directs me to the right. "Nobody is going to find us until we want them to."

We keep running. The deeper into the woods we go, the more likely our escape feels.

"Are we there yet?" My side cramps, and my lungs heave. I long to double over.

"Almost."

This deep in the forest, the trees blot out the sky and it's nearly pitch-black. Garrett throws out an arm, slamming me to a halt in front of a giant redwood tree.

"We're here."

To me it looks like every other tree in the forest, but he clearly sees something special in it. "*This* is the safe house?" I ask.

"What were you expecting? A penthouse? You Influencers are hard to please…" He kicks the side of the tree. "But don't worry, I'm sure you'll find it more than comfortable." As his foot connects with the trunk, the forest floor drops out beneath my feet, sucking me down a hole. "Have a seat."

"I hate you!" I scream, landing in a net at the bottom of the dirt pit.

Laughing, he jumps down after me. "I told you I'd hear that again tonight, though 'hot pink' makes me think otherwise."

"Then you definitely needed the reminder." I glower at his silhouette in the darkness. Standing, I rub my bruised elbow.

He pulls the trapdoor shut over our heads. Clicking on his penlight, he shines it at me. "You're looking pretty rough." As he smudges his thumb across my cheek, something hot smears toward my ear. "We'll get you cleaned up. But first, we climb." He illuminates a ladder built into the inside of the hollow tree. "Follow me."

I allow him a small head start before scaling the iron ladder. It's cold and dark inside the tree, the only light coming from the penlight Garrett holds between his teeth. We climb for what feels like forever, and I'm grateful I can't see how high we are thanks to the cramped blackness. My ears pop as the tree narrows around us, and I sense we're nearing the top.

Above me, Garrett stops and unlatches a small door, casting us in silvery moonlight. Following him through the opening, I crawl out onto a suspension bridge precariously strung between the tips of the trees. Damp wind pricks my cheeks, but I'm grateful for the sobering air as I stare through the bridge's slats. Three hundred feet below us, the forest floor is an unidentifiable black abyss. Frozen, I dig my fingers into the wood, not caring about the splinters that gouge my hands.

The bridge shudders with Garrett's footsteps. "Are you coming?" he asks, towering above me.

"Yes." Invincibility still pumping in my veins, I push myself to my feet. Nudging him aside, I take the lead, the bridge swaying dangerously from side to side until we reach a wooden porch attached to a small, redwood treehouse. It has windows on all sides but is so entangled in branches and morning glories they're barely visible. Picking the lock, he ushers me through a hobbit-sized door and shuts us inside. The interior is simply furnished with a low tweed couch, white fur rug, and a vintage red electric fireplace.

"We made it." I exhale. Collapsing on the rug, I lean against the couch, pushing my mask off my face. "Now what?"

"We wait for instructions." He flips a switch on a brown box with black knobs and white speakers sitting on a small table. The room fills with buzzing static before he turns the volume down. "Abignail will send us a Morse code message using radio waves. We'll be able to hear them on this frequency."

"How long will that take?"

"Don't know. Hopefully we hear in a few hours. We have to get the algorithm into the right hands before Simon launches his Quinn update." He props open a window.

The night breeze is welcome after our run, but the room quickly cools. "What do we do until then?" I ask. The kiss instantly flashes through my mind, and a glance at him tells me he's thinking the same. "Never mind." I grimace, rubbing my arms. "Don't answer that."

He raises his eyebrows. "Why? Is the prospect of spending a few hours alone with me giving you chills?"

"It's the wind. Definitely the wind."

He laughs.

"Aren't you cold?" I ask.

"Nope. I still have too much adrenaline, but this should help warm you up." Kneeling next to the fireplace, he turns a dial, and the logs light up, blasting me with heat. "Do you want to see if there's any food in this place? I'm starving."

My stomach growls, and I realize it's been hours since we've eaten. I drag myself to my feet and head to the kitchen.

Opening drawers and cupboards, I hunt for food. Garrett joins me and puts a pot on the stove, heating water from a jug left on the counter.

I squeal with delight when I find an unopened bag of Goldfish crackers.

"Jackpot," I say, waving the bag at him before returning to the couch.

He follows with a dishcloth and a bowl of hot, soapy water. "Before you get too comfortable, let me look at that cheek." Sinking down next to me, he lifts my chin and dabs at the cuts. "Luckily, there isn't any glass imbedded in here. That was quick thinking, Ellie. I'm impressed."

The only light comes from the full moon filtering in through the windows and the red glow of the fireplace, but his face is so close to mine I can see a tiny scar under his right eyebrow. My pulse throbs in my throat. "Why do you call me Ellie?"

"Because you're not Ella and you're not Elisha. You're someone in between. Someone I'd like to know." Without meeting my eyes, he keeps dabbing.

Butterflies flap to life in my belly. The heat from the fireplace sweeping over me, my muscles relax. My defenses fall away as he tugs me under his spell. Fearing a closet reenactment, I change the subject. "So, I was your mission and you were too busy hooking up with Faye to meet me on time?"

Frowning, he dunks the cloth into the bowl, tinging the water red. "No. I told you I never hooked up with Faye."

"Why don't you tell me the truth, then?"

He takes a deep breath. "I suppose I owe you that much." Pressing the cloth against my face, he cups my cheek. "Our mission was to steal *you*, but everything went wrong. It was my fault. The bomb was supposed to be a distraction—there would be an explosion on the yacht, and Faye would spread a rumor you were on it. Meanwhile, I'd take you to Allard. Nobody was supposed to get hurt."

His words reverberate through me, refusing to penetrate. "You planted the bomb?" I whisper, realization seeping in. "You killed my friends." Dizzy, I push him away. Covering my mouth and nose with my hands, I breathe into them, trying to comprehend.

For once, he's speechless. His lower lip trembles as his eyes search my face, and I sense his helplessness, but that night comes flooding back with a vengeance. My breath catches in my throat, the staccato bubbles rumbling past my ears. I close my eyes, thrashing in the deep, drowning. Lost at sea, I'm hunting for connection—for a lifeline—for someone who gets me.

And I'd thought I found it.

*But there is no one. I'm utterly alone in this world.*

Still.

Darkness descends, and the endless wanting for someone true cracks open. My sinuses burn, and tears prick my eyes.

When I open them, I find Garrett's haven't left my face.

Infinite apology is reflected in his glassy stare, a sorrow that cuts through to my core, that understands me maybe better than anyone—because that night is his to bear, too—but I can't look at him. I bury my face in my hands, tears leaking down my cheeks.

*My friends...my so-called friends...Adam...Nash...* I swallow, trying to catch my breath. *But he was never real. Everything was a lie... And what do I know now? More lies... But this means my parents didn't set the bomb... Maybe they did love me.* Worthless hope buoys me before reality crashes in. *You know better. That night was the end—the end of my life. The end of the lie...*

Disgust that I'm so stupid, so starved for affection I'll throw everything away to get it, descends, pinching the nerves in my neck. *Maybe I'm not worthy of love. Or maybe love doesn't exist.* I sit, paralyzed in a black void, hate for myself—for this world—reverberating through me.

Garrett touches my shoulder. His fingers are gentle at first, growing stronger as they slide up the back of my neck until his palm is applying pressure at the base of my skull.

Something about his touch is reassuring, and the dark brightens a little. I peek at him.

"I think about it all the time," he says. His voice is gravel. "The families I shattered. Those kids aren't here because of me." Squeezing his eyes shut, he breathes deep. "I think about them every day." He reopens his eyes and connects with mine, lips wobbling. "It hurts every day."

Pressing my chin to my chest, I wipe my tears and nod. "I know what that's like," I whisper.

"I got caught up in the party," he continues. After giving my neck a final squeeze, his hands find mine clenched in my lap, and he sandwiches my fist between his palms. "I'm not proud of it, but I've always been curious what Influencer life is like—what it's like to live in an augmented world—and I lost track of time. I didn't know Nash was going to be there. All I could tell from studying your Network feed was that he hurt you, and he'd completely changed since the last time I saw him. I didn't know what game he was playing—I still don't—but we used to be friends, and I thought he was on my side…" He swallows, his fingers gripping mine.

"Remember I said bad stuff happens when he's around? I trusted him to keep everyone off the boat… I don't know what happened. We haven't spoken since that night. Maybe there was a miscommunication, but by the time I realized there were people out there it was too late. I raced to get you—to get to everyone—I was on the boat with Nash, coming to dismantle the bomb. And we were fighting because he was insisting on coming with us, and I thought it was because he didn't think I could handle you alone. My pride got in the way, and I wasn't fast enough… I failed." His voice cracks.

*Nash let everyone on the boat…* I file that fact away for later, suspecting it's important. *It's not totally Garrett's fault…*

"I'm not telling you this because I want you to forgive me," he says, fingers sliding up and circling my wrist. "I can't forgive myself. I would never ask that of you. I'm telling you because you deserve the truth."

"Truth." I laugh without mirth, venturing a glance up at him through wet eyes. "Is anything real?" My throat constricts, and I choke on the words. "I need something to be real."

Grabbing my shoulders, he forces me to look at him. "We are. You and me. Here. Right now. In this moment. All of this." He gestures between his heart and mine, where the tension is undeniable. "Everything we just accomplished. Us. We are real." He searches my face, and it's like he can see straight through to my soul—like he intimately knows all of me—and he likes what he sees.

My chest tightens. "I'm sorry if I can't believe you." I practically spit the words to combat the wretched hope burrowing in my core.

"I don't blame you." The corners of his mouth turn down. "But I'll do whatever it takes to prove you can trust me."

"I'm not sure that's possible," I whisper.

"Impossible is my specialty." His mouth twitches, and his hands run down my arms, scooting me closer to him. "Honestly, when I first met you, I expected you to be a pain."

I raise my eyebrows, unable to squelch the glimmer of annoyance he always inspires in me—which is somehow reassuring—and sniffle. "Thanks."

He bites his lower lip. "All I knew was you were some sexy Influencer chick that had guys falling at her feet."

My stomach drops.

"I figured the last thing you needed was some guy following you around like a lost puppy," he continues. "And I've also never considered myself 'some guy.'"

"You're definitely not 'some guy,'" I say, pressing my lips together, suppressing the outrageous urge to giggle.

"I wasn't lying when I said my parents made me hang out with you." He wrinkles his nose. "They did, at first. But I didn't know how to get close to you without coming off as some weird stalker."

"And that's why you picked me as your partner?" Disappointment thuds in my chest.

His eyes widen. "No. Not at all. By then I'd realized you weren't some big-shot Influencer. You were cute and quirky and funny and brave, and you kept me on my toes. I *liked* you. But that was dangerous because I'm not *allowed* to like you."

Heat surges up my spine, and I nod. "Keystone Code."

"Exactly." He frowns. "I wanted you close, but I also had

to keep my distance."

An ache grows deep in my belly, a burning desire for everything to be possible, to be free of the past and barreling toward a bright future. I know it in my bones. I *want* my new life to be true. Rayelle and Sophia and Stewart and… Garrett. I *want* to believe him. I remember what Allard told me my first day at Keystone…about forgiveness changing my understanding of the past so it no longer limits my future. *I can't change the past, but I can change how I react to it. Death is a beginning. That night was the beginning of my life…*

An involuntary smile plays on my lips, and I bury the grief. *Enough.* Inhaling, I breathe in my future. "Thank you for telling me all of this. In some ways it's nice to know someone else understands where I'm coming from."

"I understand you more than you know," he says. "Do you remember I told you you're the only person at Keystone who is any competition for me?"

My heart skips. "Yes…"

He starts to say something but then closes his mouth. He blinks his eyes closed and, when he opens them, changes the subject. "I let you out of my sight that night. I should have known you were out there. I should have saved you… You know, I wasn't sure you were alive until I saw you in the Crypt that day. Do you remember?"

I think back to the first time I laid eyes on him. "You were studying the Voynich manuscript…"

"Yes. The Voynich," he repeats slowly. "I've never been more relieved. Those two days of not knowing were hell. I never want to feel that again."

"But it's not your job to save me," I say, retreating from the intensity that makes me want to be wrapped up in him.

"I have to. I can't help it."

I shake my head. "You know all my secrets. You know how

terrible I was, about my lies, my cover-ups, and you still want to protect me… Nobody has ever wanted me for me. Ever."

"Ellie, the one night I spent in the world you came from was the worst one of my life. It's left me with scars that will never heal." He runs his thumb over my lips. "I don't know how you survived as long as you did. I don't blame you for any of it."

Tears sting my eyes. I fill my lungs, and my words come out in a rush. "I don't blame you either… In fact, I like you, too."

A smile spreads over his face, and his hands move to my jaw. He presses his forehead against mine, the connection buzzing between our brains dizzying me.

Tilting my chin toward his, he presses his lips to mine. The kiss is soft at first. Warmth spreads through me as he coaxes my mouth open, and, closing my eyes, I give in to the swirl.

"We're not allowed to do this," I murmur as his mouth lowers to my throat, igniting my body in shivers.

"I know…" He settles me onto the couch, his knee parting my thighs. Coming up for air, he locks eyes with me. "But maybe if only we know…"

"It's enough." I finish his sentence, running my hands down his chest, mesmerized by his strength.

Caught in a tidal wave of adrenaline and emotion, I pull him into me, pressing my body against his. He again finds my lips. His chin is rough against mine, and my fingers are in his hair, and we are pinned together. I know I should stop it, but some part of me has already given in. I can't get enough of him, and I don't overthink it. What happens next is inevitable.

Hot pink is too much to resist.

I send out love, and it is love I receive in return.

# Chapter Forty-Seven

*March 20X6, Menlo Park*

It is with effort that I open my eyelids to return from the magical dreamland I'm floating in. Sunshine filters through the treetops, casting gentle renditions of ruffled leaves on the treehouse walls. Cocooned in cozy blankets on the fur rug, I slowly come to, stretching my arms overhead. The fire has gone cold, and I'm struck by the silence, the lack of static in the room. I bolt upright, the night rushing back to me. A quick survey of the space confirms I'm alone.

My stomach churns.

Rushing to the radio, I find no information. The dial is turned to off. *Did I sleep through the message transmission? Why didn't Garrett wake me up?* Hands shaking, I ransack the treehouse, knowing he's taken the algorithm and isn't coming back. The only evidence I find that Garrett was here is my pink *Ring Around the Rosie* dress draped over the couch.

*He delivered the algorithm without me…* Crumpling into a ball, I barricade my mind against the memories—his lips caressing mine, fingers grazing my skin, the inexplicable bond that tied us together. I press my forehead to my knees. *So much for being a team...* The tears flow, my aching throat sobbing out the betrayal. *Is anything real?* Hiccupping, I gasp for breath, the fireplace blurring before me. *Is anyone loyal?*

I wallow for a few minutes, caught in a self-loathing loop, recalling the night. His confession. *What were my instincts?* The answer comes easily. *I believed him. And I trust myself. I've never felt as complete—whole—as I did last night.* Taking a deep breath, I force myself to stop thinking the worst—to stop thinking everything is about me—and pull myself together. After I splash water on my face, I put on the pink dress and plot my next move.

*There must be an explanation. He must have been ordered to go alone.* I check my watch. *8:30... Is he still undercover? Could he be at breakfast with Nicki? For all she knows, he was taking care of me last night...* Remembering, my cheeks burn. *Maybe he's coming back.*

Two hours later, I'm still pacing the floor, beginning to lose hope.

Shoving my hand into my right pocket, I plop onto the couch. My fingers connect with a paper square, and I pull out the note from Nash and unfold it.

*We belong in nature. Among the Appalachian oaks where water falls from stone. I'll wait for you.*

*Bang, bang, bang.*

A fist pounds outside the treehouse door, and I jump. *Rayelle.* I can't help wishing it was Garrett on the other side, but my instincts tell me it isn't. I creep to the door, peek out the window, and confirm Rayelle is on the other side.

Shoving the note into my pocket, I throw open the door. "I'm so happy to see you." I hug her.

"You did it," she says, squeezing me back while moving us inside. "Quinn is dead!"

"She is?" I hold her at arm's length.

"Yes! You're a hero." She takes my hands, practically jumping up and down. "It's done. Heist complete. Everyone is in the van—Stewart, Sophia, Liam—"

*Garrett?* My chest swells with hope.

"It's time to go. Is Garrett ready?"

I shake my head. "Garrett's gone," I whisper.

Her jaw drops. "What? But he just messaged Stewart your location."

"He did?" Hope that he might be coming back blasts through me, but I know in my heart he's not. "He must have done it from...wherever he is." I shrug, unable to continue.

"No way. Garrett is a traitor?"

"No. He's not a traitor. He just delivered the algorithm without me..." Tears sting my eyes, and I wipe them away with the back of my hand. *Pull yourself together.* "It was his heist. I guess he deserved to take the credit."

"That dick. That's so unfair!" Her cheeks flush, and she rolls her eyes. "Just like a guy."

Grateful for her outrage, I smile. The day brightens, and I know exactly where I want to be.

"Thank you," I say. "You have no idea how much your friendship means to me." Gripping her hand, I hang on tight. "Let's go. Take me home."

After locking the treehouse behind us, we cross the suspension bridge and climb down the inside of the tree.

"You know what, Rayelle?" I say over my shoulder. "You deserve a ton of credit, too. We couldn't have done this without you."

"Well, I wouldn't have wanted to do it without *you*." Her voice floats up to me.

"Me neither. You or Garrett." As soon as I say his name, something in my left pocket clangs against my leg. Reaching the bottom of the ladder, I hop down and pull out the key fob with the Keystone emblem etched into it.

Back at Keystone, I go straight to Allard's cottage.

"Elisha." She wraps me in a hug and pulls me inside as soon as she opens the door. "You did it. Congratulations."

I push her away. "Why didn't you tell me Crystal stole my Book of Secrets? I told her everything. She knew all along how I felt about Adam…I mean Nash…and he's her son! I feel so stupid."

Her smile falters. "You have every right to be upset." She leads me to the couch. "I was going to tell you eventually. I'm sorry to have kept it from you. I just wanted you to get settled here. To make this home. And I thought knowing we were the ones who took your Book of Secrets might overwhelm you."

"It would have," I agree.

"Please believe me when I say we took it to keep you safe. I hope you can forgive me." She reaches out and squeezes my hand. "At first we wanted the information the book contained on your parents' Corporate friends, but once we realized your abilities, that the book might reveal your capabilities to the wrong people if it fell into the wrong hands, we knew we had to go to extra lengths to keep it—and you—safe."

"Why would anybody be interested in my abilities?"

She sighs. "Because the Simulation isn't functional yet. It requires quantum processing that nobody has figured out. Quantum cognition is imperative to making the Super Brain work, and experimenting on your brain patterns could lead to the discovery they're missing. You could be the keystone of the Simulation."

Fear creeping up my neck, I shudder. "Where is my book now?"

"Crystal has it. She's using it to help Nash know who he can trust, but as soon as she's done with it, she'll bring it back here and you can hide it in the Vault. Put it anywhere you'd like—you can be the only person who knows its location if you want."

"You know what Nash is doing with Nicki?" I raise my eyebrows.

"Yes. He's our person on the inside. He's using her to get close to Simon. He's the one who told us the Quinn update was about to launch today."

I let that digest. *Maybe Nash wasn't lying to me...*

"Why didn't you warn us Nash would be there? That he was on our side?" I ask.

"Sometimes we keep pieces of the puzzle separate. It's safer when nobody knows too much. If one person gets caught, they won't have all the information to implicate anyone else... But we don't have to worry about that." She smiles. "Because you didn't get caught. You did it. You, Garrett, Nash, Rayelle— all of you together. You won the battle for us. I'm so proud."

Staring at my shimmery pink skirt, I let everything sink in. *All of us together...*

*Two boys. Two pockets. Which code do I crack?*

The answer instantly inserts itself in my brain, and I smile.

# Epilogue

*June 25, 20X6, Keystone*

L ifting the skirt of my silk gown, I walk into the Initiation
Ball. The Lodge has been transformed with a checkered
wood dance floor and crystal chandeliers replacing the
usual dear antler ones. The decorations are actual artifacts
from the Titanic, and the attendees are wearing replicas of
clothing from the early twentieth century. After returning
from our heist, we were given the mundane task of sewing our
costumes—a Maker skill that seems ridiculous to maintain
but that Jeff and Whitney insist we know. My gown is inspired
by one of Empress Feodorovna of Russia's gowns that lives
in the Victoria and Albert wing of the Vault. Despite missing
the high of heist planning—and seeing Garrett every day—I
secretly find it relaxing to sit under the trees in the evenings
and embroider.

I scan the faces on the dance floor, hoping, as ever, one of
them might be his, that maybe he returned for this night—the
night of his initiation—the night of my eighteenth birthday.
Coming up empty, I feel disappointment dip in my belly.

Keystone isn't the same without him. It's lost some of its spark, the intrigue that made this place fascinating. Maybe that comes with familiarity, too, but his absence feels like a piece of me is lost, and I don't know when I'll find it. *But we'll see each other again. Like he said, this is only the beginning...*

It took forever to figure out how to open the key fob. For weeks I rolled the seven-letter code into endless combinations, imagining what message Garrett could have left for me. I was pretty surprised when "told-u-so" didn't work.

A month after my return, I was wandering through the Vault, thinking back to our last night together, hunting for clues. *"Impossible is my specialty..." He was right about that...* Then it hit me. *"I'll do anything to prove you can trust me."* Coming to a halt, I took the key fob out of my pocket and tried it right then and there. T-R-U-S-T-M-E.

The lid clicked, and I popped it open. Inside was a scrap of paper with a handwritten code:

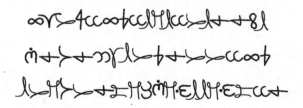

The language looked familiar, but I couldn't place it. I went straight to the Crypt, hoping some rare manuscript in the Beinecke could help trigger where I'd seen the language before. As soon as the door sucked closed behind me, I remembered. *The Voynich.*

Rushing into the glass cube, I located the manuscript and, putting on white gloves, set it on a table. I turned the delicate pages with tweezers, going as quickly as I dared, hunting for a clue. Twenty minutes later, I found it. Sandwiched between some bizarre illustrations of naked people—and I couldn't help but giggle—was a piece of paper with six compass roses, each ringed with a code. The layout reminded me of a Templar cipher, but the writing was distinctly Voynich. *Did he decipher the manuscript?* I tried a few lines from the book, and it translated to gibberish. *No…this must be* his *code.*

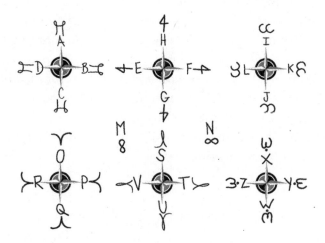

Taking the scrap of paper out of the key fob, I got to work. *N-O-T-H…*

When I finished, I sat back, admiring his handiwork, and smiled.

It read: "nothing is as it seems we're just getting started always say die"

I'm still not sure if he means we're just starting—as in me and him, together—but excitement ignites in my belly all the same.

*Yes. This is only the beginning. Always say die.*

"It's kind of morbid, don't you think?" Sophia asks as she and Rayelle join me, jarring me out of my reverie. She's gone all out with her costume, wearing a silver lamé evening gown with a drop waist and tassels. Her hair is tucked into a hat decorated with a silver plume. Half of her face is smeared with silver glitter, and she wears a small collection of rhinestones under her left eye. "The Last Night on the Titanic?"

"I think it's romantic," Rayelle says, smoothing the skirt of her red velvet gown. "It's to remind us to live every day like it's our last."

"We're definitely standing on a sinking ship," Stewart says, arriving by my side and linking arms with me. He leads me into the party. "The world as we know it might as well go to hell, since our best and brightest turned out to be a traitor."

"We don't know that," I say. "I still think Garrett was called away to a top-secret job. We got the algorithm and prevented the Quinn update this time, but Simon's still out there. Madden is still building the Simulation. They'll find another way to convince society mind uploads are a good idea. Garrett's probably on the front lines."

"If it was a job, don't you think Allard or Abignail would tell us?" Stewart asks. "They don't have to tell us what the job is."

I shrug. "Allard says she doesn't know. But maybe she's sworn to secrecy."

"Speaking of," Sophia says under her breath.

Allard taps my shoulder. "Elisha, can I talk to you for a moment?"

She's decked out in a black beaded evening gown, but I know she misses her lab coat.

"Sure." I follow her to an alcove half hidden by a string quartet.

"I'll keep this short." She presents me with an antique key. "Happy birthday."

Stunned, I take the key, rolling it between my fingers.

"I need an answer by the end of the night. And I trust you'll speak of this to no one."

Before I can respond, with a swish of her skirt, she's gone.

Dazed, I head outside. Finding a quiet corner of the porch, I lean against the railing, pretending to contemplate the moonlit trees as I twist the key's filigree head. Inside is a tiny scroll. I study the handwriting, feeling my sinuses clear as I read.

*Target: Audio tape labeled "Conversation with Jackie Kennedy, December 17, 1964."*

*Location: Andy Warhol Museum, Pittsburgh, time capsule number 78.*

*Details: Andy Warhol kept an ongoing record of his daily life by consistently sweeping the contents of his desk into a cardboard box he kept at his feet. There are 610 boxes sealed in the time capsule exhibit at the Warhol museum in Pittsburgh. Use whatever means necessary to obtain the audio tape in box 78. Once the tape is in your possession, send a message from the loft on Railroad Street.*

"What did Allard want?" Stewart asks, appearing next to me.

"Unfortunately, I can't share." I stuff the scroll back into the key and squeeze his arm.

"I figured as much," he says, smiling. "But let me know if you need a code breaker."

Rayelle and Sophia join us. "You're not coming to Vegas with me this summer, are you?" Rayelle asks.

"No." I shake my head. "There's been a change of plans."

"I'm not surprised," Sophia says. "You're definitely the

best girl for any job, but let us know if you need us."

"Thank you for being my friends," I say, resting my head on Rayelle's shoulder. "You have no idea how much it means to me."

The four of us stand, united, staring up at the stars.

"And I promise you this," I say. "I will always say die."

# Acknowledgments

When I started this book five years ago, I had no clue the journey it would take me on, how huge the world would become—how much it would make my brain hurt—or how much I'd learn along the way. At times the journey to publication felt never ending, but as I sit here at the finish line, it feels like yesterday I was staring at a blank page one. I'm grateful for every early morning, late night, and stolen moment I got to spend with these characters and that wouldn't have been possible without a massive support system. So, first and foremost, thank you to my husband Jason for always being up for an adventure (Spy School!) and for being the other half of this balancing act. I'm so happy we continue to grow together and dream BIG together. Thank you to my parents and to Joan and Joel for all the afternoons and nights at Grandma and Pap's and Nana and Papa's so that I can take a (much needed!) escape to my imaginary world.

Thank you forever and always to Jennifer Pooley for believing from the beginning and sending all the lightning bolts. To Diane Samandi for cheering me all the way—and for always bringing the deep talks. To Jeff and everyone at MGT for allowing me to make my own schedule so I can lead a double (triple?) life. To my editor Candace Havens for her incredible insight and for making me and KEYSTONE better.

To everyone at Entangled—Liz and Heather and Curtis and Stacy and Debbie and Riki and Hannah and Jessica and Meredith and everyone I've yet to meet—who have had a hand in this beautiful book. I'm so happy to be a part of this team. To everyone at the Bent Agency for looking out for me. To Donovan, Lilah, and Cece for being my greatest joys in life. And finally, to you, the readers (if you're still reading this!). Thank *you* for coming on this ride with me. You are the most important piece of the puzzle—the keystone, if you will—because without you this story would have no reason to exist. Thank you for giving me purpose. I'm forever in your debt.

Turn the page to start reading
a sneak peek of

## *Malice*

by Pintip Dunn

**What I know:** someone at my school will one day wipe out two-thirds of the population with a virus.

**What I don't know:** who it is.

In a race against the clock, I not only have to figure out their identity, but I'll have to outwit a voice from the future telling me to kill them. Because I'm starting to realize no one is telling the truth. But how can I play chess with someone who already knows the outcome of my every move? Someone so filled with malice she's lost all hope in humanity? Well, I'll just have to find a way—because now she's drawn a target on the only boy I've ever loved...

# CHAPTER 3

My breath comes in quick, shallow pants. I brace myself, preparing for the pain that's about to follow.

But it doesn't come. The zap doesn't return, the electricity doesn't intensify, and my brains don't feel like they're being boiled. What's going on?

"Move away from the sink," the Voice says evenly. It's the same one as before, but she's not impatient and angry this time. Instead, she sounds quite calm.

I perform a quick calculation. It's been seven hours since she last visited. What happened? Did she take a nap—or whatever disembodied voices do to rejuvenate—since we last talked?

I take a step back. Our dishwasher is broken, so the counter is piled high with recently cleaned plates that have yet to be put away. "Who are you?"

Which is a nicer way of saying: *damn you, you made me think I had lost my* ever-loving *mind!* But Mom raised me to be polite to strangers, even if she's not around to enforce it. Even if said strangers take the form of unexplained beings.

The Voice ignores me. "That's not far enough. Walk at least fifteen feet. To the very edge of the kitchen, where the tile meets the carpet."

I scrunch up my nose. "Why?"

"No time for questions," she says, sounding more like her original self. "Do it. Now."

There's no corresponding zap of pain. Compared to my earlier torture, this request is downright courteous. I'm not prepared to accept whatever this is as my new reality. I sure don't like being told what to do by a *voice in my head*. But I comply, more out of curiosity than any desire to obey.

"Okay," I say from the doorway. "I'm here, but I have questions. Lots of them. And if you think I'm just going to—"

*BOOM!*

The entire pile of kitchenware crashes to the floor. Pots, pans, cutting boards, knives. Plates, dishes, cutlery, and a wineglass filled with a deep-red merlot from Dad's dinner last night. It hits the floor at just the right angle and shatters, spraying drops of wine all over the kitchen.

The epicenter of the crash is exactly where I was standing.

I stare at the blue linoleum squares in front of the sink. My heart gallops, and the rain of wine all over the counter, stove, and cabinets echoes in my mind like the ringing of bullets. I sag against the doorframe, sliding down until my butt hits the floor, half on the shaggy carpet, half on the cold tile.

The Voice… She just saved me. From being drenched with wine, if not cut by the shards of glass. How did she…? The words refuse to form. Instead, images flash through my mind, like a movie sequence on fast-forward.

*Drops of wine fly through the air, splattering my skin. Up and down my bare arms, my cheeks, my forehead. My white tank top. Splashing against the fabric, staining it in a random starburst pattern, right next to Lin-Manuel Miranda's autograph. The liquid flows down my body, drip-drip-dripping like the steady trickle of a faucet.*

*Me, gaping at my tank top. The surprise gets stuck in my throat at first, but then it shakes free in a shriek so loud that Archie vaults up the stairs, taking them two at a time.*

*Archie's disgust when he realizes I'm crying over spilled wine. The hurried swipes of my finger on my phone screen as I try to figure out how to neutralize the red liquid. For an hour, I dab at the stain. Sprinkle it with salt. Add boiling water. And then I run an entire load of laundry, just to save the shirt. But it's no use.*

*My favorite tank top, made special by the black Sharpie scrawl of my idol, ruined. Forever.*

The events fly through my head like a reel of memories. Just as vivid as if they actually happened. But they're not memories. They can't be.

I stare at the white fabric of my shirt, unmarred by a single stain. And I'm jolted by clarity so deep that it must be true.

*This is what my future would've looked like if I hadn't moved.*

All of a sudden, fine tremors roll along my skin like choppy ocean waves. For my birthday last year, Archie bought me the autographed tank from eBay…and a pair of earplugs for himself. Can't really blame him. I *might* have been singing about not throwing away my shot from dawn to dusk. But more than the prospect of my nearly ruined shirt, I'm freaked out because of what this vision implies. About the Voice, about its presence in my head.

"Who are you?" I ask again.

The Voice takes a breath, a fluttering of air inside my brain. Or maybe that's me. Or the both of us together. I have this eerie sensation of breathing with this being, of our lungs (if she has them) rising and falling as one. Me, on this floor. And her… wherever she happens to be.

"I always loved that top," she says musingly. "Maybe it was silly to pick this moment to prove a point, but I might as well save our favorite shirt, if I could."

I shake my head. "What…what are you saying?"

"It's nice to meet you, Alice," she says gently. "I'm you from the future. Ten years older."

# CHAPTER 4

**M**y mouth drops. Air wheezes in and out, but it's like I've grown gills in place of lungs. The room dips and spins so violently, it's all I can do to hang on to the doorjamb and not slide across the linoleum.

She... Me... Well, flaming monkeys. We. Us.

Is it possible? The Voice is me? An older Alice Sherman?

"Ticktock," the Voice says. Or maybe I should refer to her as "me." But I can't. Not yet. I can't wrap my head around this new reality so soon. If ever. "We only have a short amount of time. Our consciousness can travel for a few minutes during each visit. Go ahead. Ask your questions."

"What questions?" I croak. It's a wonder I can still talk.

"All the things you've never told a single soul. The answers to which only you—or your older self—would know. My knowledge of the wine spill should tell you I'm from the future. The questions will prove that the rest of it is true. I am you, and you will one day become me."

A puff of oxygen slides into my chest, and the room begins to right itself. She knows me so well. She knows exactly what I need to get over this shock. Exactly what will push me into the realm of believing.

Proof. In the only form available to me.

"Who did I crush on in the first grade?" The question spills out of me like a geyser.

"Easy. Steven Chu. You pretended you thought he was disgusting, but you were giddy every time he pulled one of your braids."

I make a face. So sue me. I was six years old and clearly had a lot to learn.

"Did I ever cheat on a test?" I ask.

"Seventh grade. Mrs. Miller's class. You went to turn in a history quiz and saw that the test on top had a different answer. Panicked, you changed yours, but karma isn't kind. Turned out, your original answer was the right one after all."

My cheeks flush. Four years ago and the shame still rises in my chest. I was all emotion that day. All fear and self-doubt. The monster was so big, there wasn't room for anything else.

I take a deep breath. One more question. I almost don't want to ask. But I have to know, once and for all, if she's me.

"What's the worst thing I've ever done?" I whisper. "The thing I'll never confess to, as long as I live?"

She laughs so hard that my brain seems to vibrate. But unlike her earlier amusement, soaked with nostalgia, this laughter has no real mirth. "Oh, Alice. You're so...*idealistic*." She says the word like it's a sour candy. "I'll answer the question, but I gotta warn you." Her voice lowers. Thickens. "You'll do much worse before you become me."

I wrap my arms around myself, yearning to dive into the comforting sand dunes of the Arabian desert.

"Let's see. The worst thing you've ever done...Alice, at seventeen..." she says slowly. "Okay. At seventeen you were the Goodiest Two-shoes who ever lived."

Derision lives in the space between her words. Gone is her light teasing. Gone is the warm remembrance. She's angry with me. At herself, at this young age. But why? What did I do? More importantly: *What will I do?*

"Last year, Archie was being recruited to attend college a year ahead of schedule," she says. "By Harvard, MIT, Cal Tech. They all wanted him, and they wanted to lock him down early. You were the messenger between Dad and Archie. Most days, Dad couldn't even bother to talk to you, but that didn't stop you from inserting yourself. You took it upon yourself to act as mediator."

I close my eyes. I know all this, of course. Still, each word slices at my heart. Every sentence stings like a thousand paper cuts.

"But you lied. You told Archie that Dad wouldn't let him graduate early. Then you told *Dad* that Archie preferred to stay home another year, when the truth is, Archie can't wait to leave. Dad would've burst with pride—*he* did the same thing, after all—but you cut off your brother's dreams without a second thought."

"No," I whisper, defending myself even though she must know all my excuses. "I didn't take away his dreams; I only delayed them. The schools will still be there next year. And in the meantime, I get to keep him here. With me. So I can make sure he eats." The pressure builds behind my eyes. "You should remember this. You know he isn't ready to be on his own yet. Beyond the basics like food and laundry, he gets lost in his research. If I'm not here to draw him out, who knows how long he would go without talking to anyone?"

"I'm not judging you, Alice." Her voice softens. "In fact, I'm here to tell you that you don't need to feel guilty anymore. Turns out, that was the best thing you could've done for Archie. The more time he spends with you, the better."

"Really?" I could weep. My middle-of-the-night prayers answered right here, in this moment. I just never dreamed it would come from my older self. "You're not saying that to make me feel better?"

"Really," she says. "Pinkie swear, on the hair of a bear, with a cherry on top." The rest of the solemn promise I used to make as a little kid.

All of a sudden, I'm aware of the snores coming from the back of the house. My dad, after pulling an all-nighter at the office. Four rooms separate us. Any less, and the indistinct rumbling would sound like a faulty lawn mower.

"Is that Dad?" the Voice asks.

"Yep. Delivered the food. Reminded me about the awards banquet Sunday night. And then stumbled to his room."

I don't even blink at the fact that she's calling him "Dad." And that's when it hits me. There's no longer any doubt in my mind. She's actually my older self.

"Whose memory was that?" I blurt. "The one where I *didn't* move from the center of the crash. The one where drops of wine splattered everything."

"Mine," she says. "From my original timeline. But since I've shared my consciousness with you, as you take actions that diverge from the original thread, your memories will splinter into two timelines—what *just* happened in your life and what *did* happen in mine."

"But that's...that's absurd," I stammer. "Are you saying I'll constantly be bombarded with every difference from your life?"

"Of course not. Remember, I'm a lot older than you. I no longer have memories of every moment. You'll only experience the memory reel from my life during the big events, the ones that made an impression on me."

That's a relief. At least my mind will be my own. Mostly.

"One last question," we both say at the same time.

I shake my head, and I feel her performing the same motion, sometime in the future. This is weird. This person is undoubtedly me...but isn't.

"Why are you here?" I ask.

She hesitates. The silence is so abrupt that I think she's

disappeared. So drawn out that my mind has time to race through several possibilities.

Maybe she's here to tell me that getting a tattoo of a star on my belly is a colossally bad idea. Or to impart the winning lottery numbers so that I'll be able to cross-country ski around Antarctica. Or maybe —

"I'm only allowed to tell you what you need to know," she finally says. "Time travel is tricky. One wrong move, one detail too many, and we could create ripples that will change the future in ways we never intended."

She stops once more.

"I'm trusting you here. Trusting that you'll keep what you learn to yourself. Trusting you won't let an immature need to confide in someone ruin the future for millions of people. Saying too much to the wrong person could result in a disaster of unknown proportions."

"You have my word," I swear. "Besides, if you can't trust me, then who can you trust?"

She sighs, as though she's asked herself the same question. "We need you for a very special mission," she says slowly. "In the future, a person will invent a virus that will wipe out two-thirds of the world. It's your job to stop them now, in the present."

A blast of cold hits my core, and my mouth opens and closes, opens and closes. Seconds loop around to eternity and back again.

A fatal virus? Two-thirds of the world's population? *My* responsibility?

It's…it's too much to process. Too much to comprehend.

Faintly, I hear myself asking, "How am I supposed to do that? It's not like I know many mass murderers hard at work in their lair."

"Wrong," the Voice says. "You already know this person. The Virus Maker is a student at your school."

Pick up your copy of

# MALICE

by

# PINTIP DUNN

wherever books are sold

# Let's be friends!

𝕏 @EntangledTeen

⬜ @EntangledTeen

🅕 @EntangledTeen

📰 bit.ly/TeenNewsletter

# entangled teen

an imprint of Entangled Publishing LLC